'A terrific talent'
Peter James, author of the Roy Grace series

'I was completely immerse[d] ... [th]riller'
B P Walter, auth[or ...

'Sharply wri[tten] ... drops

Liz N[... *[cr]uelties*

'A sinis[ter ... [t]o put down'
Sar[... *Open House*

... [ke]eping

... [t]wisty'
Tammy Co[... of *When She Was Bad*

'Utterly compelling and addictive'
Samantha Hayes, author of *Until You're Mine*

Readers gave Debbie Howells five stars...

'What a rush ... I was kept guessing until
the end with this'
★★★★★

'I was gripped from the start and couldn't put it down!'
★★★★★

'She has a beautiful way of writing'
★★★★★

'A truly immersive, one-sit read'
★★★★★

'The perfect read for a rainy Saturday'
★★★★★

'More twists than your local theme park rollercoaster!'
★★★★★

'Mesmerising from the start'
★★★★★

'I highly recommend this and all of Debbie's books'
★★★★★

Debbie Howells is the bestselling author of *The Bones of You* (Macmillan), a Richard & Judy Book Club pick. It was followed by *The Beauty of the End*, *The Death of Her* and *Her Sister's Lie* (Macmillan).

The House Sitter is her third book with HarperCollins, following *The Vow*, which was a #1 ebook bestseller, and *The Secret*.

www.debbiehowells.co.uk

You can follow @_debbiehowells on Instagram or @debbie__howells on Twitter.

THE HOUSE SITTER

DEBBIE HOWELLS

avon.

Published by AVON
A division of HarperCollins*Publishers*
1 London Bridge Street
London SE1 9GF

www.harpercollins.co.uk

HarperCollins*Publishers*
Macken House
39/40 Mayor Street Upper
Dublin 1
D01 C9W8
Ireland

A Paperback Original 2023
1
First published in Great Britain by HarperCollins*Publishers* 2023

ISBN: 978-0-00-851581-2

Typeset in Bembo by Palimpsest Book Production Limited, Falkirk, Stirlingshire

Printed and Bound in the UK using 100% Renewable Electricity
at CPI Group (UK) Ltd

MIX
Paper | Supporting
responsible forestry
FSC™ C007454

This book is produced from independently certified FSC™ paper
to ensure responsible forest management.

For more information visit: www.harpercollins.co.uk/green

For Frances

I can and I will.
Watch me.

2018

I watched as the English coast came into view, taking in the white cliffs of Dover, the hovering seagulls under an already grey sky streaked with clouds. It felt weird to think about how long I'd been away and what had happened in that time, while life in England had gone on as before, pretty much unchanged.

Disembarking from the ferry, I headed for the station. I didn't have to wait long for the next train, and speeding through open countryside, I gazed out at the green fields, the distant sea I'd so recently crossed. Less than twenty minutes later, I arrived in Deal. My new life was about to begin.

1

Katharine

The house is quiet, the only sound the muted tick of the large Moroccan wall clock that Oliver bought for me. I register the time – three p.m. Going over to the window, I gaze outside. The heavy rain of earlier has let up, leaving sodden ground and grey September skies; the petals browning on the roses that climb up the back of the house, framing the window.

Our home is beautiful, a partially restored cottage in an idyllic village in the Kent countryside, with a large garden that backs onto open fields. The rooms are minimally but tastefully furnished in muted colours – the oak floor setting off the faded blue of our velvet sofa; the soft cream of the rug and curtains. A large TV and sound system are Oliver's pride and joy. We moved here two years ago, the deposit bankrolled by Oliver's parents, the mortgage easily covered by my office job and his airline salary. With our lives comfortable, six months ago, I gave up work to start my counselling business.

I've never taken any of this for granted; that I'm secure and happy, in comfortable surroundings, when so many people are not. Knowing how lucky I am, I wanted to find a way to help other people who are less fortunate. As I know only too well, there are many people struggling through life.

Glancing out of the window again, I think of Oliver. According to his roster, he should be at 35,000 feet in an Airbus A320, halfway between London and Alicante, looking out onto cloudless blue skies. It crosses my mind to call Jude, his mother, to invite them for Sunday lunch. Family's important – it's been a while since we've seen them and as far as I know, Oliver has the weekend off.

I go to check my calendar. It's in my study, a cosy room at the side of the house, where I see my clients – a quiet space with white walls, a pale rug softening original oak floorboards; a variety of plants adorning the shelves and windowsills. Apart from my desk, the only other pieces of furniture are two oyster-coloured armchairs, perpetuating the atmosphere of calm in here.

Sitting at my desk, I switch on my laptop, bringing up the notes I made about a client I saw earlier today. Reading through them, deep in thought, I don't notice the car that pulls up outside.

The knock at the door startles me. With no clients booked in for the rest of the day, I wonder if someone has their dates muddled. It happens from time to time. But when I open the door, instead of a familiar face, two uniformed police officers are standing on the step.

'Mrs McKenna?'

The police officer who speaks is about my age, with clear blue eyes and fair hair neatly tied back.

'I'm DS Laura Stanley. This is my colleague, Constable Ramirez. May we come in?'

I prefer *Ms* but I let it go. Wondering why they're here, I imagine a petty neighbourly squabble or a burglary in one of the big houses in the village.

'Of course.'

I stand back to let them in.

'Has something happened?'

She glances along the hallway.

'Is there somewhere we can talk?'

'Come through.' Leading them through to the kitchen, I gesture towards the long dinner party-sized table. 'Please. Have a seat.'

Next to DS Stanley, Constable Ramirez is younger, with clear grey eyes, a hint of makeup, her brown hair in a neat bun. Their faces are unreadable as they sit down. DS Stanley takes out her electronic notebook.

'Can I just confirm you're married to Oliver McKenna?'

At the mention of his name, I frown slightly, as my heart starts to race. 'That's correct.' I look at them. 'Why?'

She hesitates. 'I'm afraid there's no easy way to say this. I'm very sorry, Mrs McKenna, but earlier this afternoon, your husband was involved in an accident.'

My eyes widen in shock, before I shake my head. 'He couldn't have been.' I frown at the clock. 'He's at work – he's a pilot – this afternoon he's on a flight to Alicante.' But as I take in their expressions, a chill comes over me. I stare at DS Stanley, my voice husky all of a sudden. 'Is he in hospital?'

Her eyes hold mine. 'I'm afraid we're not in any doubt that it was him, Mrs McKenna. We've checked the registration of his car. He also had documentation on him.' She hesitates again. 'I'm very sorry. The paramedics tried to resuscitate him, but by the time they got there, there was nothing they could do.'

'*No.*' As shock hits me, I feel light-headed. Unable to take it in, I shake my head. 'It can't have been him. He's due home by eight. We were going to order a curry.' My eyes dart around the room, landing on the menu for the Indian in the next village. 'We're going to plan a holiday. We were talking about it at lunch time, just before he left.' As I twist the solitaire diamond on my ring finger, my voice cracks.

'I know this must be a terrible shock.' DS Stanley speaks gently. 'Is there someone we can call? A family member, or friend?'

Unable to speak, my vision blurs as I feel myself start to shake.

As DS Stanley nods towards her colleague, she gets up and puts the kettle on. 'The road was flooded,' she says gently. 'He probably lost control. We don't think anyone else was involved. We'll be checking out his car for signs of mechanical failure.'

'Who found him?' My voice trembles.

'A passing motorist saw his car.'

More tears fill my eyes as I take in what this means. Never seeing Oliver again, our plans for the future wiped out, just like that. Suddenly I remember it wasn't his car he was driving this morning. 'His car wouldn't start,' I say, only it doesn't sound like my voice. 'He was late for work – he took mine.'

DS Stanley frowns. 'But the car he was driving was registered in his name.'

'I know. Oliver took care of everything like that – bought

our cars, insured them,' I say through my tears. I let him, never questioning him. 'But it was the car I always drove.' I try to make myself clear. 'Almost always.'

'There was a flight bag inside – and one or two other things.' As Constable Ramirez places a mug of tea in front of me, DS Stanley turns to her. 'Could you get them?'

She walks towards the front door and I hear it open and close behind her. Standing up, I'm gripped by a sense of urgency as unstoppable tears pour down my face. I look around the kitchen for my phone. 'I need to call Joe,' I mumble. But as I try to walk, my legs give way.

After helping me onto a chair, DS Stanley finds my phone. 'Who's Joe?'

'His brother.' Three years younger than Oliver, Joe will be devastated.

'Would you like me to speak to him?'

Nodding through my tears, my hands are shaking as I find the number and pass her my phone, watching her go out to the hallway where she talks in a low voice.

When she comes back, she puts my phone on the table. 'He said he'll be here as soon as he can.'

Sitting there, tears stream down my face. My world is in pieces; the man I loved gone forever. But I can't deny that in the middle of it all, I feel the smallest glimmer of relief.

2

Jude

As I walk through the streets, the sky is overcast, the air damp with the promise of rain. Now and then between the houses, I glimpse sea that after the blue of summer has changed to shades of grey, as after crowded months as a buzzing holiday destination, Deal starts its annual transformation back to sleepy seaside town.

I'm on my way back to my car after a business lunch when my mobile buzzes in my pocket. Slightly irritated when I see Joe's face on the screen, I wonder what he wants this time.

'Darling. Can't it wait? I'm on my way back to work.'

'I've just had the police on the phone.' Joe sounds upset. 'Mum, it's Oliver.' He pauses. 'There's been an accident.'

Shock courses through me. I grip my phone tightly. 'What's happened? Is he OK? Does Kat know?'

'The police are with her – it's how they got my number.' Joe's obviously distraught. 'The ambulance didn't get there in time.' He breaks off again. 'Oliver didn't make it, Mum.'

'*No.*' As shock hits me, I feel sick. This can't be happening. My eyes blur with tears. My eldest son, Oliver, has a wonderful life, a brilliant future ahead of him.

'Mum? Are you there?'

'Yes.' Finding my voice, I can't think. 'I'm on my way back to work. I have a meeting this afternoon I can't get out of . . .'

I work as the manager in a medical practice. Except how can I go to a meeting? 'Can you go over there? And can you call your father and let him know?' I take a deep breath. 'Tell Kat . . .' I try to work out what to do. 'I'll cancel the meeting. I'll be with her as soon as I can.'

Ending the call, I stand there a moment, thinking about the meeting. It's important; a discussion about changing our increasingly busy appointments system. I could go, make my apologies and leave early. But on second thoughts, I dial my assistant. When it goes to voicemail, I leave a message.

I won't be in this afternoon. Please make my apologies. Something's come up.

I put my phone in my pocket and stand there, the reality sinking in, a single sob erupting from deep inside me.

3

Katharine

'Is there anyone else I can call?' DS Stanley looks concerned. 'Maybe your parents?'

I shake my head. My parents are dead. The only person I want here is Joe.

At the table, I'm conscious of the police sitting there as I listen to the slow tick of the clock as it marks the passing of time, a memory coming back of the day Oliver gave it to me. Feeling emotion welling up inside me, suddenly I want to get away from their scrutiny. Getting up, I apologise.

'Would you excuse me?'

Desperate to be alone, I go up to our bedroom. Slumping onto the edge of our bed, I give in to my emotions, wrapping my arms around myself as tears pour down my face. Everything in my life, Oliver and I have planned together. We were supposed to be together forever – each other's happy ever after, creating our own little family within Oliver's much larger one. But they're dreams that will only ever be that – just dreams.

I hold myself tightly, still sobbing when I hear a car outside before the front door opens. The murmur of voices reaches me, before footsteps come up the stairs, hesitating outside my room as someone knocks softly.

'Kat?'

Recognising Joe's voice, I pull myself upright as he comes in. His face is pale, wet with tears as, coming over and sitting next to me, he hugs me.

'I'm so sorry.' His voice is thick with emotion. 'I can't believe it. Not Oliver . . .'

'Nor can I.' Feeling my body start to shake, I bury my face in the comfort of his shoulder.

He holds me while I sob, stroking my hair gently, until eventually letting go of me, he wipes his face. 'Mum's on her way here.'

Getting up, I look for a box of tissues, trying to staunch my deluge of tears as I mumble through them. 'The police are still downstairs. I should go and talk to them.'

'I'll come with you.'

When we go downstairs, DS Stanley is talking on her phone in the kitchen. Seeing us come in, she ends the call.

'Does anyone know what happened?' Joe's voice is low as he pulls out a chair for me, before he sits down on the next one.

DS Stanley speaks quietly as she looks at Joe. 'We think he lost control of his car. A passing motorist noticed a car had gone off the road and called us. As I told Mrs McKenna, we don't have any witnesses, but an examination of his car may tell us more.' She hesitates. 'I know this is a difficult time, but would you mind if I ask you one or two questions?'

Glancing briefly at me first, Joe nods.

'Do you know if Mr McKenna drank or took drugs? Or anything else that might have caused him to drive erratically?'

Before Joe can answer, I interrupt. 'Oliver wouldn't do anything like that.'

Joe frowns slightly. 'Not to my knowledge – I mean, he drank socially, didn't he?' He glances at me again. 'But not excessively. He was a pilot. There are strict rules – if he was on his way to work, he wouldn't have been under the influence of anything.'

DS Stanley makes a note in her electronic notebook. 'So you would describe your brother as a responsible person? I suppose I'm asking, was he the kind of person who drove recklessly?'

Joe shakes his head. 'Oliver was responsible. He was proud of his car. He looked after it. I've never been aware of him driving dangerously.'

But Joe doesn't know what happened this morning.

'His car is in the garage. It wouldn't start.' My hands are shaking. 'He took mine.'

Joe looks startled. 'I hadn't realised.'

After making a note, DS Stanley looks at Joe. 'There's one more thing. We're going to need someone to formally identify the body.'

Having always seen Oliver as strong and vital, as I think of seeing his body devoid of life, horror fills me.

But Joe says quietly, 'I'll do it.'

★

It's dark by the time the police leave here. After Joe sees them out, he pulls the curtains closed before coming and sitting next to me again.

Hunched in my chair, I can't move.

'What am I going to do?' My voice trembles as I think of the people we need to tell, Oliver's work colleagues, extended family. 'About everything? Where will I live? I can't afford to stay here on my own.'

'Don't worry about the house,' Joe says quietly. 'He may well have taken out life insurance. But they're details, Kat. They can wait.'

'I just want Oliver to come back.' My voice wavers, Joe blurring as I gaze at him; my dreams shattering; shards of broken glass falling like rain. Leaning my head in my hands, my eyes spill over with tears. Feeling Joe's hand on my shoulder, my body starts to shake again.

'I know you do,' he whispers. 'We both do.'

For a while we sit there, my mind still struggling to take in the reality; regrets coming at me for everything we'll never do; for the family we'll never have.

When his phone vibrates, Joe reads the message that flashes up. 'It's from Mum. She's been held up but she should be here soon.' He gets up. 'I'll make us some tea,' he says quietly.

I watch Joe go over to the worktop, filling the kettle with filtered water, before placing it on the Aga. Going to one of the cupboards, he finds the Pantone mugs I gave Oliver for a Christmas present.

I'm used to the quiet, but this is a different kind of silence, an eerie, unwanted one of shock, sorrow, anguish; broken only by the whistling of the kettle.

Making a pot of tea, Joe brings it over.

'What happens next?' As I look at Joe, my words seem to echo. 'There are all these things you have to do when someone dies – I don't even know where to start.'

He looks at me sadly. 'We don't need to worry about that now. Let's just get through the rest of today. We can talk about it tomorrow. And you won't be on your own – I'll help you.'

Taking the mug he passes me, I shake my head. 'I should do it. Oliver was my husband.' My voice breaks. Forming the past tense is unfamiliar. But then I look up suddenly. 'I have to let the airline know. They need to know that he won't be coming in to work.' My hands shake as I reach for my phone and scroll down my contacts.

Joe gently takes it from me. 'Let me do it.'

Getting up, he walks out of the kitchen and I listen to the murmur of his voice, unable to make out his words.

'That was weird.' He comes back into the room and as he places my phone on the table, he looks puzzled. 'They said Oliver doesn't work there anymore. Apparently he left two months ago.'

'*What?*' I look at him, incredulous.

That doesn't make any sense. Oliver's been putting on his uniform and going to work. Why would they say that?

I shake my head. 'That can't be right. They must have him confused with someone else.' Picking up my phone, I find the last number on the call list and redial it. 'Hello? This is Katharine McKenna. My husband, Oliver, is – *was* – one of your flight crew.' My voice feels unsteady, my mind flitting all over the place as I talk. 'His brother just spoke to you.'

There's a brief silence before the voice answers. 'As I told Mr McKenna's brother, your husband no longer works for us.'

'Can you check? *Please?*' It feels surreal, like I'm in the middle of a nightmare.

'I'm sorry, Mrs McKenna. But there's no one of that name working here.'

Feeling the blood drain from my face, suddenly I'm light-headed. 'Can I speak to your manager? You see, Oliver told me he was on a flight today, to Alicante. I even saw his roster.'

'Can you hold please?'

The line goes quiet and I wait, feeling my head spin, my stomach churning, until a minute later another voice speaks.

'Mrs McKenna? I understand you're calling about your husband. I'm very sorry for your loss.' The voice hesitates. 'But Mr McKenna left in rather unfortunate circumstances. He was reported for being under the influence of alcohol while he was working. The first time, he was given a warning. There was no proof and the pilot who reported him was known for causing trouble. But there was a second incident when he narrowly avoided causing an accident. We didn't have any choice.'

It sounds so unlike the Oliver I know. Dazed, I shake my head. 'When was this?'

'The first time was about a year ago, the second a couple of months ago, just before he left.'

Stunned, as I turn to look at Joe, the phone falls from my hand.

Picking it up, he switches it off. 'What did they say?'

I look at him, horrified, because it's as Joe told the police. 'You know how little he drank. He was reported for being drunk at work. They said it happened twice. Once, a year ago, then the second time, there was nearly an accident. I think they must have fired him.'

Joe looks shocked. 'Has there been money coming in?'

I nod. 'His salary's always gone into his personal account

– but he's been transferring the same amount as usual into our joint account.' I've had no reason to suspect anything had changed.

Joe looks uncertain. 'If he hasn't been at work, where has he been?'

For a moment, neither of us speaks. 'I don't know.' I'm filled with anguish. 'I don't understand how I didn't know about this.'

Joe looks at me. 'I don't, either. If something had happened at work, I can't believe he wouldn't have told you about it.'

'But he didn't, did he?' There's angst in my voice. 'I feel terrible. Poor Oliver, I can't bear that he was going through this without me.'

Joe's face is pale, his eyes red from crying. 'I guess maybe he felt ashamed. But one thing's for sure – he went to a lot of trouble to keep this hidden from us all.'

I gaze tearfully at Joe. 'But why?'

2010

Gemma

As I pitched up at work, I knew Edie would be waiting for me. Sure enough, as I walked through the door of her cleaning empire, her beady little eyes swivelled around, glaring at me as she tapped her watch.

'What time do you call this? You should have been here ten minutes ago. Lucky for you the van's been held up.'

'Lucky, huh?' I said sarcastically. She was talking about the filthy minibus we crammed ourselves into to be ferried through London to the next cleaning job.

Edie's face turned a shade of puce. 'I've had more than enough of your attitude. Give me one reason why I shouldn't fire you.'

Arching an eyebrow at her, I'd had enough too. 'I work hard. I'm prettier than most of the others – plus, for good measure, it happens to be my birthday.' But as I went over to my locker, I stood there for a moment. I really didn't need this shit – not from Edie, not from anyone.

Turning around, I went back to her. 'You can poke your lousy job, Edie. I've had enough of being ordered around.' I raised my voice so everyone could hear. 'You don't pay us enough to put up with this crap.' Taking off my lanyard, I heard a snigger from behind me as I handed it back to her. 'I'd like to say it's been nice knowing you, but . . .'

'Floor show's over.' Glaring at the other staff, she snatched my ID from me. 'Get the fuck out.'

'Oooh, a little tetchy, are we?' I'd long ago mastered the art of keeping cool in situations like this. 'You really should learn to have better control over yourself.'

Before she could say anything else, I pushed the door open, relief filling me as it swung shut behind me, but as I walked down the street, already my elation was subsiding as my stomach began to churn. My rent was due at the end of the week, while the contents of my kitchen amounted to a loaf of bread and a couple of tins of beans. I had a little money put away, but given how much living in London cost, it wasn't going to last anything like long enough.

Seeing as it was my birthday, I treated myself to a pastry from an artisan bakery – what the hell, a pastry wasn't going to make any difference. As I ate it, I passed a church just as a newly married couple walked out into the spring sunshine. Hand in hand, they were radiant, exuding love as they posed for photos, firstly as a couple before they were joined by family.

As I watched them pose with parents, grandparents, nephews, nieces, suddenly I realised, weddings were for people like this, who had family and love in their lives; who were a perfect example of how manifestation worked, of love attracting more love. It was no wonder people like me didn't stand a chance.

A sense of emptiness filled me as I realised that I would never know how that felt. Once, it could just as easily have been my world – one of wealth, with the sense of entitlement that came with that – as long as you played by the rules. But by the time I was sixteen, having endured my parents' rules all my life, I couldn't get away from them soon enough — though not before helping myself to the diamond necklace my mother had inherited.

After a childhood of neglect, devoid of love, I figured that they owed me at least something. I didn't find out until later that the necklace was a fake and that the real one was probably locked away in a safe somewhere I didn't know about. That had cemented my hatred of them, as well as the values people like them stood for. Their only interest was making more money and flaunting the sense of superiority they felt.

When so many people struggled to survive, it was a philosophy I'd come to detest. But in a cruel and unfair world, there had to be an upside. If I wasn't going to be one of the rich and privileged, there was no way I was playing by their rules, either. From here on, I was going to find my own way.

As I headed back to my flat, the spring sun was already fading. I bought a can of beer from a corner shop, lifting a second while no one was watching — a tried and tested tactic that almost always worked. As I walked, I allowed myself to imagine having a well-paid job, a nice home, beautiful clothes; the difference it would make to how I felt about myself. But before I reached my flat, the bubble had burst.

Unlocking the door, I let myself in, closing it and putting the chain across, trying to ignore how dismal it was. Opening one of the beers, I placed the other in the fridge, before sitting on the uncomfortable sofa that had long since seen better days. Sipping the beer, it hit me that I shouldn't have been so reckless in packing in my job, before resentment filled me. The problem with people like Edie was that they didn't care about the people who worked for them. All they did was exploit them, working them hard, paying them too little, keeping the profit for themselves.

21

A feeling of despair came over me. I'd encountered the same attitude everywhere I'd worked. But there would always be people like me, who were desperate for any job; knowing without one, they'd potentially be homeless.

Suddenly I was frightened. I didn't have enough money to pay my rent and no one to help me out; no caring family to give me a roof over my head for a while. Since benefits didn't come near to covering the cost of living, I'd be out on the streets with nothing.

That night, I barely slept. Consumed by worry, I felt powerless. For the last three years, I'd gone from one badly paid job to the next, struggling to keep a roof over my head; wanting desperately to change the way I lived, but with no idea how to.

It wasn't until the following morning that I turned to the copy of the Evening Standard *I'd picked up. Sitting down, as I leafed through the pages towards the jobs section, a feature caught my eye. Entitled 'Try Before You Buy', it was aimed at people who were planning to move to France. Drawn by the photo of a country house bathed in sunshine, I started reading.*

We spoke to Ronnie Martinez, an estate agent in the Haute-Garonne region, about how best to set about finding your perfect home.

I studied Ronnie Martinez's photo – putting her at early forties, perfectly made up, perfect hair. Perfect fucking everything, most likely. Given where I found myself, it was nauseating. I read on, curious to see what her pearls of wisdom were.

Firstly, I advise taking your time. There are many ways to spend time in France without blowing your budget. Rental prices are much cheaper than in the UK. There is also an abundance of empty second homes or holiday homes that the owners offer as house sits. These are mutually beneficial arrangements where instead of paying rent, the house sitter maintains the house and grounds according to the owner's requirements . . .

My eyes had instantly latched onto 'instead of paying rent', before scanning the rest of the page, as I realised that this was one of those rare crumbs of hope that fate occasionally scattered in the direction of the lost and downhearted.

Usually it just as quickly whipped them away again, but no way was I letting that happen this time. Opening my laptop, I started searching for house-sitting sites, astonished at how many there were. The first charged a fee I'd really have preferred not to pay, but with the second, I struck gold. There was no fee for potential sitters. All I had to do was submit a profile.

I scrolled through the list of house sits. Some were fairly average; others however, were stunning. Slowly it dawned on me: there was nothing in the world to stop me doing this.

After studying a few listings written by other sitters, copying a few lines that sounded plausible, I started to create the profile of the perfect house sitter.

'Young woman in her twenties, seeking a sabbatical from her busy London life to start writing a novel, preferably in quiet, secluded surroundings. I have travelled extensively and love exploring new places, meeting new people and becoming part of the community. I like a quiet life, nature, walking, painting.

'I have the highest standards of housekeeping and I am also a keen gardener. Your property would be in the safest of hands, as evidenced by my references.'

After stating my availability from next weekend's date, I crafted a couple of references that waxed lyrically about how responsible, reliable and trustworthy I was, before selecting a couple of photos where I looked older than my nineteen years.

As I started perusing the available house sits again, it just kept getting better. Some of the houses were spectacular — restored farmhouses and big old manor houses, with gardens to die for, sun terraces, beautiful swimming pools.

I couldn't believe I hadn't stumbled across this before. A house sit would solve all my immediate problems, even though I'd still need to make some money. But I could worry about that when I got there.

Reading my profile back, I started to embellish this twenty-something girl I'd created. First up, she needed a name. Glancing at the Evening Standard, I took in the name of the writer of the French piece. Gemma Saunders. Gemma sounded just about right.

Instead of my own name, I typed in Gemma, after a moment's thought, adding Hargreaves, liking how it sounded, imagining her as a hard-working freelance journalist, as my mind ran away with me. When Gemma's boyfriend had just broken up with her, it was the perfect time for her to go away. All she wanted was somewhere peaceful to live — and while she was there, she was going to post endless selfies and really piss him off.

At least, that's what I'd do — but I needed to focus on what Gemma would do. I imagined her personality — calmly confident, sad over losing her boyfriend but grounded enough to know she had to move on. Her speech was well-educated, polite, the language she used enough to display her intelligence without overdoing it, the mannerisms she affected understated so as not to draw attention to herself.

I read through her profile one last time, then pressed submit. While I waited for it to be processed, I opened one of the tins of beans, and toasted a couple of slices of bread, praying that I would get lucky. If miraculously I did, it might not be long before I was out of here.

Maybe fortune had decided to favour the bold, but by the time I'd finished eating, to my astonishment, my profile had been accepted.

Scrolling down the house sits I'd marked, I applied to five, crossing my fingers as my heart started to race. I needed this so badly. But with luck on my side, it might not be long before I'd be leaving this dismal flat and on my way.

Instead of looking for another job as a fallback, I concentrated on seeing myself in shorts and a t-shirt, sitting in the corner of a shaded rose-clad garden; spending mornings drifting through little village markets, whiling away afternoons beside gently meandering rivers.

It paid off. After receiving a response from one of the house owners, we arranged a telephone conversation. Having been let down at the last minute, they needed someone to start this weekend. Channelling Gemma, I told them everything they'd want to hear in grammatically perfect language. How I loved gardening. I wouldn't dream of keeping the house anything other than spotless – in any case, I had a dust allergy. The pool was no problem at all – my family had one when I was a teenager.

Half an hour later, the deal was done. The fact that it was based solely on trust was inconceivable to me. No police check required; they hadn't even asked to see my references. More fool them – if this didn't work out, they could hardly blame me.

After being at rock bottom, I felt euphoric. I couldn't believe how quickly this had fallen into place. Going to my bedroom, I started to sort through my clothes. Picking out items I imagined Gemma would wear, I packed them into my rucksack, putting what was left in a bag for a charity shop. Ditto my meagre possessions, ruthlessly throwing them away, keeping only a necklace that had sentimental value.

I wasn't going to bother cleaning the flat, justifying that with the fact that it had been a tip when I moved in. It seemed a fair exchange. Going over to the mirror, I gazed at my reflection, feeling a thrill of excitement. This was the last day of my old life. As for tomorrow . . . whatever my new life held, it had to be better than this one.

The following morning, I got up early, wanting to be out before my landlord turned up. Ricky would stoop to anything to get his hands on his money and if it wasn't there, he'd insist on payment in kind. I remembered too clearly how he'd tried it on with me in the past. As I closed the door, I was about to post my key through the letterbox when I had a flashback to last time he came here. Pinning me against the wall, he'd forced his tongue in my mouth. I shoved the key in my pocket instead, along with the rent money I wasn't going to give him. The bastard could pay for new locks. There was no way he was going to catch up with me, so Ricky could go to hell for all I cared.

★

As the train sped south, in my mind I was already Gemma Hargreaves, knowing she could be whoever I wanted her to be; her past one that only I knew about. Wiling away the journey, I dreamed up her swanky London flat, her wardrobe of expensive clothes; the friends she went out with, the bars they drank at. I thought about the book she was allegedly going to write. A literary novel, sharply observed, about everything that's wrong in this fucking world. Who knows — maybe I'd give writing a try. In my short life, I'd gathered more material than most girls my age.

Reaching Dover, I found a cash machine and took out what was left in there in euros, before buying a couple of rather writerly looking notebooks. Showing my passport — the only link that remained to my old life — relief filled me as I put it away; as the old me was gone for good.

In no time, I was boarding the ferry. Finding a seat near a window, I peered through the salt-stained glass as England grew smaller, inwardly cheering as it vanished into the distance, before turning my thoughts towards the future. Closing my eyes, I pictured the house I was going to in Hèches, a village in the foothills of the Pyrenees. I had six months there, all expenses paid, in return for looking after the place.

Turning the thought around in my mind, I luxuriated in it. It was an opportunity the like of which I'd never known before. It was also entirely up to me what I made of it. In the meantime, however, I still had to figure out how to get there.

After disembarking in Dieppe, I'd planned to hitch to Toulouse, until a brief blip when my second ride wanted paying.

'Surely you weren't expecting to get this for nothing.' The car slewed slightly as the driver leered at me.

'Look, I just wanted a ride.' Channel Gemma, I told myself. Stay focused, keep calm.

'That's exactly what I had in mind.' He placed a large hand on my thigh. 'You and me, a cheap motel . . .'

Nausea rose in my throat. 'Fuck off,' I told him. 'I mean it, arsehole.'

His hand slid towards my crotch. 'Not so posh now, are you?'

The car was going too fast for me to risk making a run for it. Gazing out of the window, I bit my tongue, enduring his abrasive invasion of my thighs until we reached the next town, where he was forced to slow down.

As we came to a junction and the lights changed to red, I grabbed my bag and opened the door. Jumping out, determined he wasn't getting away with this, I paused just long enough to lean down and peer back into the car. 'So long, fucker.'

Slamming the door shut, I swung my bag at the window, smiling to myself as I heard the glass crack. Ignoring his angry shouts, I walked away, slipping into a shop where I took an inordinately long time scrutinising second-hand books in French that I couldn't translate a single word of.

Eventually, deciding enough time had passed for him to have gone, I went back outside. The street was quiet, only a few cars passing by, and as I carried on walking, I noticed a sign for the station. I weighed it up. Either I took the risk of another encounter like the last one, or I spent some hard-earned cash and caught a train. I paused long enough to ask myself what Gemma would do. It was a no-brainer. Carrying on, I headed for the station.

The episode with the pervy driver was soon forgotten as three trains later, I was blown away as the Pyrenees came into view. As we grew closer, their jagged peaks grew more dramatic, until I would have sworn I was on the edge of another world.

Before long, the train pulled into Hèches, a typically quiet French town nestled in the foothills, the terrain broken here and there by rivers and streams which sparkled in the late afternoon sunlight.

Outside the station, I got out the instructions I'd been given. It was about a ten-minute walk to the house, and as I set off, the early evening air was still warm, alive with insects, ringing with the sound of birdsong. I found the house easily enough. Set back from the road up a long drive, there were jaw-dropping views in every direction, of mountains, fields, a golden setting sun. The contrast with London couldn't have been more striking. It seemed incredible to me that there was no traffic noise, just the occasional sheep or resonant clang from a cowbell.

But I couldn't shake off the sense of unease I felt. So far, this whole thing had felt too good to be true and usually when that happened, it was because it was. But I found the key exactly where I was told it would be — in an unlocked shed around the side of the house that was filled with an array of gardening paraphernalia. Finding the big wooden door at the back and turning the key in the lock, I stepped into a whole new world. One I never wanted to leave again.

Taking my time, I explored the large rooms, taking in the high ceilings and comfortable furniture, the wood-burning stoves beside which firewood had been neatly piled, pausing now and then to study pieces of artwork, before making my way up stone stairs worn smooth by age.

Checking out the bedrooms, I was stunned — by the size of the beds, the beautifully made curtains, the modern en suites. Mine, I'd been told, was at the far end. Moving to that room, I took in the huge bed made up with soft linen, the enormous wardrobe that could only have been built in here. Opening the windows, I fastened the shutters back.

Gazing at the mountains bathed in the evening sunlight, I became aware of a new sense of determination burning deep inside me. Having left behind my hand-to-mouth existence in London, I knew this was the life I was supposed to have. And now I'd found it, there was nothing I would stop at to hold on to it.

4

Jude

After a call from one of the partners I work with, I reluctantly take a detour and call in at the practice, before eventually I set off for Kat and Oliver's house. Twenty miles from Deal, it's in a small village that's an easy commute and not too far from the airport. It's a lovely house – a cottage, really, that was supposed to be a forever home, with space to bring up children. Children they'll never have. I swallow the lump in my throat, as putting my foot down, I drive faster.

Struggling to take in what's happened, my eyes blur with tears as I think of never seeing Oliver again; how his death is going to decimate all our lives. As grief erupts inside me, I force myself to contain it; to think of Kat again, dreading what this will do to her. But at least she has us. She's as much our family as any of us. We'll rally round; understand each other's grief. Whether as a husband, son, brother, all of us have lost him.

The roads are rain-soaked and I drive on autopilot,

swerving to pass a cyclist I see at the last minute before forcing myself to slow down. Another accident is the last thing this family needs.

But my thoughts are all over the place, my heart breaking as I think of the son I've lost. As I take in that I'll never see him again, grief wells up inside me.

My mind turns to Oliver and Kat's wedding day – the most beautiful of weddings in a country house hotel. I remember them planning it together, how they wanted it to be the most magical of days; my heart twisting with grief as I imagine his funeral.

Knowing Kat didn't have her mother to share it with her, I was honoured when she asked if I would help her. We chose the flowers together – blush and off-white roses, with honeysuckle, the lily of the valley that was a nod to my own bouquet when Richard and I were married, a gesture that touched me. I went with her when she was looking for her dress, too. I remember how her eyes shone when she found the one she wanted; how handsome Oliver looked, how his eyes were filled with love when she walked into the church and he saw her in it.

A well of aching sadness opens up inside me as my head fills with memories of the son I've lost. The baby, the fair-haired toddler; his fascination when his brother was born. More memories of the two of them together, climbing trees, building dens in our garden. Knowing how badly Joe is going to miss him, my hands shake on the steering wheel as I force myself to think of Kat – the sadness of her childhood before she lost her parents. When she's been through so much, it's too cruel that she's lost Oliver, too.

When Oliver introduced us to Kat, I loved how bright

she was; but over time I learned the way she hid what she found so difficult to talk about, the vulnerability she rarely showed that had brought out a side of Oliver I hadn't seen before, one who wanted to protect her.

As we grew closer, when Kat told me about her past, it was heart-wrenching. Her mother had been ill most of her childhood. *You get used to it,* she told me. *It's just how life is.* But when Kat was fourteen, her mother died, and a week later, her heartbroken father took his own life. Luckily Kat had her grandmother. *We were lucky . . . We understood each other. And we loved each other.* Somehow seeing the positives in a story that to anyone else was completely heartbreaking. But her grandmother had died a few years later, too. From there on, Kat had put herself through university. *You know that handful of students who stay in halls when everyone else goes home to their families for Christmas? After Grandma died, I was one of those.*

Just as there was no one to celebrate her graduation, to feel proud when she qualified as a counsellor, every step of the way, she was alone – until she met Oliver. I've always felt so proud that he was the man she fell in love with; whom she felt she could trust, just as I was proud, too, that he went after the job he'd always coveted; of the home, the future he and Kat were building together.

But just like that, all of it is gone.

Joe will be lost without his brother. Unlike Oliver, he's yet to find a career that inspires him. Having been offered a place in his father's business, he turned it down for moral reasons. He didn't want a handout; he wanted to earn a position on merit – which is all commendable. But when all you want is for your children to succeed, Richard could have made it so much easier for him. I know Richard will be devastated. It isn't the natural order of things for children to die before their parents. Losing Oliver is going to hit all of us.

I reach the outskirts of the village, where open countryside gives way to smaller fields and neat hedgerows. Passing the pub, I turn off the main road, slowing down where the narrow lane has flooded before. A little further on, I pull into Kat and Oliver's driveway. Getting out, I hurry to the front door and, finding it unlatched, I go inside.

'Kat?' I start walking along the hallway.

'We're in here.' Joe's voice comes from the kitchen.

I pause in the doorway. 'I'm so sorry I couldn't get here sooner. I had to call in at work.' Taking in Kat's tear-stained face, I go over to her, my eyes filling with tears as I hug her tightly. '*I'm so sorry.*'

The house already feels changed by Oliver's death. Over Kat's shoulder, I meet Joe's eyes. 'The police have gone?'

He nods. 'They left a while ago.'

Loosening my arms from around Kat, I sit on the chair next to her. Her slender figure seems to have shrunk to the proportions of a twelve-year-old as she rests her head in her hands.

'I don't know what I'm going to do without him.'

'I know . . .' Putting an arm around her, I blink away tears as I speak softly into her hair. 'But you still have us.'

'It doesn't make sense, Jude.' Pulling back slightly, her face is puffy, her eyes red from crying. 'He told me he was on a flight to Alicante today.' As her eyes meet mine, they're like a rabbit's caught in the headlights. 'But he wasn't. When we called the airline, they said he doesn't work there anymore.'

I stare at her, confused, not sure what she's saying. 'What do you mean?'

'He's been lying – for the last two months.' She sounds distraught. 'To all of us.'

'I don't understand.' I glance questioningly at Joe.

'After the police left, I phoned the airline. Kat thought they should know sooner rather than later about the accident – they have flights to crew. But they told me Oliver had lost his job two months ago. So Kat called them back. Apparently he'd been reported for being drunk on a flight – twice. The second time, there was almost an accident.'

'What?' Incredulous, I try to take in what he's saying, as I turn to Kat. 'But you would have known if he hadn't been going to work, surely?'

'He's been going out in uniform.' Joe shrugs. 'There was no reason to suspect he wasn't going to work. Kat's seen his rosters, too. He must have made them up.'

'You're saying all this time he's been pretending?' I shake my head in disbelief. It's so far removed from the Oliver I know. 'Why would he do that?' It makes no sense – no sense at all, that Oliver would have been deceiving us. 'So if he hasn't been at work, where has he been? Do you know if he's been paid?'

Kat looks defeated. 'He's been paying the same amount as usual into our joint account. But his salary went into his personal account.'

'It could have come from his savings, I suppose. We'll find out from his bank statements in due course. Kat, we will get to the bottom of this.' But I'm shocked, unable to believe that Oliver could have done this. 'You should come home with me and Joe tonight.'

'I want to stay here.' Kat sounds tearful again.

Joe takes one of her hands. 'Why don't we go? Just for tonight? I'll help you pack a few things,' he says gently. 'We can come back here in the morning.'

For once I'm grateful that Joe's life isn't busy; that we can all be here for each other. As he takes her upstairs, I listen to their footsteps, before my mind turns to Oliver again, imagining him putting on his uniform, pretending to go off to a job he didn't have. What had been going on in his mind? Imagining him feeling guilty, ashamed of drinking too much, it breaks my heart that he couldn't talk to us.

It's incomprehensible that each time he's gone to work, he's deliberately been lying to Kat. I can only imagine he thought he was protecting her while he sorted out his problems. It's the only explanation that makes sense. Surely Kat must have suspected something was amiss. But as I know too well, when you're busy with work and life, it's all too easy to miss what's going on at home.

When Kat and Joe come back down again, my eyes rest on what looks like Oliver's flight bag.

I look at them both. 'Have you checked inside?'

Kat glances at it. 'Not yet.'

'Don't you think we should? There may be some clue as to what Oliver's been doing all this time.'

Seeing Kat's look of uncertainty, Joe's voice is firm. 'Kat's been through enough for one day. It can wait.'

But she shakes her head. 'Jude's right. I do want to know.' Going over, she opens Oliver's flight bag. 'His logbook should be in here.'

She's talking about the records every pilot has to keep, of the date, destination and aircraft type of every single flight they operate. She gets out his licence and a printout of a roster, then a copy of *Private Eye*, some loose euros and a couple of business cards. Frowning, she turns to look at us. 'It isn't here.'

Joe frowns. 'But if he wasn't actually flying, he wouldn't have needed it, would he?'

'I suppose not. But as far as I know, he always kept it in here.' She pauses, frowning. 'He definitely had a hard copy. I know, because he told me how some pilots use electronic versions, but he preferred not to.'

'It must be somewhere in the house.' I look at Kat. 'Do you want to look now?'

She shakes her head. 'I don't know. I don't think so.' A tear rolls down her cheek as she looks at me. 'I don't know anything anymore.'

Watching as more tears roll down her cheeks, I get up and go over to her, taking one of her hands.

'There's nothing that can't wait until tomorrow,' I say gently. 'Shall we go home?'

5

Katharine

In the large sitting room at Oliver's parents' house, I slump into the sofa, my mind filling with memories of happier times – the first time I came here, feeling nervous about meeting his parents and they were so welcoming. The many birthdays, impromptu dinners, Christmases we've spent together since.

In spite of its size, the thick carpet and subtle lighting imbue this room with a cosiness. The sofas are large, luxuriously comfortable; heavy curtains running ceiling to floor. It's a room that hints at the McKenna family's history; that echoes with the past.

I turn my head away from the photos on the wall. Mostly of Oliver and Joe when they were growing up, there are two taken on our wedding day. But it makes no difference. Even with my eyes closed, Oliver's face swims before me.

In this world without him, nothing will ever be the same. But in the space between my thoughts, the truth lingers. *You weren't happy, Kat. You hadn't been happy for a long time. You just hadn't worked out what to do about it.*

I push the thought away, wrapping my arms tightly around myself; telling myself it wasn't Oliver's fault; that it came from the pain I repressed when I lost my parents; that losing him now is bringing it back.

'You should try and eat something.' Coming in, Jude places a plate on the table in front of me.

Looking at the fish and new potatoes she's cooked, nausea rises in my throat. 'Thank you, Jude. But I don't think I can.'

She's being so kind, when she must be feeling as awful as I am. But if I eat, I won't be able to keep it down.

'I'm so sorry . . . for you, too.' My voice breaks. 'Oliver was your son.'

Suddenly Jude looks smaller, older, as though Oliver's death has physically taken something from her.

'I know,' she whispers, her eyes glittering as she swallows.

Going over to the fire, she throws on a couple of perfectly seasoned logs, before coming back.

'Try and have a little. I'll get you some wine.'

As the scent of wood smoke reaches me, I hesitate. 'Do you have anything stronger?'

After bringing me a gin and tonic, she goes back out to the kitchen, as Joe comes in.

'I feel terrible. Your mum is going to so much trouble – I should have stayed at the cottage,' I say tearfully. 'I think it would be better if I was alone.'

'Right now, it isn't going to make a difference where you are,' he says quietly. 'You're in shock, Kat – and you're grieving.'

But we all are. I look at Joe, the loss of his brother etched into his face, dulling his eyes; as mine fill with tears again.

'It isn't just about me. This is terrible for all of us.'

I listen as Richard's car pulls up outside. Seconds later, the back door opens. There are murmured voices in the kitchen, before he comes through to the sitting room.

Like Jude, in just a few hours, grief has aged him, too, and instead of the vibrant man Oliver took after, he looks haggard. In a rare show of what passes for affection from Richard, he holds out a hand towards Joe, shaking his head sadly.

'I'm sorry – for both of you.'

A man not used to sharing his emotions, he speaks hesitantly.

'I couldn't get away earlier. Blasted meeting went on and on . . .' His voice cracks as he sits at the other end of the sofa.

'It's OK.' I blink away more tears.

No one had expected Richard to come racing home. In this family, there's an unwritten understanding that work always comes first. It's why Oliver has always been the golden boy and Joe the black sheep.

'It isn't OK.' He shakes his head. 'How can it be? You and Oliver . . .' His voice cracks again.

Joe sits in one of the armchairs. 'Did Mum tell you – about Oliver losing his job?'

'Yes.' He hesitates. 'I don't know what to make of it. But he must have had his reasons for not saying anything. I can only imagine how he must have felt, but he would have hated to think he'd let you down. Of course, he should have been honest. But we all do things that are out of character – and Oliver . . .' Richard's voice wavers as he glances from me to Joe. 'You know I thought the world of him. We all did.'

'He still should have told me,' I whisper fiercely.

*

After tossing and turning most of the night in what used to be Oliver's old room, the following morning, Joe drives me back to the cottage. In our driveway, I get out, standing there a moment. The air is mild, damp from yesterday's rain; the bird song shrill, and for a moment, it's easy to believe that Oliver is inside, that nothing has changed. But as we go in, after the warmth of the McKennas' house, the cottage is cold, as if overnight, its heart has been ripped out.

In the hallway, I flick the lights on.

'At least the Aga's on.' Joe goes ahead of me to the kitchen. 'About Oliver's logbook . . . apart from his flight bag, is there anywhere else it could be?'

'I don't know.' I head for the stairs. 'I'm going to look.' Pausing at the bottom, I look at Joe. 'Last night, I couldn't sleep. I kept thinking – if Oliver lied about his job, what else might he have been hiding?'

He's quiet for a moment. 'It's probably like Dad said. He must have had reasons that made sense to him. We both know Oliver wasn't a liar, Kat. Maybe he was applying for something else and he didn't want to worry you.'

'No.' I shake my head. 'Getting dressed in his uniform and pretending he was going on a flight, you have to admit, by anyone's standards, how weird that is.'

It hasn't been twenty-four hours, yet as I go upstairs, yesterday feels a lifetime ago. I pause in the doorway of our bedroom, memories coming back to me of the first time we saw this house. I knew straight away we'd found the house of my dreams. It was everything I'd ever imagined – light, with spacious rooms, fireplaces, ancient beams; a place that seemed to feel safe, that could be a sanctuary.

When Oliver and I met, I'd envisaged us sharing the

brightest of futures, but if I'm honest with myself, too soon after moving here, things had started changing – in small ways which I'd put down to the romance inevitably wearing off, not wanting to believe that it was more than that.

Not wanting to dwell on it now, I go to the smaller of our two spare rooms that Oliver occasionally used as an office. It has exposed timbers and a window that looks onto the garden. Going to the desk, as I open the top drawer, I find the paperwork related to the purchase of the house, while another is filled with our old photos. Finding the next one stuck, I force it open to find a brochure from a pilot training organisation. But as I draw it out, underneath there's a small photograph.

Picking it up, I study it more closely. It's of a woman who looks about my age, with long fair hair, smiling at the camera. Turning it over, there's a note on the back.

Proud of you x.

Staring at it, I shiver, my eyes turning to the ring he slipped on my finger the day we were married, that I've never taken off. As well as lying about his job, had he been seeing someone else?

A cold feeling grips me inside. Sliding the ring off my finger, I place it on the desk, where it glints in the light through the window.

*

I put the brochure on the table.

'I found this. It's something to do with a flying training organisation.'

'Oh?' Joe comes over. 'Anything interesting?'

'I haven't looked – I got sidetracked by something else.'

I place the photo of the woman in front of him. 'This,' I say tearfully.

He stares at it. 'Where did you find that?'

'In his desk. It was underneath the other stuff.' I turn it over. 'Look what she's written.'

Studying it, Joe frowns. 'What's that supposed to mean?'

'I haven't a clue.' I wipe away my tears. 'It seems like quite an intimate message, wouldn't you say?'

Joe's silent for a moment. 'You've no idea who she is?'

I shake my head. 'I've never seen her before. Have you?'

He studies it again. 'I don't think so. You think something might have been going on?' But then he answers his own question. 'I can't believe he'd do that to you.'

'I don't know what to think.' My voice wavers. 'But given we were married, it's a little strange he kept a photo of someone else. Who knows? Maybe that's where he was when I thought he was at work.'

'What was he playing at?' Joe's voice is icy. 'Firstly, lying to you and now this.'

'I'm going to see if I can find her on his Facebook. She might be one of his friends.' I start walking towards my study to get my laptop.

'Leave it for now, Kat. It'll take ages. We can check later on. Did you find his logbook?'

'It wasn't in his desk.' Thrown after finding the photo, the message on the back, my mind is jumping all over the place. 'If he was having an affair with this woman, maybe she has it.' I know I'm jumping to conclusions, but at this point I don't know what to believe. 'She might know things we don't. I need to find her, Joe.'

Joe looks furious. 'I know he's my brother, but I'm so ashamed that he could behave like this.'

But I can't deal with Joe's anger. 'We don't actually know something was going on. I'm going outside for a minute. I need some air.'

Leaving him in the kitchen, I pull on my boots and go out into the garden. As I walk to the far end through grass that needs mowing, I listen to a pigeon in a nearby tree. The leaves are turning, the garden filled with autumnal colour – tall purple asters, orange crocosmia and red dahlias. I've loved planting this garden, one day imagining our children playing here. Dreams that have gone on hold forever; that Oliver's death has shattered.

Feeling the chill in the air, I go back in to find Joe leafing through the brochure. 'Maybe the photo means nothing,' I say to him. 'She could be someone he knew before we met.' I'm trying to give him the benefit of the doubt, but however much it's what I want to believe, it feels a step too far.

'What's the brochure about?'

'It's about training courses for Citation Longitudes – long-range private jets,' he says. 'Maybe Oliver was hoping to get a job flying them. He loved flying. Even if he was having problems, I can't imagine him giving it up easily.'

As I look at the photograph of the unfamiliar aircraft, there's something else I need to check. 'Oliver had an annual medical. I'm sure he renewed it recently.' Going to my office, I get the calendar we shared, flipping the pages back until I find what I'm looking for.

'Here.' I show Joe. 'This is his appointment – last month. If he'd lost his job, why would he have bothered with it?'

'Maybe he did it in case you'd notice if his medical had

expired – to stop you asking questions. Or maybe he didn't keep the appointment,' Joe says quietly. 'Where did he go to renew it?'

'There was a place in Horley, near Gatwick. I suppose we could check.'

'If he went, it may well mean he was applying for another job.' He frowns. 'Do you know where his phone is?'

I shake my head. 'Either it's in the car or the police must have it.' A wave of desolation comes at me out of nowhere. 'None of it matters, does it?' I blink away my tears. 'It won't change what's happened. Oliver's dead, I have a funeral to plan, all his stuff to sort out . . .' Suddenly overwhelmed, I look at Joe. 'I hate asking, but would you help?'

'Of course.' Joe's voice softens. 'I've already said I will. Look, this may not be what it appears, Kat. He was probably embarrassed about losing his job. Thought he'd let you down.'

'And the photo . . .' I shrug.

'The photo.' Joe's silent for a moment. 'I don't know, but I don't think we should jump to conclusions. Do you think we should say anything to the police?'

The mention of the police startles me. 'Do you think they'll be interested?'

'They will be if they think his death is suspicious.'

Startled, I look at Joe. 'They said the roads were flooded. He lost control. I don't think they were implying anything more sinister than that.'

Joe pushes his chair back. 'How about this: if they think his death is suspicious, then obviously, we have a duty to tell them. But if they decide it was a genuine accident, there's no reason to, is there? I mean, it's hardly evidence of anything more than a possibility that Oliver cheated on you. It's a personal matter. If you don't want to tell them, I'm with you on that.'

As he speaks, my emotions swing between sadness and anger at Oliver's duplicity; the bare-faced lies that undermine the life we shared, before my grief comes back, for everything I've lost. Despairing, I turn to Joe.

'I don't know how to deal with any of this.'

'I know.' He looks troubled. 'God knows what Mum and Dad would think if they knew about the photo.'

When Jude's been so kind to me, when she's lost her son, I can't put her through this. 'I do think we should keep the photo between you and me. Your mum is already upset enough.'

Joe nods his agreement. 'OK. If you're sure that's what you want.'

'It is.' But there's another reason, too. And that's me. When it hasn't been easy living with Oliver these last few months, it would be too humiliating to have to explain it to anyone.

*

That evening, when we tell Oliver's parents about the missing logbook, Jude looks uncertain.

'Maybe the police should know. Someone may have taken it.'

'It's not as if there's a crime investigation going on,' Richard says quietly. 'At least, not at the moment. I agree with Kat and Joe. Let's see what they say when they've examined the car. Unless they think his death is suspicious, anything else is simply personal.'

'And it's not like his logbook is any use to anyone else,' Joe points out.

I glance at him, grateful. The thought of talking to the police again is something I'd rather not think about.

'The only other thing we found was some literature on flying training,' Joe says. 'On Citation Longitudes. And Kat remembered him planning to renew his medical last month, which would have been after he lost his airline job.'

'Interesting.' Richard frowns. 'It can't be difficult to find out who operates those jets in the UK. I can get someone to look into it.'

Getting up, I look at them both, horrified. I've faced enough for one day. I know there are unanswered questions, but I'd give anything for this to stop, for it to be over; not to go on poring over unimportant details or imagining fictitious scenarios. We need proof, but it can wait, surely, until tomorrow.

'*Please.*' They both turn to look at me. 'I'm sorry – but this is already difficult enough. Can we leave it – at least for now?'

6

Jude

I want to know what's happened as much as anyone else, but Oliver's death is too recent, my emotions too raw to think straight.

'Kat's right.' Aware of her distress, I try to divert her. 'Let's make some tea.'

We go to the kitchen together. Sitting at the table, Kat's silent as she watches me fill the kettle and switch it on. Before I get out some mugs, I pause.

'I noticed you'd taken your ring off.'

'Oh.' Kat's cheeks flush. I try to make out if her surprised glance at her hand is genuine or not, as she goes on. 'I was rubbing in some hand cream earlier. I must have forgotten to put it back on.'

It's a plausible enough reason. In the strange place we inhabit in the light of Oliver's death, our minds are elsewhere. I hesitate before bringing up a subject none of us want to think about.

'Kat? Have you given any thought to the funeral at all?'

The question seems to hang in the air before she shakes her head.

'I haven't been able to face thinking about it.'

It's like it was on her and Oliver's wedding day, when she had no family to help her plan it.

'I'll help you – we all will, if you want us to.'

'Thank you.' Her knuckles are white as she clenches her hands together. 'Joe's already offered.' She hesitates. 'Every time I think about it, it keeps taking me back to when my gran died.'

It's what grief does; triggers the latent memory of other losses. When we prefer not to think about death, planning a funeral is an alien process. 'I don't know whether you remember much from when your gran died,' I say gently. 'But the first thing we need to do is register his death, for which we need his death certificate. To some extent, that will depend on whether or not the police think his death was accidental.' When you are unfamiliar with dealing with a death, these are huge things to get your head around.

She nods. 'I remember now.'

Looking at her again, I pause. 'Would you like Earl Grey or Darjeeling?'

'Earl Grey.' Kat stares at the table.

'Then after that . . .' I hesitate. 'I imagine Oliver has left a will?'

Continuing to stare at the table, she nods. 'We both wrote wills – after buying the house. Mark Osborne advised us to.'

'Good.' Mark Osborne has been our family solicitor for years – and it will make the next stage easier. 'We'll need to contact him. Then you'll need to apply for probate.'

'Where do we start with the funeral?' As she says *funeral,* her voice breaks. 'My gran's was small – at the crematorium. But there'll be loads of people who want to come, won't there?'

'Probably.' I swallow the lump in my throat. 'It depends where you would like to hold it – if you want a service in a church or crematorium. We should also think about publishing a death notice.' While I try to keep my composure, to think of Kat, as I think of burying my son, the pain I feel is visceral. 'Oliver never used to be religious – unless anything had changed?'

'No.' Her voice is tiny. 'Neither of us were – are.' She can't work out which tense to use. In her head, instead of divided by death, she and Oliver are still together. 'I suppose a church is traditional.' She raises her eyes to mine. 'After all, we were married in one. And he could have a grave then, couldn't he?'

Religious or not, sometimes there's comfort in having somewhere to go to sit for a while and remember someone.

'If that's what you want,' I say gently.

'*None of this is what I want.*' It bursts out of her. 'I want life to go back to how it was before. I wish for yesterday to never have happened.' Leaning forwards, she buries her head in her hands.

There's nothing I can say. I know how she feels; because I feel exactly the same. Going over, I crouch down next to her.

'Kat? When something like this happens, there is no rhyme or reason to it; no understanding, no good to come out of it.' I pause. 'Now and then, life throws these things at us. We just go on putting one foot in front of the other. And slowly, eventually, I promise you, it will get easier.'

As she looks at me, her eyes are wide as she seems to struggle with some kind of inner turmoil.

'Are you sure? Because that's the thing,' she whispers. 'I can't imagine it's ever going to.'

★

Later that evening, after Joe drives Kat home, Richard comes to find me.

'Hideous, isn't it?' He sounds deeply weary, a man from whom several years have been shaved off, but that's what Oliver's death has done to both of us.

As I gaze at him, my eyes fill with tears. I've been holding it together for Kat's sake, but without her here, I let my guard down.

'Not so good.' Suddenly I'm sobbing.

Coming over, he rests a hand on my shoulder. We are not an affectionate couple, but in our mutual loss, our pain is equal; an integral part of our lives has been brutally ripped out of us.

'I already miss him more than I imagined possible,' Richard mutters.

When his default is cold detachment, this smallest display of emotion is utterly surprising from Richard, as I wonder if this could be a turning point; if after years of drifting apart and leading separate lives, Oliver's death has the potential to reunite us.

★

I awake early the next morning. As I lie in bed, for a split second the world is as it used to be, before the reality of Oliver's death comes flooding back. As grief hits me anew, I get up and go downstairs to make some coffee.

But before Richard goes to work, there's something on my mind.

'Did you ever see anything to indicate that things weren't quite right between Oliver and Kat?'

Richard looks surprised. 'No. Should I have?'

'I don't know.' Frowning, I shake my head. 'It's just a hunch – but it's so out of character for him not to tell her about something as big as losing his job. Equally, it's just as odd that she hadn't noticed something was wrong.'

He seems dismissive. 'They've always seemed fine when I've seen them together – though I haven't spent much time with him the last couple of months.'

'Me neither.' I hesitate. 'That's another thing. A couple of times we arranged to meet for lunch, but at the last minute, he cancelled.' I shrug. 'A guilty conscience, perhaps? Or perhaps he didn't want to put himself into a situation where he knew he'd be forced to lie?'

'About losing his job?' Richard raises his eyebrows. 'In the circumstances, it's entirely possible.'

'I just regret that he didn't feel he was able to talk to us,' I say sadly.

'For goodness' sake, Jude.' Richard speaks abruptly. 'He has no one to blame for this other than himself. I have to go. I'll see you tonight.'

His lack of empathy leaves me speechless. But in our new world of suspicion and secrets, anything is possible. It's a world that takes a more sinister turn, when the following day, Kat calls me.

'Kat . . . Slow down. It's a terrible line. I can't hear you.'

'The police called me.' She sounds hysterical. 'They've

53

examined the car. They think someone may have tampered with the brakes.'

Shock hits me. 'Are they sure? Who would do that? Did they say any more?'

She mutters something about fingerprints I can't properly make out.

'Kat? Can you say that again?'

'They're checking the car for fingerprints. They want to take mine,' she sobs. 'Of course mine are on there – it was my car. You don't think they'll think it was me, do you?'

I try to calm her. 'The police know it's your car – they'd expect to find your prints.'

'I have to go to the police station.' Kat sounds beside herself. 'But Joe isn't here. I don't think I can do this on my own.'

I try to take in what she's saying; to imagine who could have tampered with the brakes. Does this make this a murder enquiry? Dazed, I say to Kat, 'Don't worry. You don't have to. I'll take you.'

2010

Gemma

As I adapted to my new life in the foothills of the Pyrenees, I quickly realised how easy this was. OK, so I had a long list of so-called duties, but I didn't need to worry about those until the owners were coming back. I soon settled in, spending lazy days lying by the pool, my skin tanning and my hair lightening. I was growing used to life in the sun. It suited me far more than life in London had.

But there was an air of unreality about it, caused by one looming problem: cash flow. Having gone through all the pockets of the clothes that had been left in the house, I'd acquired the princely sum of fifty euros — better than nothing, but I needed more.

Scouring the surrounding countryside, there were riches to be had for free — as long as I was savvy. An orchard of peach trees, a strawberry farm. If I timed it right, there was no one around to stop me picking fruit. That was when I realised — if I gathered enough, I could sell them at one of the markets.

Collecting a sizeable basket full of peaches by moonlight, I filled another with figs from the garden. Sitting in the shade of a tree close to where everyone parked, I'd sold the lot in the first hour. Forty euros richer, I knew it was survival-level money that would cover my food. Meanwhile, I'd discovered the house had a cellar and if I fancied a bottle of wine to go alongside dinner, there was plenty to choose from.

Just as this life was seeming sustainable, one Tuesday afternoon there was a knock at the door. Opening it, I found a woman standing there.

'You must be Gemma!' She held out her hand. 'I'm Allison – I'm a friend of Ray and Sally's. They've probably mentioned they asked me to pop by and make sure you were getting on OK.'

'How lovely to meet you!' Forcing one of my brightest smiles, I tried to ignore the feeling of foreboding that came over me. 'They probably did – and I've probably forgotten!'

Ray and Sally were the owners of the house. I watched Allison frown slightly as she glanced past me towards the sitting room. Knowing she'd seen the clothes and bed sheets I'd washed piled on the furniture, I did my best to reassure her.

'Everything's wonderful,' I smiled brightly again, grateful that she couldn't see into the kitchen. 'I'm having a bit of a laundry day – I'm afraid things are rather all over the place.'

'You do know there is a laundry room?' Her smile faded slightly.

'I do! I just love the light in this room.' I glanced back at the sitting room. 'I'm nearly done. I'm in the middle of putting it all away.' I tried to deflect her. 'Actually, one thing I have had a problem with is the mower. But there's a man I've found who's coming out to take a look at it – just in case you were wondering why the grass was so long. I'm pretty good with mechanical things but for some reason, this mower has defeated me.'

Giving her a full-wattage Gemma smile, I was lying. I hadn't even attempted to start the mower.

'He said he'd try and come tomorrow — so kind of him.' I paused. 'Where is it that you live?'

'We're about ten miles from here — towards Lannemazan . . .' As she carried on about all the work they'd had done to their house, about the builders who'd come and gone, stifling a yawn, I pretended to listen intently. When she paused for air, I gave her another smile.

'It's been so nice meeting you, Allison.' I crossed my fingers behind my back. 'Next time, you really must come for lunch.'

'Thank you,' she beamed. 'Yes, I really should be getting on. When I talk to Sally next, I'll tell her you're looking after things beautifully.'

'Splendid. Thank you.' Standing in the doorway, I watched her walk out to her car, holding my breath that she didn't think of anything else, before she got in, waving once as she drove away.

Going back inside, my smile dropped as my anger came back. I had no compunction about lying. It was fine for people like her, with their cosy little lives and private pension funds; the smug rich with their self-worthiness and sense of entitlement. In short, people like my parents. People who didn't give a shit about anyone else.

Closing the door, I breathed a sigh of relief. But I was kicking myself. That was a close shave. If she'd come in, she'd have found the kitchen in a mess with an array of empty wine bottles; the entire house in disarray. I'd be a fool to be rumbled when life here was about as good as it got. From here on, I needed to make sure that if anyone called by, they would see nothing out of place. A little gardening wouldn't go amiss, either.

The following week, as I finished selling that day's fruit, I noticed a girl watching me. The guarded look on her face reminded me of myself pre-Gemma as she came over.

'Where did you get this?'

'I grow it,' I flashed her a super-powered smile. 'The garden's full of it — I can't bear to see it go to waste.' I passed her a fig. 'Try this.' I paused. 'I'm Gemma.'

'I'm Nadia.' She took the fig. 'Cheers.'

'You doing anything? Or would you like to get a beer?' When I spent so much time alone, I fancied the idea of some English conversation.

'Sure.' She spoke through her last mouthful of fig.

'I know a place.' But as we started walking towards a bar I knew, I heard footsteps coming from behind me as a voice called out.

'Madame?'

I knew who it was — the guy who collected the fees for the pitches, who until now, hadn't taken any notice of me.

'Run,' I urged her.

Turning down a little side street, Nadia was ahead of me.

'In here.' Ducking under a low roof, she disappeared from sight. In the nick of time, I followed.

Abandoning the bar idea, I invited her to come back with me, taking the long way around the town to avoid being caught again, before we headed away towards the house.

'This is frigging awesome.' As we walked inside, Nadia's eyes darted around, taking it all in.

'Nice, isn't it?' I said casually, going to the fridge and getting out a couple of beers. I passed her one.

'So how come you're here?' Gazing up at the high ceiling, her eyes were constantly on the move as she took in the fixtures and fittings. 'Does it belong to your family or something?'

'It belongs to a couple I've never even met.' I watched her face. Her eyes widened. 'So what's the crack?'

I shrugged. 'It's simple. I look after the place.'

'Yeah, right.' She glanced around the messy kitchen. 'Do they pay you?'

'No,' I said nonchalantly. 'But I get the run of the house and garden — and the pool.'

'Pool?' Her eyes gleamed.

'Come on, I'll show you.' Leading her outside, I followed the path around to the back of the house, then under the arch over which the roses were in full bloom, breathing in air that was heady with their scent. Reaching the paved area around the swimming pool, I stopped.

'What do you think?'

'I think you're bloody lucky.' She gazed at the glistening water. 'Can we swim?'

'Go ahead.' Taking my beer, I sat on one of the loungers that was shaded from the sun, watching as she stripped off her clothes and dived in, staying submerged for a few moments before coming up for air.

'I've forgotten how that feels.' Coming to the side of the pool, her hair was slicked back, her skin glistening with water droplets. 'Aren't you coming in?'

I shook my head. 'Not now.' I may have invited her here, but truth was, I was still trying to get the measure of her. 'So where are you living?'

'All over . . . I'm travelling — I stay wherever. Hostels, sometimes people's houses; barns even, when I'm desperate.' Watching me raise an eyebrow, she sighed. 'OK. I met this lousy guy. He screwed me over in every sense. The upshot of it is I don't have a lot of money left. There's nothing in the UK for me anymore. So my plan is to keep moving while I work out what I'm going to do next.'

I tried to weigh up if she was lying or not, but in many ways, it was a story I could relate to. 'Stay here a night if you like,' I offered. 'There's plenty of room.'

'You're sure?' She sounded surprised. Then before I could change my mind, she added, 'Fuck, Gemma. I'd really love to.'

It was my first real trial of maintaining Gemma in front of someone else. But as it turned out, a worthwhile one. After starting the mower, Nadia made short work of the overgrown lawn, leaving it looking better than it had in a long time. Meanwhile, I got on with the far less arduous task of raiding the larder to put another meal together.

But by the third day, when Nadia showed no sign of leaving, I decided it was time to confront her.

'OK. So I said you could stay a night, but I think it's time you moved on.'

She frowned slightly. 'What's the problem if I stay a little longer?'

'For starters, it isn't my house.'

'Does it really make any difference to you?' Her voice was hard, all traces of friendliness gone, as suddenly I saw through her. She was desperate; in it for herself — just as I was.

'Before we met, you would have had to find somewhere else to stay,' I tried to sound reasonable. 'I'm just saying, maybe it's time.'

She shrugged. 'What if I don't want to?'

I was starting to get irritated. 'Look, the owners don't want me to have people staying. A friend of theirs comes by sometimes — supposedly to check everything's OK. But I think it's more about checking up on me. I have to fulfil my side of the arrangement — otherwise they're quite within their rights to get rid of me.'

'So? They don't have to know anyone else is here. And let's face it, judging from how the garden looked, I've done far more than you in the short time I've been here.'

I folded my arms, struck by the irony that, in becoming Gemma, I'd run up against myself. I thought hard for a minute.

'OK. So here's the deal. You can stay until the weekend, but in exchange . . .' I gave her a list of chores that badly needed doing

– windows cleaning, paths sweeping, the sort of shit I preferred not to be bothered with. Desperate as she was, she went for it.

I watched her like a hawk. The saying 'keep your friends close but your enemies closer' had never felt as true as it did here. But life had become rather too quiet and while Nadia's refusal to leave was cause for concern, it added a certain jeopardy to being here.

There was something about her I didn't trust, and on Saturday afternoon, while she was swimming, I went upstairs to the bedroom she was using. Like me, her possessions were few and I'm not sure what I was looking for, but when I went through her rucksack and pulled out a small bundle tied up in a headscarf, I knew I'd found it.

'What the fuck do you think you're playing at?'

My voice was icy as I confronted her with the jewellery she'd stolen from the master bedroom. I knew it was from there because I'd already checked it out.

'Why are you doing this to me?' Her eyes were wounded as she looked at me.

I could see what she was doing, turning it around and playing the victim when the reality was, she was anything but.

'Save the gaslighting for someone who gives a shit,' I said harshly. 'You can't waltz in and take what doesn't belong to you.'

'Why not? All I'm doing, in a very small way, is redistributing some unnecessary wealth. People who own a house like this can afford to be a little generous.' She shrugged. Then she gave me a sly look. 'You've been thinking the same, haven't you? How else would you know they were from this house?'

I stared back at her. 'I trusted you.'

'More fool you, Gemma,' she mocked, 'for trusting people. But you don't really, do you? Why else would you have run away here?'

'I have not run away,' I said coldly. 'I have every right to be here, while you have none.'

'So what are you going to do? Call the police?' she taunted.

While I'd rather not be bothered with dealing with the local gendarmes, I would call them if I had to. 'If you don't leave, that's exactly what I'm doing.'

Watching her face pale, I marched out of the kitchen. Going upstairs, I started packing her things, zipping up her rucksack before lobbing it out of a window at the front of the house.

Back downstairs, I stood in the doorway to the kitchen. 'Your stuff is outside in the drive. It's time for you to leave.'

As she got up, her eyes glittered with rage. Pushing past me, she stopped suddenly, before turning and taking a swing at me. Somehow I managed to dodge out of the way, but as her fist connected with the door frame, she completely lost it. Hurling herself at me, she tried to get her hands around my neck. As we fell to the floor, I struggled to free my arms, using all the strength I could muster to shove her backwards, away from me.

Wincing at the horrible splintering sound that followed, I stared at Nadia's motionless body, silence filling the house, a feeling of horror taking me over as I noticed blood seeping from the back of her head. As she'd fallen, she'd hit the bottom step of the stone staircase. I watched, transfixed for a moment, before I pulled myself together. Running to the laundry room, I collected some towels, piling them around her to soak up the blood, thinking quickly. It had been an accident, but if I called the police, I'd probably get banged up in a French jail.

Standing there, I could feel my heart racing. It was my own stupid fault – I should never have invited her here. But I'd seen death too many times for it to hold any real shock value. The fact was, people died every day – for all kinds of reasons – particularly people like Nadia who took risks. While other people might be emotional about it, I saw it for what it was – at some point, death would come for all of us.

All I had to do now was dispose of any evidence. But as I thought about the best way to do that, I realised that Nadia herself had secured the means to her own disposal. The tractor mower started first time, as methodically, I drove it as close as I could to the house, before dragging her body outside and as best I could into the grass box.

Trundling across the garden, I was praying that Allison wouldn't choose this moment to turn up. At the furthest end of the lawn, I carried on as far as I could into the woods until, under the trees, I came across a half-drained pond. There were thousands of miles of woodland around here and I'd often wondered what might be hidden there. Stopping the mower, I somehow manoeuvred Nadia's body into the water, before looking around for branches, logs, anything to pile on top in order to conceal her.

Two hours later, you wouldn't have known anything had happened. Every last trace of the blood-stained towels had been incinerated in the firepit designed for garden rubbish, Nadia's possessions with them. Tidying the bedroom she'd used, I cleaned it and wiped the surfaces down, until every remaining trace of her had gone.

I scrubbed every inch between the kitchen and stairs, was still scrubbing the next day when Allison turned up. Suitably flustered, I didn't have to pretend. But her timing was perfect – the house was the cleanest it had been since I arrived.

'Allison! How are you? Sorry – I'm in the middle of cleaning.' I stood back to let her in. 'But come and have a cold drink. It's so hot again, isn't it?'

Her pink face glistened with sweat. 'That would be lovely – if you're sure?'

'Of course! Come through.' I led her towards the kitchen, maximising the opportunity for her to feed back to Sally. 'I can't offer you wine. But would you like water or orange juice?'

'Water.' Coming in, she gazed around the kitchen. 'Such a lovely room, isn't it?'

'It really is.' I passed her a glass of water. 'So how have you been?'

'So busy, you wouldn't believe.' She raised her eyes to the ceiling. 'I honestly thought living in France would be quiet – but it's anything but. I'm sure you know what I mean.'

'I really do,' I said honestly.

Suddenly she looked startled. 'What's that?'

As she pointed towards a patch of marks on the wall, my blood ran cold.

Thinking quickly, I pinned on one of my brightest smiles; my eyes fixed on the small flecks of what I knew were Nadia's blood. 'After a glass or two of wine, I'm always spilling things! Probably pasta sauce. Us girls, hey?' I crossed my fingers, hoping she'd go for it, but there was never any real danger she wouldn't. It would be beyond someone like Allison to even imagine what had gone on in here.

She winked conspiratorially. 'I know! Terrible, aren't we?'

7

Katharine

It's another half-dark day as I wait, on edge, for Jude to come over. When she comes into the house, my distress is impossible to hide.

'Thank you for coming.' My nerves are taut, my stomach churning. 'It's horrible knowing the police think someone tampered with my car. But whoever it was couldn't have known Oliver would be driving it. Someone must have been trying to kill me.' I'm shaky, tears filling my eyes.

Jude looks startled. 'My God. Why?'

'I don't know. I just keep imagining someone out there – when Oliver and I were sleeping. If only I'd woken up . . . none of this would have happened.'

'I know this is a huge shock.' Jude's eyes are troubled. 'But try not to think about it too much. We should probably get over to the police station. Are you ready?'

Under her pale face, behind the redness of her eyes, Jude's the epitome of calm, a measure of the strength she possesses.

Not trusting myself to speak, I nod, picking up my door

keys, pulling on a woolly hat against the elements. Neither of us says much as she drives, both lost in our thoughts, my eyes turned to the grey landscape, to the rain that's barely let up since Oliver died. The road into Deal is quiet, and turning into the police station, Jude parks and switches the engine off.

I sit there for a moment. 'I've never had my fingerprints taken before.'

'It isn't because they think you're a criminal. The police are doing what they have to,' she tries to reassure me. 'It won't take long. Come on. Let's get it over with.'

Inside, we're met by DS Stanley and escorted into a room just off the reception area. Jude's right. It doesn't take long. But before we leave, DS Stanley stops us.

'Given it was your car that was tampered with, there's a very real possibility that it was you, rather than your husband, who was the intended target. Is there anyone you can think of who'd want to hurt you?'

As she confirms my worst fears, the blood drains from my face. 'I've thought the same – and no.' I pause. 'I can't think of a single person.'

'I suggest that until we know more, you stay vigilant. Keep your doors locked – and if you see anyone suspicious hanging around, call us straight away. In the meantime, we're treating your husband's death as suspicious. It means there will be a post-mortem, and possibly an inquest further down the line, but we won't know for sure until we gather more information.'

Knowing Oliver's death was probably intentional, as I try to take in what she's saying, suddenly I don't feel safe at all. I glance at Jude. 'I wasn't expecting there to be an inquest.'

'When a death occurs in circumstances such as your husband's, we have to report it to the Coroner,' DS Stanley explains. 'It will be up to them to decide whether to hold one or not.'

*

As we drive back to the house, Jude sounds worried. 'Maybe you should come and stay with us for a while. If there's someone out there trying to harm you, it might be safer.'

I falter, thinking about it. In one sense, it's tempting, but I'd rather have familiar surroundings around me. 'There are things I need to sort through at home. I'll keep everything locked – and I have neighbours if I need someone.'

'Well, if you change your mind, you only have to say. It's unbelievable, isn't it? That someone got to your car without you or Oliver noticing.'

Beside her, I'm rigid. 'They could easily have done it at night. No one passing by can see the garage from the road – the hedge is too tall.'

'You're going to need a car, Kat. I'll ask Richard to get someone to come over and fix Oliver's.'

Anxiety rises in me. 'What if someone's got to his, too?'

Jude tries to reassure me. 'Don't worry. We'll make sure it's thoroughly checked over.'

Back home, I keep the windows and doors locked, my phone on me at all times, thoughts churning around my head as I wonder what the police will find. When Joe doesn't mention the photo again, I keep it out of sight, hidden in my bag, as in the days that follow, he helps me go through the pockets of Oliver's clothes. I look for some clue as to where Oliver's been, but we find nothing of any significance and after packing them into plastic bags we carry on, separating his possessions from mine.

I try to keep a lid on my emotions, but now and then they erupt out of me. 'He's a bastard,' I sob furiously to Joe, as we fill a bag with Oliver's shirts. 'A fucking, lying bastard. *And I was so stupid . . .*'

Standing up, Joe takes me by the arms. 'You weren't stupid. You loved him. Honestly, I thought he loved you too – the day you got married, I'd never known him so happy.'

'He fooled me,' I cry, shaking as I pull my arms away. Picking up a mug, I hurl it at the wall. 'He fooled all of us. Why didn't I know, Joe? *Why*?'

'Because you're you,' he says quietly. 'You trust people. You don't expect to be duped by people you love. It's Oliver who was the fool. Not you.'

Between us, Joe and I notify all the financial companies with which Oliver had accounts. More than once, he queries the way Oliver and I have handled our finances.

'Everything is in his name – the utility bills, everything to do with the cars.' He frowns. 'Surely they should be in both your names.'

'It's how Oliver did it. I know it looks old-fashioned.' What I mean is, I know how weak it looks, as though I expected Oliver to look after it all for me. 'But we shared the costs – we both paid money into our joint account.'

'What about the mortgage?'

'That's in both our names.' The paperwork is upstairs in Oliver's office. 'There's a file. I'll go and get it.'

Going upstairs, I take it out of the drawer in Oliver's

desk, and go back downstairs to Joe. 'Look.' I show him the documents where both our names are clearly stated.

Looking through them, he nods. 'It looks straightforward enough.'

I frown at him. 'Shouldn't all his finances be? Given that we were married?'

Joe frowns slightly. 'You need to see his will. And you'll need probate to access everything that isn't in your name.'

'Do I need that to change the utilities and cars?' I gaze at Joe. 'I've no idea how this works.'

'We can find out easily enough – also about council tax.'

'There's also his personal bank account.' I hesitate. 'He banked online – he did everything online.' All his personal information will be there. Why hadn't I thought of this before? 'I'll get his laptop.'

Oliver always left it in the same place and, picking it up, I take it over to the kitchen table. But when I turn it on, I gaze at Joe. 'I've no idea what his password is.'

'Try his birthday, your birthday, your wedding day.' Joe suggests, watching over my shoulder.

'Nothing's working.' Locked out, I wait to try again, but each time I try to think of something significant in Oliver's life, it doesn't work.

'Leave it for now,' Joe suggests. 'Maybe something will come to you.'

*

Nothing gets any easier over the next few days, as my entire life seems to hang in limbo. Now that the police have my fingerprints, all I can do is wait to hear from them; while alone in the house, I search every corner of it for clues as to what Oliver had been doing.

Outside, the countryside is lashed by gales and heavy rain, a summer's worth of leaves falling overnight. Meanwhile, as word spreads about Oliver's death, the cottage fills with flowers, as well as cards filled with messages of sympathy, words that in the circumstances feel misplaced.

Having contacted my clients to explain why I'm not available, the days are long, the future uncertain. But as I think back over recent months, only now that I'm alone do I acknowledge that Oliver and I weren't the perfect match everyone wanted us to be.

Just as I feel I'm going out of my mind, the police call around.

'Mrs McKenna? May we come in?'

It's the same two officers that came here last time. I stand back as DS Stanley and Constable Ramirez come inside.

'Come through to the kitchen.' I walk ahead of them, then gesture towards the table. 'Would you like to sit down?'

'Thank you.' DS Stanley undoes her jacket and gets out her electronic notebook. Beside her, Constable Ramirez is silent. 'The first thing to say is that we have conclusive evidence that someone deliberately caused damage to your car, rendering the brakes unsafe.' She hesitates. 'Seeing as it was your car, we need to try to establish whether it was your husband or you who was the intended victim.'

As she speaks, I feel the blood drain from my face.

She goes on. 'Can you tell us how often your husband used your car?'

I try to remember how regularly Oliver drove it. 'Not that often – though he had more recently, particularly when he was supposedly going to work. His had been playing up.'

'It's possible that whoever did this might have known

70

that.' DS Stanley speaks slowly. 'Or even tampered with his car, too – disconnecting the battery or intentionally flattening it, in the knowledge that he would end up taking yours. We've checked and, out of the two, your brakes would have been more easily accessible. I know we've already asked you, but I need you to think very carefully. Is there anyone in your life, or from the past, even, who might hold a grudge against you?'

The thought makes me shiver. 'No.' Shaking my head, I say it emphatically. 'I've already told you. I genuinely can't think of anyone.'

'No disgruntled clients?'

'No. My clients are very happy with me.' My voice shakes, but as I pause, I'm thinking of the photograph. If there was another woman in Oliver's life, could it have been her? Not wanting to hurt Oliver, but wanting me out of the way.

If Joe was here, I know what he would say. He'd want me to tell the police about our suspicions that Oliver was having an affair.

But DS Stanley is ahead of me. 'I have to ask this.' She looks uncomfortable. 'But is it possible your husband was having an affair?'

Confronted with her question, I'm torn as to whether I should tell her about the photo. Whoever the woman is, it's possible that she might be a suspect. And if Oliver was cheating on me, he deserves to be exposed. But I think of Jude, how disappointed in Oliver she would be; how demoralising it would feel, how stupid people would think me, if it became publicly known that I was the victim of his betrayal. I shake my head. 'I had no reason to think he was. I always thought we were happy together, but I suppose anything's possible . . .'

'You'd been married how long?'

'Two years.' My eyes fill with tears. 'Whoever's done this to my car, they're responsible for Oliver's death. You have to find them.'

DS Stanley looks at me sympathetically. 'I understand how distressing this is. I can assure you we're doing everything we can.'

Suddenly I remember something. 'The fingerprints . . . What did you find?'

'Yours and your husband's . . .' She glances briefly at her colleague. 'There was also a third set – female, hence my question about your husband. Did anyone else use your car? A friend, perhaps?'

I think of how many times Oliver has borrowed my car, my stomach twisting as I picture him driving it with another woman sitting beside him. I shake my head. 'No.' Hesitating, I try to think. 'There's something else you should know. I told you he was on his way to work the day of the crash – but we've found out since that he wasn't.'

'Oh?' DS Stanley looks at me sharply.

'When I called the airline he worked for to tell them about the crash, they told me he'd lost his job two months ago.'

DS Stanley frowns as she writes in her electronic notebook. 'And until that point, you didn't know?'

'I had no idea.' I gaze at her blankly. 'As far as I was concerned, for the last two months, he's been going to work. He went out wearing his uniform. I even saw his roster. I had no reason to think otherwise.' I tell her what Oliver's manager told me about why he was fired. 'I genuinely had no idea he had an alcohol problem. Oliver wasn't irresponsible. It seems the most bizarre thing that he would drink when he was at the controls of an aircraft.'

'Can you give us his manager's contact details?'

I get out my phone, scrolling down my contacts before reading out the number.

'Going back to the car,' DS Stanley looks curious. 'Clearly at some point, there's been another woman in the car your husband was driving. But you really have no idea who she might have been? No friend of yours, or possibly of Oliver's?'

'No.' I fold my arms, hating her earlier suggestion that Oliver had been cheating on me. 'But if he hasn't been going to work, I've no idea where he has been.' I'm silent for a moment. 'This woman's fingerprints, can you identify her?'

'Only if she has a criminal record — and if the prints match any we already have on file.' She pauses. 'We will be talking to his brother again. Your husband may have confided in him.'

I need to warn Joe not to mention the photo. 'If he had, I'm sure Joe would have told me.'

She looks surprised. 'Joe would have betrayed his brother's confidence? You're sure about that?'

But I know how Joe's mind works. 'He would have hated knowing Oliver was deceiving me. And Oliver would have known that.'

DS Stanley makes another note.

'On the subject of money, do you have access to your late husband's bank statements?'

'Only for our joint account. I've checked it — and there's nothing unusual showing. But we had separate accounts, too. I have an appointment with our solicitor about the will in a couple of days. There's no reason to think it won't be straightforward, but I guess I'll see what it contains and go from there.'

'But you'll be applying for probate?'

'Yes.' As I look at her, something else occurs to me. 'How long before we can hold the funeral?'

'Once the results of the post-mortem come through – which should be in the next three to five days. A Liaison Officer from the Coroner's Office will contact you once they've finished their investigation. Have you organised an undertaker?'

I shake my head. 'Not yet.'

'It might be advisable to do that now. Explain the situation, so that you can let them know when your husband's body is released.'

As I take in more unfamiliar words, I sense the inevitable next stage is looming closer.

'Mrs McKenna, I know I've said this before, but if you do see anyone unusual hanging around, or if anything strange happens, please call us straight away.'

As she speaks, a chill comes over me as I suddenly don't feel safe. They leave shortly after that and as I listen to their car drive away, I sit there a moment, thinking, my hands shaking as I text Joe.

The police were here. They're treating Oliver's death as suspicious. They asked if he might have been having an affair. I didn't tell them about the photo.

Almost immediately, he calls me. 'You should have told them, Kat. They need to know.'

My heart sinks. 'It still doesn't prove anything.'

'That may be the case, but we agreed, didn't we, that if

74

Oliver's death turned out to be suspicious, we'd have to tell them. If they're trying to build a picture of what was going on in Oliver's life, they need to know everything.'

I'm uncomfortable, imagining the police asking questions, scrutinising every corner of my personal life. 'Not this, Joe.'

After the call ends, my thoughts are all over the place. As I gaze blankly through the window, it seems impossible that just days ago, he was alive – putting on his uniform, allegedly going to a job I didn't know he'd lost, with an alcohol problem that I didn't know about.

As for me, I believed I'd found love; had a husband, a future to look forward to. But I've lost it. I've lost everything. I think of my car again and what the police said, that they can't be sure who the intended victim was. I imagine Oliver driving too fast, the fear he must have felt as he lost control on the flooded roads, the car spinning; the impact as it hit a tree; how the police aren't sure if it was intended to have been me.

As I sit there, I feel as though the walls are closing in. Overwhelmed, starting to panic, I pick up my phone and call Jude.

2010

Gemma

In the kitchen of the French farmhouse, as Allison gazed at the flecks of Nadia's blood on the wall, I assumed a frown to hide my surprise, before rolling my eyes.

'Actually, I've just remembered where that came from. This cat keeps coming in. He's a big old tabby cat. The other day, he brought in a rabbit. It was gross' I pulled a face. 'I thought I'd cleaned it up.' Going over, I bent down with a cloth and rubbed them away. 'Thank goodness you noticed. I'd have hated Ray and Sally to have come back to that.'

'Ray and Sally would have understood perfectly,' she said, smiling conspiratorially. 'They probably know the cat. Cats know a soft touch when they see one, don't they? They're going to be so pleased when they get back and see how much care you've taken of everything.'

*

With each day, my concern grew that someone would find Nadia's body, but after a month, when no one had, I guessed that between the heat and the wild creatures, there probably wasn't too much left to find.

Much as this life suited me down to the ground, the trouble was it hadn't solved my problems. It had simply kicked them six months down the road. With the end of my time here not far away, my fear and uncertainty were back.

While my initial plan had been to escape my old life, now that I'd stumbled across this way of living, I knew I couldn't give it up. Instead, I needed a way to maintain it, which first and foremost meant I needed money.

I waited until two weeks before Ray and Sally were due to come back, before sending them an apologetic email explaining that my father had been taken ill and that I needed to rush back to the UK. They couldn't have been more understanding as they asked me just to leave the house tidy and put the key back where I'd found it.

The day I left, Allison came by one last time. I took the opportunity to show her around the rooms, to check the kitchen, so that she could see everything was immaculately tidy. Closing the house up together, I turned to her.

'I just need to leave the key where Ray and Sally asked me to.' After putting it back where I'd found it the day I arrived here, I went to find her again.

Allison looked wistful. 'I'm so sorry you have to rush off like this, Gemma. Would you like a lift anywhere?'

This was getting even better. 'That's so kind, but I wouldn't want to put you out. Unless you happen to be going anywhere near the station . . .'

'I'm not — but it's no trouble at all to drive you there.'

Driving into Hèches, she stopped outside the station. 'Well, bon voyage.' She smiled.

I lingered a moment. 'I don't like to think of the house empty. I feel terrible leaving earlier than I said I would.'

'Don't worry. I'll pop by now and then, just to check everything's OK.'

'That's so kind of you. It's been wonderful meeting you.' I smiled back at her. 'Who knows — maybe our paths will cross again?'

Crossing my fingers that they wouldn't, I watched her drive away, before going inside and finding a bench to sit on while I waited.

As dusk settled over the town, I started the walk back to the house. As luck would have it, not a single car passed by. Finding the back-door key, I let myself in, carefully staging it to look like a burglary, taking the items I'd already singled out before placing them in the bottom of my rucksack.

Replacing the key, I went back down the drive. Twenty minutes later, after paying cash for my ticket, I was on a train speeding away.

*

After arriving in Perpignan late that night, I found a cheap hotel and the following day, carefully set about working on my appearance, pulling on a wig and making up my face to look much older.

With the items from the house safely inside my rucksack, wandering the streets, it didn't take long to find the right kind of antiques dealer.

'My grandmother left me these.' I made my voice tremble just enough. 'It's the last thing I want to do, but things haven't been going so well. Can you tell me how much you'd give me for them?'

When his eyes gave me more than a passing glance, for a moment I wondered if he was suspicious. But in silence, he scrutinised each of the items before making an offer.

It was probably less than they were worth but it was way more than I'd expected. I pretended to hesitate. 'Is there any way you could give me a little more? I mean, they are such beautiful things.'

Dabbing a tissue to my eye, I apologised. 'I'm so sorry. It's just difficult to hand them over – to a stranger.'

As he handed me tens of thousands of euros, I bit my lip, hiding my euphoria until I stepped outside. After a visit to a pharmacy for hair dye, I bought a couple of new outfits before returning to my hotel. Settling down with my recent purchases, Gemma Hargreaves was getting a makeover.

I imagined that at some point I'd hear from Sally, so two weeks later when she called, suitably prepared, I feigned my horror that their house had been burgled.

'That's terrible, Sally . . . I can't believe it.'

'It happens more often than you might think. There are too many people struggling at the moment. It's why we like to have house sitters.' She sounded upset. 'It's just such bad luck you had to leave early.'

'It really was.' Relief washed over me at how well I'd taken them in. I filled my voice with regret. 'I can't tell you how bad I feel.'

Apparently the police had found a credit card registered to a Nadia Delaney – it was maxed out – presumably in desperation, she'd turned to burglary. It had been an inspired idea on my part to leave the credit card. Knowing by now how unlikely it was that anyone would find her body, leaving it there would draw the heat away from me. It seemed the police had failed in their efforts to track Nadia down. They weren't even sure if that was her real name.

After suitably expressing my condolences for everything they'd been through, I took down my house sitter listing – at least for the time being.

Meanwhile, I had enough money to survive for the foreseeable future, while I worked out what to do next. With Perpignan to *explore, and trains and buses to the whole of the rest of France, I could feel my horizons opening up. With new people to meet and new places to see, it wouldn't be long before I'd be living the good life again.*

8

Jude

Having taken compassionate leave from work, my world grinds to a halt around me. Losing Oliver so suddenly has shown that nothing is certain; a reminder that death can strike any of us at any time.

That afternoon I get a phone call from her. Clearly on edge, she speaks too quickly.

'The police have just left. They have evidence someone sabotaged the brakes . . . But they still don't know who the intended victim was. What if it was me? What if whoever did it comes after me?'

'Slow down, Kat.' My initial shock at what she's saying gives way to disbelief. We knew it was a possibility, but that it's been confirmed is horrifying. 'Are the police sure it isn't possible the damage was accidental?'

There's a brief silence before she goes on. 'There's more, Jude. They found three sets of fingerprints in the car. Mine, Oliver's and someone else's – a woman's. I don't know who else has been in my car – not a woman. I don't know what to think.'

I feel a secondary wave of shock, before dismissing it. Oliver was devoted to Kat. There's no way he would have been having an affair. 'There's probably a perfectly reasonable explanation. He was giving someone a lift, for example.'

'Do you think so?' She doesn't sound convinced. 'I should have said that to the police.'

'I'm sure they'll consider every possibility.' Trying to stay calm, I frown slightly. 'Did Oliver often use your car?'

'He did recently, since his started playing up. Nothing adds up, Jude. That day . . .' Her voice trembles. 'Before the crash, he was in a hurry. I remember him saying he was going to be late for his flight. The weather was awful – I thought he must have driven too fast. But now . . .'

'If he wasn't in a rush to get to work, where else was he going?'

'That's what I was thinking. How would I know?' She's clearly agitated. I hear the doorbell ring in the background as she goes on. 'I'm sorry, Jude. There's someone at the door. I have to go.'

But even her doorbell ringing has me worried. When potentially there's someone out there who wants to harm her, she's right to be concerned. The conversation hangs over me, my mind working overtime. If Oliver hadn't been driving to work, where had he been going? I think about the friends he's had since he was a teenager. Might he have confided in any of them? But they've drifted apart in recent years. To the best of my knowledge, any contact between them now is only peripheral.

Still worried about Kat, early that afternoon I drive over to see her. It's a quiet autumnal day, shrouded in mist that has lifted slightly but still lingers across the fields. I've always believed that whatever is going on, it's better to know the worst than be left in limbo. But without any answers, it's tough on all of us.

When Kat opens the door, the strain on her is obvious. 'You didn't have to come over.' She looks wired, taut, as though she's waiting for the world to cave in. But in her mind, it already has.

'I did,' I say gently as I go inside. 'I was worried about you. Did you have a visitor earlier?'

'A neighbour. They brought those.' She points to a vase of autumnal flowers clearly picked from someone's garden.

'They're lovely.' I glance at the basket I'm holding. 'I've brought some soup – and a loaf of bread. I thought we could share it.'

She shakes her head. 'I don't really have an appetite – it's kind of you, though.'

As I follow her towards the kitchen, her shoulders are hunched; her usually glossy hair lank and in need of washing. In the kitchen, I take off my coat before going over to the cupboard and getting out one of her saucepans. Pouring the soup into it, I put it to warm on the Aga.

I try to get her to focus, to talk to me about how she's feeling.

'Are you sleeping, Kat?'

'A bit.'

Her mind seems miles away. But as I watch her closely, I try to imagine how it must feel to know your husband had been keeping secrets from you. She's silent, only now and then emotion exploding out of her like steam from a pressure release valve, leaving her temporarily calmer until the next time.

'The police said they'll have the post-mortem results in the next few days.' Her eyes fix on me. 'Once they have them, they'll release Oliver's body. I've found an undertaker. They understand the situation – I just have to call them when the time comes. Once that's done, we can plan the funeral.'

My heart goes out to her. 'Richard and I would have done that. There's no need for you to take all this on alone.'

'It gives me something to do.' Her face is haunted. 'I can hardly work at the moment. I can't do anything.'

I wonder if the funeral will give her closure, but when we lose someone close, there is no quick fix. Each of us has to find our own way. I watch Kat, restless, not sure what to do with herself, wondering if there's something she isn't saying. But this is no ordinary grief. How can it be?

Joe's lack of motivation has long been a source of irritation to me, but since Oliver's death, he seems to have come into his own. Not a day passes I'm not grateful to him. He and Kat have always got on well, evidenced today when as I serve up the soup, I hear him let himself in.

'Hey, Mum.' Coming into the kitchen, he hugs me. There's genuine warmth in his embrace.

'I wasn't expecting to see you.' My heart unexpectedly twists as, for a moment, I see his resemblance to his brother. 'How are you?'

'Not so bad.' He glances at the soup. 'Is there enough for three?'

'Plenty.' Forcing brightness into my voice, I nod towards Kat. 'While you're here, see if you can persuade this one to eat.'

Joe turns to Kat. 'Mum's right, you know. You need to eat.'

Sighing, she joins us at the table. Slicing the loaf I bought on the way here, I pass her a piece.

'How long are you off work?' Joe asks.

'For as long as I need to be,' I say quietly, noticing Kat dip into the soup; not wanting to mention the funeral again. It presents another dilemma that plays on her mind, between playing a woman who was wronged or the grieving wife.

As she eats the soup, Kat is silent. Not for the first time, I think about the unhappiness of her childhood, as well as the people she's lost. When burying emotion has become her way of survival, it makes dealing with grief so much harder.

'The police will have the results of the post-mortem soon,' she tells Joe. 'The police were asking if we had an undertaker – so I found one. Once his body's been released, we can plan the funeral.' She glances from Joe to me. 'Knowing that Oliver lied to me makes it so much more difficult.'

Joe leans forward. 'Try to remember all the reasons you fell in love with him. In his heart, I'm sure he realised he was making a mistake. No one at the funeral is going to know what's been going on.'

'You think?' Her eyes flit anxiously.

'Yes.' I glance gratefully at Joe. 'He's right, Kat. For all you know, Oliver was waiting to find the right time to talk to you.'

'He drank at work,' Kat says starkly. 'For an airline pilot to be drunk at the controls of a jet is unforgivable.' She shakes her head. 'There's part of me that finds it really diffi-cult to accept.'

'Maybe his drinking wasn't that bad. If there was something

on his mind, maybe a quick drink was his way of dealing with it.' But I know as far as flying goes, the rules are black-and-white. Yet again, I wonder if there's more Kat isn't saying. It's the harshness in her words, her lack of sympathy. But in the circumstances, I suppose neither is surprising.

'I know you're angry, and with good reason. But I know you loved him, Kat.' I watch her sigh. 'Right now, you feel betrayed. But you'll get through this. On the day, you're going to stand there with all of us beside you, and you're going to grit your teeth. It will be over sooner than you think. No one's going to know about him losing his job or lying to you. Let them remember Oliver as the man you fell in love with.'

Kat looks worried. 'But if the truth comes out, it will make me look as bad as he was.'

As she uses the word *bad*, I realise the impact Oliver's deception has had on her. 'Nothing's going to come out. What's happened is between us and the police,' I say firmly. People come to a funeral to share their memories and offer words of comfort. It's a formula, Kat. A ritual. No one will be expecting anything other than that.'

She hesitates. 'You're right. I'm so sorry . . . I just have so many things going around in my head. I think it's what the police said earlier – it's freaked me out a bit.'

'What did they say?' Joe's voice is sharp.

'They reminded me to be careful. The brakes were definitely sabotaged – but because it was my car, they can't be sure who the intended victim was.' The fear is back in her eyes. 'There's every chance it was meant to have been me.'

A look of alarm crosses his face. 'You really do need to

be careful,' he says quickly. 'If someone's out to harm you, they may not have given up.'

Kat hesitates. 'The police said to call them anytime. But I'll be fine.'

Joe looks uncertain. 'I'm not so sure. I really don't think you should be alone.'

'He's right. I think you should come and stay with us. Unless . . .' My eyes flicker towards Joe. 'If you want to stay here, how about Joe stays with you? At least that way, you won't be alone.'

'I don't want to put anyone out,' she says obstinately. 'I have neighbours if I need anyone.'

Joe turns to Kat again. 'I don't mind staying. We could start putting together ideas for the funeral.'

She looks undecided, before she gives in. 'If you're really sure . . . OK. Thank you,' she adds, albeit reluctantly. 'Both of you. I don't mean to sound ungrateful. I know I'm lucky to have you.'

I drive away, only mildly reassured that Joe will be with her. It's clear that Kat isn't looking after herself. Constantly on edge, there's a brittle fragility to her that's come to the fore. But none of this is easy for any of us.

At home, I get out the box of old photos I've collected over the years. There are so many of Oliver and Joe – as babies, toddlers, schoolboys. On family holidays; as teenagers before they grew into men.

Tears fill my eyes as I touch Oliver's face with one of my fingers. He was such a determined child. Slightly anxious, too. Frowning, I study a photo of him with Richard. Richard's hand is on his shoulder, the worried look that I remember on Oliver's face. Richard's, however, is austere.

I put the photo down, suddenly questioning myself. What kind of parents have we been to our children – not materially, but emotionally? Have I been so busy over the years that I've missed something? I flick through more photos, a feeling of unease filling me. Not a single one shows any emotion on Richard's face – and it's taken until now for me to notice.

Placing the photos in the box again, still uncomfortable, I make a mental note to talk to Joe about it. Life has been so fast-paced; about dealing with the everyday; the nuts and bolts of life, it's only now that I'm taking time to consider our relationships.

As I reflect on the past, I'm aware of Oliver's death causing me to reassess what I've always taken for granted. *But a mother doesn't expect to lose a son.* And losing Oliver is so hard, as is fielding the memories it's triggered. I wonder if it would have been easier if he had been ill for a while; if an anticipated death is any more manageable. But at the root of it all is the realisation that someone wilfully wanted him – or Kat – dead. It's devastating.

★

That evening, Richard comes home early. 'I've been doing a little research into these private jets in the brochure Kat found. I now have a list of all the companies who operate them flying in and out of the UK. If Oliver was flying for any one of them, he'll be on their books.'

I frown slightly. 'Surely if he'd found another job, he'd have told Kat.'

'Given what's happened, who knows what he was thinking? Anyway, I should know soon enough.'

'That's insane.' Frowning, I look at Richard. 'What about

data protection? They're hardly going to give out information about their employees.'

He at least has the grace to look slightly awkward. 'You and I both know, Jude. There's always a way.'

'I think you should leave it,' I say firmly. 'Oliver's dead, Richard. Digging around into what he may or may not have been doing isn't going to bring him back.'

'Don't you think Kat would like some answers?'

But I know the way his mind works and it isn't Kat he's thinking of. It's his need to satisfy his curiosity; maybe even to lord it over a son that he can prove had let him down, even in death. It's an abhorrent thought, but Richard does nothing without an agenda.

'No. I really don't. She isn't coping at all well. Her nerves are already stretched. I'm worried about her. The police went to see her today. The brakes were definitely tampered with. They're still considering the possibility that whoever did it may have been after her, not Oliver. After all, it was her car.'

Richard looks horrified. 'Why would anyone want to hurt Kat?'

'Why would anyone want to hurt Oliver?' I say simply. 'I can't help thinking there has to be more to this.'

'Which is why I'm checking out these companies,' he says briskly. 'Who knows what it may turn up? Even the smallest piece of information, Jude, can shift a line of enquiry.'

Taken aback by his lack of emotion, I shake my head. 'This is Oliver we're talking about. Our son, Richard. I know you like to leave no stone unturned, but just for once, I think you should let this go. Surely it would be better for everyone.'

2014

Gemma

I'd soon got into the swing of this way of life, interspersing legitimate house-sits with others that were less so; for a short while crossing the border into Spain, too. I was managing to save money and hiding it inside an invisible lining in my rucksack. With luck, it might not be too long before I could fulfil my dream of having my own little place; somewhere no one could take away from me.

But until then, this life was working for me just fine and by 2014, I was back in France, on the move again. Gazing at the map, I turned to look at the house in front of me. Over the last few years, I'd become adept at spotting opportunities by various means, using different names. I knew which bars to hang out at; the restaurants where the expats went to squander their private pensions. Portraying myself as one of them, I developed a radar for them — there was nothing they loved more than to show off about their luxury second homes and private yachts. Pretending to flatter them, I liked to see how far I could push them.

And as I'd found out, there was no shortage of random empty country houses, such as the one I'd come to today on a tiny country lane, miles from anywhere. Set back up a gravel drive, it was large and imposing, its roof gothic in the way I'd learned was typically French; its windows shuttered as they always were when a house was uninhabited. I'd found out about it from a British couple I'd met in a bar one night. Having just closed up their house for several months, they were returning to their home in England.

It had been music to my ears – especially when they showed me a photo. Just when I needed another hideaway. It was perfect.

'This is definitely it,' I said to Nathan, remembering the photo.

Nathan and I had hooked up a couple of months earlier, both of us solo travellers happy to casually overlap for as long as it suited us. To start with, I'd thought we were like-minded, but after leaving my last house sit, as I was finding out, Nathan wasn't nearly as brave as I was.

To avoid drawing any attention to the car, I drove a little further on past the house, pulling up at the side of the road under some trees.

Getting out, he was silent as he stared at it. 'It's bigger than I thought,' he said at last.

'Cool, though, isn't it?' Getting my bag out of the car, I slammed the door. 'Come on. Let's check it out.'

Climbing over the wall, we headed through the trees, reaching the manicured lawns that surrounded the house. Walking towards it, I took in how beautiful it was, how well-kept the shrubs were; the brightly coloured geraniums; the neatly mown lawns giving away the fact that they had a gardener.

Around the side, I quietly tried the solid wooden door. Finding it locked, I tipped the large flower pot where I'd heard the owners say the key was usually left, but when I felt underneath, it wasn't there.

After checking under the doormat, I reached up and felt along the top of the door frame, a smile crossing my face as my fingers found the key. I dangled it in front of Nathan.

'Shall we go in?'

Standing there, he looked slightly nervous. 'I don't know. What if someone comes here?'

'They won't,' I said impatiently, deliberately not telling him about the gardener, knowing it would freak him out. 'I've already told you. The owners only use it in June and July. The rest of the year, no one comes here.'

'Yeah, but you can't be sure.'

'For fuck's sake.' I stared at him. 'I know so – I met the frigging owners not that long ago. If anyone does arrive to stay – which they won't, we'll scarper. Are you up for this or not?'

Reluctantly he followed me inside. With the door closed behind us, the house was airless. It smelled of stale wood smoke and dusty stone. 'I'm guessing the kitchen could be this way.' I headed along the panelled hallway and opened another door. I stood there for a moment.

It was a glorious kitchen of titan proportions, a catering-sized gas cooker set among pale wood kitchen units, while the floor with original tiles was to die for.

I heard Nathan come up behind me. 'This is a fancy house, Gemma.'

'It'll do, won't it?' Going over to the window, I opened it enough for the spring air to filter through. 'Better leave the shutters closed – at least, for now.'

I started checking out cupboards; going through another doorway, I found the larder. 'Le cellier'. My eyes were gleaming as I turned to Nathan.

He gazed at me blankly.

'It's French for larder.' My eyes took in the floor made of slabs of stone that kept the temperature down; the shelves piled with tins and dried foods of the region — mushrooms, tomatoes, containers of olives. 'Wow. We have really lucked out — and I mean really. Are you hungry?' Grabbing one of the bottles of wine, I passed it to Nathan. 'Can you open it?' I reached for a jar of olives and a vacuum-packed cheese.

After a glass of wine, Nathan was starting to relax — thank fuck, because he'd been starting to annoy me. Cutting a chunk of cheese, I put it on a wooden board I found with one of the baguettes we'd bought on our way here, adding the bowl of olives, as surveying it, I felt pleased with myself.

'Bon appetit.' Sitting down, I cut myself a slice of cheese and tore off a hunk of bread.

As he ate, Nathan started to look less on edge. 'I can't believe houses like this sit empty most of the year.'

'Well, they do — and they are ours for the picking. There are loads of them scattered across France — hidden among trees without any neighbours. Easy to break into. With well-stocked larders. All you have to do is find them.' I raised my glass. 'Cheers!'

Nathan clinked his glass against mine. 'So what next?'

I shrugged. 'We just see what tomorrow brings. We need to keep an eye out for pool guys or the gardener, but that's probably a once a week job. If we hide out, they'll never know we're here.'

I grinned at him, loving the frisson of potentially being caught out, knowing I'd make sure it wasn't going to happen. We already had a back way onto the lane where I'd left the car. As long as we made sure no one saw us arrive or leave, even if there was anyone around, there'd be no reason for them to suspect we were living here.

Meanwhile, we had days, if not weeks, of free and easy French living. Liking how that felt, I got up. Going over to Nathan, I kissed him. 'Shall we check out upstairs?'

*

Over the days that followed, I found an escape route from upstairs if we needed to get out in a hurry. I also got to know the house. The well-stocked library, the spacious bedrooms with en suite bathrooms; the drawer filled with kinky sex toys, the dressing table stocked with expensive perfumes; the cave where shelves ran floor to ceiling, packed with dusty bottles of wine. I picked one out.

'Oh man.'

The label was dated 1945 – it must have been worth a fortune. I took another. When there were this many, no one was going to notice if a couple went missing.

I carried them up to the kitchen, smiling as I waved them at Nathan. The side of salmon I'd found in the freezer was already defrosting.

'Tonight, we are going to dine like kings.'

Creeping around the back of the house, I breathed in the scent of the roses as I gathered fresh herbs and a bowl of wild garlic – with olive oil, they'd be perfect with the salmon.

Making my way back, I froze momentarily as the sound of footsteps on gravel reached my ears. Someone was walking towards the house. Dashing inside, I quietly closed the door and locked it, my heart starting to thud as I ran to find Nathan. 'Someone's outside,' I whispered.

Nathan looked panic-stricken. 'What are we going to do?'

This was the bit I loved. The jeopardy; knowing that even if someone came in and started checking the house out, by the time they came upstairs, we would be long gone.

Putting down the bowl of herbs I'd just gathered, I grinned at Nathan.

* 'Hide.'*

9

Katharine

Even with Oliver's car thoroughly checked over and running again, the majority of the time I don't venture far. But there are things I can't put off and after the Coroner's Liaison Officer gets in touch, I force myself to drive to Deal to register his death.

It coincides with the day I have an appointment to see our solicitor. With a couple of hours to kill, I cross the road onto the beach. The sea is flat, a milky grey, the horizon brought closer by the layer of sea fog that lingers. Folding my arms, I breathe in the salty air, letting my mind wander as I stand, enjoying the sense of briefly being removed from the world.

Stepping onto the shingle, I walk towards the sea, thinking of the times I've been here with Oliver. Hot summer days when we've sunbathed and swum; cold days when we've walked here, watching the wind whipping up the waves. I wonder what this afternoon is going to bring. Watching a grey seal swim past, swivelling its head to look at me, for a moment I crave the simpler life I used to have. Death makes everything so complicated.

I glance at my watch. Before I find out the contents of Oliver's will, I have another appointment. Walking back through the town, I head for a disused church that's been creatively repurposed as a community centre. The church is stark, its tall spire home to hundreds of birds, its windows dark in comparison to the small modern building that's been built alongside in the churchyard. It's a place I discovered by accident, that seems oddly relevant right now; resonant of how we constantly live so close to death. Understated, the centre is tucked away; in summer the trees offering shade to the tables set among the flowers and gravestones. But today it's too cold and I go inside.

The girl behind the bar is young, the prices cheap, the bar a venue for anyone and everyone.

'Coffee, please.' I wait while she makes it, then hand over the money, before taking it over to a table in the corner.

Everything is exactly as it was when I was last in here and in moments like these, it's easy to imagine that nothing has changed; that an alternative world exists, in which none of the chaos in my life is happening. But the steady passage of time keeps me resolutely grounded in the here and now, my stomach lurching nervously, as I think how, before long, I'll know the contents of Oliver's will.

I watch a man wander in. Clearly drunk, he weaves his way over to the bar and orders a pint. This place draws a lot of people like him, trading more lavish surroundings to shave a few pence off the price of a pint. Maybe that's why I've always liked it here.

Someone calls over to him from across the bar. 'You OK there, Derek? Only you look a bit . . .'

'I'm fine, mate. Nothing a bit of the old . . . won't sort out.' Befitting his intake of alcohol, slurring his words slightly, he mimics the gesture of injecting himself.

I don't know what surprises me more – that someone would publicly allude to injecting drugs, or the lack of concern shown by either of them. I catch the eye of the girl behind the bar, wondering if she caught the exchange. But it's none of my business.

A few minutes later, I catch my breath, glancing towards the door just as another man comes in. He turns towards me, the last person I want to see, and as I take in his familiar eyes, a sense of loathing fills me.

★

The rain may have stopped, but days have passed since the sun last showed its face and an hour later, I pull my coat around me against the cold as I walk head down towards the solicitor's office. Last time I came here, I was with Oliver. Walking hand in hand, we were excited about the house we were buying, our heads full of ideas of how we'd put our stamp on it. It's a life I barely recognise, but in the two years since, so much has changed.

I turn into Madrigal Street where Mark Osborne's office is. When he's been the McKenna family's solicitor for years, it made perfect sense that Oliver and I would use him, too. As I walk, the street is quiet and I take in the beautifully maintained buildings. It's what I've always liked about Deal – the juxtaposition of thriving town and quiet coast.

Reaching the office, I hesitate in front of the immaculately painted door, before ringing the doorbell. I'm immediately buzzed in, and I go inside. The receptionist who looks up is new. Young, her makeup is immaculate, her clothes under-stated, her manner bright and professional.

'Mrs McKenna? Do take a seat. Mr Osborne will be with you in a minute or two.'

'Thank you.' I head over to the small seating area, slipping off my coat and folding it over my arm, just as a door opens and a balding man in a dapper suit walks through.

'Katharine, how good to see you.' He adopts a professional expression of regret. 'I was so very sorry to hear about Oliver.'

'Thank you.' Meeting his eyes, I shake the hand he's holding out.

'Shall we?' He gestures towards the door he's holding open.

It's the first time I've come here alone and I follow him along a hallway, then through a second door into his office. One wall is given over to shelves of books, the others panelled, while behind him the window looks out onto trees still holding on to the last of this year's leaves, while beyond there are glimpses of the sea.

'Please have a seat.'

'Thank you.' I take one close to his desk.

'I can only imagine how difficult a time this must be for you. I really am so sorry. I was very fond of Oliver. As you know, I've known the family a long time.'

'Thank you,' I say again as he pauses.

He picks up some papers on the desk in front of him. 'Anyway, to business. When you bought your property, I remember I advised you both to make wills – which you did.' He pauses. 'I'm not sure if you're aware . . .'

As he speaks, I get a sense that I'm not going to like what I'm about to hear.

'About six months ago, your husband came to see me. There were some changes he wanted to make to his, as you will see in due course. You remain the beneficiary of a large part of his estate.' He lists out a portfolio of shares and savings accounts I already know about, adding a couple I wasn't aware of, before going on. 'It amounts to a sum in the region of half a million pounds. The exception is one other account he opened relatively recently.'

'What's that?' I'm on my guard all of a sudden, because Oliver hadn't mentioned it to me.

'There's quite a sizeable sum involved.' Mark doesn't meet my gaze. Picking up the piece of paper in front of him, he clears his throat. 'A million pounds, to be precise.'

'*What*?' I'm stunned. 'Oliver doesn't have that kind of money.'

'My dear,' Mark looks slightly upset. 'Surely you're aware you married into an extremely wealthy family.'

'Yes. But,' I'm trying to think, 'I know Richard has his own business and Jude's a medical practice manager. But . . .'

'There's a little more to it than that.' He hesitates for a moment. 'We're talking about family money.' He studies me intently. 'You genuinely didn't know?'

'I had no idea. When Richard and Jude helped us with the deposit, I'd assumed it had come from their savings.' Ever since, Oliver and I had paid into an account from which our mortgage payments came out. 'But with this amount of money we could have been living mortgage free. Why didn't he tell me?'

But as I ask the question, I already know the answer. He clearly didn't want me to know, adding to the list of things Oliver had been keeping from me.

Mark tries to reassure me. 'Sometimes families are protective about inherited wealth. There may even have been some kind of stipulation on him inheriting.'

'But if that was the case, surely you would know about it?' I say pointedly.

'I can understand you saying that – and it's fair to say that in this case, if there was, I was unaware.'

Folding my arms, I take a deep breath. 'I suppose the money will go back to his family.'

'It doesn't.' Looking at me, he takes off his glasses. 'He's left it to someone – a woman. Her name is Ana Fontaine.'

Frowning, there's a rushing sound in my ears as I try to take in what he's saying. 'What did you say?'

'This is rather awkward.' Mark looks troubled. 'I hoped you would have known her.'

This can't be happening – not when Oliver and I were married. 'I've never heard of her. I'm sorry. I don't feel very well.' Leaning forward, I rest my head in my hands, suddenly light-headed; gasping for air.

I'm aware of Mark getting up and placing a glass of water in my hands. As I sip it, my light-headedness starts to dissipate as anger suddenly takes over. He should have left his money to me. But thinking of the unaccounted-for time when he should have been working, of the photo of the woman I found, there's no longer any doubt in my mind that he was having an affair.

'Do you know who she is?'

Mark looks hesitant. 'He didn't tell me anything about her – and it's not my place to ask. I questioned his decision, but he was adamant. I assumed, as most people would, that he would have informed you. I can only apologise that it's come as such a shock to you.'

'It has.' I shake my head. 'A complete shock. I had no idea. I've never even heard of her.' I'm trying to think. 'Do you have an address for her?'

'I'm afraid as Oliver's executor, I can't give out personal information.' Looking troubled again, he adds more quietly, 'There can't be too many Ana Fontaines.'

My mind is all over the place as I walk back to my car. Reaching into my bag, I get out my phone, my fingers fumbling as I call Joe.

'Do you know someone called Ana Fontaine?'

'Hang on . . .' The line crackles. 'Can you say that again?'

'Ana Fontaine,' I repeat more slowly. 'Ever heard of her? I've just come from Mark Osborne's office. Your brother's left her a million pounds. It's twice what he's left me. I think that's pretty incontrovertible proof that he was cheating on me.'

'Shit.' Joe falls silent.

'It is shit.' Tears pour down my face. 'It isn't so much the money – though it is a lot of money. Who the fuck is she?'

'Are you still in Deal?'

'Yes.'

'Come over to the house. I came back to get a few things. Mum and Dad have both gone out.'

'OK.' I wipe my face. 'I'll be there soon.'

★

I'd always assumed Richard's business was the source of their wealth, but as I pull in to the McKenna family home, I see it with new eyes. There's nothing understated about the proportions of this house – the tall stone porch, the two columns either side of steps worn smooth with age.

I'd always seen it as a slightly tired seaside town house, but now I realise it's anything but. It's the same when I go inside – the artwork on the walls, the pieces of antique furniture I'd always thought were reproductions. Every single one is probably genuine.

'At least we have a name,' I say bitterly. 'Not that it helps. Mark Osborne wouldn't give me her address.'

'He wouldn't be allowed to.' Joe places a cup of tea in front of me.

'I don't understand why Oliver didn't tell me about this money.' I take the mug of tea, suddenly seeing Joe differently too. It explains the way he manages not to work for months at a time, yet always drives a nice car, buys expensive shoes. 'I'm guessing it's the same for you?'

'Yes,' he says quietly. 'There's more that will come to us – I'm not sure how much exactly. It's not something either of us talked about. People are different with you when they know you have money. Our parents instilled in us how important it is to work and have a career – hence my father's view of what he perceives as my idleness.' For a moment he sounds slightly bitter. 'Being a commercial pilot, Oliver fulfilled all their expectations. You know how much they loved talking about what he did. He was lucky to find something he loved, while for me . . .' he shrugged. 'I guess I'm still trying to find my own version of that.'

But I feel sick inside. 'Oliver could have paid off our mortgage.'

'I know from the outside it doesn't make a lot of sense.' Joe sighs. 'But would it honestly have made a difference to anything that's happened since? You have a gorgeous home, Kat, in a lovely part of the world.'

'We could have had a bigger gorgeous home – and no mortgage.'

'Maybe that was why Oliver kept quiet,' Joe says softly. 'He didn't want bigger – and that's what always happens with money. It becomes about always having bigger, faster, better. Always wanting more, more, more. What he had was enough for him. I think he was more interested in the quality of the life he had with you.'

I shake my head. 'But even that wasn't enough for him, was it? It's why he hooked up with Ana Fontaine. I can't believe I haven't given the police the photo.' Cursing myself, I reach for my phone. 'I need to talk to them, Joe. She may even be the person who tampered with my car. Doesn't it stand to reason that she might have wanted me out of the way? She'd probably discovered how wealthy he was. It could have been his money she was after. If she knew how much he'd planned to leave her, it could even have given her a motive for killing him.'

Joe looks at me. 'You're right. It's all possible.' Getting up, he picks up his phone. 'I'll call them, Kat, and let them know we're on our way over there.'

10

Katharine

After speaking to DS Stanley, Joe and I head over to the police station.

As we drive, I'm quiet, still shaken by the contents of Oliver's will. But there's more no one knows about our marriage; the way Oliver had begun to treat me, my every word seeming to irritate him, often enough for him to lose his temper altogether. I should have told someone about this earlier, because if the police find out now, my hiding it might make them think I had a motive for killing him.

Joe glances sideways at me. 'You definitely have the photo, don't you?'

I nod. 'It's in my bag.'

'Presumably the police will be able to find this woman, whoever she is.'

'I hope so.' Another thought occurs to me. 'If they still have his phone, surely they'll be able to check it for messages from her?'

'What the fuck was he playing at?' Joe sounds angry. 'Stupid bastard – when he had you, the house, his job.'

'But he'd fucked that up too, hadn't he?' I say quietly. 'He'd fucked everything up.'

Inside the police station, we don't have to wait long before DS Stanley appears. 'Thank you for coming over. Would you like to come with me?'

We follow her along a corridor. Stopping next to a door, she opens it and stands back to let us into a small room with a table and four chairs. 'Please take a seat.'

Joe and I sit side by side, as sitting opposite us, she turns to me. 'I understand you went to your solicitor earlier today.'

'Yes. He's Oliver's executor. I found out something I wasn't expecting.'

'Go on.'

'He told me what Oliver had left me, but also that Oliver had recently opened another bank account – one I didn't know about – and deposited a million pounds. My guess is it's family money.' I'm aware of Joe stiffening beside me. 'I didn't know it existed until today.'

'Is that a problem?'

'Well, yes.' I clasp my hands together under the table, trying to hide how upset I am. 'He's left it to a woman I've never even heard of. Her name is Ana Fontaine. Given all the time he had when he was supposedly working, I'm guessing he was having an affair with her. I can't help thinking it could have been her who sabotaged my car. She might have wanted me out of the way – or wanted Oliver dead, knowing she was going to inherit the money.' My hand shakes as I pass her the photo we found in Oliver's desk. 'This might be her.'

Frowning, DS Stanley studies the photo. 'Where did you get this?'

'Kat found it after the crash, when we discovered Oliver had lost his job,' Joe tells her. 'We were trying to find his logbook – which is still missing. The photo was in one of the drawers. We didn't think it was worth telling you about before. At the time, it looked as though the crash was an accident.'

'But you now know that's unlikely.' Turning it over, DS Stanley studies the back, before passing it to her colleague. She looks at me again. 'Do you have any idea what that message might mean?'

I shake my head. 'I haven't a clue.'

She frowns. 'Why didn't you give this to me before? We asked if it was possible your husband might have been having an affair and you didn't mention it.'

'I haven't been thinking straight.' I shake my head, hiding the fact that I'd been trying to avoid intrusive questioning. 'I suppose I didn't want to believe it. And I was thinking of Jude – Oliver's mother. I'd still prefer she didn't know. I'd rather she remembered the son she thought he was.'

DS Stanley doesn't react. 'Do you know anything at all about Ms Fontaine?'

Joe and I shake our heads.

'He's never mentioned her,' Joe says quietly.

'Bizarre, isn't it?' DS Stanley frowns, then her guard slips. 'Had a few secrets, didn't he? Makes you wonder what else he was up to.' She looks at me. 'Given what you've found out, has there been anything else in recent weeks that in the light of what we know, might have seemed suspicious?'

'He used my car more often.' I shrug. 'I think I told you

111

there was a problem with his. Maybe the third set of finger-prints belongs to her.'

'We'll see if we can track down this Ana Fontaine. Presumably your solicitor must be in contact with her – could you give me his details?'

Scrolling down my phone, I find Mark's number. 'He has her address. But he wouldn't give it to me.'

'Considering he has a professional reputation to uphold, I wouldn't expect him to. Thank you.' After making a note of it, DS Stanley turns to me, then Joe. 'However tempting it is to look for her yourselves, can I advise you to leave this to the police?'

★

Having held my silence to protect Oliver's enduring memory, after Mark Osborne's revelation this afternoon, if this is family money, his parents should know.

When I tell Jude about Oliver's will and about the money he's left to Ana Fontaine, her face goes pale.

'How could he?' The anger in her voice turns to tears as she takes hold of my hands. 'It's absolutely dreadful that he's done this to you.'

She says little more and I'm not in the room when she tells Richard. But when he comes to find me, his face is like thunder.

'It's wrong, Kat, whatever spin he might have put on it to himself. You were his wife. By rights, that money should be yours.'

I look at him. 'I think it's more upsetting for you and Jude. It's inherited money that I didn't even know about. What I don't understand is why he's left it to this woman.'

'There must be some way of tracking her down.' Richard sounds mutinous.

'The police said to leave it to them.'

'I'm sure they did,' Richard says angrily. 'But there's no law to stop you trying to find someone.'

★

If Richard tracks her down, he doesn't say. Over the next few days, we're distracted, planning a funeral that none of our hearts are in, more for show than anything else. While Jude and Richard choose traditional readings and hymns, we all write something benign to form the eulogy.

'We must have flowers.' Jude looks upset. 'I just wish this beastly day was far behind us.'

'It will be soon.' I try to push my anger with Oliver aside, to put myself in her shoes and imagine how she must be feeling. 'Let's have autumn colours, Jude. Oliver loved them.'

Looking at me gratefully, she squeezes my hand. 'Will you come with me to the florist to order them?'

After we finalise the orders of service, Joe lines up a pub in Deal with a function room, for anyone who wants to join us after the funeral. Richard, however, remains aloof. I put it down to his feeling that when Oliver knew what the family's expectations were, all he'd done was let him down.

I spend the night before the funeral alone. In the house I shared with Oliver, after lighting a fire, I take out our wedding photos. Studying our faces, I think of the happiness that hadn't been faked; that had been tangible in every aspect of our wedding day.

Going through the photos, I take in the pride on Jude's

113

and Richard's faces, lingering on one of Joe – it was one of the rare occasions I'd seen him wear a suit – his face so similar to Oliver's, yet at the same time so different. More distant members of the McKenna family; our friends – friends who since that day, we seem to have lost touch with.

One photo stands out – of us, under the floral arch outside the church. The breeze has lifted a lock of hair across my face and as I smile at Oliver, he's stroking it away. The photo encapsulates the tenderness he used to display – tenderness that vanished after we were married.

I think of the future I've lost, that should have been everything I'd dreamed of; how in recent months, there was a tension between us. I'd put it down to Oliver working hard; to us adjusting to married life; the amount of money we were spending on the house that he was trying to rein in, which now that I know the extent of his estate, doesn't seem plausible. At the start, I'd been so sure we loved each other – enough to get over any differences between us. But now I can't help seeing things differently. Two years on, maybe there had been no hope for us. It wasn't what I'd wanted but maybe we'd reached the end. Maybe that's why I feel this fleeting, inappropriate sense of relief.

A tear rolls down my cheek. When we could have been so good together, why did it have to go so wrong?

Shame, betrayal and sadness swirl inside me. In spite of my efforts, I wasn't – never could be – enough for Oliver. Picking up the photo again, I rip it down the middle, then into smaller pieces before scattering them into the flames.

2014

Gemma

This latest French house offered everything I needed – not only free living, but luxury, invisibility, the sense of awaiting discovery – and above all, the delicious tension that came from knowing I was walking a knife edge. It empowered me to the point that I started to care less about being caught, opening the shutters, letting the warm air into this dusty old mausoleum; spending time in the beautiful gardens.

At the same time, Nathan was growing more fearful. 'Stupid fucking bitch,' he hissed at me as he slammed the shutters closed again. 'Do you want to get us caught?'

Staring him back in the eye, I shrugged. So he was annoyed – who gave a fuck. 'Time's ticking. We're going to have to get out of here at some point. In the meantime, we may as well have some fun.' I was winding him up, but as I'd discovered, he was too frigging sensitive. 'I'm going for a walk.'

He grabbed my arm. 'You can't go out there.'

'Excuse me, I'll do whatever I like.' My voice was icy. 'If you wouldn't mind.' I shook off his grip.

'It's the day the gardener guy comes.'

'So it is.' I glanced at my watch. 'I better go now before he gets here.'

As I wandered across the garden, away from Nathan, a feeling of relief settled over me. The fact was I was getting bored with him, which was why I'd come out here – to shake things up, bring a thrill of excitement into my life. After all, being here was just a game. But we'd come here together and I felt I owed it to him to see this through. When we left here, however, I was going to tell him it was over, before moving on, alone, to something new. It would be too risky to break up with him now, when he knew where I was staying and could easily exact revenge.

Across the garden, I sauntered under the trees, taking in the shadows they cast, the sunlight glistening through the leaves. Glancing up at the house, I felt a flicker of irritation as I watched one of the closed shutters move slightly. At this rate, it was going to be Nathan who gave us away – not me.

Hearing the mower start, I waited from my vantage point. Anyone lost in the woods could happen across this garden. From under the trees, I watched the regular motion of the tractor mower leaving its wake of neatly striped grass, until picking my moment, I wandered out.

As I'd predicted, the driver came straight over. 'Bonjour. C'est privé.' He spoke in a manner that wasn't exactly friendly.

He was younger than I'd expected, with tanned skin, dark hair and intense eyes I didn't want to look away from. 'Pardon.' Feeling something stir inside me, I tried my hardest to look embarrassed. 'Dans le maison?' I pointed to the house, then to the sting forcibly inflicted on my hand from when I'd encountered a convenient bumble bee. 'J'ai été piqué.'

He looked less hostile. 'English?'

Meeting his gaze, I nodded.

'You want something for your sting?' He shook his head. 'No one is there. No one comes this year.'

The whole year? That was unexpected. 'Oh.' Trying to look downcast, I turned my gaze towards the house. If Nathan was watching, he'd be freaking out. 'It's so sad when the house is so beautiful.'

The gardener shrugged. 'Is just a house.'

'Oui. Et merci. Pardon,' I apologised. 'Le village?' I pointed in the direction of where I thought the nearest village was.

He nodded. 'Is about two kilometres.' His eyes wandered lazily over my body before he looked up again. 'Bon journée. Au revoir.'

'Au revoir.' I felt his eyes on me as I wandered in the direction I'd pointed, before the mower restarted. Once I was out of sight, I waited until he'd finished; giving him the few more minutes he usually took to finish up and put the mower back, before getting in his van and driving away.

I had no idea if Nathan was watching me, but as quiet fell, I had something else up my sleeve. Making my way through the trees, I went back towards the house, letting myself in quietly. Tiptoeing along the hallway towards the kitchen, I followed the waft of whatever Nathan was smoking.

No way was I telling him the house was going to remain empty. He'd probably want to stay. Stopping in the hallway, I could see him sitting at the kitchen table. With his back towards me, I could tell he was on edge, inhaling frantically on one of his thin roll-ups, now and then tapping his fingers on the table.

Noticing the earphones he was wearing, I knew he couldn't hear me creep up behind him. Standing there a moment, I think he became aware of my presence a split second before I put my hands around his neck.

117

His arms started flailing as I held him, long enough to frighten him, for him to know that I had the power if I wanted to go all the way. But though Nathan was irritating, he was harmless enough.

As I let him go, gasping for breath, he got up and staggered away, his eyes terrified as he turned to look at me. 'What the fuck, Gemma?'

Casually picking up an apple, I took a bite. 'You should be more careful, lover boy. What if it hadn't been me?' Enjoying his discomfort, I took another bite. 'Ever heard the saying, keep your friends close but your enemies closer?'

He looked at me as if he didn't understand. 'I thought you were my fucking friend.'

'I am your fucking friend,' I said casually. 'For now, at least.' This wasn't the time to tell him that it wouldn't be for much longer. 'Besides.' Tasting a rank bite of apple, I spat it out. 'Asphyxiation is supposed to be a bit of a turn on – heightens sexual pleasure. Didn't you like it?' I pulled a look of mock disappointment. 'Shame. I thought we could maybe try it out.'

Nathan went visibly pale. 'You're fucked.'

'Not yet . . . but I want to be.' This afternoon, the encounter with the gardener, the element of risk, had combined to leave me feeling gloriously aroused. 'On the table?' I started slowly peeling off my clothes until slipping out of my underwear, I stood naked in front of him. I looked at him provocatively. 'What are you waiting for?' I pulled a pose. 'Don't you want me?'

Nathan never could resist me. This one last time, I promised myself, enjoying the feel of his body against mine. The sex was good, but after this, when tomorrow came, I already knew what I was going to say.

The moment I woke up the next morning, I got on with my plan. After a shower, I went downstairs. After tidying the kitchen, *putting away the plates and cutlery we'd used, I wiped down the surfaces. Unless you noticed the one or two items that were missing, no one would know we'd ever been here. Already I was imagining where I'd go next. If I sold some of the silver packed in my rucksack, I'd have enough money to tide me over for some time. Maybe I'd head for the coast — find an antique shop on the Côte d'Azur — a dodgy one — they were everywhere, as I already knew — and realise some cash.*

Lost in my thoughts, I didn't notice Nathan walk in.

'What are you doing?'

Turning around, I saw him standing in the doorway watching me. 'Tidying up,' I told him. 'Time to go, lover boy. We don't want to outstay our welcome.'

He looked suspiciously at me. 'What's the rush?'

'Time waits for no man,' I quoted. 'I need change, Nathan. I'm getting frigging bored, aren't you?'

'No.' He folded his arms. 'I'm not ready to leave.'

'Stay, then.' I shrugged. I no longer cared. 'But you'll need to keep your wits about you without me to keep you on your toes.'

'That's not what I'm saying.' His voice was angry. 'You can't just go off and leave me here.'

His neediness was pissing me off. 'Look,' I stopped tidying. 'This was always going to come to an end. You and me . . .' I hesitated. 'It's been cool hanging out with you, but I'm moving on. It's time for a change.'

'Just like that?' He looked at me in disbelief. 'You con me into this . . . whatever this is . . . and then walk out when you feel like it.'

'For fuck's sake.' I stared at him. 'You seem to have your wires crossed. We have no obligation to each other. None whatsoever. Got it?'

'See, that's where you're wrong.' His voice was deceptively soft. 'You're not the only one who's got this figured out. I could go to the police. Tell them I know this girl who breaks into empty houses. They're probably looking for you all over France. I have so many photos . . .' Taking his phone out of his pocket, he started scrolling through them. 'How about this one?' He held up a photo of me holding one of the bottles of wine I'd helped myself to. 'Breaking, entering and stealing?' he sneered. 'Your fingerprints are everywhere in this house. You leave without me, you won't know what's hit you.'

For the first time in our relationship, I felt a flicker of fear. 'Don't fucking threaten me.' I brazened it out. 'You're as guilty as I am. The police will know that — don't forget, you're not the only one with photos.'

When he didn't respond, I went on. 'In any case, we both know you don't have the balls. I mean, look at you — while I was out in the garden talking to the man on the mower, where were you? Hiding like a baby — that's where. You're always scared, Nathan,' I taunted. Seeing his reaction, I knew I'd hit a nerve. 'Scared of being caught, scared of being alone,' I mocked. 'You won't go to the police. You're not fucking brave enough to take the risk.'

While I was speaking, his face had turned red, but by the time I finished, it was white.

'You really are a first-class bitch, Gemma.' He spoke quietly. 'Fine. Play it your way. I'm going — and I'll take my chances with the police.' He paused. 'I know you've stolen some silver, by the way. I saw it in your bag. If I were you, I'd get myself a very long way from here.'

I couldn't believe I hadn't seen this coming. But until then, I really didn't know Nathan had it in him. 'Don't worry. I'm out of here.' I could feel my heart thumping as, pushing past him, I went upstairs.

In what had been our bedroom, I gathered the last of my things, folding them roughly and squashing them into my rucksack, before picking up the car keys, as a thought occurred to me.

Making the bed, I pulled the covers over it. If the house was going to be empty for a year, whoever was here next would surely change the bed linen. It was a waste of precious time doing it twice.

Going back downstairs, I looked at Nathan. 'Seeing as it's me who'll be taking the car . . .' I paused. 'Can I give you a lift somewhere?'

He looked at me incredulously.

I raised my arms in a gesture of exasperation. 'We've spent the last three months together. When we're miles from anywhere, is it really so weird to offer you a lift?'

'What's the catch?'

I shrugged. 'There isn't one. I'll drive you to the village. I'll even drop you outside the gendarmerie . . . then you'll never see me again.' I glanced at the clock on the wall. 'Are you ready?'

In silence, he went upstairs to get his things, minutes later coming back down again.

'Right.' I picked up the keys. 'Let's go.'

Locking the door, I replaced the key where I'd found it. As we had since we first arrived here, we avoided the main entrance. Taking the narrow path through the woods, we walked in single file towards where we'd left the car.

Suddenly I stumbled. 'Fuck.'

Behind me, Nathan stopped. 'You OK?'

'I've twisted my ankle.' Doubled over, I was hiding the knife I'd taken from the kitchen. 'Can you help me up?' Leaning on the arm he was holding out, as I stood up, the rest was easy.

However much of a risk Nathan had become, I didn't enjoy watching someone die. Many times, I'd wondered, if pushed, how far I'd be prepared to go, but I'd always known that if it came to it, I'd do what I had to; that in a cruel world, when you had no one on your side, you had to look out for yourself.

After the initial intensity of the moment, as I stood there watching his life ebb away, seconds became hours, before suddenly it was over. Looking down at his motionless body, I allowed myself a flicker of regret. But if Nathan had only been smarter, less needy, more accepting of our parting of the ways, this needn't have happened. In essence, he'd brought it on himself.

Focusing on the practicalities, I started going through his bag, taking his passport, before finding his wallet and phone. It was all he had — ever since we got here, I'd been watching him. I'd checked his bag, too, to see if he was hiding anything. But unlike me, he wasn't. If anyone discovered him before his corpse decayed, they'd find a twenty-something white male with nothing to identify him. Getting up, I put everything in my bag, wiping the knife on Nathan's t-shirt before hiding that in my bag, too. I'd deposit things in bins once I was far away from here — scattering everything that might have identified him.

But it wasn't just Nathan who had to disappear. A new chapter called for a new persona — hair, clothes, and this time, name too. She'd done me proud, but after what had just happened, she'd had her day. Gemma Hargreaves was no more.

11

Jude

Infidelity is at the heart of the rot in many marriages and when Kat tells me about the woman mentioned in Oliver's will, I find it hard to hide my anger that he could do that to her. More than once, I wonder what was going on between them, as with each passing day, Kat becomes more closed off, as though she's absorbing each element of Oliver's deceit, while inside it's slowly corroding her. When it comes to grief, people will excuse anything, but I worry that the funeral will tip her over the edge. *It will soon be over*, I keep telling myself. After, I've no idea what she plans to do. But given enough time, that will come.

On the day of the funeral, the wind picks up, scattering a golden carpet of autumn leaves. As the four of us gather in Kat's house, Joe is composed, sombre in his dark suit. Kat's face is pale, her black dress hanging off; her fragility never more evident. Upright and calm, Richard remains silent.

As we wait, I have the strangest sense that at any moment, Oliver could walk back in; until, through the window, I catch sight of the car as it pulls into the driveway. I watch Kat draw herself up, summoning her strength before she and Joe leave to join the funeral cortège.

Richard and I follow behind in the black BMW SUV, as I try to focus on Kat rather than my own feelings. 'Today isn't going to be easy for her.' I watch the first of the rain-drops spatter on the windscreen.

'It isn't going to be easy for any of us,' Richard says abruptly.

'No.' My voice wavers as I seek to distract myself. 'After this is over, why don't you talk to Joe again? You never know, he might be rethinking things.'

'About coming to work for me?' Richard sounds taken aback. 'Knowing Joe, I imagine he's counting the days until he can leave the country again – especially after what Oliver's done. He's always idolised him – and Kat. All of this will have rocked him.'

'He's really been there for Kat – for all of us, actually. But he has his own life to live.' Suddenly I realise how little Joe has said; just shored us all up, selflessly pushing his own grief aside for later. A feeling of sadness fills me at the thought of him going away. 'I'd just like to understand why Oliver did what he did.'

'That's exactly why I want to make some enquiries,' Richard says smoothly. 'Two months, Jude, when he was supposedly at work. Where the hell was he?'

Given he's about to attend his own son's funeral, he shows an extraordinary absence of emotion. As the church comes into view, Richard slows down behind the funeral car. I turn to him. 'I know I said I thought you should let it go – but maybe you should try and find out. Depending on what you uncover, we can decide whether or not we tell Kat.'

'Good – because personally, I'd very much like to know. I always used to think Oliver had integrity. I trusted him – he was our son, for Christ's sake. Why the hell wouldn't I? But he's pulled the wool over all our eyes.' For a moment his anger shows through, before he continues in a more conciliatory tone. 'Let's get today out of the way. We have plenty of time to think about it later.'

Pulling over, he parks at the side of the road. Sitting there a moment, we glance simultaneously towards the sea of black umbrellas gathered outside the church. Fleetingly I wonder if Ana Fontaine will dare to show up today – but among the crowd of unfamiliar faces, if she was among them, there's no way I'd know.

Getting out of the car, Richard comes around to the passenger door with an umbrella. Climbing out, the cold hits me as I take his arm. Side by side, we cross the road to the church. Inside, I'm grateful for the flowers Kat helped me choose; their warm colours bringing softness to the austere stone; beauty on a day that resonates with the darkness of betrayal. At the front, I take my place next to Kat. Her tension is palpable, soaking into me. My hand finds its way to one of hers and as I squeeze it, I realise she's shaking.

'OK?' I whisper.

She inclines her head, the slightest movement. 'No.'

But as I gaze at my son's coffin, I know none of us are. Not long ago, I'd believed we were a united family. But Oliver's duplicity has shaken up all our lives and turned them into something unfamiliar.

As the service goes on, I forget what's gone on in recent

days. Instead, my mind drifts back to the day I gave birth to my first child. Memories fill my head, of watching him grow into a tousle-haired toddler; his passion for all things that flew, from birds to helicopters, before he obsessed about learning to fly. His determination, the sacrifices he made, the successful career he achieved – until . . . until he made a misjudgement and it all went wrong.

When at last it's over, Kat and Joe follow the coffin up the aisle, as Richard and I take our places behind them. Outside, beneath cloudy skies and drizzle, under the scrutiny of the crowd that's gathered, Kat holds up stoically, Joe never far from her side. Now and then I watch her eyes flicker across faces. I know she, too, is wondering if Ana Fontaine is here.

The family-only service at the crematorium is brief, after which we steel ourselves to join the wake at the pub. Kat's face remains blank, her shoulders rigid, as she circumnavigates the people who have come to pay their respects.

I'm touched by how far people have travelled to come here; distant family, old friends who have moved away. I catch sight of a brief exchange between Richard and Beatrice. She used to look after the boys when they were little. They liked her, but she could be too outspoken and Richard said it wasn't what we paid her for. I've always regretted that it hadn't ended well.

Throughout, Kat stays impressively calm. But when we get back to the house, she crashes, overwrought, the strain pouring visibly from her like a river in full flow.

'It's too much, Jude,' she sobs. 'It's the not knowing. I feel like I'm losing my mind. Today, in the church, I knew that woman was there. She had to be,' she says hysterically. 'If I'd been her, I would have wanted to see who Oliver's wife was.'

Over her shoulder, I catch Joe's eye. Going to the kitchen, he comes back with a tot of brandy.

'Shh . . .' I hold her firmly. 'This is awful, Kat. Really awful. But it won't always be like this. You're going to take each day, one at a time,' I say quietly. 'And it isn't going to be easy. But you won't be alone. You'll never be alone.'

'I keep thinking of the way he'd walk in, telling me about his day at work or his stories about the crew. It never entered his head that I wouldn't believe him. All the time, he must have been laughing at me.' She clenches her fists until her knuckles are white.

All the clichés come to mind, about invisible lines that life is full of – between light and darkness, day and night; love and hate; but in the context of what she's suffered, they're pointless, trite.

'You're angry, Kat. And you're hurting. You have every reason to. I'm angry, too. But in spite of what he's done, you're grieving – and you mustn't forget. We still can't be sure there wasn't a reason that Oliver kept things from you.'

'Such as what?' Lifting her tear-stained face, her eyes are filled with angst.

But I can't think of a single one. 'I don't know – maybe he wanted to surprise you. But even if he made a mistake, we all do things we regret. None of us are perfect.'

There are no answers to her questions, no soothing of her pain, just difficult days that lie ahead as she waits for more time to pass.

12

Katharine

Even with the funeral behind us, I'm still in limbo, waiting for probate to be granted so that I can access Oliver's accounts; to hear from the Coroner's Office; for the police to find out who sabotaged my car, while the desire to find Ana Fontaine consumes me.

I attempt to struggle back into some kind of routine for the sake of my clients. Oliver's death has disrupted their therapy for long enough. And being forced to focus on someone other than myself helps me too, to some extent. I hear nothing from the police. Meanwhile, the evenings are long, filled with unsettled thoughts and decisions I can't yet make, about where to live, or what I'm going to do with the house. While Oliver's left me enough money to pay off the mortgage, given what I've found out in recent weeks, I'm not at all sure I want to stay here.

More often than not, Joe comes over to visit. 'I've spent most of the morning googling Ana Fontaine. I'm sick to death of it, but I'm determined to find her,' he says on one of those days. 'Sorry. It's probably the last name you want to hear.'

I shake my head. 'I've been doing the same – but I haven't found anything.'

'I'd really like to know if the police have contacted her,' he says. 'I suppose we're going to have to wait.' He settles into one of the kitchen chairs. 'Have you thought any more about selling the house?'

'I have, but I have to wait for probate. I keep changing my mind about what to do. Everything feels so uncertain at the moment. This house is about the only security I have. I think, right now, I probably need that.'

'If it's in your joint names, I don't think you have to wait.' Joe watches me make two mugs of tea. 'But it's probably wise not to make any hasty decisions.'

'What about you?' I take the mugs over to the table. 'Are you still planning to go away?'

'I feel a bit like you. Uncertain about pretty much everything. I can go away any time.' He pauses. 'Plus I think the old man is gearing up to ask me to go and work for him.'

'Again?' I know how Joe feels about his father's business. 'Surely he knows what you'll say.' I pause. 'If you could do anything, what would you really want to do?'

'Do you know how many times I've asked myself the same question?' Joe sighs. 'I always envied Oliver knowing he wanted to fly. Ages ago, I looked into training as a football coach – you can imagine what my father had to say about that.'

I can, all too easily. The idea of being a football coach wouldn't have impressed Richard. 'If that's what you want, just do it. It's your life,' I say quietly.

'I know.' Joe stares at his tea. 'But everything's different since Oliver died. Losing your brother . . .' His voice is emotional. 'It makes you see everything differently. You realise you can't take anything for granted – while going off on another adventure seems frivolous, somehow.' He swallows. 'I may stick around for a while. I'm not sure yet.'

I look at him sympathetically. 'Nothing prepares you for something like this, does it? But if you still want to go to Australia, maybe you should. You already have a visa, don't you?'

'I know. It just doesn't hold the same pull.' His eyes meet mine. 'Weird, isn't it, how much has changed?'

Getting up again, I'm silent as I go over to the window. Outside, everything is damp with rain, the only colour the bright red berries on the holly tree – evidence of the relentless passage of the seasons, that stop for no man. Yet Joe's right. In our hearts, everything's changed.

'Have I said something wrong?' Joe's voice comes from behind me.

Folding my arms around myself, I shake my head. *But it had already changed.* I hear him push his chair back, then the sound of him coming closer, my heart starting to thump as he turns me to face him, before his arms snake around me, pulling me towards him as he kisses me.

I stiffen, taken momentarily by surprise before I sink into his arms. But then reason sets in. Gently pulling back, I look into his eyes. 'It would be so easy, Joe. But we can't do this.'

'No one needs to know, Kat. And no one's going to guess. For heaven's sake, even my mother has virtually pushed us together.'

'That's different,' I say quietly. 'There's too much to sort out. It isn't that I don't want to,' I add. I've always been drawn to Joe, especially during the more difficult times with Oliver. But life is complicated enough without making it more so.

More than ever, I'm in turmoil. But shortly after, when Joe goes out to do some food shopping, something clicks into place inside my head. I'm almost sure Oliver took out life insurance – I remember us discussing it when we finalised our mortgage. The mortgage we needn't have had.

Going to the kitchen table, I start sifting through the pile of paperwork that's growing bigger by the day, my heart lifting when I find a quote in Oliver's name. Finding my phone, I call the insurance company, but any hope I have is short-lived when they tell me that the quote was never confirmed.

I think about calling other companies – but given how many there are, it would be like looking for a needle in a haystack. At least once probate is granted, I'll be able to search Oliver's bank statements. If only I could access them now.

My eyes wander towards his laptop. Switching it on, my fingers hesitate over the keys. Knowing more about my husband now than I ever have before, I try to log in.

AnaFontaine1

I keep trying, with different numbers, until I'm locked out. Then I try again, with *Fontaine,* then *fontaine,* using every combination of upper and lower case with different numbers.

Two hours later, I have one last attempt. *fontainea1.* Pressing return, I wait a second before somehow, miraculously, I'm in.

Almost immediately my mobile rings. Picking it up, I take in the unknown number.

Listening to the voice the other end, a frown crosses my face. And when the call ends I put my phone down and just sit, stunned.

It isn't long before Joe comes back with the shopping.

'I had a call while you were out,' I tell him as he puts the shopping away. 'It was from the Liaison Officer from the Coroner's Office. You're not going to believe this. The post-mortem results showed Oliver had diabetes. The symptoms can include confusion and slurred speech – and appearing drunk. It could explain the accident, Joe. But also . . .' As he turns to look at me, I go on. 'It means it's possible he wasn't drunk when he was at work.'

Joe's eyes widen. '*What?*'

'I know.' I'm relieved on the one hand. I've hated the thought of him being drunk at the controls of an aircraft, but it doesn't resolve anything else. 'We should tell your parents.'

Joe nods. 'Let me finish doing this. Then I'll drive us.'

On the way to Deal, while Joe drives, I google diabetes. Convinced Oliver would have known something was wrong, according to what I read, it turns out that the symptoms can come on so slowly, it's possible he wouldn't have. Maybe he went to see our GP. I add it to my mental list of things to check out. But for the first time it presents an acceptable reason for his secrecy – that he hadn't wanted to worry any of us.

But it does nothing to explain Ana Fontaine.

'Joe? If we can't find anything about her on Oliver's laptop, I'm going to search all the online directories and make a list of any Ana Fontaines within a radius of here. There can't be that many. Then one by one, I'm going to call them.'

'I'm not sure the police will be too happy about that.'

'They can't stop us, can they? From making a few calls?' Getting out my phone, I google her, wondering why I haven't done it before. 'I can't find anyone in Kent.'

'Try Facebook,' Joe suggests.

Scrolling down, my heart sinks. 'There are loads – not in the UK, though. It seems to be a French name.'

'Well, Mark Osborne must have an address for her. Maybe Dad can speak to him.'

'I hope so.' A part of me wants to know who she is. But even if I found her, what would I say to her? When I wouldn't be able to face her telling me that my husband had fallen in love with her, is there any point?

13

Ana

I knew something was wrong when Oliver went silent. When news of his death reached me, I somehow held myself together, while around me I was aware of my world shattering. When Oliver and I met, love was something I'd closed the door on; an emotion I never thought I'd feel again. I never expected to fall for him and in so many ways, it would have been easier if I hadn't. But at a time when both of us felt desperately alone, we were inexorably drawn together.

There was something about him I felt I could trust; that brought back a part of me I thought I'd lost forever. He was my second chance, one I never once contemplated losing. Imagining we'd be together, always, we'd started making plans.

Before he died, from what he told me about his family, I'd been prepared for things not to be straightforward. They'd have been against him divorcing Katharine, for one thing. Since we'd started spending more time together, worried that our affair would somehow slip out, I'd prepared myself for an angry encounter with Joe at some point, the little brother, who according to Oliver was in love with his wife; with Jude, who loved her career more than her children; with Richard, for whom making money was the sole purpose of being alive.

Believing any woman worth her salt would pick up cues if her husband was having an affair, I'd even been prepared for Kat to show up here. In her shoes, I would have left no stone unturned in my quest to find out where my husband was. But so far at least, I've seen none of them.

It's unbelievable how much has happened in such a short time. Prior to meeting Oliver almost a year ago, I'd been at my lowest ebb as I'd stumbled across a basic truth I most needed to find, that the only way my life was going to change was if I took control back and stopped letting things happen around me.

Life had been hard for so long, alcohol had become a place to escape to; somewhere to hide my pain, my loneliness; an inconstant friend while life was passing me by in a progression of wasted, unproductive days. As I told everyone at the first AA meeting:

I'm Ana. I want to be sober, and I want my life back.

The AA group were a varied crowd when I started going there. Eleven weeks before Oliver arrived on the scene, I was taking my first steps on my journey towards sobriety, while others were getting ready to leave the group. A few weeks later, I was saying goodbye to one of them when Oliver walked in.

Out of the corner of my eye, I took in his sweater – I was pretty sure it was cashmere. The jeans that were the right shade of faded blue, the dark eyes that avoided everyone else's. He was a little older than me, I guessed.

My gaze slipped to his shoes. He was well-off, that much was certain.

I was curious as to what brought a guy like this to a small community centre near the centre of Deal. There were far more established places if you could afford to pay for rehab, while this one was quirky, built on the grounds of a deconsecrated church – the bar firmly off limits for the duration of our meetings. I'd been astonished there'd even been a bar – but it wasn't my place to question the logic of such things.

When he missed the next meeting, I wondered if he'd written the experience off – it wasn't uncommon for people to show up once and never be seen again. But the third week, to my surprise, he was back. In running clothes this time, I wondered if that was his cover for coming here – not just ordinary running gear either, I noticed, my eyes wandering over the subtle branding.

Five weeks after he'd first come here, I was into my twelfth. Having discovered a new sense of control, my head was clearer, my mind more focused. I'd reached a point, I'd suddenly realised, where I was ready to step back out into the world.

When my turn came, I stood up. 'My name is Ana. I've been coming here for twelve weeks – and I've been sober for ten. Being here,' I glanced around at the group, 'and meeting all of you, I can honestly say it's the best thing I've done. I knew it wasn't going to be easy and when I first started coming, I wasn't sure I could do it. Alcohol had become a crutch . . .' I faltered, swallowing the lump in my throat; thinking of what had started me down that road. 'But I don't need it anymore. I just want to thank you for supporting me. To those of you just starting . . .' My eyes rested briefly on Oliver. 'All I can say is keep going. It does get easier — and whatever regrets you might have in your life, I promise you, coming here won't be one of them.'

I detected a flicker of interest from Oliver as I spoke, that was confirmed afterwards when I was pouring myself a cup of tea.

'Interesting speech.'

The voice came from behind me. I knew immediately who it was. I paused a moment, before I turned around. 'Ah, the new guy.' I smiled into his eyes.

He winced. 'Not feeling so new — more like quite a jaded old guy.'

'It will pass,' I said quietly. 'Cup of tea?'

'Thanks.'

Pouring another cup, I passed it to him. 'Finding it tough?'

'You could say. It's just one more thing that isn't as it should be. But hopefully I'll get there. You, however . . . congratulations.'

'Thanks. I won't say it's been painless.' I sipped my tea. 'Especially at the start — but honestly, it's true what I said. It does start to get easier. Maybe it's partly my personality — plus mine wasn't a gin for breakfast kind of problem. But I was drinking enough for it to affect me . . .' I paused. He really didn't need to know the details. 'Once I'd decided to stop, I engaged all the available help. And it's worked. At least, so far.' I was highly aware that this was only the beginning; that I had to stay sober.

'You've done well.' He raised his teacup.

'Thank you.'

When he hung around, we carried on talking a little longer, peripheral stuff, about Deal and the community centre, until finishing my tea, I pulled on my jacket.

'Well, I guess this is it.'

He looked at me, confused.

'I don't suppose I'll see you again. I'm not going to be coming anymore,' I reminded him, adding gently, 'Good luck.'

'Thanks.'

But something in his eyes made me linger as he looked at me hesitantly.

'How about I buy you another cup of tea?'

I smiled. 'I'm kind of a bit tea-ed out, but I'd love a Coke.'

This time, he smiled back. 'I'm not the greatest fan of tea anyway. You're on.'

After saying my goodbyes, we slipped away through the churchyard, the gravestones washed orange in the dull glow from a street lamp.

'You're going to have to get over that,' I said lightly.

'Over what?'

'The tea thing. It's a major part of those meetings – a prop, I guess you'd call it. There's a lot of talking, crying, laughing, staying silent, that all goes on with a cup of tea in our hands.'

We carried on walking, finding a cafe further along the seafront, where we sat at a corner table with our Cokes.

Oliver eyed his glass. 'After years of drinking wine, this is going to take a bit of getting used to,' he said wryly.

I raised an eyebrow. 'You mean talking to a stranger without the social lubrication that alcohol affords?'

He looked amused. 'Something like that.'

Over the AA weeks, I'd become used to talking about it. 'I've asked myself so many times why I've let myself become dependent on it. Except I think it's hardwired into us. I mean, as human beings, since the beginning of time, we've always sought out a means of escaping from ourselves.'

A cloud crossed his face. 'That's exactly it – we need a way of forgetting stuff.'

'But it comes back, doesn't it?' I say sadly, wondering what his stuff was. 'In the cold light of day?'

'Yes.' His face wore a heavy expression. 'So, if it isn't too personal a question, what were you escaping from?'

I took a deep breath. 'Let's just say, I fucked up.' I smiled through my tears. 'More than once. Drinking blotted it out, but it didn't solve anything. It's taken until now for me to face that.' It was the sketchiest of outlines, but as much as I could bring myself to say to someone I'd only just met.

He was silent for a moment. 'Can I see you again?'

I looked at him, slightly unsure. 'I don't even know your name.'

'Oliver.'

'I'm Ana.' I was forgetting he already knew from the meeting.

There were any number of reasons why I should have said no. But something stopped me. The strangest thing was, I already knew I wanted to see him again. After giving him my mobile number, he hurried off into the night, while I made my way along the seafront back to my flat, as I walked, going over the events of this evening in my head. It had been a long time coming, but at last, something in my world was slowly shifting.

2017

Margot

As the ferry pulled out from Valencia, I felt the sea breeze ruffle my hair. I was embarking on the kind of life that until now I'd only dreamed of. A few months in the most stunning of villas set high in the hills of Ibiza.

I'd seen photos of the place – its stunning Mediterranean gardens and exotic planting; stone sculptures, multiple shaded corners furnished with day beds or comfy sofas. In return for living here, all I had to do was keep the place tidy and look after it.

It was a thing about wealth, I was realising. The more people had, the less they cared about their houses – well, in this case, second or third houses. The villa belonged to an Italian businessman. I didn't know how he'd made his money. I didn't care. He'd never met me before, but my carefully worded profile had clinched the deal.

Young woman seeking inspirational environment in which to write and paint. I'd like to meet similar quiet, peace-loving people – my party days are long gone. I'm single, sober and vegan, seeking as we all should, to walk respectfully in this world, thoughtful to all living creatures.

I'd included a couple of photos – a recent headshot, and one of me on a beach in a bikini. I also written myself a couple of references from past hosts I'd dreamed up – I'd agonised over them for hours. There was no way anyone could tell they were written by me. I had a new name, too. Margot Jameson. Slightly romantic, a little unusual; a name that made me feel rebellious.

As the Spanish mainland faded into the background, I picked up my bag and went to find my cabin. I needed to sleep, waking up with enough time for an identity change, to ensure I was ready for tomorrow.

As the ferry docked in Ibiza the following morning, the sun was rising in a cloudless sky. Having embarked in my cut-off shorts and cropped t-shirt, I was leaving the ferry in style – my hair newly washed and sleekly straightened, my makeup on trend. My dress was a piece I'd picked up in the south of France – floaty, reeking of class and style. There was one item I never stinted on and that was perfume. If you were in the know, you could judge a person's wealth by the scent they wore.

With my sun hat in one hand and bag in the other, I waited for the doors to open. To my left, the walls of Dalt Vila glowed in the early morning sunlight. Looking towards the distant hills scattered with sugar-cube villas, I felt my heart quicken. Maybe I'd found where my destiny lay.

Having arrived on a one-way ticket, already I couldn't imagine leaving here. As I walked out of the ferry terminal, a lone taxi driver stood holding up a placard on which Jameson had been written. Walking over, I smiled. 'That's me.'

'Good morning.' A look of surprise crossed his face. 'No luggage?'

I shook my head, the lie practised. 'It's been sent on separately.'

As he drove towards the north of the island, I watched the landscape flash past. It was beautiful out there — a sky of the deepest blue, the beginnings of a heat haze evident; the dusty hills scattered with rosemary and pine trees.

The driver caught my eye in his rear-view mirror. 'You stay here for long?'

I nodded. 'I think so.'

'Holiday?'

'Not exactly. I got to know someone who lives here. He's lending me his house.'

Gazing out of the window, already I could tell how different life was going to be. If I played my cards right, it really wasn't far-fetched to imagine that my future could lie here. Twenty minutes later, as the taxi driver turned off the main road, feeing a thrill of excitement, I smiled to myself. Then a few yards on, as we slowed down, my smile grew broader.

The taxi driver turned to look at me. 'This is the house?'

'This is it.' I couldn't believe my luck. The photos hadn't done it justice. Up close, as well as big, the house was glorious. Nestled among palm trees, it consisted of a modern extension tacked onto a four-hundred-year-old finca, immaculate white walls contrasting with beams of sabina wood, while halfway along, deep red bougainvillea cascaded.

'You are lucky,' he said quietly.

I nodded. 'I am.'

After paying him, I carried my bag towards the house. Going up some steps, I found myself in the shade of a terrace, at the back of which a door was open. Frowning, I went closer. I had no idea anyone else was going to be here. Reaching the door, I knocked. 'Hello? Hola?' I corrected myself.

I heard another door open, before an older woman came hurrying towards me. In a neat, fitted dress, her eyes were bright as she smiled at me. 'Are you Margot? I wasn't expecting you today.'

'I am. Oh, really? Is it OK that I'm here?'

'Of course it is!' She was mumsy and warm as she smiled at me.

I held out my hand. 'Sorry – you are?'

Shaking my hand, she beamed at me. 'I'm Gabby. I live here, too – I've looked after the family for many years. They are very kind. They let me stay. Come in. Welcome!' She hesitated. 'You have no bags?'

Why was everyone so fixated on how much luggage I had?

'I've had them sent on. They'll probably arrive later today.'

She nodded. 'Let me show you to your room. I do hope you're going to be happy here.'

Taken aback, I followed her. I didn't understand why Giuseppe needed me here when he already had Gabby. Following her along a passageway, I took in walls decked with black-and-white photos of Ibiza in the sixties, broken up with abstract art, before she showed me to a room at the far end of the house. My irritation was forgotten as I looked out at the view. Framed by trees, beyond the gardens, the sea sparkled at me. It was as though I'd arrived in paradise.

'Do you like it?' Gabby beamed at me. 'I've been looking forward to you coming here. Giuseppe said you like peaceful-minded people. I hope we can become friends.'

'Me too.' I flashed her a smile that vanished as soon as I turned away. The villa was perfect, no question – I just hadn't planned on sharing it.

'Shall I leave you to unpack? Then come to the kitchen and I'll make you breakfast.'

I turned on the smile again. 'Thanks, Gabby. That would be great.'

I closed the door behind her, listening as her footsteps disappeared down the corridor, annoyed that this wasn't quite as I'd planned. My understanding had been that the house was empty, leaving just me, Ibiza and a whole glorious summer of hedonism. Gabby's presence was mildly inconvenient to say the least. Sitting on the bed I gazed around the room. Even with her in situ, though, there were some serious advantages to being here, starting with this enormous wood-framed bed, the en suite that was bigger than most people's bathrooms. I stroked the sheet – top notch, soft linen – probably Italian, I was guessing, given the owner's heritage.

Using the time to think, I unpacked my few possessions, arranging them in the bathroom, putting away my shorts and bikini before going to find Gabby.

'That dress won't be any good.' Putting her hand over her mouth, she giggled as she reached for something. 'Here. You have this. It's mine, but you may borrow it.'

Taking the fabric she was holding out, I frowned.

'Put it on.' Hands on her hips, she stood there watching me.

Her smile was starting to annoy me. Holding up what she'd given me, I realised it was an apron. I gave it back to her. 'There's been a mistake.'

Her smile vanished. 'You are here at Giuseppe's invitation, yes?'

'That's right.'

'I thought so. This is a big house – very beautiful, but it takes a lot of cleaning. We do it together!'

I frowned at her. 'You've got this all wrong. I haven't come here to be a cleaner.'

'But you are the house sitter. Am I correct?'

'I am. Let me get this clear, Gabby. There seems to have been a misunderstanding.' No way was I scrubbing floors or making beds or any such things. 'Of course, I'll keep the house clean and tidy, I wouldn't dream of doing anything else. And it will be immaculate by the time Giuseppe comes back. But I really was hoping for a little downtime.'

'But I have a list.' Going over to the table, she picked up a piece of paper. 'I do this for Giuseppe, to make sure his house is cared for.'

My eyes scanned the notes she'd made – washing and ironing on Mondays, scrubbing all the floors on Tuesdays, the windows on Wednesdays. Handing it back to her, I'd read enough. 'I have a better idea. While it's just the two of us here, why don't you take a break?'

She looked confused. 'But if you are not cleaning, why are you here?'

'It's very simple. I live here. Look, Giuseppe knows I'm an artist and a writer. He's asked me to be guardian of his house while I am working.'

She frowned. 'But you have no paints with you.'

'Like I said, my luggage has been sent on.' I tried not to show my irritation. 'It just hasn't arrived yet. Look, I know this probably seems very strange to you, but if you don't believe me, why don't you call Giuseppe?'

'I have to.' The smile faltered. 'I tell him this is what happens when a stranger comes to his house. Is not good – for him, for me, for you.' Glancing around, she went to get her phone.

My visions of summer in Ibiza were fading before they'd started. 'I have a better idea. I'll speak to Giuseppe myself.' Getting my phone, I scrolled through my contacts before dialling his number.

'Giuseppe? Buongiorno. It's Margot! Si! I am here! No, not next week – it's today – obviously! Your house is very beautiful. I'm so grateful you've entrusted me with it.' I glanced at Gabby. 'I will dedicate my next book to you.' I paused again. 'Yes, we've met. Really?' Surprise trickled into my voice. 'She hasn't mentioned anything.' I frowned slightly. 'I'm not sure. I think it would be much better coming from you.' I listened for a moment. 'OK. I will tell her that, too. Ciao, Giuseppe. Yes, speak soon. Safe trip! Ciao!'

I turned to Gabby. 'It's a good thing I called him when I did. He's just boarded a flight to Dubai. He wants you to join him – for a holiday. He said you work so hard, you deserve some time off. He's emailing the ticket desk at the airport in Ibiza.'

She frowns. 'So why didn't he tell me?'

'He was planning to – but he didn't think I was arriving until next week. He was going to call you tomorrow – after he arrives in Dubai. He's clearly got his wires crossed, but he's a busy man, isn't he?'

'He is.' She looked at me uncertainly. 'He is also a good man. I will go to his family. When is the flight?'

'He said to arrive at the airport for six in the morning. There's a flight to London, where you'll get another to Dubai.' I looked at her. 'About the list – can I take it? You were right, Gabby. As Giuseppe's guest, I will keep this house as beautifully as you have.'

Gabby's smile reached her eyes again. 'I am so pleased for Giuseppe – and for you. I will go and pack.'

'I really envy you. I've never been to Dubai,' I said enviously. 'Is it OK if I make myself some breakfast?'

'Of course. Here.' Going to the fridge, she got out eggs and avocado.

'Shall I make some for you?' I offered.

Her face lit up. 'That would be very nice, thank you.' Walking towards the door, she hesitated. 'I am excited to go to Dubai, but I am sorry I won't be here. It would have been nice to get to know you.'

'You too,' I said wistfully. 'But we have the rest of today. Later on, if you have time, why don't we take a picnic to one of the beaches?' I pretended to think. 'I'm sure Giuseppe mentioned a private one. Do you know where it is?'

'After I finish packing, I will show you,' she said happily.

As her footsteps faded, my smile vanished. I knew where the beach was. I'd looked it up, reading about a secluded cove reached by steps from a corner of the villa's garden. Going through the drawers, at last I found what I was looking for. Perusing the knives in front of me, I picked one, running my finger along the edge of the blade, before raising it up and bringing it down hard, slicing clean through a watermelon.

14

Ana

Having given Oliver my number, I was far from convinced I'd hear from him again. Facing your personal struggles can be too uncomfortable for most people and, given where we met, I would only be a reminder of his. But the next afternoon, I had a call from him.

I didn't want to invite him to my flat. It was my personal domain and I was careful who I shared it with. It was chilly as I walked along the promenade, my breath freezing in clouds, the streets and windows adorned with Christmas lights. Turning away from them, I gazed across the water. I almost hadn't taken Oliver's call, but at the last minute, I'd picked up. Hearing the same desperation I'd glimpsed last night, it was like a siren call.

Today he was wearing a grey sweater pulled over navy trousers that didn't quite resonate with what I'd seen him wearing before. As he got closer, I took in his troubled look, the dark circles under his eyes.

'Hey. You OK?'

He looked like a man who was uncomfortable in his skin. 'I'm sorry. I didn't know where else to go.'

'It's OK. Talk to me.'

Glancing sideways at him, I was surprised by the single tear that tracked down his cheek. It was about the only visible clue to the silent, restrained battle he was having with himself, but I could feel it, palpably. Feeling his hand reach for mine, I was taken by surprise, as instead of heading back towards town, we walked towards the beach.

The main road was quiet. As we crossed over, he was still holding my hand. Reaching the shingle, we kept going until close to the water's edge, we stopped.

'Are you OK?'

I wasn't sure what else to say, just that I knew he needed to share whatever burden he was carrying.

'I feel like I'm going mad,' he muttered. 'Sometimes I just want to scream at the craziness of life. At the degree to which we're forced to push ourselves. At the game-playing, the mask-wearing, the always saying the right thing . . .' As he turned to face me, his grip on my hand tightened. 'Do you ever feel like that?'

'Oh, I have done – many times.' Right now, life was going through one of its better phases, but it was something I never took for granted. 'Tell me, what is it that's so bad in your life?'

For a moment he was silent. 'If I told you . . .'

I stared at him, suddenly curious. 'Try me.'

A look of agony crossed his face. 'I have a well-paid job, a career people would die for. I'm married to a beautiful woman. I have a nice home . . .' He was silent for a moment, before words started erupting out of him. 'I feel like I'm having some kind of breakdown.' His eyes looked haunted. 'I go home and pretend everything is fine. I listen to Kat – my wife – going on about Christmas presents, telling myself I'll only pretend to have a glass of wine – I can't talk to her about how I'm feeling, because if she gets wind of my problems, I'll never hear the end of it. Believe it or not, Kat's a therapist. Some joke, isn't it, that she can't see what's under her nose?' He paused again. 'Last night I ended up drinking most of the bottle. Then this morning, I was supposed to be on my way to work, but I phoned in sick. It was crazy. I felt badly hungover – like I'd had twice as much. I'm a pilot, and there was no way I could have flown feeling like that. I'd have been an accident waiting to happen.'

It explained the trousers. But there's a question I had to ask. 'You weren't still drunk were you?'

'God, no. I could never do that.' He looked ashamed. 'But you wouldn't believe how many times I've flown with a hangover. I don't seem to have any tolerance for alcohol these days. But it's not even that. My mind feels like it's coming undone. I can't think straight.'

I was taken aback. 'And no one's noticed?'

'Not yet.' His voice was grim. 'At least, I don't think they have.'

'All the more reason to go to the meetings,' I said gently. 'Maybe you should see your GP, too.' I paused. 'If you're really as unhappy as you sound, maybe you owe it to yourself to make some changes.'

When he didn't say anything, I went on. 'I meant what I said at the AA meeting. It's one of the best things I've done. When you're with other people who understand how you're feeling, you can be honest without any fear of being judged.

You also feel less alone. I guess it's kind of weird – being united by our failings – but there are a lot of us broken people in the world.' For a moment, I wondered if I'd gone too far including him in my generalisation.

Suddenly I was wondering what I was doing here. I eased my hand out of his. 'So what the fuck are you doing on a beach in winter with a total stranger?'

'It's real,' he said quietly. 'The cold, the sea, the damp air, you . . .' Pausing, he looked at me for a moment. 'And everything else isn't – not any of it. My marriage is a sham; I don't enjoy my job but there's no way I can say that because everyone you meet wants to be an airline pilot. My home, it's nice, but it's just stuff. Meanwhile my parents are too busy with their own lives to notice anyone else's. As for my brother . . .' He laughed, a dry sound. 'He hasn't had a job for years. He drifts around – *finding himself,* for fuck's sake – and to top it all, he's in love with my wife. So there you have it. Up till now, I've played along.' He shrugged. 'So I suppose I have only myself to blame.'

I was slightly taken aback. 'Being a pilot must be pretty cool?'

'Yeah.' His outburst seemed to have taken it out of him. 'I used to love it – but now, it just feels like endless pressure jumping through hoops and living up to expectations. My whole bloody life revolves around living up to other people's expectations. I drink to forget how miserable and shallow it all is. But now, even that doesn't seem to be working.'

I looked at him sympathetically. 'Does your wife have any idea how you're feeling?'

'Kat sees what she wants to see – that's half the problem.'

He stopped suddenly. 'This conversation is the first honest exchange I've had in a long time.'

I was quiet for a moment. 'Lacking in this world, isn't it? Honesty?'

*

When I think back, it seems bizarre that we met through a shared battle against alcoholism; that just as easily, our paths might never have crossed. But through each other, we'd rediscovered hope; both of us glimpsing an unexpected future opening up.

It became obvious very soon that this was no passing thing; that Oliver was deeply unhappy. When he described his marriage, I couldn't understand why he stayed with his wife. As our relationship developed, I knew how he felt about us; that we were each other's second chance, but when his wife was emotionally fragile, he felt responsible for her.

In the months that followed, we shared afternoons together; occasionally a night. A high point was a trip to Paris, which given his job had been easy to hide; our happiness tainted by the deception and betrayal that didn't sit well with either of us.

I first became suspicious something was wrong the morning Oliver didn't call me, a feeling that intensified when he failed to turn up here. Ever since we met up that second time, he used to message me several times a day, returning mine as soon as he could. When twenty-four hours passed without hearing from him, I had a churning feeling in my stomach. Knowing how unlikely it was that he'd had a change of heart about us, it could only mean something had happened to him.

Checking the local news online, when I read about an accident, my heart was in my mouth. Beside myself, my heart was hammering as I pored over the news, a few hours passing before I found a description of the car involved. Recognising it, I only just made it to the bathroom before I was sick.

Slumped on the floor, I'd leaned back against the bath, my eyes closed, my fingers pressed into my forehead, tears pouring from my eyes as I sobbed, completely heartbroken. After too much tragedy in my life, I thought I'd found a reason to live again. But as I sat there, everything I'd strived to rebuild lay in ruins around me.

There was no one for me to call, no one to share this agonising pain I had. Unable to move, I wasn't even sure how I was going to survive this. Or maybe I had this wrong. Maybe, this time, I wasn't meant to.

The days that followed tested me to the limit. Alone in my flat, what used to be my sanctuary had become a prison, one that resounded with memories of us. The first time Oliver came here, the dinners we shared, the way we'd slip out at night sometimes to stand on the beach and gaze at the moon.

For so long I'd dreaded Oliver's family finding out about us; even turning up here. But as an inescapable sense of loss settled throughout my life, I had to stop myself from contacting them. They were my only link to him. *But it wouldn't help,* I kept telling myself. *Oliver's gone. There's nothing you can do to bring him back.*

Knowing they'd be planning a funeral, there was so much they didn't know about Oliver – what he'd recently discovered he loved to read; the classical music we'd fallen in love with together; the calmer, more honest world he was slowly shifting towards.

I constantly scoured the news for more details until I found a post on the Facebook page of Kent Police that horrified me. Stating that his death was being treated as suspicious, they were asking if anyone had witnessed the accident. It rocked me to the core. The thought that someone had wanted to harm him was devastating. But my mind was racing. In spite of what we shared, Oliver had been hiding something, even from me. *Something that involved other people,* he'd told me. At the time, it had unsettled me and now, I couldn't help thinking about it. Had someone wanted him out of the way? Should I tell the police?

Checking local obituaries for announcements about his funeral, I'd thought about attending. Standing at the back, knowing there wouldn't be anyone there who recognised me; wondering how it would feel knowing I was in the vicinity of his family. But when this was about Oliver, I had to be there.

Gazing out of the window, I cast my mind back to the funeral. Knowing how connected Oliver's family was, I'd guessed it would be well attended. Dressing unostentatiously in black, I'd arrived in good time, blending, unnoticed with the congregation. When the hearse pulled up, it had taken all my self-control to keep my emotions in check. Emotions that had spiralled when my eyes settled on the woman I knew was Oliver's wife. Even thin, she was a striking-looking woman, her long hair sleek, her face white, closed; Joe, the faithless, feckless brother at her side. I'd scrutinised him with interest, a man who on first glance appeared insubstantial, a pale imitation of the brother he'd lost. Shortly after, the unloving parents had turned up, upright, expensively dressed, their faces suitably sombre.

From my seat across the aisle, it took all my strength to hold myself together, while throughout the service, I observed no visible display of emotion among the four of them. After, they hung around briefly outside the church, stiffly acknowledging a few people before conveniently departing for the family-only cremation.

Knowing it would be at least another hour before they'd return, I'd made my way to the pub. I wanted to know what kind of people were associated with Oliver's family; if there was any clue to the secret he wouldn't tell me about. An ex-wife he hadn't mentioned? A love child no one knew about? But something in my bones told me it was probably more sinister than that.

By the time I reached the pub, a number of people had arrived ahead of me. Inside the function room, I was aware of the usual atmosphere that follows a funeral. A buoyant gratitude for being alive that seemed somehow inappropriate; a sense of relief, juxtaposed against the knowledge that death waited around the corner for all of us.

Taking a glass of wine, I cast my eyes around the room, taking in people similar in age to Oliver's parents, clearly of similar backgrounds. I could tell instantly, from the way they dressed, their ludicrous accents, the jewellery they wore. More than once I'd wondered if from somewhere otherworldly, Oliver had an eye on today. I imagined his cynical laugh. His voice: *Load of hypocrites, Ana, every last fucking one of them.*

A middle-aged man came over. 'Oscar.' As he'd thrust his hand towards me, I caught his whisky breath.

'Nice to meet you,' I said politely. 'Would you excuse me?' Turning, I'd had no compunction about walking away, my snub deliberate, a display of solidarity with how Oliver felt about these people. I had no desire to fraternise with any of them.

A couple more approached me, before I'd noticed an older woman standing away from everyone else, in this room of fake melancholy, her sadness standing out as genuine. Going over to her, I took in her tear-stained eyes, the modest navy dress and plain shoes she was wearing. 'It's a sad day, isn't it?'

'So sad.' Her voice trembled. 'I still can't believe that Mr Oliver died like that.'

I'd taken her use of the word *Mr* to suggest an old-fashioned note of subservience to the family. 'Had you known him a long time?'

'Since he was a child.' She dabbed at her eyes. 'I used to look after him and Mr Joseph. I wasn't going to come today, but I had to.'

I looked at her, surprised. 'If you'd known him that long, surely there's every reason for you to be here.'

Shaking her head, she mumbled something I couldn't hear above the background noise of voices.

I leaned closer. 'Sorry?'

'I shouldn't say. You're probably a friend of the family.'

'I most certainly am not. I'm here, like you are, because I knew Oliver.'

She glanced around. '*They* wouldn't want me here.'

'I don't understand. Who are *they*?'

'His parents.' Her eyes glittered with tears. 'If you can call them that. I'm sorry. I shouldn't have said anything. It's just that I always feared Mr Oliver would come to harm. I know he seemed confident enough, but underneath, I knew there was this little boy who desperately wanted to be loved.' Her voice trembled, before it hardened again. 'They didn't show their feelings or love their sons. It was all about turning them into men just like their father.'

A shiver went down my spine as I watched her face. 'That still doesn't explain why his parents wouldn't want you here.'

'It got too much, watching them coming and going with their important jobs and fancy social life. They spent so little time as a family – and I could see what it was doing to the boys. All Oliver wanted was his parents' approval – particularly his father's. I kept quiet until I couldn't any longer. I felt it was my duty to tell them. I remember that day, asking if I could talk to them both – in private. I was nervous about it, but I had to say something for the boys' sakes. Anyway,' she tried to compose herself. 'When I told them my concerns, they didn't take it too well. You can imagine.' She turns to me, slightly anxious. 'You *can* imagine, can't you?'

I nodded. 'Oh, believe me, only too well. What happened after that?'

'They sacked me. *Let me go* were the words they used. They felt their sons needed someone more socially attuned to their ways, was how they put it. They paid me off, but I didn't want their money. I made a donation to the local children's hospice – in the boys' names. It broke my heart not seeing them again.'

'If you want to be here, you should stay.' I was outraged. Every word she'd said resonated with what Oliver had told me. But it had also explained his inner vulnerability, his obsession with maintaining a facade that fitted with everyone's expectations of him. Maybe Joe, the brother, wasn't as weak as I'd thought. Unlike Oliver, he hadn't been pushed into signing his life away for something his heart wasn't in.

'How did you know him?'

I smiled sadly. 'He was a friend.'

'I'm Beatrice.'

I almost told her my name, before deciding it might be simpler not to. 'It's really nice to meet you, Beatrice. I just wish it had been in happier circumstances.' Out of the corner of my eye, I noticed Oliver's family walk in. Drawing themselves up, you would never have known it was their son's, husband's or brother's cremation they'd just come from.

'They're here.'

Beatrice looked anxious again. 'I should go.'

'No.' I laid a hand on her arm. 'Wait. Let them know you're here – for Oliver.'

Beside her, I took in Oliver's wife, her shoulders tight, eyes nervously flitting around the room; Joe's hand now and then gently touching her back. Jude, mother superior, so outwardly perfect, so unmaternal. My eyes turned to Richard, Oliver's father. He was a good-looking man, but a ruthless one, I wouldn't mind betting. My assumption was confirmed when he glanced towards Beatrice, his eyes hardening as he looked firstly at her, before his gaze swung around towards me.

Suddenly he turned and came towards us. 'Beatrice. Nice of you to come. I hope you're keeping well.'

As Beatrice looked at him, she made no attempt to hide her dislike of him. 'I was very sorry to hear about Mr Oliver. He was a good man.'

'Yes. Thank you. He was.' He looked at me. 'Richard McKenna. I don't believe we've met.'

As I met his eyes, there was a coldness about them that made me shiver. Keeping my voice cool, I matched it. 'I don't believe we have.'

Before I could say any more, a woman came over and interrupted. 'Richard, darling . . .' Everything about her screamed of wealth, from her designer clothing to the jewellery she was dripping with; absolutely nothing about her was subtle.

There was a part of me that wanted to linger; to reveal the cracks, expose this so-called family that Oliver had detested. But as the woman engaged Richard in conversation he couldn't escape, I looked at Beatrice. 'I've had enough of this charade. Shall we get out of here?'

'That is one cold fish,' I said to Beatrice as we walked away. After the stifling atmosphere in the pub, the cool air was welcome.

'He can be charming,' she said quietly. 'He knows how to turn it on.'

'I know his type.' I shuddered. I'd seen under his facade immediately.

'I've never understood,' she said. 'If people don't want to be parents, why have children?'

'Beats me.' But I didn't want to talk to about them anymore. 'In Oliver's case, I imagine it was about keeping up appearances — and keeping money in the family. But some people just don't know how to be parents. Tell me more about Oliver when he was a child — what was he like?'

As she started to tell me about the curly-haired boy who delighted in all things that flew, I thought of the man who on the face of it had everything he'd dreamed of; who underneath, had been deprived of the single most basic need all children have, one that money couldn't buy. His parents' love.

Before we went our separate ways, I turned to her. 'I hope you don't think this is odd, but can I have your phone number?'

Beatrice looked surprised. 'I don't see why not.'

I tried to explain. 'It would be nice. You're the only person I've met who knew Oliver.' When she nodded, I got out my phone and typed it in. I didn't tell her I had a hunch it might be useful.

15

Jude

I'm not sure how I feel as I go back to work, but since Oliver's death, nothing's the same anymore, my motivation no longer what it used to be, my mind elsewhere. The practice seems busier than ever, with too many issues demanding my attention. Given the sheer quantity of work to catch up on, it saps what little energy I've regained since the funeral and by the end of the first week, I'm exhausted.

I'd hoped Joe would be here, but when I get home the house is empty. Going upstairs, I change out of my work clothes, clipping up my hair and showering quickly before pulling on leggings and a loose-fitting sweatshirt.

Back downstairs again, I put the kettle on, as for the first time I seriously consider whether I can go on with my job. Over the years, I've worked hard to keep the practice running smoothly, but I've lost the drive and sense of purpose I used to have. Maybe it's time to hand over to someone else, younger and more ambitious. The fact that the practice ran so easily without me proves that not even I am indispensable.

But I'm already thinking, if I resign from my job, what will I do? Imagining empty days stretching ahead of me, I feel a weight lift. There are so many things I could fill them with – the garden, walks along the coast, volunteering for one of the local charities, helping out the neighbours.

Deciding to sleep on it before talking to Richard, I'm starting on supper when the door opens and Joe calls out.

'Mum? Are you there?'

'In the kitchen.'

As he walks in, he's followed by Kat. Tonight, there's a flush of colour in her face as she comes over and kisses my cheek. 'Sorry to walk in on you like this. I had a call earlier from a Liaison Officer at the Coroner's Office.'

When she glances at Joe, he goes on. 'They have the results of the post-mortem. The tests showed that Oliver was diabetic. The Liaison Officer said it could have been a factor in the crash. His reactions would have been affected. It could also explain why they thought he was drunk at work. It would have been very hard to tell the difference.'

'Oliver, diabetic?' The news is unexpected, though it's possible his symptoms were mild enough not to bother him. But in some ways, it's a relief to have an explanation.

From the way Kat stands there, it's clear she feels the same. 'The strange thing is I saw someone the other day,' she says. 'I was getting a coffee in town. He was slurring his words and couldn't walk straight. I was convinced he was drunk. But maybe he wasn't. I guess you never know with anyone, do you?'

'The symptoms can be similar.' I can't believe no one noticed. But it's true of so many conditions – symptoms can

164

come on insidiously; go undetected until they're extreme. 'Poor Oliver. He probably wasn't feeling at all well. I'm surprised he didn't mention it.' I pause. 'Did you notice anything when he was at home, Kat?'

'Not really.' She frowns. 'I guess there were one or two nights when he seemed a little drunk, but we'd been drinking some wine.'

Joe's face is guarded. 'But there's still the fact that the brakes had been tampered with.' He glances at the clock. 'Mum, we're not staying. We're going to pick up a takeaway and head back to Kat's place. There's some stuff we want to go through.'

'Let me know if you find out anything important, won't you?' I try to inject some normality into a world that feels anything but. 'And if you're not doing anything, why don't you both come for lunch on Sunday?'

*

It's about an hour later when Richard arrives back. He looks as tired as I feel, but it's been a long week for him too.

'You just missed Joe and Kat.'

'Oh?'

'She heard from the Coroner's Office. It's possible that Oliver hadn't been drinking at work. The post-mortem results showed he was diabetic. Appearing drunk is a common symptom.'

Richard shakes his head dismissively. 'It isn't exactly conclusive though, is it?'

I frown at him. 'You can't honestly believe that Oliver would have knowingly been drinking when he had the lives of hundreds of passengers in his hands? It would have been

165

totally out of character. At least this offers a reasonable explanation for him not being himself.'

'Right now, my expectations of Oliver aren't very high,' he says dryly. 'Wouldn't his medical have been revoked?'

'I don't know. I suppose we can find out. But it's possible he wasn't even aware he was ill.'

'Another thing we'll never know.' Richard sounds dismissive.

'Glass of wine?' I ask quietly.

Nodding, he seems distracted. 'I'll do it. I'll just get out of this suit.'

I listen to him go upstairs, the sound of his footsteps somehow weary as he goes into our bedroom. He takes longer than usual before coming downstairs in jeans and his slippers. Going to the wine rack, he chooses a bottle of red and opens it, pouring some into two glasses before offering one to me.

Seeing the look on his face, I frown. 'What is it?'

'I made a few calls earlier today. I've been doing some digging into the companies that operate these private jets, in the brochure Kat found,' he reminds me. 'Most of them are operated by five companies, so I've been in touch with all of them. Four of them are above board – but the fifth is another matter altogether.'

I look up from the vegetables I'm chopping. 'How do you know all this?'

'I have a contact we use when we want to check out new investors – all done in the strictest confidentiality, of course. She found out that this particular company had recently offered Oliver a contract – apparently he applied a while ago. It seems he'd been for an interview with them before he lost his airline job. I couldn't imagine why he hadn't told

166

any of us.' He hesitates. 'But then I found out something else about this fifth company. They're called Skyro. They're based at Brighton City Airport – Shoreham, to you and me. They operate five aircraft – two of these new Citations that were featured in that brochure, plus three turbo props. They're high-spec and long-range – and can carry both passengers and freight, but according to my contact, their CEO and one of their crews were arrested a couple of years ago on suspicion of smuggling illegal firearms to Saudi Arabia. It may have been a set-up – they were never charged – and if there was any evidence, it was never found. But if they were operating outside the law, if Oliver had been working there and he knew what they had been involved in, it would explain why he didn't want us to know about it.'

My mind refuses to take it in. 'But even though they'd offered him a contract, it doesn't mean Oliver took the job, especially if he'd discovered anything illegal going on there. He had principles, Richard. Anyway, who's to say this company actually is involved in smuggling arms? As you've just said, there was no evidence.'

'I had another thought.' He looks at me. 'That money he left to this woman, Fontaine, maybe it isn't his inheritance. Maybe this job was a way to make himself a fortune. I can imagine the way he'd justify it; that if he didn't do it, someone else would. That kind of thing.'

'This is pure speculation.' Anger flares in me that Richard could suggest such a thing. Anyway, it sounds more like Richard's logic than Oliver's. But now doubt has crept in. Could he have? Maybe Richard's right. Everyone has their price. It isn't impossible that, tempted by the offer of a large sum of money, Oliver might have succumbed.

Opening his laptop, Richard brings up a page he's bookmarked. 'Basically, this describes what they were allegedly involved in. It doesn't make for easy reading.'

It's a website belonging to a charity. As I scroll down the page, it soon becomes clear that their main aim is to halt the massive humanitarian crisis resulting from an ongoing war. I read on about their attempts to expose countries that are shipping arms to Saudi Arabia, thereby fuelling conflicts that result in mass devastation and the displacement of millions of people.

I frown at him. 'But there was a ruling in the UK. It was declared unlawful.'

He nods. 'But the trade is worth billions to the government and sales were resumed. They kept it quiet, of course. And the official line from the Tories was that only isolated incidents of civilian casualties resulted. Pure spin, of course. Obviously it wasn't true. Everyone knows that. They ship missiles and bombs, for Christ's sake, knowing full well they're contributing to war – in Yemen, for example.' There's a look on his face I haven't seen before. 'It gets worse, though, because along the way, a huge proportion of the weapons go missing and end up in the hands of groups like ISIS or the Taliban.'

I'm horrified. 'Should we tell the police about this?'

'Of course we should.' Richard looks drained. 'I'll call them first thing tomorrow.'

'We still don't know for sure that Oliver was working for them.' I'm clutching at hope. 'But you should probably tell Joe and Kat what you've found out.'

He nods. 'I'll call her.'

I only catch the occasional word as he makes the call from

his study. From the tone of his voice, it's clear she's shocked. He tries to placate her, but I know Kat. That Oliver appears to be implicated in something so unethical will have upset her terribly – Joe, too.

It's impossible to concentrate as I carry on cooking and I burn the fish. Not that it matters. After Richard's bombshell, neither of us are hungry. For the rest of the evening, I scour the internet for more information on the shipping of illegal arms, still unconvinced that Oliver would have gotten caught up in it.

2017

Margot

Once I'd seen to it that Gabby was conveniently out of the way, my summer could begin in earnest. Checking out the four garages, an Aston Martin and vintage MGB caught my eye but in the interests of anonymity, I decided against them. Settling instead for a dusty Jeep, it was the perfect choice — kind of cool, yet commonplace enough around the island that it didn't stand out. Pulling away from the house, I drove with the roof folded down and music loud, my hat protecting me from the sun, my hair blowing behind me in the breeze.

Driving towards Ibiza Town, elation filled me as I thought of the summer that lay ahead. Reaching the town, I decided to park on the outskirts and walk. As always, I'd done my research and as I made my way along the streets, in my long dress and sandals, my carefully applied fake tan, the highlights that made my hair look as if I lived in the sun, already I looked as though I belonged there.

So much so, at the first bar I pulled — kind of.

'You live here?' The guy serving drinks spoke broken English.

'Yeah.' I swept my sunglasses on top of my head to get a better look at him.

'Which part?'

'Near Sant Carles.' I tried to sound nonchalant. 'You?'

'I have a place in town, about twenty steps from here.' He nodded in the direction of Dalt Vila. 'Tiny little place. I share with another guy, but very good when we close late.'

'Nice. Can I get a beer?' Too late, I was kicking myself. If I had a reputation to create, it was all about champagne, but I had plenty of time to make up for that. 'Hey, if you're local, you might be able to help me. I'm interested in chartering a private boat for a few days. I have friends coming over in a couple of months. I want them to see the island, so obviously it has to be from the sea.' I tried to sound as though I did this all the time. 'There will only be ten of us. It has to be high end, though – quality bedlinen, en suites, cocktail bar. Do you know anyone?'

He looked slightly astonished. 'You realise how much you're talking about?'

'Obviously.' I dropped my smile. I wasn't having anyone question my ability to pay. 'If you think you can help, I'll put you on commission. Otherwise, there's someone I'm meeting later on today who says he knows someone.'

He took the bait. 'I know many people on the island. I will find you the perfect boat.'

'Cool.' I smiled again. 'How much do I owe you?' But I knew what he was going to say.

He didn't disappoint. 'It's on the house.'

'Thank you. I didn't expect that.' I held his gaze a little longer than necessary.

'It's my pleasure.' He bowed his head slightly. 'I'm Nico.'

'I'm Margot.'

'Excuse me.' Noticing a group of customers that had just come in, he turned away to serve them. I watched, liking his manner, his easy way with them. Before long, after taking their money, he was back.

'So, what's your mobile number?' As he gave it to me, I typed it into my phone, then rang it. 'That's me.' I hesitated. 'Nico, it's been really nice meeting you. I have to go now, but I will come here again very soon.'

After leaving the bar, I wandered along the marina, checking out superyachts from behind my sunglasses. Another day, I planned to come back here and stake it out, incognito — see which people came from which boat. Being here was about forging connections, of the right kind. If you had a plan and you had patience, there were ways to get what you wanted, and right now, I had plenty of both.

But today, I wandered through the narrow streets, taking in the architecture, soaking up the vibe, pausing now and then to look in a shop. A short stroll later, I was a dress and a kaftan better off as I headed back towards my car. As I drove out of town, I pulled over to take in the view. In the foreground, palm trees encircled a white-painted villa, while in the distance, I could make out the coves and inlets of Ibiza's east coast. But it was the sea I couldn't get over; its colour so blue it was almost navy, glistening silver where the sun caught it.

As places went, this was pretty much perfect. As was the villa — where I did a tour of a couple more of the bedrooms, borrowing some toiletries, striking gold when I found a designer bottle of Jean Patou Joy and an Yves Saint Laurent makeup palette.

That evening, I pulled on the dress I'd lifted from the fancy little boutique in Ibiza Town, styling my hair into soft waves before adding a spritz of my new perfume. I gazed at my reflection in the mirror for a moment, feeling a surge of satisfaction in my stomach. Margot Jameson was ready to take on the world.

★

I had some money, but not enough to sustain me for long. But to meet the right kind of people, you had to be seen in the right kind of places and tonight was one of those calculated risks.

The cocktail bar had a sunset view and from my corner table, I sipped a margarita, watching the sky change colour. It was still early when I ordered dinner – fish and a side salad, a glass of champagne, and as more people filtered in, it wasn't long before I was aware of someone watching me. Out of the corner of my eye I watched the party at a table over by the bar, as one of them came over. In a skinny black dress, her skin was tanned, her makeup subtle, a perfect example of understatement, until I clocked the enormous diamond ring she was wearing.

'I noticed you were alone. My party wondered if you would like to join us.'

'Oh.' I faked surprise. 'I'm really quite happy dining alone.'

'It's more fun with other people.' She winked at me. 'I'm Tati.'

'Margot.' Glancing past her at the other people at her table, I pretended to think. 'OK!' I held up my hands. 'Why not?'

Hours later, after too much champagne, I was slightly woozy as I stood up. 'I've had a wonderful evening meeting you all. But I should go now.'

'No, no, no, Margot.' Taking my hand, Tati pulled me down again.

'No, really,' I laughed. 'I have a deadline for my book, and I'm not one for clubs.'

'You're kidding, right?' Judging from her face, I might as well have said that I was flying to the moon.

'Seriously'. As the waiter brought the bill over, catching sight of it, my eyes were watering as I got out my purse. 'Let me get this.'

'I think this one's on us.' Adam, Tati's boyfriend, moved it out of reach, before turning beseeching eyes on me. 'Come with us, Margot. When she doesn't get her own way, Tati's a pain in the ass.'

Glancing at Tati again, a smile broke out across my face as I gave in. 'OK! If you insist.'

★

I paid for it the next day with a headache that felt like I'd been hit by a rock. But I had some new friends and I'd proved a point to myself. It cost far more to eat in the cheaper places on the island. If you went for the top, as long as you knew how to play the game, there was almost always someone else to pick up the bill.

That afternoon, as I lay on a sun bed, a text from Nico came in about a possible boat charter and early that evening, a fashionable thirty minutes late, I headed for his bar.

Unlike the day before, it was crowded, but as I made my way towards him, across the sea of heads, Nico was already looking out for me.

Reaching the bar, I smiled. 'Hey! Busy, isn't it?'

'It is always like this at sunset. People go crazy! What can I get you?'

'Champagne,' I said. 'But this time I'm paying.'

'Actually, he is.' Nico nodded towards a guy sat alone at a table. In a white shirt and jeans, he was sipping a beer. 'That's Andre. He has a very nice boat. I'll come over when the bar is more quiet – but he is waiting for you.'

Walking over, as I reached Andre, I smiled. 'Hi! I'm Margot!' I held out my hand.

'Andre. Please . . .' Taking off his sunglasses, he shook my hand

175

before gesturing towards the seat next to him. 'I'm delighted to meet you. How are you enjoying our little island?'

'I love it here.' Taking in the heavy gold chain around his neck, it took no effort to inject passion into my voice. 'I've been staying here a while. A friend has lent me his villa. But I'm thinking about moving here permanently. Meanwhile, and this is the reason Nico got in contact with you, I have friends coming over. Not until late August – there will be ten in our party. Nico says you have a boat.' I paused. 'Before we go any further, I should probably explain. You see, I'm not looking for an average boat.'

'My boat is not average.' Andre's eyes were piercing. 'You tell me what you would like, and I will tell you the price.'

'Perfect.' I allowed my face to light up. 'Well, my requirements are eight bedrooms, all en suite. A cocktail bar, a comfortable lounging area, a chef. My plan is to circumnavigate Ibiza, docking here and there to swim or eat at restaurants. I've done something like this before – as a guest – and it really is the best way to see the island.'

'For how many days?'

'I think probably five.'

'OK.' Andre nodded. 'My boat has an excellent chef. You will need to give him a list of dietary requirements, of course.'

'Of course.'

'All in, we're talking in the region of . . .'

It took all my self-control not to recoil at the sum he mentioned. 'That sounds fine, but before I sign on the dotted line, I would like to see it for myself.'

'Of course. Are you busy tomorrow? I am holding a party, to which I am now inviting you as my guest.'

'Then I will accept with great pleasure.' Smiling, I held his gaze. 'Thank you.'

Andre stood up. 'I am sorry but I must go. I have another

engagement.' Lingering, he looked reluctant. 'But I will see you tomorrow? There will be a small boat here at seven p.m. to ferry the guests.' He pointed towards a jetty. 'It will bring you to my boat.'

After Andre had walked away, finding Nico, I passed him the two hundred-euro bills that were neatly folded, designed to impress on him that I was serious. 'This is just to say thank you. There will be more, but the meeting was good.'

Looking surprised, he slipped them into his pocket. 'Can I get you another drink?'

'No, thank you. I have to be somewhere else.' I paused, smiling. 'But I'll see you.'

As I drove back to the villa, I knew I could pull this off. It was easy enough to attract money – all it took was a little sass, a shitload of confidence, the right clothes and a talent for telling people what they wanted to hear. My summer here was going to be easy, and above all, as long as I was careful, it was going to cost me very little, provided I made sure nothing went wrong.

The following day, I perused the impressive contents of Giuseppe's wife's wardrobes. She had good taste, I'd give her that, and one or two quite stylish pieces. Checking the labels, I picked out a strappy dress made of a sheer fabric with a split up one side. Trying it on and finding it only slightly on the loose side, I decided it would do for Andre's party.

That evening, standing at the marina, I watched from a distance as other guests arrived and made their way to the jetty; breathing a sigh of relief that I seemed neither over or under dressed.

'Thank you.' I took the hand that was held out as I stepped into the boat – and even this was a cool boat, if not exactly by millionaire standards. Making my way into the cabin, I found a seat. Much as I'd have loved to be sitting on deck, with my image to protect I didn't want to arrive with my carefully arranged hair in disarray.

I watched the marina grow smaller behind us as we headed out of the port before turning west towards the sunset. Even out at sea it was warm, the sky fading to peachy shades that reflected off the walls of the town, while around me, everything screamed money: perfect clothes and hair, jewellery, scent; and the intangible confidence exuded by those with wealth. I considered the irony of cutting myself off from my parents, only to seek out similarly wealthy people. But instead of on their terms, strictly on mine, I reminded myself.

Moored close to a small cove, Andre's boat was something else and as we drew closer, music filtered towards us across the sea. Another boatload of guests had clearly arrived before us – the party had already started and as I stepped on board, Andre noticed me immediately.

His pristine white shirt showed off his tan. 'Margot.' Taking my hand, he raised it to his lips. 'Welcome.'

'Thank you, Andre. Your boat is very beautiful.'

'Yes.' His eyes were twinkling. 'I will give you a tour later. But first . . .' Taking my hand, he led me towards a waiter holding a tray of champagne, before taking two glasses.

'For you.' He held my gaze for a moment. 'Salud.'

I clinked my glass gently against his. 'Salud.'

'I must introduce you to some people.' He led me over to a couple standing away from the others. 'Nina, Mike, this is Margot. She is new on our island.'

I beamed at them. 'Hi. So nice to meet you both.'

They were rich, no question. I discovered that Mike's father had made a fortune doing something he couldn't talk about. But they were nice, too. Another glass of champagne later, I was already feeling very at home with these people.

As I moved among the guests, it was almost dark by the time Andre came to find me. 'Would you like a tour?'

Catching his eye, I felt a flicker of lust. 'Do you say that to all the girls?'

Holding my gaze for a moment, he didn't reply. 'Come with me.' Swiftly turning, he headed for the front of the boat, then down a flight of steps. 'The cocktail bar.' He held out an arm towards a beautifully constructed bar, colourfully decked out with tropical fruit and state-of-the-art cocktail ware.

Going through another doorway, I found myself in a panelled hallway, off which there were several doors. Andre opened one.

'Come and see.'

Stepping inside, I reminded myself to channel Margot as I took in the luxurious bed, the subtle furnishings, a view from the window that was to die for. I turned to Andre. 'And the en suite?'

He opened what until now had been an invisible door, beyond which there was a beautiful bathroom.

I turned towards him. 'The other rooms are the same?'

'I will show you.'

Each room was individual, yet the theme of unbridled luxury continued. After he'd shown me the last, I smiled at him. 'This is perfect.'

When he stepped closer, I wondered if he was going to try it on. Secondary to that, seduced by the surroundings, by the riches of this other world I found myself in, I knew I was probably up for it.

But stepping back, he gestured towards the deck. 'So now, you think about it.'

'Thank you.' As we headed back to join the party, it crossed my mind only fleetingly that I was on thin ice. But I wasn't causing any harm. I was simply being a little economical with the truth. OK, so a lot economical, but no one was getting hurt, and no one was going to find out. And in the meantime, I stood to meet some wealthy and connected people, who might open doors. After that, I was open to whatever might follow.

*

I spent the next couple of days lying low at the villa, topping up my tan, now and then dipping into the pool for a couple of leisurely lengths before flopping onto my sunbed again. But it wasn't long before I went back to the bar to catch up with Nico.

'Hi!' I waved a hand in greeting. But instead of his usual friendly response, his face was clouded. 'What's up?'

'It's not a good day.' He shook his head. 'A body was found this morning – a woman's. She was washed up on the beach at Cala Jondal.'

As he spoke, I felt the blood drain from my face. 'Nico, that's terrible.'

'It is.' He raised his eyes to look into mine. 'It is bad for this island and all the people who live here, but mostly, it is bad for her family. The police are there, but . . .' He shrugged. 'Maybe they will find out what happened – or maybe not.'

'I'm so sorry.' There was an expression of shock on my face. 'Do the police know who she was?'

He shook his head. 'They haven't released any information yet.'

Seeing how downcast he was, I rested a hand on his arm. 'Let me buy you a coffee. My treat.'

He glanced at his watch. 'I would like that, but I don't have time. Later, maybe?'

'Sure.' Arranging to meet him again later this afternoon, I left him to get on. Wandering along the marina, I bumped into Andre.

'Margot!' He kissed me on both cheeks. 'What a nice surprise!'

'Thank you for the party, Andre. I really enjoyed it!'

180

He looked pleased. 'I am glad. It's a beautiful day, is it not? What are you doing with it?'

'It is — just a little less than it was a few minutes ago.' I told him what Nico had just said about the body that had been found.

Frowning, he shook his head. 'It may just have been an accident. It's a peaceful island — but now and then, occasionally someone ruins it. So, I am meeting some friends for lunch. Can I invite you to join us?'

I hesitated. But then I thought, why the fuck not. Wasn't this the whole reason I'd come here? 'Thank you, Andre. I'd love to.'

Lunch was at a restaurant set alone at one end of a sandy beach. In chill-out seats close to the water, we sipped chilled wine and ate the most sublime fish. Andre's friends were interesting — Sebastian, a musician from Seville; Kayla, who owned a chain of high-end clothing stores; and Christos, who owned several villas he rented out during the season — a classic case of how you needed money to make money. Listening to them, suddenly I was torn between a very real possibility of finding a job, or maintaining the illusion that I didn't need one. Glancing at Andre, just as I was wondering if there was a way of doing both, Christos turned to me.

'Margot, I'm sure you are very busy, but I will ask anyway because I think you could be the right person. Now and then I need someone to host parties. We're talking the most exclusive, private parties — in my villas. Are you interested?'

'I'm sure I could do that.' I had to stop myself biting his hand off. How hard could it be? I had no illusions as to what the nature of these parties might be, but my need to earn money was becoming desperate.

He nodded slowly. 'Good. Perhaps we can meet to talk about this some more. Maybe next week?'

Smiling as I gave him my mobile number, I glanced at my watch, suddenly remembering Nico. I was already late. Standing up, I made my apologies. 'I hadn't realised the time. I'm supposed to be meeting someone.'

Andre stood up with me. 'I will drive you.'

I thought about taking him up on it — it would have saved me time and money. But I didn't want the responsibility of ruining the party. 'No, you stay. I will get a taxi. But thank you.' I kissed him on both cheeks. 'Ciao.'

After waiting for a taxi to arrive, by the time I got back to Ibiza Town, I was almost an hour late. Jumping out of the taxi, I hurried to the bar. 'Is Nico here?' I asked one of the waitresses.

'I think that's him over there.' She pointed in the direction of a bench further along the marina, where a single figure sat, unmoving.

'Thanks.'

Head down, he was staring at the ground as I hurried towards him. 'Nico? I'm so sorry. I lost track of time.' I sat down next to him.

'It's not a problem.' He didn't look at me. 'We all have our priorities. I understand. I know your type, Margot. You play with us for as long as it suits you. But you don't really care.'

I gazed at him in disbelief. 'That's hardly the case. It's like I said. I lost track of time and as soon as I realised, I got in a taxi and came rushing over here. But if that's what you think of me . . .' As I started to get up, I felt his hand on my arm.

'I apologise, Margo. I didn't mean that. I have had a really bad day.'

'What's happened?' I packed as much sympathy into my voice as I could muster.

'There is a rumour — you know the woman I told you was murdered?' He rests his head in his hands. 'I don't know who she

182

was, but it has happened before. Two years ago . . .' He broke off. 'There were a couple of teenagers backpacking on the island – the police thought it was them. They had been caught stealing food, but always they got away. When the police identified the woman's body, her house had been ransacked. Her money, her valuables, everything was taken. There was no sign of the teenagers, of course – and no proof. But it's obvious. They were fucking opportunists . . .' His voice trembled. 'They took advantage of a helpless old woman who couldn't defend herself.' As he finished speaking, he looked furious.

'God, Nico.' I wore a look of shock, but everyone knew these things happened from time to time. Unpleasant, but given there were some desperate people out there, sometimes they were unavoidable. I didn't understand why he was so upset.

'You think I'm overreacting.' He turned to look at me. 'But that woman who died two years ago . . . . she was my grandmother.'

This time my shock was genuine. I looked at him, horrified. 'That's awful, Nico.'

'It was. Really awful.' He went on. 'Ever since, I look for clues as to who did that to her, and now it's happening again.'

'Hey,' I said as gently as I could. 'This time may well have been an accident.'

He shrugged sadly. 'I have a bad feeling, Margot.'

'Why not wait and see what the police come up with?' I suggested. 'I understand,' I added more quietly. 'It must have been a terrible time for you.'

'It was. My grandmother was kind. She never hurt any living thing. No one had the right to do that to her.'

I was starting to get uncomfortable. But he stood up.

'My shift's about to start.' His eyes met mine. 'Thank you for coming.'

Getting up, I hugged him lightly. 'I'll see you soon, OK?'

As I watched him walk away, a sense of foreboding came over me, but I brushed it aside. I hadn't wanted to kill Gabby, but she'd been an obstacle between me and everything I'd come here for. In the end, I hadn't needed the knife. When she showed me the secret beach, it had been her idea to go for a swim. It was hardly my fault she swam out of her depth, that there wasn't enough strength in her tired limbs when I held her under. Anyway, at least she'd had a nice enough life. However unfair, however brutal something seemed, sometimes, the old had to give way to the young. Life could be cruel, but sometimes it was a matter of survival.

16

Ana

After the funeral, when the solicitor's letter arrives, I wonder how long it will take for the police to come here. Given Oliver's wife will know the contents of his will, she will also know the solicitor was in contact with me. And knowing the suspicious circumstances of Oliver's death, I'm certain that at some point the police will want to talk to me.

They arrive a few days after the funeral, and I'm unsurprised when I open the door to find two uniformed police officers standing there.

'Ms Fontaine?'

'Yes?'

'I'm DS Laura Stanley, Kent Police. This is my colleague, Constable Ramirez. We'd like to talk to you in relation to Oliver McKenna. May we come in?'

DS Stanley has fair hair, immaculately pinned back. As her eyes rest on me, an uneasy feeling comes over me. That the police have taken so long to come here only confirms how well Oliver had covered his tracks.

Silent, I stand back and open the door wider. As they come in, there's something about DS Stanley that gives me the impression that she wouldn't miss the smallest detail. 'Come through.' Closing the door behind them, I lead them into my sitting room. 'Have a seat.'

'Thank you.' DS Stanley sits on my sofa, her uniform somehow incongruous with the plush green fabric, as Constable Ramirez sits next to her.

She gets straight to the point. 'I understand you knew Oliver McKenna?'

I nod. 'I did.'

'How long had you known him?'

'We met about a year ago.' A memory of the AA meeting flashes into my head.

'Do you mind if I ask you what the nature of your relationship was?' Her blue eyes are frank.

Taken aback by her directness, I hesitate, but only for a moment. They may as well know. 'We were lovers.'

She passes me a small photograph. 'Is this you?'

Taking it, as I look at it, I remember giving it to Oliver. It was an old photo taken before my hair was blonde. I'd written on the back: *Proud of you x*

Turning it over, the words are as I remember. Wondering if it was in Oliver's wallet, I pass it back to DS Stanley. 'It is. He wanted a photo and it was the only one I had on me at the time. He'd just left his last AA meeting.'

'So the message presumably was related to his new-found sobriety.' DS Stanley glances at her colleague. 'Could you give us your mobile number, Ms Fontaine?'

'Of course.' I recite my number, wondering if they're going to check it against Oliver's phone.

Having made a note, DS Stanley looks up again. 'We understand from Mr McKenna's solicitor that he's left you a considerable sum of money.'

I'd known from the moment I received the letter from Mark Osborne Associates that the money was going to draw attention to me. 'I had no idea he'd left it to me,' I say hastily. 'The first I knew was when I received a letter from his solicitor.'

'How well did you know Mr McKenna?'

'Like I said, we were lovers. We were close, enough for him to confide in me.'

'What about exactly?'

I hold her gaze. 'He wasn't happy, for a number of reasons, his marriage being one.'

'He told you that?' She sounds surprised.

It's hardly unexpected.

'People who are happily married don't have affairs, Detective Sergeant. At least, not in my experience. Oliver wasn't a serial adulterer. I think he just found that in a dishonest world, he could be honest with me.'

DS Stanley frowns. 'What do you mean by a dishonest world?'

I shrug. 'His family, his marriage.'

She makes a note. 'According to his wife . . .' She hesitates. 'She's painted a picture of what seemed ostensibly a happy enough marriage.'

I try to hide my annoyance, but my sharp intake of breath gives me away.

DS Stanley frowns. 'Did Mr McKenna talk to you about it?'

'He did. Would you like to know the truth?' I gaze at her.

'Of course, I only know what Oliver told me. Put it this way. I'm not surprised she's told you that. Of course, I can't tell you what conversations went on between them, but I can tell you he was spending more and more time here. His clothes are in my wardrobe. There are books. He was building up to telling his wife he was leaving her.' I watch her closely, wondering if she believes me.

'And she had no idea?' DS Stanley looks thoughtful.

'The honest answer? Oliver thought not, but I don't know.'

Both police officers watch me as DS Stanley goes on. 'Can you give us your version of the McKennas' marriage?'

'It's Oliver's version,' I remind them. 'But by all means. He and his wife married two years ago. But soon after, things started going wrong. He said they argued all the time, and that every time he went away, she became increasingly neurotic. He was a pilot, as no doubt you know. She'd harangue him with calls and voicemails. If you have his phone, you'll probably find some.' I hesitated. 'Though thinking back, he probably deleted them because there were so many and he didn't want them cluttering up his phone. Anyway, each time he came home from work, he never knew what he was going to find. Sometimes she was the epitome of the loving wife, other times . . . let's just say, she attacked him, not just verbally. More than once.'

DS Stanley's frown deepens. 'Given Mrs McKenna is a qualified therapist, it's hard to relate this kind of behaviour to her. How sure are you that Mr McKenna wasn't overdramatising things?'

'I believed him.' I hold her gaze. 'I had no reason not to.' I go on. 'He also had suspicions that Kat was taking his money. He used to pay some into their joint account every month, but often it was spent in no time at all. When he challenged her, Katharine always had a reason – a new piece of furniture or artwork, an expensive dress she'd wear once. In the end, he felt it was easier to keep his money where she couldn't get to it.'

After noting everything down, DS Stanley twists her pen between her fingers. 'Isn't it possible she'd discovered her husband was having an affair? Maybe for reasons of her own, she kept it to herself, but that would be enough to drive many women to quite extreme behaviour.'

'Is that what she's told you?' I wonder if that's really the case, or if DS Stanley's trying to wrong-foot me. She doesn't respond.

'After he died, she found your photo in the bottom of a drawer in a desk her husband used. It was the first time she suspected something was going on.'

I'm silent for a moment; surprised that the photo had been left somewhere Katharine might stumble across it. 'I don't think she ever confronted Oliver exactly, but he did say her behaviour had become more unstable in recent weeks. I was convinced she must have found out about us.' I frown. 'It seems odd Oliver would have left my photo in their house. From what you've said, I wonder if perhaps she found it much earlier than she admits to.' I pause. 'Tricky, isn't it? From your point of view?'

Ignoring my comment, DS Stanley goes on. 'How did you and Mr McKenna meet?'

'At an AA meeting. He'd just signed up as I was leaving. We got talking.' I shrug. 'That was how it started.'

'When did he tell you about the problems with his wife?'

'He was quite open about the fact that he wasn't happy

– from the start. But it was obvious, too, that he was at a personal crossroads. Work was one part of it. His marriage another. Meanwhile, his parents were self-obsessed. He didn't feel he had anywhere to go.'

'What about his brother? Did he talk about him at all?'

'You're talking about Joe?' I look from one to the other. 'The drifter brother who lives off his parents' money? The same brother who is in love with Katharine?' I watch them. Surely if they had their eyes on the ball, they must have suspected it by now. 'You didn't know?'

DS Stanley is silent for a moment. 'Let me get this straight. You say Mr McKenna's brother is in love with his wife. Did he tell you anything he'd seen or heard to corroborate that?'

'He didn't need proof. When you know people intimately, it goes beyond words, doesn't it? You read body language, mannerisms, silences, chemistry. I'm no expert, but Oliver was good at things like that, and he knew both of them.' I sit back. 'I suppose in your position, you need evidence. But I'm sorry, I don't have any.'

'Did he talk to you about his relationship with his parents?'

'Relationship?' I gaze at them. 'I think that's an overstatement. Oliver described them as disconnected strangers whose lives only overlapped occasionally. They were far too busy with their careers to be concerned about their children. They weren't parental towards him, Detective Sergeant. I'm not sure they ever were.'

'Did Mr McKenna talk to you about work at all?'

'I'm assuming you know he was fired from his job?' Seeing from their faces that they do, I go on. 'The stress was getting to him – the hours, the demands of the company, the environment. His parents had always made such a thing of him

190

being an airline pilot. He knew if he told them, all manner of retribution would kick off. He was already having enough problems. It was easier to keep it to himself.'

'Are you aware of the reasons he lost his job?'

Sighing, I'd hoped to avoid this subject. 'I do know Oliver was suspected of being drunk at work. He had been drinking more than usual to relieve the stress he was under, but he was trying to do something about it.'

DS Stanley looks at me sharply. 'So he acknowledged that he had a drink problem?'

I nod. 'He was slightly mystified, to be honest. It was more that he felt hangover a lot of the time. He said he didn't have the same tolerance for alcohol he used to have.' I imagine his family finding out, hiding his secret, because being an alcoholic was a problem that wouldn't be acceptable to them; wouldn't fit with the image of the Oliver they wanted to believe he was.

'But it was clearly enough of a problem for him to get noticed at work.'

'I know. I never fully understood that.'

She goes on. 'Did you know he'd applied for another job?'

'Yes.' I frown slightly. 'I think he hoped that flying smaller aircraft would take some of the pressure off. But this is what doesn't make sense. Shortly after he went for the interview, there was a change in him. He'd started the training, but instead of feeling enthusiastic, he was preoccupied.'

'Did he tell you why?'

Remembering Oliver's reticence when I asked him what was worrying him, I shake my head. 'He refused to talk about it.'

'I imagine you're aware that we're treating Mr McKenna's

death as suspicious. Did he allude to anything specific after starting this new job?'

'Nothing. Like I said, I couldn't get him to talk about it.'

'Ms Fontaine, we will need to take your fingerprints, to see if they match those we've found in the car.'

I don't bat an eyelid. 'Of course.'

She goes on. 'Going back to Mr McKenna, did he ever confide in you that he had concerns about his safety? Or if anyone might have threatened him?'

'Never. But something was definitely bugging him. It just struck me as odd that he wouldn't talk to me about it. All he said was that there were other people involved and he'd tell me one day, just not yet.'

She looks up sharply. 'Did he say anything else?'

I shake my head. 'No. I tried again, several times, but it was always the same. He said he would tell me.' I pause, remembering. 'But he never got around to it. From what he said, though, there is one obvious person in his life I wouldn't trust.' Surely, from everything they already know, it must be obvious. Taking in their questioning faces, I go on. 'His wife.'

DS Stanley writes in her electronic notebook. 'Did he specifically say he felt threatened by her?'

When I've already told them that Katharine could be abusive, I can't believe she's asking. 'She attacked him, for goodness' sake. Who knows what she's capable of?'

DS Stanley doesn't comment. 'It's a very nice flat.' She glances around the room. 'You have quite a view.'

I follow her gaze towards the window, where beyond the end of the road, there are views of the sea. 'Thank you.'

'Do you work, Ms Fontaine?'

I frown. 'What does that have to do with anything?'

She's matter-of-fact. 'Well, I imagine living here can't be cheap. Did Mr McKenna support you financially?'

Suddenly I see what her game is. Thinking I was after Oliver's money, she wants to know if without him, I'm financially viable. 'For your information, I used to be a nurse. I'm not working at the moment, I haven't been well, but I can assure you I'm financially self-sufficient, Detective Sergeant,' I say coldly. 'Not that it's of any relevance.'

After making a note, she looks up. 'When did you move here?'

'About three years ago.' I remember coming here that first time; the appeal of living somewhere no one knew me, that was close to the sea. 'I wanted somewhere to settle for a while and it seemed like a nice enough town.'

'Where were you before that?'

'Here and there,' I say carefully. 'My marriage ended. I lived with a friend for a while.' When she doesn't comment, I can't resist adding, 'Do you want her name and phone number?'

'That won't be necessary at this stage.' There's an uneasy silence before she goes on. 'Given you were in love with Mr McKenna, the funeral must have been a difficult time for you.'

I nod, barely trusting myself to speak. 'It was. Very.'

'Did you attend it?'

Feeling my eyes blur, I blink away my tears.

'Yes.'

*

After the police leave, I lock the door behind them and wander back to the sitting room. Picking up the letter from Oliver's solicitor, I read it again. Now that his family know the contents of his will, not for the first time, I wonder if they'll come here.

Or maybe the police have warned them off. In any case, apart from Oliver's solicitor, no one else has my address. But I'm sure you can find anyone these days, if you really want to. My mind drifts back to the funeral; going to the wake, fronting up to Oliver's father. Maybe I'd been reckless. Suddenly I'm uneasy. He's exactly the kind of man who would pay a private investigator if he was determined enough to try and find me.

Maybe I should move away from here. With the money coming to me, my life is going to change forever. My eyes fill with tears. Without Oliver to share it with, my vision for the future has gone; while instead of feeling like home, Deal has come to represent everything I've lost. I really thought this time around, it was going to be different; that at last I'd found the happiness I'd never expected to find. But for whatever reason, it wasn't to be.

But the police coming here has left me uneasy; realising I'm no less a suspect than anyone else. A feeling of despair fills me, as I imagine them coming back with more questions. It seems that wherever I go, whoever I meet, the past is never far behind me.

17

Katharine

If I was starting in any way to adjust to this new status quo, the call from Richard is another setback as my husband's obvious duplicity plummets to new depths.

'Apparently Oliver had been offered another job,' I say bitterly to Joe. 'You'll never guess what it was.' When he looks at me blankly, I go on. 'Flying illegal arms.'

Joe looks shocked. 'Do you know for a fact that he took it?'

'No, but it's a possibility.' But I don't know for sure, and I don't know what else this company ships, but if Oliver had been employed by them, he must have had his suspicions. 'Your dad's been digging. The company is called Skyro. He was offered it a while back, presumably before he was fired from his old job.'

Joe frowns at me. 'How the fuck did Dad find that out?'

'He has a contact that rakes up dirt for him about potential new investors. Maybe Oliver knew it was dodgy. What other reason could he have had for not telling any of us?

Your father's calling the police in the morning.' Oddly matter-of-fact, I gaze at Joe. 'Maybe it's time we found out what else he was up to.'

As I sit at the kitchen table, the warmth from the Aga reaches me as I fire up Oliver's laptop, while Joe pours us both a glass of wine.

'The password is *fontainea1*,' I tell him, as I type it in. 'Tells you all you need to know that he used this woman's name.'

'Here.' Joe places a glass in front of me. 'Kat?' He pauses. 'Are you sure you're up for this? You may not like what you're about to see.'

'It can't be worse than not knowing.' But this latest piece of news has motivated me to find answers. 'I have to do this. Don't worry. I'm ready. Where should we start?' I click on Oliver's emails. Scrolling down, I pass spam, emails about the cars, my heart skipping a beat when I find one titled *training schedule*, sent from *admin@skyro.com*.

I click on the attachment. When it opens, it gives a list of dates and training venues, from simulator up to his first flight, followed by a roster. 'I don't think there's any doubt that he did start working for them. But he went to a lot of trouble to hide this,' I tell Joe. 'Including faking rosters that looked like his old ones. It makes you wonder why.'

I scan the list of routes – Paris, Milan, Belgium, Israel, Riyadh, instead of Alicante, Malaga, Palma, Rome, the typical tourist destinations that he used to fly to.

Beside me, Joe studies the page. 'It doesn't really tell us anything. They're all civilian airports. For all we know, they were regular flights.'

I check the dates. 'The training started a couple of weeks before the accident – that still leaves six weeks when he was pretending to go to work.' My fingers hesitate over the keys. 'I want to see if I can look at his bank accounts.'

'Do you know his passwords?'

'No.' I hadn't thought of that. 'But he's the only person who uses this laptop. It may well remember them.'

For the most part I'm right and I access his personal account without any problem. The transactions fit with what we know – his airline salary ending after they fired him, replaced over the following two months by a payment from his savings, followed by a first from Skyro for almost twice the amount.

I stare at the figures, astonished. 'No wonder he took this job. Look.' I point them out to Joe.

'What's that one?' Joe's finger hovers over another payment. 'Can you click on it?'

It's for a huge sum of money, alongside what appears to be an obscure set of letters and numbers. Copying them, I paste them into the browser but they show up nothing.

'Money to buy his silence?' Joe suggests.

'Or blackmail?' In the circumstances, I'm not sure there's a difference. 'I want to look at his photos.' I start on the most recent ones – of airports he's landed at, a couple of the house last summer. There's one of me, taken on our wedding anniversary, before any of this started; photos of family occasions. But noticing a separate folder, when I open it, the face of a woman comes up on the screen. Clear eyes gaze back at me, holding a knowing look. Her hair is long and pale blonde – expensively coloured, I wouldn't mind betting – her skin smooth, delicate gold hoops in her ears.

'That's her, isn't it?' I think of the photo I found, that the police now have, turning to Joe. 'I mean, I know her hair and makeup are completely different. But facially, there's a strong likeness, don't you think?'

He nods. 'Are there more?'

There are several. One of her at a restaurant, sitting at a table, in London – the Thames is clearly in the background; another of her smiling happily as the picture's taken, the Eiffel Tower behind her. 'They've been to Paris together.' As I stare at them in disbelief, the penny drops. 'He told me he was on a night-stop. He must have been with her.'

'It looks that way, doesn't it?' Joe's hand rests on my shoulder. 'I'm sorry, Kat. Are you OK?'

But as I stare at the photos, I'm oddly calm. I turn to look at him. 'It's weird, but I don't feel anything. It's like this isn't the Oliver I married.' I pause. 'Do you think we should print these off for the police?'

'Maybe. But after Dad talks to them about Oliver's new job, they'll probably want to pick up his laptop.'

I go back to his emails, searching for exchanges between him and Ana Fontaine. 'Maybe if she emailed him, he deleted them.' But when I go to his sent folder, it's another matter. There are dozens, if not more, he's sent to her. Clicking on the first one, there's no question they were intimate.

You know how much I love you. I'm sorry about earlier. I'm worried about leaving Kat. I know how much she's come to rely on me.

As Joe reads over my shoulder, I hear him sigh. 'Sounds like he felt torn.'

198

But I'm unrelenting. 'Not so torn he wasn't planning to leave me.' Carrying on, I scroll through the rest of the folder, until I reach what appears to be the first he sent her. 'This goes back eleven months.' I look at Joe, aghast. 'Eleven months of living a lie. He was bloody good. I didn't have a clue.'

Consumed by a need to know more, I click on each of his early emails.

You have no idea how wonderful it was to meet you.
    You've opened my eyes, Ana. I've spent too long living the life everyone expects me to live. The time has come to do something to change that.

And as I click on the next email, so it goes on, evidencing the way this woman has influenced him. 'She really got to him, didn't she?' My voice is hurt.

Eventually, as I reach more recent emails, his tone changes.

If I'm not careful, there's going to be so much fallout from this. This isn't just about my house and job. I stand to lose absolutely everything

'What's that supposed to mean?'
'I don't know.'
'Unless it's a reference to money. Maybe he thought he'd be disinherited if he divorced me, but surely that's too archaic, even for the McKennas,' I say archly.

Closing the laptop and getting up, I pace over to the window. Outside, winter has well and truly arrived, evidenced in the greyness of the landscape, the heaviness of the sky; the lack of daylight only adding to the desolation I feel.

'It's supposed to get easier with time, Joe. But every day, it seems to get worse.' As I stand there, I wrap my arms around myself. 'I don't know how much more I can take, to be honest.'

Coming over, Joe stands next to me. 'You're not sleeping. It doesn't help. Maybe you should see your GP. See if there's something they can prescribe to take the edge off things.'

'Maybe.' I turn to look at him. 'You're so supportive to me. I mean it. Thank you.'

Seconds pass before he speaks, seconds during which he holds my gaze. 'You know, don't you? I'd do anything for you.'

Reaching a hand to touch his face, suddenly I'm dizzy.

Noticing, Joe frowns. 'Are you OK?'

'I don't feel so good. I think I'm exhausted.'

'It's hardly surprising. Poor Kat. You've been through so much.' His voice is full of sympathy.

Suddenly I'm craving human contact, from someone who cares. As if he knows, stepping closer, Joe's arms move around me.

2017

Margot

For as long as good fortune flows your way, you owe it to yourself to make the most of it. In the summer of 2017, that's what I did, gathering acquaintances, experiences, money. The private villa parties were lucrative by anyone's standards, guests going to new lengths in the pursuit of pleasure and self-indulgence, sexually, chemically or whatever turned them on. I simply turned a blind eye and took the money.

I knew I was seeking the same as they were, in my own way, if not to the same extreme. But what was hedonism if not the avoidance of physical pain, or disorder of the soul? I couldn't think of a single person alive who didn't seek that.

At some point I knew I had to tell Andre there wasn't going to be a boat charter. The question was how to do it without losing face. In the end, I invented a reason that only the most insensitive person couldn't have empathised with.

'I'm so sorry.' I let tears fill my eyes – a trick I'd long perfected. 'Natalie's just been diagnosed with brain cancer.' Natalie was one of the mythical friends I'd invited on the boat trip. 'Knowing she's ill, none of us feel right about this.' A tear rolled down one of my cheeks. 'It's so awful. I need to go back and see her.' I gazed at him. 'I feel terrible about letting you down, Andre. You could have hired your boat to someone else for those days.' I bit my lip. 'I must compensate you. Tell me how much.'

It was one of those moments of jeopardy. Saying what he'd expect me to say. Bluffing, I had about enough money to cover five minutes on his wonderful boat.

But shaking his head, he held a finger to my lips. 'We are friends, Margot. There is no need.' Gently, he wiped my cheek. 'Book a flight, and I will take you to the airport.'

I gazed at him, my eyes filled with what I hoped was gratitude. It wasn't the perfect solution. I had no intention of going to the airport, but if it assuaged his need to be the alpha male, I was happy to oblige.

'You're so good to me, Andre.' I reached for one of his hands. 'I'll go home now,' I said tearfully. 'Can I text you when I've booked a flight?'

Having checked the flights, I'd earmarked one for the following morning. When Andre turned up late, I was already walking down the road to meet him.

Pulling over, he pushed the door open. 'I'm sorry, Margot. I overslept.'

'Don't worry. I'm so grateful to you.' Getting in, I kissed his cheek, before glancing at the clock on the dashboard of his car. 'I should still be able to make it.'

'Have you spoken to your friend?' He sounded concerned.

'I called her last night.' My voice wavered. 'She's going in for surgery next week. I'm going to help look after her kids while she recovers.'

'That's nice,' he said softly. 'I like when people do something selfless.'

'She's one of my oldest friends.' I paused. 'When something like this happens, nothing else matters, does it?'

'You are right. And when you are back, I will take you somewhere special,' he said gently.

'You don't need to do that.' I placed a hand on his leg. 'Really, Andre. You've already done so much for me.'

After he dropped me at the airport, I waved as he drove away, before heading through the doors into departures. Heading for the restrooms, I went into one of the cubicles and taking off my beautiful dress, changed quickly into the clothes I'd packed – shorts, a faded t-shirt, scrunching my hair up into an unflattering topknot before scrubbing off my lipstick and putting on my shades.

Knowing the only common denominator between the Margot who walked into the airport and the one that walked out again fifteen minutes later was a rucksack onto which a brightly coloured scarf was now tied, I blended inconspicuously into the crowd that had just arrived and was spilling out of arrivals into the Ibiza sunshine.

Outside, I made my way to the taxi ranks and a minute later I was on my way back to the villa.

For a week, I kept a low profile. To start with, it wasn't hard. I did a little housekeeping; sunbathing until I remembered I was supposed to be in the UK, where typically the English summer wasn't happening. But three days in, I was getting restless.

With the island full of tourists, I thought about losing myself among them for a few hours, incognito, taking the risk that no one would recognise me. But not wanting to jeopardise everything I had here, for once, I curbed the urge. And it was just as well, because on the fourth morning, I had an unexpected visitor.

Hearing a moped stop by the gate, I went to an upstairs window. When I saw Nico outside the villa, I shrank back. I had no idea what had brought him here. As far as anyone was concerned, I was still in England, but suddenly I realised, I hadn't told him.

I was getting too complacent. This was another mistake that could have been avoided. When I'd let Nico think he was my friend, I should have told him about Natalie and the charter being cancelled.

Coming over to the front door, he knocked loudly.

'Margot?' He tried again. 'Margot? Are you in there?'

I heard him try the door. Thank fuck I'd thought to keep it locked. The crunch of his feet on gravel became silent as he reached the paving stones at the side of the house. Imagining him going around to the back, I sank to the floor.

In my pocket, I felt my phone vibrate. Carefully removing it, Nico's name flashed up on the screen. Putting it down, I let it ring, thinking quickly. If Nico had known I was in England, he would have been expecting an English ringtone rather than a Spanish one. But if he'd known, surely he wouldn't have come here?

It was another scenario I hadn't thought through. If he ever questioned me, I could easily explain that I had two phones. Upset by Natalie's illness, I'd simply forgotten to take this one with me.

Half an hour passed, as on the floor, I didn't move. At last I heard Nico start his moped, revving the engine, before driving away. Still on the floor, I contemplated how to get out of this. I couldn't risk using my mobile to contact Andre, either. If he and Nico spoke, the cat would be out of the bag.

Still anxious about being caught out, I crawled to my bedroom and found my laptop. Deciding to use Facebook, I was about to send Nico a message about where I allegedly was and the reason for it, when I stopped myself. It might seem less suspicious if I left it a few hours.

That evening, my fears were allayed when Nico responded sympathetically. I breathed a sigh of relief. But even for me, this had gone a step too far beyond the jeopardy I thrived on and I was starting to feel the pressure mounting.

The only saving grace to my self-enforced confinement was Giuseppe's cinema room. Below ground, I could at least binge-watch TV until my mythical return from the UK, or so I thought. That night, in the darkness of the villa, I went to the fridge to get myself another beer. As I opened the door and the light inside it came on, there was a loud rap on the window.

'Margot? Are you going to let me in or am I going to have to smash this window?'

I was pretty sure the glass was toughened, but I knew when the game was up. Going to the door, I unbolted it.

As he stepped inside, Nico looked furious. 'What the fuck are you playing at?'

'What the fuck are you doing here?' I countered.

We stared at each other. 'So many lies, Margot. You invent a friend with cancer. It is not good.' Nico smoothed his hair off his face. 'And you forget one small thing. I've known too many people like you. I know what you are doing.'

'It isn't what you think. It's complicated.' Turning, I walked back to the kitchen, thinking on my feet. 'If I tell you . . .'

'I think you must tell me.' Helping himself to a beer from the fridge, he leaned against the worktop.

'Come downstairs. I was about to watch a movie,' I said lightly.

'I do not come here to watch a fucking movie.' He didn't budge. 'Or are you frightened of being seen by someone else?'

I paused, but only for a split second. 'Fine,' I shrugged. 'Stay there if you like. I'm going downstairs.'

My heart was starting to race. I knew I was pushing him. But

205

if he turned up uninvited, what did he expect? There was silence behind me, before I heard him follow. Going down into the cinema room, I arranged myself on one of the sofas.

Coming in, he sat down and for a moment, he didn't speak. When he looked at me, his eyes were filled with distrust. 'I am not sure I know you, Margot. I thought I did, but not now.'

I formed a look of embarrassment on my face. 'I'm sorry. I know how bad this looks. But I have an explanation, Nico. It's just.' I lowered my gaze, just a fraction. 'It's not something I wanted anyone to know about.'

'Then you tell me. I stay here until you do.' Nico sounded uncompromising.

Thinking quickly, I sighed. 'OK. But it's actually fucking embarrassing. I was set to inherit some money from my grandfather. A whole lot of money as it happens. I received the first instalment just before I came out here. I was due the next a couple of weeks ago. But . . .' I paused. 'This is the embarrassing part. Someone came forward. They said my grandfather owed him hundreds of thousands from a business deal they did years ago. He says he has the paperwork. My solicitor seems to think his claim won't stand up. But in the meantime, the estate has been frozen.' I'm aware of Nico's eyes fixed on me. 'It doesn't affect my day-to-day life, but there's no way I can afford to charter Andre's boat.' I rested my head in my hands. 'I know I should have been honest with him. But I didn't want anyone to know that my grandfather hadn't paid his debts.' I shrugged miserably, watching him closely to see if he fell for the act. 'It was wrong, but it was easier to lie.'

Nico looked slightly less angry. 'You are right. It is wrong. It is also wrong to spend money before you have it.'

'I know.' I gritted my teeth. 'I honestly believed that coming here was the start of wonderful new chapter of my life.' If I was

going to be honest with him, I may as well tell him about the house, too. 'This house . . . I'm not renting it, Nico. I found an advertisement for a house sitter and when I applied, I was offered it. It's all perfectly above board. There's an agreement and everything. The only thing was . . .' I frowned slightly. 'I thought the house-keeper would still be here. But it was really strange. When I arrived, she wasn't.'

'If there is any chance of us staying friends, I want you to tell Andre the truth,' Nico said quietly.

I looked at him, horrified. 'I can't.'

'If you don't, I will.' Nico shrugged. 'He is a good man. He was prepared to let you charter his boat on trust. He does not deserve your lies.' Nico paused. 'You may not know this, but the boat does not belong to him, Margot. He looks after it for someone else. Andre works on commission. Your lies have cost him thousands.'

I was taken aback. But it wasn't my fault. 'Well, perhaps he should have been more honest, too.' Taking in the look on Nico's face, I decided I needed to be more repentant. 'OK. That was unfair of me. I suppose I assumed.'

'Yes.' Nico's eyes are grave. 'You should not assume.'

Getting up, I stood there awkwardly. 'Would you like another beer? Or some food?'

'A beer,' he said briefly.

Going out to the kitchen, I was thinking on my feet. No way was I telling Andre. But how else was I going to get out of this?

Taking the beers back, I passed one to Nico, looking at mine before swapping them over 'Mine's the zero.'

Sitting down, I was silent for a moment. 'Have you ever been down on your luck?' I said at last. 'I mean really down, without a job, with no money to pay your rent, with no family to turn to, without any hope that anything will change for the better.'

He spoke coldly. 'I have been without work more than once. But I have always been honest.'

I wished he'd stop banging on about honesty. 'So have I,' I said hastily. 'Until now. I'm desperate, Nico. Since coming here, it's felt like the beginning of a whole new life. The people I've met, this island . . .' I paused, watching him drink his beer. 'Nico, I really don't know if I can tell Andre.'

He looked at me. 'You don't have a choice.'

'You're wrong.' I watched him drink more of his beer. 'My friend, you should know by now. There is always a choice.'

★

There were just two rules to living the way I did. Say whatever it takes to get you whatever you need, and when the going gets too hot, get the fuck out. The problem was I was far from ready to leave here.

But events had forced my hand. As the ferry chugged out of the port, I felt a genuine pang of sadness as the lights of Ibiza Town faded behind me, wondering if I'd ever come back. Sitting in the darkness, I tried to work out a plan, but all I could picture was Nico, shaking his head, making no attempt to hide his disgust with me.

'I was right about you. You didn't come looking for people. It was all about money.'

He was referring to the day he'd been upset; the day I'd been late meeting him because I'd lost track of time at some fancy lunch with Andre. But the villa parties had paid off in more than one way. As the Rohypnol I'd spiked Nico's beer with took effect, he was starting to slur his words.

'In vino veritas, Nico?' Dropping the act, I was done with this. 'I'm not telling Andre a single fucking thing. You shouldn't have come here. If you could have kept out of this, everything could have just stayed the way it was. But now . . .' There was regret in my voice.

Trying and failing to speak, it wasn't long before Nico was unconscious. Gazing at him, I had two choices as I thought about administering the lethal dose of heroin I'd lifted from one of the villa parties. But I'd stopped myself. Nico was an innocent in this. He didn't need to die. Minutes later, I fetched the trolley I knew was outside, used to transport firewood in for the oversized fireplaces. Rolling his inert body onto it, I pulled the trolley into the lift up to the ground floor.

It made it so much easier when a villa was kitted out like this one. I didn't have to use strength. Outside, I switched on the electric motor and steered the trolley outside. Briefly I considered dumping him on the roadside, but I couldn't take the risk that someone would see me. Heading past the pool towards the garden, reaching a shaded corner, I put the brakes on, before rolling Nico onto the ground.

But after what I'd done, I knew I couldn't stay. After putting the trolley away, I'd cleaned up the house and packed, taking one or two souvenirs in payment for my trouble, pausing only to send Giuseppe an apologetic email. This time it was my mother who'd been taken ill. After locking the house and leaving the key hidden, I'd gone out to the taxi I knew was on its way. Not an official one – I wasn't taking any chances. There were plenty of taxis that did rides for bargain prices, no questions asked.

As the taxi headed for the port, I thought fleetingly of Andre. I'd be sorry not to see him again, but what I was most sorry about was leaving this glitzy life I'd created here. With the police already sniffing around Gabby's death, I was sure it wouldn't be long before Nico told them what he remembered of tonight. So I bought a ticket on the first available ferry, which happened to be going to Valencia. With a whole night to think about what came next, I watched *the lights of Ibiza fade into the darkness as I considered mainland Spain, Italy, or maybe France again. With any number of places to check out, one thing I did know was that Margot Jameson's moment had been cut short. I just bitterly regretted it couldn't have lasted longer.*

18

Katharine

After Joe goes to bed, like most nights, I lie awake, unable to sleep. Stretched out on the sofa, I take in how quiet the house is, the image of Ana Fontaine filling my head. I wonder if the police have spoken to her yet. Then I think of the job Oliver had allegedly applied for and the implications of that, the restlessness I feel gnawing under my skin, before it subsides to numbness, almost as though someone's flicked an emotional off-switch. I read somewhere once that nothingness is the root of insanity. But as I lie here, I know what's worse. When trust has been hard won, betrayal cuts deeper; is magnified a hundredfold.

But I've learned the hard way never to count on anyone, and I find myself winding the clock back to my childhood, to somewhere that should have been carefree and happy. Except even back then, nowhere was. I've talked to Jude about my mother's illness, how it hung over my life until she died when I was a teenager, how my grieving father took his own life. As the numbness starts to wear off, a wave of grief, unhappiness, desolation, washes over me. Feeling the walls close in, it takes superhuman effort to do what I've taught myself to do. Deep breaths, Kat. Start counting, keep going, through the tens, twenties, hundreds and thousands, for as long as it takes for this to pass.

Eventually I must have drifted off, because the next morning, I'm still lying on the sofa when I'm awoken by a knock on the door. Suddenly realising what the time is, I get up, pausing in the hallway to glance in the mirror. My pale skin exaggerates the dark circles under my eyes, my hair unkempt. I make an attempt to smooth it, before going to answer the door.

'Good morning, Mrs McKenna.' DS Stanley is there with the same colleague as before. She's everything I don't feel – bright, her makeup perfect, her hair newly washed and neatly pinned back. 'I hope this isn't too early. I was hoping you might have a moment.'

'Of course,' I say wearily, knowing I don't really have a choice. 'You'll have to excuse me. I didn't sleep at all well last night. Come through to the kitchen.'

They follow me into the kitchen, where getting a glass of water, I gesture towards the table. 'Please, do sit down. Can I offer you a cup of tea?'

'No, thank you.'

Watching as DS Stanley gets out her electronic notebook, I pull out one of the chairs opposite them.

'There were one or two things we wanted to ask you about.' She frowns slightly. 'Your father-in-law has already contacted us regarding the job your husband had applied for. I understand you didn't know about it?'

'I knew nothing about it.'

'Can you think of any reason why your husband hadn't told you? Had he referred to it in any way, even in a way you might have missed at the time?'

I shake my head. 'No. Not once.'

'The second . . .' She pauses. 'It's a little awkward. It's regarding your relationship with your husband. I know you told us that everything was fine between you. It's just we have new information that suggests that wasn't the case.'

'Excuse me?' As I gaze at her, a feeling of uncertainty comes over me. 'Who told you that?'

DS Stanley opens her electronic notebook. 'We've been to see Ana Fontaine. She told us quite a few things, actually. According to her, your husband was about to leave you.'

Shocked, my mind starts to race. 'That's insane.'

'Apparently you and your husband argued constantly. That's what he'd told her.'

I shake my head. 'Why would she say that? Did you believe her?'

'I'm simply stating her side of events. She didn't know about the money he'd left her, or so she says.'

I stare at her. 'Have you considered that she might be lying?'

'It's possible.' DS Stanley goes on. 'But your husband also gave Ms Fontaine quite a detailed account of your behaviour. He described it as paranoid. He never knew what he was coming home to. He also told her you'd attacked him verbally and physically. Does this sound at all familiar to you?'

A feeling of helplessness builds inside me. Knowing how bad she's making me look, how can she say these things? 'I've no idea where she's got that from. I've told you what our marriage was like. It's obvious she's determined to cause trouble. Don't you wonder why?'

It isn't right that the police should believe her, when it's me they need to believe. But without Oliver here to corroborate her story, it's her word against mine. I shake my head. 'I've no idea why he would have said those things to her, or even if he actually did say them. But whether he did or not, it sounds like my husband was going through some kind of crisis. It probably explains why he hid things from me.'

'You seem very calm, Mrs McKenna.'

I look from one of them to the other. 'What am I supposed to say? I don't know what Ana Fontaine's agenda is, but what she's told you isn't true. She's definitely up to something. I can assure you I am neither paranoid nor unstable. I suppose he might have told her that in order to gain her sympathy. I'm a therapist, as you know. I have an understanding of these things.' But even I can hear the uncertainty in my voice.

Sitting there, I look at her. What can I say if DS Stanley has already decided that for whatever reason, this Ana Fontaine is more plausible than I am? But her next question shocks me.

'According to Ms Fontaine, your husband was concerned about your spending habits. He told her that he was intentionally keeping money where you couldn't access it. Were you aware of this?'

Disbelief fills me. 'We had one or two disagreements about the cost of items for the house. We've been doing it up,' I say through gritted teeth. 'Oliver liked nice things. They don't come cheap.'

The two police officers glance at each other. 'Your husband also told Ms Fontaine that his brother was in love with you. Was the feeling mutual?'

'*What*?' I gaze at her incredulously. 'That really is pure fiction. Joe and I are friends – good friends – but that's all we are. We've always got on well, but there is nothing more between us. Just for the record, whatever my husband may have been up to, I was never unfaithful to him.'

She makes a note in her electronic notebook. 'Were you aware your husband had started attending AA meetings?'

Another shockwave hits me, another wave of denial. 'Oliver did not have a drink problem.'

'Mrs McKenna, he lost his job because he'd been drinking. Surely that's indicative of a problem at some level?'

Puzzled, I frown. 'But if he was diabetic and hadn't been diagnosed, isn't it possible he might have misinterpreted his symptoms?'

'If he was going to AA meetings, he clearly thought he had a problem.' DS Stanley studies me. 'It's a pity we can't check with the local group, but of course, they don't keep records. You never suspected anything?'

Before I can answer, a creak comes from upstairs.

DS Stanley looks up. 'Do you have someone here?'

I shake my head. 'Probably just the cat,' I say slightly more loudly than usual after her earlier comment, glad that Joe's car is parked outside on the road and not in the drive. 'I imagine you need this.' Trying to pre-empt more questions, I slide Oliver's laptop across the table towards her.

Mercifully Joe waits until they've gone before coming downstairs.

'They've spoken to Ana Fontaine.' As my eyes fix on his, I'm numb again. 'Get this. She told the police that Oliver and I argued all the time. Apparently he'd told Ana that I was paranoid, and that I'd attacked him. It's nonsense, Joe. She's made

215

it all up.' My voice is tight. 'Now the police think I'm aggressive, and I'm not.' Breaking off, I'm tearful as I look at Joe. 'According to her, Oliver had told her he was going to leave me. You read about women like her, don't you? Conning people out of their money. For all we know, she orchestrated this whole thing. She must have known exactly what she was doing.'

Joe looks shocked. 'It's starting to look that way. But if it is the case, the police will see through her.'

'What if they don't?' Nothing is certain anymore. 'She told the police about something else Oliver said to her, allegedly. He told her that you were in love with me.'

Joe's cheeks colour slightly. 'Nothing's happened between us, Kat. Though I'm not saying I don't wish it was different . . .'

'Don't, Joe.' My body is rigid. 'Can't you see what this looks like? Ana Fontaine is stacking up all these reasons for me to want Oliver out of the way – my paranoid, abusive behaviour, our so-called unhappy marriage, the fact of you being in love with me. It's obvious to us what she's doing, but what if the police don't believe me?'

'The truth will out, Kat. It usually does.' Coming over, he takes one of my hands, frowning slightly. 'What was really going on between you and Oliver?'

I react as if I've been stung. 'Nothing. I've already told you.'

'I mean the truth,' he says gently. 'If Oliver had been seeing someone else, things couldn't have been great between you.'

'We were fine.' I swallow the lump in my throat. 'What makes you think we weren't?'

'I know you,' he says softly. 'You're hiding something. Don't you think it might help if you tell me?'

Pausing, I'm caught between telling a truth I've tried to hide, or continuing with this charade. But as Joe looks at me, I can no longer keep it to myself. 'What Ana Fontaine told the police . . . the reverse was true.' My voice trembles. 'It was Oliver who bullied me. I've never said anything before. I didn't think anyone would believe me.' I pause. 'He had a controlling streak. I never saw a sign of it until after we were married. He always wanted to know everything I was doing. He also wanted me to account for everything I spent. He didn't like me going anywhere without him – it's the reason we've lost touch with all our friends. There have been so many cancelled dates, they've given up on us. But he knew what he was doing. It's classic abusive behaviour – in pushing them away, he knew he was isolating me. He was even looking at rigging up CCTV inside the house, just so that he could keep an eye on me while he was out.'

'That's insane.' Joe looks horrified. 'It's not like he could keep track of you while he was flying.'

'I think that's what he couldn't bear. Knowing he couldn't keep tabs on me was driving him out of his mind. At least with CCTV, he could play it back.' I pause for a moment. 'But you don't know the half of it . . .' Unless you've been there, no one knows what an abusive relationship feels like. 'It's affected my work. I've had to be so careful about who comes here when Oliver's been at home. He'd been acting as though he was suspicious of everyone – and I've no idea why. I'm not even sure there was really a problem with his car. He probably manufactured it deliberately so that he'd have to take mine, knowing he'd be leaving me marooned here.'

'That's crazy.' Joe sounds outraged.

'It was about control,' I say quietly. 'Everything was always on Oliver's terms – down to the furniture, the meals I cooked. He let me choose the plants because he wasn't interested in gardens, but have you ever looked outside and asked yourself why there are so many empty flowerbeds?' I shook my head. 'I planted them – beautifully, lovingly – and as the plants started growing, Oliver ripped a load of them out. He didn't want me to have the pleasure of seeing them bloom. He wanted me to look like a failure.' Folding my arms, I try to stop myself shaking. 'Remember you asked why the bills were in his name? For the same reason . . . control. He didn't want me to believe I could cope without him.'

Joe looks shocked. 'How long has this been going on?'

'Since just after our wedding.' I take a shaky breath. 'The first time, I thought he was joking. He criticised what I was wearing – not in a nice way, but telling me I looked ugly and inappropriate. See that clock?' I turned to the Moroccan clock on the wall. 'I used to have one that belonged to my gran. I didn't have much of hers and it wasn't anything fancy, but I loved it. Anyway, he got rid of it without telling me, and replaced it with that one. There's more . . .' I go on, listing examples of Oliver's undermining and ridicule, building up to the times he was physically violent towards me. 'It starts in such a small way – and escalates. I've learned all about it in my therapy training. But even with that behind me, I can't believe I couldn't see what was happening in my own life.' I look at Joe, wondering if he gets it. 'I've tried to understand why he behaved like that towards me. I've wondered if in some way, his behaviour stemmed from his childhood.'

Joe frowns. 'In what way, specifically?'

'I don't know.' I shrug. 'Maybe he was mirroring the way your father behaved. I don't know how he was when you were small, but he certainly has high expectations of everyone. He can be pretty critical – and demanding.'

'He was never abusive towards us.'

'Maybe not physically, but emotionally?' I fix my eyes on Joe. 'It isn't always obvious, Joe. And what about your mother?'

Joe's jaw drops open. 'Are you suggesting he abuses her?'

'I don't know. People become so good at hiding things, and over time, abuse becomes less shocking. But you'd never go to him with a problem, would you? He wouldn't be interested.'

He looks taken aback. 'But he's successful, he's provided for us.'

'Did you grow up feeling loved, Joe?'

I want him to properly think about it. But he doesn't know what to say.

I go on. 'I'm talking about being made to feel safe and cared for. Cuddled when you were upset, reassured that your parents would be there for you, no matter what. I don't think you and Oliver ever had that.' I wipe away the tear that rolls down my cheek. 'It happens surprisingly often. I think your father's been emotionally abusive towards both of you. He's done it all your lives. Look at how he tries to manipulate you into joining his company; the way he freezes you out when you don't do what he wants. Until you do, you'll never receive approval from him. But the thing is, you don't see it, because it's what you've grown up with. And to question it would be deeply uncomfortable, because it's so ingrained in you. It's really difficult to dismantle that kind of programming.'

Joe looks stunned. 'Why haven't you said anything before?'

I wipe my face again. 'I honestly thought we could work it out. I really wanted us to. I hoped we could. And pitted against Oliver, if I'd said anything against him, I don't think any of you would have believed me. But that's the age-old trap of abuse.' Breaking off, I gaze at Joe. 'And now, it's a hundred times worse, because after the accident, when the police said the car had been tampered with, there was no way I could tell anyone.' More tears fill my eyes. 'The cards on the table answer? I haven't done anything wrong, but I'm terrified of being arrested, Joe. *Please* don't say anything,' I beg. 'If the police know he was abusive towards me, they'll think I killed him.'

When Joe doesn't speak, suddenly I'm afraid that he doesn't believe me. 'You have to talk to the police, Kat. They need to know what Oliver was really like. He's obviously been spinning this Ana Fontaine a whole pack of lies.'

'Either that, or she's made it all up,' I say tearfully. 'She probably found out how wealthy he was, then lured him in with the hope of getting her hands on his money – and she's succeeded, hasn't she?'

'We still don't know what Oliver's left you. Try not to worry, Kat. If this woman is up to something, the police will get to the bottom of it.'

But will they? It could go either way. Not only is it her word against mine, it's completely impossible to prove anything now.

19

Jude

Late Saturday morning, Richard's out, leaving me alone in a house that echoes with memories. As I walk through its quiet rooms, for the first time it strikes me how ludicrous it is that most days, weeks, months, it's just the two of us here.

It's a house I've always taken for granted. When the boys lived at home, it was filled with life, but as I look at it now, though, it's no more than a bloated status symbol, an impressive address, which when our lives are so transient, seems utterly meaningless.

I'm taken by surprise when the doorbell rings. Opening the door, a cold wind blows in as I find DS Stanley and Constable Ramirez standing there.

DS Stanley's face is grave as she looks at me. 'Do you have a few minutes, Mrs McKenna? There are one or two things we'd like to talk to you about.'

Uneasy, I wonder why they've turned up without warning. 'Of course. Please come in.'

As they come inside, I close the door behind them. 'Would you like to come through to the kitchen?' I lead the way through the hallway, then across the kitchen, gesturing to the slate-topped table and cushioned chairs. 'Do sit down.' I take a seat opposite them. 'How can I help you?'

DS Stanley takes out her electronic notebook. 'We've just been to see your daughter-in-law.'

'I imagine you saw Joe, then.' From their exchanged glances, I take it they didn't know Joe had stayed over. 'Or maybe he'd gone out.'

DS Stanley hesitates. 'We didn't see your son, Mrs McKenna. But prior to that, we'd been to see Ana Fontaine. She tells quite a different story to what we've heard from anyone else.'

As she speaks, a feeling of dread fills me. 'How do you mean, different?'

'For one thing, her account of your son's marriage. According to her, your son was deeply unhappy – about a number of things. He'd told her he was planning to leave his wife.'

'No.' Frowning, I shake my head. 'That's impossible.' Oliver and Kat separating? Even the idea is incomprehensible.

'Is it? Why would you say that?'

'They were so happy. You only had to see them together. Everyone knew they were.' Under their scrutiny, I'm lost for words.

'Are you sure about that? The very fact that your son was having an affair suggests otherwise.'

'She has to be making it up,' I say firmly. 'She probably

found out how wealthy he was and thought she could get her hands on his money. Richard and I have always encouraged Oliver – and Joe – not to talk about money. You know what people can be like.'

DS Stanley doesn't comment. 'According to what she says your son told her, his wife had become unstable, to the point that she could be abusive towards him.'

I'm outraged. 'I'm not sure she's being straight with you. I can absolutely tell you I've never seen a hint of anything remotely like that.'

DS Stanley makes a note before continuing. 'She also had some interesting insights into what he'd been going through at work. Apparently – according to her – the pressure of airline flying had been getting to him. Your son told her he had a drink problem – enough for him to join an AA group locally, about a year ago. That's where he and Ms Fontaine met.'

'That tells you everything you need to know.' I'm not usually judgemental, but the words are out before I can stop them. 'She's clearly a woman with problems. Why else would she have gone along there?'

'I imagine for exactly the same reasons as your son,' DS Stanley says coolly. 'It sounds as though she was someone he felt he could confide in – about work, his marriage, his family . . .'

When she mentions family, it touches a nerve. 'Exactly why would you believe her over any of us?'

'I'm simply putting two sides of the story across.' DS Stanley speaks calmly. 'She told us that you weren't close. Your son felt there were expectations of him to be a certain kind of person – successful, confident, happily married.'

As I gaze at her, I'm uncomfortable. 'But whatever she's told you, he was all those things. You only have to look at what he's achieved. As for not being close, that's ridiculous. Ask anyone in the family. The McKennas have always looked out for each other. Really, Detective Sergeant, this Ms Fontaine seems to have been stringing you a line.'

DS Stanley doesn't react. 'There was something else she mentioned. She said Oliver was preoccupied about something. She said it involved other people, and for that reason, he refused to talk to her about it, though he planned to later. Have you any idea what it might have been?'

'No.' I shake my head. 'Whenever I saw him, Oliver always seemed the same – happy with Kat, busy with work.'

'Which rather begs the question, doesn't it, as to why he was having an affair?'

Under their scrutiny, I try to gloss over it. 'These things happen in a lot of marriages.' As I know to my detriment. 'It doesn't make the situation terminal. So Oliver fell for a pretty face. It's not to say there was any more to it than that.' I pause. 'And all this is based on the assumption that Ms Fontaine is telling the truth.'

'Whether she is or not, it was your son's decision to leave her the money. And given the sum involved, I'd say there was quite a lot more to it than just a passing fling. Maybe we'll know more after probate is granted.' She pauses again. 'In light of your comment earlier, about your youngest son staying with Ms McKenna, there was something else Ms Fontaine alluded to. Oliver told Ms Fontaine that Joe's in love with Kat.'

Shock hits me. 'That's an outrageous suggestion, and completely unsubstantiated. Joe has been nothing but

224

supportive since Oliver died. He's been selflessly there – not just for Kat, but for all of us. I don't know what we would have done without him.'

DS Stanley frowns. 'How can you be so sure that's all he's been?'

Her question leaves me floundering. *Joe and Kat?* Was something going on between them? Is she suggesting that Joe could be a suspect – that he might have had a reason for wanting Oliver out of the way? I think of his willingness to drop everything to be with her, his solicitousness towards her. But if it had come to betraying his brother, there's no way Joe would have done that.

'What exactly are you suggesting?' I ask coldly.

'Families can be complicated entities – and love is found in the most unexpected, sometimes most inconvenient of places. Wouldn't you agree?' It's a question that doesn't demand an answer as DS Stanley moves on. 'How was your son's relationship with your husband?'

'Perfectly fine, thank you, Detective Sergeant.' Sitting back, I fold my arms, not appreciating the direction this conversation is taking. 'Are you any closer to finding out who damaged the brakes on the car Oliver was driving? Because in all this, it's quite possible Kat was the intended victim.'

'We're very much aware of this, and we're still in the process of gathering evidence.' She looks at me. 'You do realise how important it is that we build an accurate profile of your son's life and relationships? Someone clearly wanted to hurt either him or his wife. There has to be a clue somewhere as to who that was.'

'I agree.' I draw myself up. 'But you're barking up the wrong tree, Detective Sergeant. You're not going to find anything in this family.' Hearing the front door open, I'm relieved when Richard calls out.

'Jude? Everything OK?'

He will have seen the police car parked outside. 'Fine. We're in the kitchen.'

Coming in, he looks at the police officers. 'Good afternoon. Is there a reason for your visit?'

DS Stanley nods. 'There is. We've received some conflicting information about what was going on in your son's life in the weeks and months before he died.' She pauses. 'As I was explaining to your wife, Ms Fontaine met your son at an AA meeting.'

There's a split-second silence before he reacts. 'That's impossible.' Richard sounds dismissive. 'Oliver wasn't an alcoholic.'

DS Stanley hesitates for a split second. 'He clearly considered he had a severe enough problem if he was attending meetings.'

A look of hostility crosses Richard's face. 'Now just a moment. It wasn't so long ago that you told us that he was a diabetic. That's the explanation for his symptoms. There's absolutely no reason to think he had a drink problem.'

'Mr McKenna, I really don't think anyone goes to those meetings for fun,' DS Stanley says drily. 'Most likely, your son didn't tell you because he didn't want you to know, which given your response just now, seems entirely plausible.' Looking at Richard, she pauses for a moment before going on. 'According to Ms Fontaine, he drank because he was under a lot of stress – as is so often the case. In your son's case, the stress was related to his work and his marriage. He didn't feel he had anyone to turn to, until he met Ms Fontaine, that is.' She pauses. 'While you're here, Mr McKenna, it appears something else was bothering your son, something he refused to talk about, even to Ms Fontaine. Do you have any idea what that was?'

'None whatsoever,' he says shortly. 'Is this going to take much longer? I have to go out again.' He glances at his watch. 'In about ten minutes.'

She ignores his question. 'We've contacted the airline he used to work for. We're making enquiries to see if he'd talked to any of his colleagues.'

'They won't be able to tell you anything,' Richard says smoothly.

DS Stanley frowns at him. 'Why do you say that?'

'I know my son. All of this is fabrication, by this Ana Fontaine. If you're looking for a potential murderer, I'd suggest you start with her.'

*

After the police leave, Richard looks thunderous. 'Who do they think they are, making judgements about our son?'

I try to pacify him. 'They're just doing their job.' But I don't like it any more than he does. 'Where are you going?'

'Nowhere,' he snaps. 'I wanted to get rid of them. It's the weekend, for Christ's sake.'

I'm just about to tell him what the police said about Joe being in love with Kat. But knowing what his reaction will be, I stop myself. I need to talk to Joe myself, first.

'Ana Fontaine has a lot to answer for,' I say instead. 'Passing comment on what goes on inside this family.'

'I'll tell you exactly what she is: an imposter,' Richard says shortly. 'An imposter and a gold digger.'

'That's not what the police think. They seem fairly convinced that she and Oliver were having an affair. It's odd – the comment they made about him being under some kind of pressure. If that was the case, it could have explained why he drank. Before you came in, she mentioned something about him having too many expectations to live up to.' I frown slightly. 'I never thought I'd say this, but maybe we were too hard on him.'

'This is getting more and more ridiculous. Oliver was bloody lucky.' Richard sounds angry. 'He had a privileged home life, a private education, a successful flying career. He was more than up to any pressure that went with that.'

I gaze at Richard, suddenly wondering if all this time, we've both been blind to the truth. 'So why did he feel the need to drink? And why did he lie?'

My question wrong-foots him. 'Probably because this bloody woman, whoever she is, led him astray. I've seen it happen all too often. Unscrupulous young women setting their sights on someone else's wealth, doing whatever it takes to get their hands on it. I wouldn't be at all surprised if it turns out to be her who sabotaged the brakes. Once she'd persuaded Oliver to change his will, she wouldn't have needed him anymore.'

His denigrating rant only serves to increase my discomfort. If Oliver had been having problems, the truth is neither of us would have known. Richard has no empathy. He sees himself as worthy of his wealth and privilege; while in his mind at least, he sees other less fortunate people as deserving of their struggles. But Oliver should have felt able to come to me. I'm his mother. Except I've been too caught up in work. I've never been there for him when he's needed me, not when he was younger and not now. In short, I've failed him.

The knowledge hangs over me as I make a light lunch of poached eggs on granary toast, throughout which we say little before, as he always does on a Saturday afternoon, Richard heads for his study. Left alone again, a tentative feeling of relief settles over me as I make a cake, trying to dispel my feeling of guilt, until an hour later, Joe turns up.

'Hi, Mum.' Coming into the kitchen, he kisses my cheek. 'You're alone?'

He nods. 'Kat didn't sleep much last night. She's resting. She had a visit from the police this morning.'

'They said. They've been here, too.' I pause. It looks as though Joe hasn't been sleeping too well, either. In worn jeans and a blue sweater, there are circles under his eyes. 'Your father's in his study.' I glance down the hallway where Richard's door remains firmly closed. 'If you're not rushing off, can we talk?'

Making a couple of mugs of tea, we take them into the conservatory, where with the door closed, there's no way Richard will overhear us. Glancing outside, I take in the panoramic views across the garden, extending to the old walls on either side, to the beech hedge at the far end. I make a note to self to ask the gardener to rake the leaves up.

Sitting down, I sink into the comfortable cushions, savouring the warmth magnified by the glass as I look at Joe. 'How are you bearing up?' I ask gently.

'It's weird.' Joe's eyes are filled with sadness. 'I still expect him to walk in at any minute and this will all turn out to be a horrible nightmare.'

'I know.' I feel the same surreal sense. 'The police, Joe.

They said all these things. I'm not sure what to make of them. They said Oliver had been planning to leave Kat, that he had alcohol problems most likely because of the pressure he was under . . .'

'Kat said something this morning.' He looks uncertain. 'She said that Oliver had become abusive towards her, undermining and ridiculing her. She also said he was controlling – about who she saw and how she spent money.'

My face creases into a frown. 'Surely not Oliver? He was always so gentle.'

'That's what I thought. But the way Kat was talking . . .'

'Has she told the police?'

'No. She's worried they'll think she had a motive to kill Oliver. She begged me not to tell them.'

I'm as mystified as Joe is. 'I should try to talk to her. I mean, if it's true, I suppose the police should know.'

'It might be good if you do.' Joe looks troubled as he goes on. 'The thing is, she was describing the form emotional abuse can take. She reckons Dad is abusive in the way he controls us. She used the example of the job he wants me to take. But because I haven't, look at the way he speaks to me.'

As he speaks, a chill comes over me as I realise he's summarising exactly how Richard operates. 'She isn't wrong.' To my horror, my eyes fill with tears. 'All this time, I've let him do it. I haven't been much of a mother, have I?'

Joe's eyes widen. 'Mum, Oliver and I . . . we've always known how lucky we are.'

'I know you have.' I'm grateful for small mercies, but it's the answer he wants me to hear, rather than the truthful one. 'I wasn't there for him.' Pausing, I swallow the lump in my throat. 'If things were going wrong for him, he should have felt able to come to me. But he didn't.' My voice breaks.

Leaning forward, Joe looks distressed. 'None of this is your fault, Mum. It's like you said to Kat. Things happen sometimes, not always for a reason. It's life.'

I try to pull myself together. 'Like being in love with your brother's wife?'

Joe's face colours slightly as he sighs. 'I don't know what Oliver was thinking, saying that to Ana Fontaine.'

I shake my head sadly. 'She's stirring things up all right, isn't she?'

Joe tries to reassure me. 'Nothing has happened between us, I promise you. Kat would never have betrayed Oliver – ironically, as it turns out. Whether it ever will in the future,' he shrugs, 'time will tell.'

But as he speaks, I can't help reading between the lines. Kat may not have been prepared to betray Oliver, but suddenly I'm not so sure about Joe. A feeling of disappointment fills me as I look at my son. 'Did you know Oliver was going to AA meetings?'

He shakes his head. 'It's as much a surprise to me as it is to you.' He's silent for a moment. 'I've been thinking. Maybe I should try and find Ana Fontaine. I want to talk to her. See what she has to say.'

'You and me both,' I say fervently. 'From everything the police have said, it looks as though Oliver really did confide in her. I haven't told your father what they said about you and Kat, and I don't intend to. He was out at the time, thank God.' I look him straight in the eye. 'I do believe you, Joe, when you say nothing happened.' I pause. 'And I'm sorry. I know I haven't been much of a mother to you, either. When you were growing up, my career always seemed so important. But I realise now, what a mistake that was. It doesn't mean I didn't love you.' My voice cracks again. Love isn't a word that features in this family. 'Anyway,' I swallow the lump in my throat. 'It's all going to change. I'm leaving my job.'

Not because of Joe, I know he's an adult . . . but losing Oliver is making me reassess all kinds of things.

Joe looks shocked. 'Does Dad know?'

'I haven't told him yet. You're the only person I've told. Nothing's the same anymore. It hasn't been since Oliver died. I suppose I've realised I've spent most of my life chasing something that sounds impressive but hasn't made me happy. I can't make up for the time I've lost . . . and I know you have your own life, but I really would like it if you and I could spend some time together.'

Joe speaks quietly. 'So would I.'

I look at him gratefully. I'd give anything to be able to wind back time, to give my sons the love they should have had, to mediate in Richard's harshness, to be someone they knew they could always have come to. Instead, I have to live with my regrets because it's too late now.

★

Later that afternoon, I drive over to see Kat. When she opens the door, seeing how pale her face is, how dull her eyes are, I wonder if it's the fallout of what she confided in Joe about.

'How are you doing?' I ask her as we head towards the kitchen.

'Muddling through.' She goes to the kettle. 'Tea?'

'Thank you.' I wait for her to make two mugs before telling her why I've come here. 'Joe came over earlier.' I hesitate. 'He told me, Kat. About what Oliver did to you.' I pause. 'Joe said he was abusive and controlling – about money, too.'

Her eyes are wide with fear. 'I shouldn't have told him, Jude. It probably wasn't as bad as I made out.' As she picks up her mug, her hands are shaking.

I study her closely, trying to read between the lines. 'If he hurt you, Kat, you should tell the police,' I say quietly.

'There's no point, is there?' she says tearfully. 'It's not like there will be any consequences for Oliver. All it will mean is answering difficult and painful questions, at the end of which they'll probably think I had a motive for killing him.'

I can see her point, but it goes against my instincts. 'I still think you should tell them,' I try to persuade her. 'They're investigating his death. They need to know what was going on.'

But she shakes her head. 'I'm frightened about what they'll think.'

'When it comes to the police, the best bet is honesty. I don't know about Joe, but if they ask me directly, I'm not going to lie to them.'

Something flashes across her face briefly. 'I'll think about it.' She sounds resentful.

Knowing I can't force her, I change the subject. 'I should thank you, by the way.'

She looks surprised. 'What for?'

'For what you said to Joe about Richard's behaviour. He needed to hear it. We both did,' I add, as our eyes meet.

2017

Hannah

After the Margot debacle, I decided to change things up. Enter Hannah Price, social media blogger and travel journalist. Feeling a pang of sadness, I ditched my Ibiza wardrobe. My highlights would have to go too, but a new chapter called for a new image, and in my case, the sooner it happened, the better.

The first thing I did was to turn my trophies from Giuseppe's villa into hard cash. The dealer scrutinised me briefly, but didn't ask questions, just handed over fifty thousand euros. I was taken aback. I'd expected a fraction of that. But it seemed that when I left Giuseppe's, I'd chosen well. As for the money, if I was careful, there would be no more scrimping or stealing. For the first time in my life, everything would be above board.

With that done, I cut my hair to shoulder length and dyed it a shade of brown close enough to my natural colour, before finding a salon.

'I let a friend cut it.' I raised my eyebrows at the stylist. 'Sadly, she didn't do that great a job of it.'

A couple of hours later, I walked out with a fringe and auburn highlights, ready to go in search of a brand-new wardrobe. Boyfriend jeans, cargo pants, washed linen tops, an oversized jumper. Even if I'd walked past Andre, he wouldn't have recognised me.

I re-adopted the way I used to speak — no nonsense, littered with f-words, already liking Hannah Price. Blunt and to the point, she took no prisoners, but if you kept on the right side of her, she was also pretty nice.

Meanwhile, the old city and cobbled streets of Valencia were growing on me, as were the sandy beach and the promenade that stretched for miles, flanked by palm trees. The only obstacle in my mind was that the port was a prime crossing from the Spanish mainland to Ibiza. And given how many people I'd met in the previous months, it would be less risky were I to move further away.

Working out where to go next, I got on a bus and headed north, in true travel journalist style, hopping off now and then to jot down notes, taking photos to post on a new Instagram profile I'd set up, before waiting for the next bus to come along. I decided to aim for the Pyrénées-Orientales. It seemed to me to be the best of both worlds, where the eastern end of the mountains sloped down towards the northern Mediterranean coast.

I had planned to spend some time on the Spanish side of the border, before eventually crossing over back to France. The first night I stayed in a small hotel, tucked away up a narrow street with a modest frontage that belied its cavernous interior. In a large room with a tiled floor and shuttered windows, the mountain views reminded me of when I first came to France.

Thinking back, I thought of my first house sit, feeling a flicker of self-satisfaction that out of sheer determination, I'd made this work. But I couldn't go on moving from place to place. With the money I'd saved, I was looking for something a little more permanent.

The hotel room was beautifully furnished and as I looked around the fixtures and fittings, it was almost too tempting not to pick out one or two to take away. But I stopped myself. If I wanted my life to change, the first thing I had to do was to stop thinking like this.

After tapas in a buzzing local bar, I lay in bed, using the hotel Wi-Fi. Holding my breath, I looked at the Ibiza news, relieved when, so far at least, there was no mention of Nico reporting me to the police. Nico. If only he hadn't challenged me and been so fucking self-righteous. I would still be in Ibiza, living the life I loved there. No one would have been any the wiser.

Not for the first time I considered that maybe I should have killed him. It would have made life simpler. I'd had the perfect alibi in Andre, who'd taken me to the airport to fly to England.

The trouble was I'd had a soft spot for Nico. But the very real risk of him going to the police and them coming after me was enough motivation to keep moving. The sooner I left Spanish territory behind me and headed into France, the less likely it was that anyone would catch up with me.

The following evening, I crossed the border and headed for Collioure. As I set eyes on the picturesque town and my beloved Mediterranean Sea again, I felt my spirits lift. With the holiday season still in full swing, there was a buzz here.

As Hannah Price began to establish herself, I was very soon starting to feel at home. A month on, the summer crowds were subsiding and slowly the town was beginning to change. From various vantage points in the cafes and bars I frequented, I soon worked out who was local   as did they, as I found myself gravitating towards a bar that overlooked the harbour. Run by a woman who I guessed was a little older than I was, I often stopped there for coffee and a croissant.

'I have seen you here a lot,' she said to me one morning. In a patterned shift dress, her shoulder-length brown hair glinted where the sun caught it.

'I arrived a few weeks ago. I'm writing a set of pieces about travelling in France. I'm Hannah.' I held out my hand.

'Colette.' Her eyes were warm as she shook my hand. 'Are you staying long?'

I smiled back at her. 'I'm hoping for the winter, or maybe longer. I haven't decided yet. It's beautiful here.'

'It is. But I am glad the summer is over. We have been busy.' She paused. 'I don't know if you have anywhere to stay, but I have a room upstairs I want to rent out for a few months. Well, probably until Easter. Are you interested?' She named a price that seemed ridiculously cheap.

It was a nice part of town, and close to the sea. Plus I liked it when things like this happened seemingly effortlessly. 'Could I see it?'

She nodded. 'I have an appointment in a minute. But if you come back tonight, I'll show you.'

I idled away the day, taking photos and creating arty-looking Instagram posts, suddenly remembering it was days since I'd checked the news. Clicking onto an Ibiza news feed, I felt my blood run cold. Not only had Nico spoken to the police about me after all, but they were now out looking for an English woman in her early twenties with long fair hair, who'd been recently seen in Ibiza Town. Posing as a house sitter in a luxury villa, she was also wanted in connection with the murder of the villa owner's housekeeper.

Feeling my head spin, I took a deep breath, reassuring myself that there was nothing to link me to Margot or Ibiza. I didn't look anything like her anymore. I didn't even sound like her. There was absolutely nothing for me to worry about.

When I went back to Colette's that evening, she showed me the room. It was large and airy, with views of the harbour and its own bijou bathroom.

'It's frigging amazing,' I said, Hannah-style. 'How much rent would you like up front?'

After paying her a month, I took the keys and went back to my hotel to pick up my stuff. It was the smartest thing I could have done, as it turned out. Not only was Colette's bar open all winter. It was where the expats gathered and as Hannah Price quietly integrated herself, in no time, everyone had forgotten she'd just arrived here.

With a new persona established as well as a base, the need to plan longer term was starting to niggle at me, as was a way of making money. But even that was going my way, as with Christmas on the horizon, the town was getting festive. As the bars grew busy again, I started working for Colette. It was just the sort of thing Hannah would turn her hand to – pouring drinks and waiting tables; helping out her new friend; quietly making herself indispensable.

One evening just before Christmas, Colette came and knocked on my door.

'I've been meaning to ask you, Hannah, are you going to England for the holiday?'

I shook my head. 'I don't have anyone to go back for. My mum died,' I explained. 'For all kinds of reasons, I'm not in touch with my dad.'

'Then you must spend it with us,' she said firmly.

I hedged. 'I can't. You have your family coming.'

'And friends, too,' she insisted. 'We will be about twenty-five. We would love you to join us.' She raised one of her eyebrows. 'Plus, I would really like your help.'

I gave in. I'd never seriously intended to refuse her offer. 'OK. Merci bien mon ami!'

When I'd spent many a Christmas alone, it was wonderful to be included in this gathering of family and friends. On Christmas Eve, I worked in the kitchen with Colette preparing the food, so that on the day, it kept coming – one delicious course after another, the wine chosen accordingly, all in an atmosphere of warmth and celebration.

'Where is Leo?' I heard Colette say more than once. 'He's late! He promised he was coming.'

Other than a vague family connection, I'd no idea who Leo was. But when at last he walked in, I froze. Either I was hallucinating or this was some kind of sick joke.

I watched the man I knew as Andre go from person to person, shaking their hands, kissing them on both cheeks. Quietly, I got up before he noticed me and slipped away. What the fuck was he doing here?

Upstairs in my room, I contemplated my options. Either I ran while I still could, or I stayed and brazened it out. I felt angry suddenly. Just when I thought my life was settling down, fate had thrown me one of its curveballs. Except . . . if Andre went by more than one name, clearly I wasn't the only one with an interesting past.

To hell with it. Checking my makeup, I went back downstairs to join the party. Going back to my place at the table, it wasn't long before I heard a voice behind me.

'Mind if I join you?'

Hearing the familiar voice, my skin prickled. As I turned around, he started to smile, before his face froze and a look of contempt registered in his eyes.

'Hi Leo,' I said slightly sardonically. 'I don't think we've met before. I'm Hannah.'

His eyes glinted at me. 'You should be more careful about covering your tracks.'

*

Guessing he might be in touch with Nico, I had to find out what his agenda was. Half an hour later, huddled in my coat, I sat outside with Leo on a bench overlooking the harbour. In darkness lit by twinkling lights behind us, I was unnerved. 'Before we go any further, one question. Are you Andre or Leo?'

'Are you Margot or Hannah?' He paused. 'I'm guessing you probably know that Nico reported you to the police. He thinks you gave him Rohypnol. Other than going to the villa, he has no recollection of that evening.'

'He was lucky,' I told him, remembering the heroin I'd thought about giving him. 'It would have been a lot worse if I hadn't liked him.'

'I'd hate to see what you do to your enemies.' He spoke with icy calm.

'That's for you to guess at and me to know.' I gazed out across the water. 'How do you know Colette?'

'She's married to my cousin,' he said briefly. 'You never had any intention of chartering that boat, did you?'

But I wasn't Margot anymore. I got into part. 'I'm not into boats. I think you're confusing me with someone else.'

Shaking his head, he lapsed into silence.

I looked at him. 'Why didn't you mention that it wasn't your boat?'

Throwing back his head, he laughed, a cynical sound. 'That's rich, coming from you. You're not the only one who's perfected the art of creating the perfect illusion.' As he turned towards me, his

241

face was wary. 'You know, so many times I thought you'd rumbled me.'

'Well, I hadn't. Of course, I know now the real story is you were employed to run the boat and charter it for ludicrous prices. But what you were really doing was looking for connections to wealthy people and opportunities to take their money.'

'Just like you.' He shook his head. 'Pity we hadn't known. We could have joined forces. It would have been a lot of fun.'

I was silent for a moment. 'So what now?'

'I am Leo and you are Hannah.' He shrugged. 'We met briefly once, a while back. I'm going to ask you to dinner and you're going to accept graciously.'

Not sure I wanted more than a fleeting association with him, I frowned. 'What if I don't?'

'You're forgetting, I know a lot about you,' he said smoothly.

'Ditto,' I said warningly.

'True.' He paused. 'But at least I haven't killed anyone.'

'You're forgetting, Leo. You're short of facts. You also have no proof.' He was starting to annoy me. 'There is nothing to connect Hannah Price to either Margot or Ibiza. Whatever you might think, I've covered my tracks. As far as anyone knows, Margot Jameson is hiding out somewhere on the island. The border forces have no record of her leaving.'

'Very smart. So who did leave?'

Getting up, I was done with being questioned. 'Do you really think I'm going to tell you that? I'm going inside. Are you coming?'

*

I should have listened to my instincts when it came to Leo – or Andre as I found myself calling him. But not sure that he wouldn't shop me, too soon I felt myself being sucked into his game of cat

242

and mouse. So much for trying to build some semblance of normal life. With Andre intent on bringing me down to his level, it was impossible.

'There's a party, Hannah,' he said authoritatively. 'Come as my guest.'

'No thanks.' Outside the bar, I didn't want to be associated with him.

'Let me ask you again.' This time, he sounded menacing. 'I need a date, that's all. Given what I know about you, it is not much to ask.'

'Fine. But no funny stuff.' I ignored the glint in his eye.

After borrowing a dress from Colette, I pinned up my hair, and spritzed myself with some of the perfume I'd pilfered.

'You look very beautiful.' When Colette was the epitome of elegance, it was praise indeed.

Somehow Andre had procured a vintage Aston Martin for the occasion. Heading away from the town, I buried my misgivings about the evening as we followed a road that twisted into the hills. As the house came into view, I was gobsmacked and as we pulled up outside, heads were already turning to look at us.

As we got out of the car, the views were breathtaking. Looking down towards the sea, the lights of Collioure twinkled against the majestic backdrop of the Pyrenees. Threading my arm through Andre's, we made our way up the steps to the ornate door, hesitating a moment before stepping into a hallway obscured by flowers.

Wandering through to the ballroom, I couldn't take my eyes off the priceless art adorning the walls. Beside me, I was aware of Andre smiling.

'How the fuck did you get yourself invited here?' I muttered to him.

'Connections, Hannah. Watch and learn.' Noticing an older man, he went over and introduced himself. 'Leo Matisse.' He pretended to frown. 'I'm sure we've met before.' He pretended to think. 'Countess Savana's Midsummer Party? But forgive me. I'm forgetting myself. This is Hannah.'

Taking my hand, the man kissed it. 'Enchanté.'

As he proceeded to engage me in conversation, Leo put a hand on his back. Then as I watched, he slipped a hand into one of the man's pockets.

I felt sick. Since arriving in Valencia and deciding to play it straight, this blatant contradiction was making me nauseous. This wasn't even a con. Andre was nothing but a common thief. Making my apologies, I made my way outside.

'Wait,' he called after me as he caught me up. I kept walking. 'I don't want a part of this. It isn't how I want to live anymore.'

'Drop the holier than thou act,' he said sharply. 'You've killed someone, Hannah-Margot. All I've done is to appropriate some of the obscene wealth in this world that we both know is in dire need of redistributing.'

'I don't want any part in it,' I said firmly.

'But you're not going to shop me, either, because you know, don't you, that as far as anyone at the party's concerned, you're my accomplice.' He spoke quietly, dangerously.

I remained silent, knowing that for now at least, I was stuck with him. The bottom line was, Andre knew far too much about me. But that night, I couldn't sleep. Instead, I lay awake, wondering how I was going to get out of this, my mind churning relentlessly – until at last I found the solution.

'Here's how it is,' I said to Leo-Andre the next morning. 'You see, I have inside info that you met Nico at the villa that night. He'd found out you were scamming people, overcharging them and keeping the additional profit for yourself.' Watching his face turn pale, I knew I'd struck a nerve. 'I imagine if the owner of the boat found out, he'd want that money back. I know I would.'

'Your point is?' He spoke icily.

I shrugged. 'The deal is this. Fucking leave me alone, Leo or Andre or whatever you want to call yourself – I don't give a shit. Otherwise, I might just make a call to your employer. Planning to go back next year, were you? When he's heard what I have to say, he won't touch you with a bargepole.'

'Bitch,' he hissed.

'Touché.' I raised an eyebrow, feeling calmer now that I was back in control. Draining my coffee cup, I got up, passing him the bill. 'Your round, I believe. I'm off. I have more important things to do.'

I was walking away when I heard him push his chair back. The next second I felt his hand grip my arm.

'You haven't heard the last of this.'

Gone was what I used to think of as the charming host with the luxury boat. His eyes were malevolent, his voice menacing as his grip tightened.

'I want you to know how it is to feel frightened, Hannah Price. Powerless, terrified for your life. Everything Giuseppe's housekeeper must have felt.'

I stopped short of telling him that she probably wouldn't have felt a thing well, not much after the water closed over her head Staring back at him, I tried to stay calm, to hide the fluid fear that filled my veins. In that moment I knew that if Andre was going to stay here, this town simply wasn't big enough. I'd have to move again. I didn't want to walk down the streets, terrified of seeing him, fearful of whatever stunt he was planning to pull next.

20

Ana

While I wait for the fallout of what I've told the police, I'm driven to learn more about Katharine. Online, I find her LinkedIn profile. I study the photo of the woman with warm eyes who bears little resemblance to the brittle widow I observed at the funeral.

Clicking on the link to her website, I read a contrived profile about her qualifications and her interest in helping people, before my eyes scan the testimonials that she probably wrote herself. I think about reporting her. If she can't see what's under her own nose, how can she possibly assist other people?

It occurs to me to check if she genuinely is a therapist. I look up the BACP register, but to my surprise, as I scan through it, there is no record of her. Staring at the photo on her website again, I take in dark lashes, smooth hair, high cheekbones. She's an attractive woman on the surface, giving nothing away about the person who lies beneath.

It has crossed my mind that Oliver had lied about her –

that maybe he and Katharine were simply a mismatch; a marriage that shouldn't have happened. In blaming their problems on her, he had absolved himself of guilt. But when he had nothing to gain by being anything other than honest with me, it doesn't make sense.

Still unconvinced, I stare at her photo.

Who are you, Katharine McKenna?

As I carry on searching, I find a photograph taken at their wedding in an archived copy of an online glossy magazine. There's no denying Katharine looks beautiful in her elegant dress, that Oliver looks breathtakingly handsome. The venue is stunning – an ancient castle bedecked in climbing roses. I swallow the lump in my throat. Even on that day, there was a guarded look about him. It's hardly surprising, given his monstrous family. Under the photo, a brief paragraph describes *the fairy-tale marriage of Katharine Armstrong and Oliver McKenna.*

But when I google Katharine Armstrong, I find little other than a mention of her graduation from Canterbury University. Finding her Facebook page, I scroll through her photos. The oldest are a couple of landscape shots obviously taken on holiday, but the earliest that feature people date from after she and Oliver met. Reading her posts, it's the same.

It's almost as though she's deliberately erased everything that came before. But why would she do that? I pause for a moment, uncomfortable, thinking of my own past, the social media profiles I've taken down from public view. Anyway, I'm probably wasting my time. These days, people use Facebook less and less. Given the chance, most of us have episodes we'd rather leave behind.

Given their family wealth, I wouldn't mind betting Oliver's father had her checked out, and if there were any skeletons in her closet, no doubt he would have found them. Thinking of him, I shudder. I'd already known from Oliver what kind of man he was, but when I met him after the funeral, everything about him repulsed me. His overpowering air of self-assuredness, the way he looked at me; the absence of obvious grief given his son had just died.

I find it hard to imagine what Jude ever saw in him – until I realise it's obvious. She was after his money, as no doubt Katharine was after Oliver's. Out of curiosity again, I google Richard, finding pages of links to businesses he's been involved in, numerous photos showing him shaking the hands of the rich and famous. Richard McKenna clearly has his fingers in many pies, and I wouldn't mind betting that not all of them are above board. In my experience, people like him tend to have a sparse relationship with social media, but to my surprise, when I click on his Facebook, he turns out to be an exception. Scrolling down, there are photos of family and social occasions, accompanied by pseudo-affectionate comments, spinning out the facade of a network of old friends and a close, united family.

The word *hypocritical* comes to mind as I continue searching, stopping at one of the photos. Something about it looks wrong. As I stare more closely, I check the date. It's October 2018 – a photograph of Richard at a dinner standing next to a colleague. But it's the women in the background I'm looking at.

Shocked, I realise one of them is Katharine. Her hair is shorter, a little lighter than in the other photos; her long dress casual in style compared to the minimal elegance she dresses with now. The date is definitely before she and Oliver met. So what was she doing with Richard?

Surely this has to be more than coincidence. I wonder if that was when she first set her sights on the McKenna family. Reading the post, the evening is described as a charity dinner to raise funds for St Margaret's, a local hospice. I take in the grand surroundings, the beautifully set tables and lavish flower arrangements. The money they cost would surely have been better spent donated to the cause?

Curious to know what Katharine's connection had been, I look up St Margaret's Facebook, and start paging back through the posts. The charity dinner appears to be an annual affair. At last reaching 2018, I go more slowly, then stop. There are twenty photos of that evening, and it isn't long before I find one of Katharine, then to my astonishment, another of her with Richard. Side by side, they're smiling into the camera. Underneath, there's a comment.

We are grateful for the support of local businessman Richard McKenna, seen here with Katharine Armstrong, representing another generous beneficiary, Skyro, an airline operated by a subsidiary of . . .

My mouth falls open. There's no way Katharine would have been in any doubt about Richard's wealth. But it's the mention of *Skyro* – the company Oliver had applied for a job with. Surely he must have known Katharine used to work for them. So why he didn't mention it to me?

As everything about this family gets stranger by the moment, unease passes over me. Any one of them could have a motive for wanting Oliver out of the way – Katharine, with her marriage in tatters, making sure she got her hands on his money; drifty Joe, coveting his brother's wife – with

Oliver dead, there'd be nothing to stop him making his move. Even Richard – if he'd discovered the problems Oliver was having, he'd probably rather he was dead than have the world know the truth about what he would undoubtedly have perceived as his son's failings. The only person I'm not so sure about is Jude.

If only I knew what Oliver had been keeping to himself. I think about telling the police about these photos, before deciding to wait in case anything else comes up. But I've learned from experience, there are times you can't sit back. You have to act.

Suddenly restless, I make a decision. Getting up, I pull on my boots and find my coat. Outside, I walk purposefully down my road towards the sea. I need to find Joe, Oliver's brother. If he's as weak as Oliver suggested he was, when it comes to getting any inside information, he has to be my best hope.

The McKennas' house is at the opposite end of Deal, and as I walk along the seafront, the air is cold, damp with a hint of drizzle. I breathe in the salty freshness, hoping Joe's in, wondering how he'll react when I turn up at the family home. It's oddly quiet today, the grey sky befitting my mood, the pavement devoid of the usual cyclists and skateboarders, as now and then I turn to take in the sea, its green-grey shades merging with the sky, so that it's impossible to tell where one ends and the other begins.

Forty minutes later, I turn up the road where the McKennas live. It's a wide street, where impressive-looking houses are set back up perfectly maintained driveways, separated from each other by ancient trees. It's the first time I've seen their house and as I gaze at it from the road, it has grandeur in an old-money kind of way. Understated, one half of it is clad with strands of creeper, but on first glance, it's the proportions that give it away. The generous windows; the stone steps leading up to a porch flanked with columns; the huge wooden door in its weathered frame.

I feel a pang of sadness as I imagine Oliver growing up here, rattling around in its cavernous rooms as he absorbed the dysfunctional parenting of Richard and Jude. Glancing at my watch, knowing it's a weekday, I imagine Richard will be at work. Jude, too, but I can't be sure. I hesitate. The last thing I want is to come face to face with Richard again.

But having come here, I have to do this. It takes all my courage as I take a deep breath, before walking up the steps and ringing the doorbell. For a minute, nothing happens. But then the door opens.

I saw him at the funeral, but up close, the likeness to Oliver is startling. In jeans and a long-sleeved t-shirt, Joe wears a guarded look.

'Can I help you?'

'I hope so.' I pause. 'I wanted to talk to you about your brother. You see . . .'

But before I finish, he's already shaking his head. 'I'm not speaking to the press.' Stepping back, he starts to push the door closed.

'I'm not press.' Seeing him hesitate, I go on. 'You'll definitely want to talk to me, Joe.' I pause, holding his gaze. 'I'm Ana Fontaine.'

21

Ana

Now that I have Joe's attention, I relax slightly. 'I just want a few minutes of your time. That's all.'

As I study him, he's less like Oliver than I initially thought. His hair is a shade darker, his eyes less intense.

'You have a nerve, coming here.'

I have to persuade him. 'Surely you must be curious.'

He hesitates a moment, before standing back. 'There are a few things I'd like to ask you, too. I suppose you should come in.'

I shake my head. Setting foot onto McKenna turf was never the plan. 'Not really. I was thinking we could go for a walk.'

He goes back inside and I wait, peering through the cracked-open door, taking in the plush carpet, the warm glow coming from a lamp in the hallway, until he comes back wearing a jacket. Tying a scarf around his neck, he closes the door behind him.

'This is very weird.' As we walk down the road, his hands are in his pockets.

'It is.' At the end, we cross over and head for the beach.

'Is it true you met my brother at an AA meeting?' Joe sounds guarded.

'Yes.'

'Didn't he tell you he was married?' he says accusingly.

Suddenly I'm wondering if I was rash to come here. 'Yes. He did.' I take a deep breath. 'But he clearly wasn't happy. He wanted someone to talk to and I suppose I thought I was helping him.'

'Screwing up his marriage, more likely,' Joe says tersely. 'Assuming everything you've said is true.'

'I haven't lied to anyone.' On the defensive, I remember what Oliver told me. 'And if you're talking about screwing up his marriage, I'm not sure you're entirely blameless.' In the brief silence that follows, I know I've touched a nerve. 'Oliver and Katharine . . .' I hesitate, wondering how much to say. 'Let's just say, when he needed support, there wasn't any.'

'So why have you come here?' Joe's jaw is set.

'Too many unanswered questions,' I say quietly. 'I didn't know what else to do.'

'You're not wrong about that.' He seems to drop his guard slightly.

I take the opportunity to tell him what's on my mind. 'I don't know what you're thinking, but from where I am, so much about your brother's death doesn't add up. I'm sure Katharine thinks it was me who tampered with the brakes, but I wouldn't have a clue how to do anything like that.' I pause. 'I'm guessing she must hate me.'

Joe nods slowly. 'What do you expect? She's lost her husband – she's had a tough time of it. She'll be OK. She needs to deal with Oliver's financial affairs, but once they're out of the way,' he shrugs, 'I guess it will get easier.'

'It's never easy losing someone.' I force myself to focus, to suppress the memories that are never far beneath the surface. 'I don't know if you were aware, but there was something nagging at Oliver. He refused to talk to me about it. He said it was because it involved other people. I've been going around in circles trying to figure out what it was. It's one of the reasons I've come here, to ask you if he'd hinted at anything.' But even if he had, Joe wouldn't have noticed. He would have been too busy ogling Katharine.

'I hadn't,' Joe says carefully. 'What were the others?'

'Sorry?'

'The other reasons you've come here.'

I think about asking him what he knows about Katharine and Oliver's marriage. But if he's in love with her, I can't imagine he'll want to hear what Oliver said about her. Not wanting to put his back up when he's already cagey, I give it a miss. 'There's just one, really. It's probably nothing . . . but did you know Katharine already knew your father before she and Oliver met?'

'I don't think so,' Joe sounds remarkably unfazed. 'If they had, I'm pretty sure one of them would have mentioned it. What are you suggesting?'

Does this man not get worked up about anything? 'I'm not suggesting anything,' I say lightly. 'I'm just stating facts, and I'm curious. There is one thing I have found out, though. Did you know that Katharine used to work for Skyro, the company Oliver had started working for?'

'What exactly are you trying to get at?' Joe sounds irritated. At last, a reaction from him. 'I genuinely don't know if it's relevant to anything. I just wondered if you knew,' I persist.

'I didn't. But it's none of my business what Kat did before she and Oliver got together.'

'St Margaret's hospice Facebook page, charity fundraiser, 2018,' I tell him, guessing he won't be able to resist checking it out. 'Take a look. But you must have known he was offered another flying job?'

'Only because Dad found out. Oliver had kept a brochure about a flying training course. It was in a drawer in a desk he used to use. Dad did some digging around into who operated the aircraft type. There aren't that many of them in the UK. Then somehow he found out one of them had offered Oliver a job.' He frowned. 'When he told us about it, Kat didn't mention she used to work there.'

'Strange, don't you think?' It's like taking candy from a baby as he reveals yet another layer of deception. 'Sounds like your brother wasn't the only one with a secret,' I say lightly. 'Maybe you should ask her about it.'

He's silent for a moment. 'Why did you tell the police I was in love with Kat?'

'Because it's true, isn't it?' I frown. 'I don't understand this aversion to the truth you all seem to have. It drove Oliver mad. Why can't you just be honest?'

But Joe won't be drawn. 'Why did he leave you all that money?'

'I don't know. I didn't know he had until his solicitor got in touch.' It's what I told the police, even if it isn't quite true. Oliver had expressed his concern that he didn't want his wife to have it more than once. 'Presumably he's left Katharine well provided for.'

'I'm not sure that's something I should be discussing with you.'

'Fair enough.' Getting the feeling our conversation is drawing to a close, I pull my coat more tightly around me. 'Cold, isn't it?'

'Why don't you give me your mobile number?' Joe says suddenly.

I shake my head slowly. 'Probably best not to. I know where you are. If I need to talk to you again, I'll come and find you.'

As I walk away, I'm no closer to knowing what was going on. But it's an interesting twist that no one talks about Kat's old job. Maybe something went wrong and she left in awkward circumstances. But after our conversation, I wouldn't mind betting Joe will ask her.

22

Katharine

That evening, after Joe texts me to tell me he's on his way over, I'm on edge as I wait for him. But these days, I'm almost constantly on edge. Pouring myself a drink, I check my emails. Seeing one from our mortgage company, I open it, feeling horrified as I read it.

Reading it again to make sure there's no mistake, I hear Joe's car pull up outside, before the door opens and closes again as Joe lets himself in.

'Hey,' he says quietly. 'How's it going?'

'Not so good.' My heart is racing. 'Take a look at this.'

Pulling out a chair, he comes and sits next to me. 'When did this arrive?'

'Just now.' I turn to look at Joe. 'It says our mortgage is in arrears. According to this, the monthly payments haven't been kept up.' I frown. 'But the payments have been going out. I'm sure they have. If something was wrong, they should have let me know before.'

'Have you searched your emails?'

I shake my head, already typing the name of the mortgage company into the search bar.

'You are sure the mortgage is in both your names?'

'Yes. I showed you the paperwork. Unless . . .' I try to think. 'Oliver must have arranged for all correspondence to be sent to him. I didn't receive anything until I contacted them and told them about his death. I'm going to check our account again.'

Opening another window, I log in to our joint bank account and study the list of transactions. 'Look.' Relieved, I point them out to Joe. 'The payments have been going out, for the same amount as usual. The mortgage company must have made a mistake.'

'Why not call them?' Joe suggests.

I'm already picking up my phone. Fortunately I don't wait long before I'm put through to an adviser. But my relief is short-lived. After explaining the problem and listening to what she says, I'm light-headed.

'You're kidding.' But as I listen, she assures me there's been no mistake. 'Can you leave it with me? I'll call you back tomorrow.'

Ending the call, I look at Joe. 'She said the house has been re-mortgaged and the mortgage payments have trebled. Oliver must have done it without me knowing. Apparently they've been sending him emails which he hasn't responded to. Why would he have done this?' But then the penny drops. 'I get it.' Hatred fills me for my husband, for the woman he betrayed me for. 'He's been moving all his money, hasn't he?' I shake my head in disbelief. 'After I pay off the mortgage, there's going to be next to nothing left.' I feel myself start to panic. 'What am I going to do?'

'Let me sort out what's outstanding.' Joe speaks quietly. 'You can pay me back when you either have access to Oliver's money, or if necessary sell the house.'

I shake my head. 'You can't do that.' It isn't for Joe to sort out this mess.

'Look, it's my brother who's screwed you over. I have the money in the bank. If it's too much for you to cover, I'd like to help you with this.'

'I hate this.' But I make the decision quickly. 'If you could, it would really help, Joe. I'll pay you back as soon as I can.'

Getting out his phone, he busies himself, before a couple of minutes later, he looks up. 'It should be in your joint bank account. If I were you, I'd pay them straight away. It'll be one less thing for you to worry about.'

'Thank you,' I say quietly.

'You're welcome.' But he looks slightly preoccupied. 'Why don't you do it now, then we can talk.'

As I make the payment, I wonder what it is he wants to talk about. Once it's done, I close my laptop. 'Glass of wine?'

'In a bit.' He sounds hesitant. 'Kat, I need to tell you something. I met Ana Fontaine earlier.'

A rushing sound fills my ears. '*You what?*'

'She came to the house. She must have worked out that Mum and Dad would probably be at work. She wanted to talk. She said there was something on Oliver's mind before he died. She wanted to know if I knew what it was.'

Getting up, I go over to the window, trying to take it in. 'What's she like?' I say at last.

'Normal. Average. Not what I was expecting.' Joe pauses. 'She'd been digging into Oliver's past. Dad's, too.'

A frown crosses my face. 'What for?'

'She's looking for answers.' Gazing at me, he drops a killer blow. 'When you and Oliver met, you'd already met Dad, hadn't you?'

A cold feeling comes over me as I wonder where he's going with this. I think about denying it. But something in the way he's looking at me changes my mind. 'I knew who he was,' I say shortly.

'So why the secrecy? I remember the big family evening the first time Oliver brought you over. Wouldn't it have been more natural to say you'd met before, even if it was only briefly?'

'It wasn't anything. I didn't want to bring it up, because I honestly didn't expect him to remember me. I was a secretary. We were introduced, said hello, before he moved on to the next person. I didn't really know your father, and coming to the house that first time was a little intimidating.'

'You know, I could actually buy into that, Kat.' Joe pauses. 'But why didn't you tell me you used to work for Skyro?'

I feel sick all of a sudden. As I look at him, there's an expression of distrust on his face. 'They fired me, Joe. For something I didn't do. I was ashamed, if you really want to know. The last thing I wanted was to talk about it.'

'But presumably Dad knew.' Joe shakes his head. 'Ana found a photo, Kat. It was of Dad at some charity dinner a few years back, raising funds for St Margaret's. There are quite a few of them on Facebook. The thing is . . .'

'What?' Dreading what's coming, I steel myself.

Joe looks unhappy. 'When she said you were in the photo, I didn't believe her, so I looked. There are a couple. One where you're in the background, but in the other one, you and Dad are standing side by side. If you like, I'll show you.'

But he doesn't need to. The whole episode had been a nightmare, one I'd desperately wanted to leave behind. But I should have known these photos would come back to haunt me. I glance at the photos Joe has screen-grabbed.

No one knows how hard it's been for me since that time. How meeting Oliver felt like a lifeline; the start of a future I'd only ever dreamed about. Damn Ana Fontaine, coming into my life and ruining it. 'Look, we only met the once, briefly, as I said, at the charity dinner. His company and Skyro were major donors to the hospice. I was only there because at the last minute, someone was ill and my boss invited me. Honestly I'd be surprised if your father even remembers it.'

'Oh, I'd say he'll remember all right.' Joe looks ashen. 'You have, haven't you? I don't understand the big secret, Kat. That faked shock when Dad told us that Skyro had been involved in smuggling illegal firearms.'

'All right. So I did know about that.' Sighing, I think back to the episode that changed everything. 'If you really want to know, it was the whole reason things blew up with my job. I tried to talk to my boss, to persuade him that what they were doing was wrong. But instead of listening, he fired me.'

'Really?' Sitting back, as Joe studies my face, I'm not at all sure he believes me. As he goes on, there's sarcasm in his voice. 'It will be interesting to see what Dad has to say. All this stuff going on in the background . . . if Oliver found out, it's hardly surprising things weren't great between you, or that he had a drink problem.'

As he shakes his head, suddenly I'm frightened. Joe's the one person I've always believed I could count on to have my back, to see my side of events.

'Tell me the truth, because I'd really love to know. Are you actually a therapist, Kat? Or is that another of your lies?'

I've never heard Joe talk like this before – cynical, untrusting. 'Of course it's true. You know I am, Joe. I haven't lied about anything else. I haven't lied about *this*. I just haven't talked about it. Surely you can see that?' I plead.

'I thought you trusted me enough to be honest,' he says gently. 'But right now, I'm not sure what to think.'

'I know how it looks.' I blink away the tears in my eyes. 'I went through a really tough time, Joe. I'm not like you. I had no home, no parents to go back to. The episode with Skyro was horrible and traumatic. I was made to feel as though I'd done something wrong, when the reverse was true. Being treated that way by an employer . . . even when you know you're innocent, it stays with you. Do you have any idea what that's like?' I pause for a moment. 'After, as well as alone, I was unemployed. It was part of the reason I started to train as a therapist. I needed to make a positive change in my life.'

Joe's silent for a moment, before raising his eyes to mine. 'I'm just sad you didn't feel you could trust me.'

'I told you about Oliver being abusive,' I blurt out.

'Was that actually true? Really?' Getting up, as he stands there, his eyes bore into me. 'I'm going out for a bit. I need some space.'

'Joe?' I swallow. 'Thank you for helping me. I do appreciate it. And I'm sorry if you feel I've been deceiving you. It was never my intention.' Holding his gaze, I watch him soften slightly.

'You're welcome,' he says quietly. Picking up his phone, he takes his car keys out of his pocket.

As he turns and walks towards the door, I have to stop myself running after him and grabbing hold of him. But right now, there is no point. Instead, I listen to him close the door behind him, before he starts his car and drives away.

Sitting there, I'm not sure what to do next, before I do the only thing I can. I pick up my phone, my hands shaking as I make a call.

'Hello. It's me. Can we meet?'

2018

Hannah

Over the days that followed, I managed to stay out of Andre's way. But I knew it would only be a matter of time before he came to find me again. Two weeks had passed by the time one Friday night, he did exactly that.

Uninvited, he pulled out a chair and sat down, sitting in silence for a moment. 'I want you to do something for me.'

'Really.' It was amazing how much sarcasm you could load onto a single word. 'Give me one good reason why I should want to do anything for you.'

'This is different.' He rested his head in his hands. 'I'm ill, Hannah.' He paused. 'I'm dying.'

'Yeah, right. Nice try.' Did he really think I was going to fall for that?

I was about to get up, but something in his eyes stopped me.

'I'm not lying to you,' he said quietly. 'Not about something like this.'

Looking at him more closely, I noticed his eyes were red, with dark circles underneath them. He looked terrible, as if he hadn't slept since I last saw him.

'No one knows.' As he spoke, I noticed that even since I'd last seen him, the weight had fallen off him. He went on. 'A couple of years ago I found a mole. It was malignant. I had treatment and last year, I was well. You saw me. But very suddenly, I've started getting pain. And now . . .' Clenching his fists, he battled visibly with himself. 'This bastard cancer has not only returned. It seems to have spread.' His voice trembled.

As I sat there, my mind filled with doubts. Was he really ill or was he spinning me a line? And why confide in me of all people? But as I looked at him, I hated myself for even thinking that.

'It is true.' It was as though he'd read my mind. 'I will show you. This is from the hospital.' Getting out his phone, he brought up an email. From the hospital in Toulouse, it described the nature of his illness.

My hand went to my mouth. 'This is shit, Andre.'

'Probably what I deserve,' he said quietly.

'No one deserves this.' I tried to sound sympathetic. Then I frowned. 'You said you wanted to ask me to do something.'

He nodded. 'There is a treatment, in the USA. It is probably my only hope of surviving. Without it . . . I have a few months, if I'm lucky.'

I was starting to guess where this was going. 'And . . .'

'It is expensive, as you might expect. I need to find a hundred thousand dollars, Hannah. I don't know who else to ask. Will you help me?'

'How?' I folded my arms. Ordinarily I would have told him where to go, but knowing he was ill, I couldn't quite bring myself to.

'Criminally,' he said cryptically. 'I know how this makes you

268

feel. But I wouldn't ask if I wasn't desperate.' His eyes were wide as he stared at me. 'This is about my life.'

My instincts were telling me to walk away. 'I'm sorry, Andre. I know it's shit. But there's nothing I can do. I'm trying to sort myself out. I'm not getting involved in anything criminal.' Getting up, I turned to go.

His voice came from behind me. 'I had a message from Nico a few days ago.'

I froze. 'Saying what?'

'He was asking where I was. He was thinking he might come and visit his old friend.'

Disbelief filled me. The timing was too convenient. But if I was wrong and Nico was coming here, it would be disastrous. 'What did you tell him?'

'I haven't replied yet. But maybe I should invite him here. If I don't have long, it would be nice to have a familiar face around.'

My instincts were telling me to run, get far away from here. But I'd be trading my freedom for Andre's life; risking Andre going to the police. Could I really do that? 'If Nico comes to see you, you do know I'm going to be out of here.' My eyes were blazing as I looked at him. 'So what the fuck, Andre? What do you fucking want?'

The faintest glimmer of hope returned to his eyes. 'I have a plan.'

Andre knew someone, but Andre always knew someone. This was a woman who ran a catering business. I was to be employed for one night only, at a grand soirée for southern France's rich and famous.

'There's a small painting in one of the rooms – a miniature. It's nothing to look at. But there is someone I know who is willing to pay extremely good money for it. For centuries, it has passed between two families. Now it is time for it to exchange hands again.'

I really didn't like the sound of this. Getting caught between warring factions had never interested me. 'Is it alarmed?'

'You don't have to worry about that.' Andre waved his hand dismissively. 'There will be a distraction. An alarm is the last thing anyone will be taking notice of.'

I had to take his word for that. 'Andre . . .' I hesitated. 'How sure are you that this will give you the money you need?'

He bowed his head. 'It has been guaranteed.'

In any other circumstances, I would have said no. For all I knew, this was a set-up to beat all set-ups. But until I was ready to leave here, I couldn't chance Nico turning up.

Reluctantly, I agreed. The afternoon of the soirée, I pitched up at Andre's contact's warehouse. When I gave her my name, she nodded, her eyes lingering briefly on me before she passed me a uniform. Standing there while she briefed us about the service, in no time we were loading vans and on our way to the venue.

The house was imposing, with vast landscaped gardens; in prime position to take advantage of views of the Mediterranean. Inside, it was ludicrously, obscenely grand, symbolic of the kind of wealth I utterly detested. As we set up trays of glasses and platters of canapés, I watched the others closely, observing their mannerisms, the care and precision with which everything was done, so that by the time the guests started arriving, you wouldn't have known I wasn't one of them.

Andre had told me to wait until six minutes past eight. I was walking out with a tray of glasses when I heard a commotion outside. Putting down the tray, as everyone started to panic, I heard an explosion.

Glancing at my watch, I registered the time. Knowing this was my chance, as everyone fled outside, I ran back to the kitchen, taking the servants' stairs to the second floor, pausing briefly to check the coast was clear, before making it to the study where the miniature was.

Thirty seconds later, I was back outside, the miniature concealed under my uniform. Observing the pandemonium going on around the garden, I slipped out of the gate and disappeared into the night. It had been easy – too easy, almost. When Andre came to meet me later that evening, I handed him the miniature. 'Don't ask me to do anything like that again.'

As he raised one of his eyebrows, I really looked at him. The dark circles were gone from under his eyes, and instead the glint was back. I should have listened to my hunches. Andre wasn't ill. I wouldn't mind betting Nico hadn't been in touch, either. In my attempt to do the right thing, I'd been had.

'You bastard,' I said under my breath.

'That's no way to speak to a dying man,' he said sarcastically. 'Sit down, Hannah. I'll give you commission.'

'I don't want fucking commission,' I said furiously. 'I want to never have anything to do with you ever again.'

He jabbed me in the chest with one of his fingers. 'You fuck with people, expect to get fucked in return.'

'You're a jerk.' Getting up, I picked up my glass of red and threw it at him.

There was a deathly silence as he looked at me. 'You really shouldn't have done that.' His voice was menacing as he held up the miniature. 'You have ruined a piece of priceless art. You know what this means?'

But I was way past caring. 'I don't give a fuck. You tricked me, Andre. You brought it on yourself.'

'You don't understand.' There was fear in his eyes. 'There are many people involved. I owe money to the people who rigged the explosion. I was meant to pay them after handing this over. Look what you've done to it.' He thrust the soiled miniature in my direction.

'If I were you, I'd think about leaving the country.' I shrugged. 'Might be safer. And don't even think about putting this one on me. Oh, and just so you know, I've recorded our conversations.' I dangled my phone just out of his reach. 'An insurance policy, I think you'd call it. I left out the bit where I agreed, obviously. Something about your illness seemed a tad too convenient.' Not wanting to admit he'd caught me out, I was bluffing, hard.

His eyes were sorrowful. 'You have no idea what you've done.' The reality he wasn't going to get his money was clearly sinking in.

'Like I said, I don't give a fuck.' Getting up, I walked off.

Outwardly I may have looked calm, but underneath, I was seething — with Andre, for duping me; with myself for not seeing through him. But it was too late for recriminations.

I couldn't believe what a fool I'd been. When I came here, I'd really thought it was a chance to turn my life around. But now . . . this called for a major rethink.

I didn't rush into anything. What I did next would have to stand the test of time. Changing my name and appearance was the easy part. But when I yearned for a different way of life, what I really needed to change went much deeper.

I still had most of the money from the items of Giuseppe's I'd sold. Maybe it was time to cut my losses and head home.

On edge, I was preparing myself for some kind of comeback from Andre, reconciling myself to the uncomfortable truth that for as long as he was alive, I wasn't safe. In my mind, I killed him a thousand times. In the end, he made it easy for me, when a week later he begged me to meet him. He was desperate and I knew he'd decided I owed him.

I had it all worked out, leaving Colette's the back way so that no one saw me go. Everyone would be busy while lunch was going on. By the time it was over, I'd be back.

Walking out of town, I headed towards the little cove where I'd arranged to meet Andre. I had no qualms about what I had to do. Andre himself had made it a necessity. By the time I got there, he was sitting on the sand, waiting for me.

After the walk, sweat was pouring off me. 'I need to swim.'

'You're not going anywhere. We need to talk.' His voice was grim.

'Talk away.' I sat on the sand next to him.

'I have a shortfall of fifty thousand dollars.' He stared ahead of him.

'Surely someone like you can lay their hands on that kind of money. I mean, it's not that much, is it?'

He looked defeated. 'Do you have it?'

I shook my head. 'No, sadly.' I was silent for a moment. 'I've been thinking, Andre. It was never my intention to damage the miniature. I was mad as hell at you for lying to me about being ill. You should never have done that. Anyway.' I knew I was taking a risk as I handed him the envelope that held most of my remaining money. 'It isn't fifty grand, but I want you to have it.'

There was a look of disbelief on his face as he took it. 'I misjudged you.'

'Unlike you, I have principles,' I snapped. 'Take it or leave it. It's up to you.'

I watched him count it, waiting for him to take the bait as I started peeling off my clothes.

'This helps,' he said quietly. 'Thank you. Now it's me who owes you.'

'I prefer it that way, and maybe there is something you can do, but first I need to cool down. Coming for a swim?'

Lured by the turquoise water, Andre took off his t-shirt, before running towards the sea and diving under the surface. I followed more sedately, waiting until I was under the water to remove the pocket knife I'd hidden inside my bikini top. Catching him off guard, I knew he was distracted, thinking about the money. I was too quick; by the time he knew what I'd done, it was too late.

There was just one thing left to do. Unfastening his watch, I swam towards the shore. Wading onto the sand, I squeezed the water out of my hair. I hadn't expected Andre to fall for my plan so easily. I could only guess it was a measure of how desperate he was. The cove was private, the beach belonging to one of France's exclusive country houses, where no one was home – I'd checked. It would be a while before anyone found him.

Picking up my envelope of money, I got dressed and wrapped the knife in Andre's t-shirt, before heading along the beach, climbing out along some rocks to where the water was deeper, holding out the knife still wrapped in the t-shirt before throwing it in, watching until it disappeared from sight.

Breaking into a jog, fifteen minutes later I was back at Colette's, sneaking in without being seen and tiptoeing along to my room. After spending the rest of the afternoon there, that evening, when I went downstairs, Colette was behind the bar.

I faked a yawn. 'Do you have anything for a headache? I lay down for a bit. I've only just woken up but it hasn't shifted.'

'Poor you.' She looked sympathetic. 'I will get you a drink.' She picked up a glass. 'Wine?'

'I think just water,' I said pitifully. 'I'm still not feeling that well.'

I maintained the facade for the rest of the evening, but the next day, I was fine again.

*

It was a fishing boat that came across Leo's body. Mercifully it had drifted well away from Collioure. With nothing to identify him, another week passed before a photo was circulated and the police had a name.

'Poor Leo.' Colette was distraught. 'Who would do such a thing? Everyone loved him. He was one of those people who made you feel better just by being around. I'm going to miss him.'

It took all my self-control not to put her right; not to tell her he was a thieving, devious conman. 'I know.' I squeezed tears into my eyes. 'It really is so sad, Colette.'

'We have to think about his funeral.' She dabbed her eyes. 'After, everyone must come here.'

'Leo would have really appreciated that,' I said softly. 'I will help you.' Having granted myself a reprieve, it was the least I could do.

For all his fraudulent ways, Andre's funeral attracted a large turnout. Beside Colette, I displayed an appropriate level of sorrow, hiding the elation I felt. I really had killed two birds with one stone. In eradicating Andre, I'd also broken the remaining link between me and Nico.

After, at Colette's bar, I served drinks and trays of the food we'd prepared, using my role as waitress to scrutinise faces and eavesdrop on conversations, for snippets of rumours about what had happened to Andre. But according to popular opinion, the belief was he'd been mugged, most likely for his expensive Cartier watch, the same Cartier watch that was now hidden in my room.

With the funeral over, I took a walk past the harbour towards the beach. Sitting on the low wall, I gazed at the mountains, taking in the sweep of their soft green as they sloped down to meet the sea, while beneath me, the water was clear enough to make out the ripples in the sand on the sea bed.

I loved this place, the buzz of the town, the feeling that you were surrounded by the elements. With Andre gone, I'd planned to make it my home, but his death had left it tainted, his blood mingled forever with this beautiful clear water, so that all I knew was, I couldn't stay.

After this latest unfortunate event, I probably needed to move sooner rather than later. Where to, I'd yet to decide, but this time, I had to make sure there was no chance the past could catch me up again.

23

Ana

After talking to Joe, by the time I get back to my flat, dusk is falling. Locking the door behind me, I close the curtains before switching on a lamp that fills the room with soft light. Finding some classical music that Oliver and I used to listen to together, I curl up on the sofa and start listing what I know about his family, adding the unexpected link between his wife and his father; Katharine's determination to paint her own version of the story; the refusal of all of them to accept the truth.

This undercurrent of the unknown is the backdrop to the strangest of times, in which my life seems to be on hold, while too much stays unresolved. A restless night passes, the sound of the sea reaching me through the open window, the curtain billowing gently in the breeze. I'm awake early the following morning, still preoccupied when the police call to see me again. I show them into my sitting room.

'We've confirmed the third set of prints we've found in the car are yours,' DS Stanley says as she sits down.

'I thought you would.' When we'd been out in that car a number of times, it comes as no surprise to me.

'You've been causing a bit of a stir.' Her face is unreadable as she gets out her electronic notebook.

I gaze at her. 'I haven't done anything wrong.'

She gets straight to the point. 'I understand you found some Facebook photos.'

So they've been talking to Joe again. I wonder how news of this went down with Katharine. 'I take it you've seen them?'

'As a matter of fact, we have.'

'Do you believe in coincidence, Detective Sergeant?' I gaze at DS Stanley. 'Only it's some quirk of fate that Katharine worked for Skyro, the same company that Oliver was offered a job with. He never mentioned anything to me about Katharine working there, so I can only assume she hadn't told him.'

As I speak, I watch DS Stanley making notes, before turning to me again. 'Ms Fontaine, can I suggest you stay away from the McKenna family? I'm sure you have unanswered questions, as do we. But if you discover anything else, it might be better to contact us, rather than them.'

'If you think it's important, then absolutely. I don't know if you've tried to investigate Katharine's background,' I say cautiously. 'But it's very hard to find out anything about her. I only discovered her maiden name from the Facebook photo. Actually, that's not quite true. I found another photo online, of her and Oliver on their wedding day.' I remember something else. 'I thought I'd check the BACP register. They have a list of accredited counsellors and therapists. There's no Katharine McKenna on record. No Katharine Armstrong, either. You may already know that, but it's strange, don't you think?'

From their expressions, it's obvious they haven't yet thought to check. But I haven't finished. 'I know that Katharine's tried to create a picture of her marriage, but . . .' I hesitate. 'You should probably know that Oliver spent quite a lot of time here. She may have been under the impression that he was away on night-stops. I genuinely don't know what he told her. But he has clothes in the bedroom, toiletries in the bathroom.' My eyes fill with tears. 'Do you want me to show you? Only so that you know the reality,' I add.

'Very well.' Getting up, DS Stanley takes in the drawers I open, the contents of the bathroom, before sitting down again and making more notes.

As she finishes writing, I go on. 'There's something I've forgotten to mention before. I think I told you, I went to the funeral. I went to the wake, too, only briefly.' I know how weird it probably sounds, that I'd choose to be in the same room as Oliver's family. 'I left as soon as the family arrived back from the cremation. I didn't want anything to do with them. But before that, I got talking to a woman called Beatrice. She used to mind Oliver and Joe when they were young, until the McKennas fired her. I think she'd expressed her concerns at their style of parenting, or rather, non-parenting,' I add. 'It was an interesting conversation. Richard wasn't at all happy to see her there.'

DS Stanley looks interested. 'Do you have her full name?'

'No.' My hunch pays off. 'But what I do have is her mobile number.'

Making a note, when she looks up, she's frowning. 'It isn't

just Mrs McKenna's background we've been looking into.' She pauses. 'It's yours.'

A cold feeling comes over me. 'Mine? I have nothing to hide, I can assure you.'

'There's surprisingly little information available about you, too, Ms Fontaine. If that's your real name?'

My heart starts to race. I've been worried this might happen. 'There isn't much to know about me,' I summon as much dignity as I can. 'After my husband died, I moved here and changed my name. It was a very painful episode of my life that I'd rather not revisit, if it's all the same to you.' I wait with bated breath, praying she doesn't ask more.

'Was that when your problem with alcohol started?'

I grab the lifeline she's thrown me. 'Yes. Like I said, it wasn't a good time.'

But she hasn't finished. 'The truth is you don't own this flat, do you, Ms Fontaine?'

I look at her sharply. 'I don't think I ever said I did. You asked me if I was financially independent. I told you I was.'

DS Stanley frowns. 'We made some enquiries about owner-ship of your flat. It turns out Mr McKenna had approached the owner about buying it, but at the last minute, he pulled out.' She pauses. 'Why was that, Ms Fontaine? Was he getting cold feet about leaving his wife?'

Taking in the implications of what she's saying, my heart starts to race. I shake my head. 'It wasn't that,' I say quietly. 'He was thinking we should move further away.'

'Have you any proof of that? Any property details or meetings with estate agents?'

'No.' Aware of the accusatory nature of their questions,

I try to hide my unease. 'We hadn't got around to it yet. Oliver had enough going on.'

'According to what we've found out, you've had quite a lot going on, too, Ms Fontaine.'

I force myself to stay calm. 'I'm not sure I know what you're talking about.'

'I'm talking about France. Specifically four years ago, in a small town in the south,' she says quietly. 'I have a colleague over there. He recognised your photo instantly, just not your name.'

As memories start flooding back, it takes iron will to suppress them. Gazing at the police, my eyes fill with tears. 'If you already know what happened, you'll understand that there's nothing more I can say to you.'

After they leave, I'm shaken. I should have known when I came here, you can't outrun the past forever.

Going through to my bedroom, the pale curtains are open, the bed made up with soft cotton linen and as I look around, my eyes fill with tears. Everything in here is the same as the day Oliver was last here – his jumper still hanging over the chair, the drawer of t-shirts and socks, the shirts hanging in the wardrobe, the pile of books he'd picked up in a second-hand shop. It didn't matter that the flat was small, he'd told me. It was homely, something he'd never felt. It meant so much more to him than big rooms and expensive furniture. When he walked in, he felt he could be himself.

By the bed, there's a photo. It's of us, a selfie taken on the beach, six months to the day after we met. There's something akin to hope in Oliver's eyes. It corresponds to a time when for a while he was sober. But alcohol was his pressure release valve and when the stress inevitably ramped up again, sobriety didn't last.

I can't help wondering if Katharine's come clean about how little time Oliver had been spending with her, or whether in her deluded mind, he was simply away more. But from what I understood from Oliver, Katharine's take on most things had become questionable.

I've yet to look more closely at Skyro. Maybe they are the missing link in all this. Going back out to my sitting room, I take my laptop over to the table by the window. I start googling. *Skyro airline Oliver McKenna.* A random set of links come up, about Skyro taking delivery of new aircraft, about contracts they have with various businesses. Oliver's name doesn't come up, but when I add Katharine's name, I hit on something.

Secretary blamed for leak of confidential information. A previously unidentified whistle-blower has been named as Katharine Armstrong. Ms Armstrong is suspected of disclosing a contract detailing the export of allegedly illegal firearms. Her position has been suspended, pending further investigation. Skyro, the company who employ Ms Armstrong, have so far refused to comment.

Astonished, I read it again. If I was looking for something to incriminate Katharine, what I've found does completely the opposite. To stand up against something so obviously immoral, she must have balls.

Googling further, eventually I discover the identity of her boss, a Jonathon Myers. The name means nothing, but as I google him, it starts getting interesting again. Either it's my imagination, or there's more than a passing acquaintance between Richard McKenna and Jonathon Myers. But as I look more deeply, there are just as many links between these men and anyone else. And as everyone knows, it's a small world.

Gazing through the window down at the street, a figure of a man catches my eye. Stationary, he seems to be staring towards my flat. Making out his face, I shrink back.

What is Richard McKenna doing here?

Moving away from the window, my heart is racing again, but I've already worked it out. It's intimidation tactics – he's warning me off. As if it isn't enough that Oliver's left me the money, he would hate that I've been to the house, spoken to Joe.

Going to the door, I check that it's locked before sliding the bolt across. Then picking up my phone, my hands shake as I call the police. Keeping half an eye on his figure in the street, I wait only a minute before I'm put through to DS Stanley.

After the police visit this morning, I'm already on edge. I try to sound calmer than I feel. 'I don't know if it's anything, but Richard McKenna is outside in the street staring at my window. I'm worried he might try something.'

She doesn't hesitate. 'We'll send someone over. In the meantime, keep your door locked and don't let anyone in until we get there.'

Given the time it will take before the police arrive, her words do little to reassure me. Perched on the sofa, I'm on edge, terrified at any second I'll hear a knock on the door.

What feels like an eternity passes before I hear a woman's voice outside.

'Ms Fontaine? It's Constable Ramirez. Can we come in?'

Opening the door, I see her familiar face. Instead of DS Stanley, there's another uniformed officer I don't recognise.

'We've had a good look outside, but there's no sign of him.' She looks concerned. 'Are you OK?'

Relief that he's gone is tempered by the possibility that he'll come back. 'To be honest, I felt really intimidated. I imagine that was the intention.'

'Quite probably. He may have gotten wind of you finding those photos of him and Katharine.'

I'd guessed as much. 'As long as he doesn't come back.'

She shakes her head. 'If he does, call us immediately.'

After they leave, I lock the door again. Keeping my phone in my pocket, I'm still uneasy as I go through to the kitchen. What if Richard does come here? What if he tries to break in? But surely he wouldn't be stupid enough to take the risk of me calling the police. Putting the kettle on, I'm aware of my mind whirring as I try to distract myself. There has to be more information somewhere about Katharine. I just have to find it.

Settling in for the long haul, I close the curtains, moving my laptop over to the sofa. Sitting at one end, I put my feet up, resting my laptop in front of me. Then, opening Facebook, I type in Katharine Armstrong and start working my way through every last one of them.

24

Katharine

The conversation with Joe leaves me racked with guilt. It had been naïve of me to imagine the episode at Skyro would go away. Why couldn't have I been honest with him, told him how, sometimes in life, you have to take the rough with the smooth? That incident at Skyro was one such time, one I've tried to leave behind. But from within the confines of his privileged life, Joe can't see that. As another layer of my life is exposed, I start to wonder if there's any point in me staying here. There are too many memories, as well as all these possessions that Oliver and I chose together, that in the light of his deception I have no desire to keep.

Going around the house, I start photographing items to advertise on Marketplace. The Moroccan clock is first to go up, followed by the sofa, Oliver's sound system, the kitchen table, the chairs. The more I think about anything in this house, the less of it I want to keep.

Once I can access Oliver's affairs, I'll know where I stand. I'll also find out whether he'd taken out life insurance. But even without probate, as our house is in both our names, there's nothing to stop me putting it on the market – after what Joe said, I checked. Sitting down, I check out a list of local estate agents, before going upstairs and beginning to sort through my clothes, pieces I've carefully selected over the last few years. Uncharacteristically ruthless, anything I haven't worn in recent months, I place in a bag for the local charity shop. I do the same with my boots and shoes, then books, remembering how I felt when we moved in and I first unpacked them; swallowing my grief for the dreams I've lost.

I'm mid-sorting, the house in disarray, when the police turn up again. Irritation flares inside me as their car pulls into the drive, as I wonder what they want this time.

Going downstairs, I open the door to find DS Stanley and Constable Ramirez again.

'Mrs McKenna? May we come in?'

Without speaking, I stand back, closing the door behind them. 'The house is a mess. I'm sorting through what to keep and what to sell before it goes on the market.' Reaching the kitchen, I gesture to the table. 'Please.'

Nodding, DS Stanley sits next to her colleague. Her hair has been cut, and there are highlights that weren't there before. Suddenly aware that my own hair needs cutting, that it's a long time since I've made any effort with my appearance, I envy her the luxury of uncluttered time for such indulgences.

I pull out a chair opposite. Sitting down, I look at them. 'How can I help you?'

'A good question.' DS Stanley's quiet for a moment. 'Why didn't you tell us you worked for Skyro?'

While I should have been ready for this, I'm taken aback by her directness. 'It was years ago. It has no relevance to anything that's happened recently.'

'How sure are you about that?'

'Completely.' But it's obvious why she's asking. 'Have you spoken to Joe?'

Frowning, DS Stanley shakes her head. 'Not recently. But some new information has come to light.'

'Not from Ana Fontaine, by any chance?' I say sarcastically.

'As it happens, yes, though indirectly.' DS Stanley puts down her pen. 'There are some interesting photographs of you and Richard McKenna – taken, what, a year or two before you met his son?'

Knowing it must have been Joe who told them, I'm shaken, wondering what else he's told them. My heart starts to race as I shrug. 'I haven't mentioned it because there wasn't anything to tell. I honestly didn't expect Richard to have remembered it. Our paths crossed fleetingly. It's a small world, Detective Sergeant. These things happen.' Getting into my stride, I've had enough of their thinly veiled accusations.

'Did your husband know?'

I gaze at them both. 'I haven't a clue. I wasn't hiding anything. There wasn't anything to hide.'

'Except maybe this.' Passing me her notebook, she shows me a photograph of a press release.

But I don't need to read it. I feel cold all of a sudden. It seems wherever I go, whatever I do, it's only a matter of time before this awful chapter of my past catches me up. 'It's exactly as it looks. I lost my job for standing up for what I believed in. It didn't go down well.'

287

'Did your husband know? I mean, your principles were admirable.'

'I didn't talk about it.' I shake my head. 'I wanted to leave it behind. It wasn't an easy time. After losing my job, money was tight.'

'But of course, in this world of social media and Facebook, nothing ever really goes away, does it?'

'Clearly not,' I say shortly.

DS Stanley looks curious. 'What did you do before you worked for Skyro?'

I have a sudden yearning for a time when life was simpler. 'It depends how far you want to go back. I used to work in a school. When I left, I travelled. I went to Australia for a year. Then when I came back to the UK, I did whatever work I could get until Skyro offered me a job.'

'So how did you fit in training as a therapist?'

'During evenings and weekends. It wasn't easy. But I guess when you want to do something, you prioritise, don't you? I made the time.'

'And would you say your business is successful?'

I frown slightly. 'It has been, but more recently, it's been quieter.'

'I imagine you keep client notes?' She seems inordinately interested in my work all of a sudden.

I nod. 'All therapists do, but they're confidential.'

'I wasn't suggesting we look at them. But one thing does puzzle me. There's a BACP register of accredited counsellors. I was surprised to see you weren't on it.'

'It isn't a prerequisite,' I explain. 'When it comes to practising counselling, there are no laws, only guidelines.'

She sits back in her chair.

'Where did you train?'

'It was a course associated with Canterbury University.' I shake my head. 'If you check with them, they'll confirm I completed it. I don't see how any of this is relevant, though.'

'I can assure you it is, for one simple reason. We're trying to establish facts. But we're hearing two very different stories. Yours, that your marriage was going through a rough patch but was allegedly sound, while your husband, from what we've gathered, was building a life with Ms Fontaine, at the same time keeping a foot in the door here with you.'

I stand my ground. 'I'm still not convinced Ms Fontaine wasn't lying about him planning to leave me.'

DS Stanley looks disbelieving. 'Surely you had your suspicions? And now, of course, you know he wasn't flying these last two months. Isn't it plausible he was spending time with her? He's had a lot of hours to account for somehow. If he wasn't flying, he must have gone somewhere.' As she looks at me, I don't have to say anything as she goes on. 'Unless you have any other explanation, I think it's pretty clear he must have been with her.'

25

Jude

Having handed in my notice, I'm aware of the pressure lifting, a sense of relief filling me, though I've yet to tell Richard about my decision. The opportunity hasn't presented itself, but I'm also slightly worried how he'll react.

Taking the leave I'm owed and craving quiet, I alternate between spending time in the garden and going through the mementos of our children's childhoods. I'm not sentimental, but as I look at the old school books and reports, the school yearbooks, certificates for sports courses, I'm overtaken by an unfamiliar nostalgia.

One such afternoon, I'm at home alone when the police call me. Half an hour later, they pull up outside. Letting them in, I'm grateful Richard's at work. After the last time they were here, he was in the foulest mood. Showing them into the kitchen, I gesture towards the table. 'Do sit down. Would you like tea?'

'Please.' Unusually, DS Stanley accepts. I can't help noticing that today she seems preoccupied. 'Is your son at home?'

'No. I'm not sure where he's gone. He could be at Kat's.'

'We've just come from there. We didn't see him.'

Bringing over a tray of tea and mugs, I place it on the table. Pouring it, I offer them milk and sugar.

'Thank you. We have discovered some new information, and we're still looking into it, but it appears that when Katharine met your son, she already knew your husband. Were you aware of that?'

'Surely not.' I'm incredulous. 'That can't be right.'

Thinking back to that evening, I don't remember any sign of recognition on either part. If Richard and Kat had met before, when Oliver first introduced her to us, surely he would have said something.

DS Stanley passes me some photos.

'These were taken at a charity evening to raise money for St Margaret's hospice.'

My confusion clears. 'That I do know about. Richard's business has always been generous towards them.'

'Apparently so was the company that your daughter-in-law worked for, or Katharine Armstrong as she was then.' She pauses. 'The company was called Skyro.'

A frown settles across my face. 'You mean the same company that had offered Oliver a job?'

'So it would seem. Odd that she didn't mention it when she found out, don't you think?'

I'm silent, thinking. It is extremely odd.

DS Stanley goes on. 'She told us it was because she left in difficult circumstances and she wanted to leave it in the past. We found a press release. In many ways, it's understandable.' She passes me her notebook. 'But even when your husband discovered that Skyro had offered Oliver a job, she didn't say anything?'

'No.' As I read the press release, I'm mystified, remembering Kat's anger that Oliver would accept a job with an airline alleged to be connected with illegal firearms. 'But nor did he. And to be fair to her, this press release makes it clear she was against what they were doing.'

'Don't you think that makes it even stranger that she stayed silent?' Her question hangs in the air.

She's right. It is strange. As I turn it around in my mind, I can make no sense of it. My tea goes untouched in the light of this latest bombshell, as an uncomfortable feeling comes over me. 'Have you spoken to Richard about this?'

'Not yet. But we will ask him to come in for questioning at some point.'

After they leave, I think about calling Kat, but before I can, Joe arrives. Seeing my face, he frowns.

'Are you OK, Mum?'

I'm distracted, still taking in what the police told me. 'I'm not sure. I've just had the strangest conversation with the police.' I sit down. 'Really strange. They said that Kat worked for Skyro, before she met Oliver. But also . . .'

'She knew Dad.'

I look at Joe in surprise. 'You already know?'

'I've only just found out. I've seen the photos. I found out about them after a conversation with Ana Fontaine. She came around here while you and Dad were working the other day. She wouldn't come in. We went for a walk. It's obvious Kat's been deliberately hiding this from us.' Joe clearly feels let down. 'I told the police about the photos.'

Taken aback that he's spoken to Ana Fontaine, I frown at him. 'Does Kat know?'

'She may have worked it out, but that's not my problem. I'm giving her some space. I understand her reasons for keeping quiet, but I honestly thought she trusted me.'

'I'm not surprised.' I touch his arm briefly. 'The police showed me a press release. It sounds as though Kat was standing up for what she believed in. It wasn't anything for her to feel ashamed of.'

'That's what I thought.' Joe looks confused. 'It makes it even weirder she didn't say anything. God, I remember the shock she faked when she took the phone call from Dad, acting like she'd never heard of Skyro.'

I'm silent for a moment. 'There has to be more to it. I'll talk to her about it. I'd love to know what her reasons were. Anyway, are you here for dinner?'

Joe nods. 'Yeah. If that's OK.'

There are shades of normality when Richard comes in, and I make pasta carbonara, passing Joe a bottle of red. 'Open that, will you?'

Buoyed up by Joe's presence, I take the opportunity to tell Richard about the decision I've made. 'Richard?' I'm nervous all of a sudden, before telling myself how ridiculous it is when I have every right to make a decision about my life. 'I've been wanting to talk to you about this for some time now, but everything's got rather sidetracked lately, for obvious reasons. Anyway, I've made a decision. I've handed in my notice.' When he's silent, I go on. 'Since Oliver died, I've realised I've spent most of my life focused on this job. I've missed out on so much family time. I think we both have. We don't need my salary. I thought I could do something to the garden, get involved with a local charity. There are so many more worthwhile things I could do than working another ten years at the medical practice.'

A look of disapproval settles across his face. 'You've actually done it? Without extending me the courtesy of discussing it with me?'

'Yes,' I say obstinately, noticing Joe's anxious look. 'I've been a working mother the entire time our children were growing up. And looking back, it was a mistake – one I bitterly regret. I could have worked part-time while they were small. I was offered the option. But I didn't take it. I wanted the money and prestige that came with being successful, and I was wrong to put that first.' I shake my head at my husband. 'We both were. We didn't have to bring children into the world. We made a choice, and I don't think we did the right thing by them.'

Slamming down his wine glass, Richard's face is white. 'Our hard work has given this family everything it has.'

I shake my head. How dare he? 'You know as well as I do that isn't true. There is more money in this family than any of us could ever need. I'm talking family money, Richard. I think we should do something decent with some of it.'

'You've lost it, haven't you?' Richard's voice is icy. 'Losing Oliver's triggered some kind of breakdown.'

'Don't speak to Mum like that.' Joe's voice is quietly angry.

Richard turns on Joe. 'Stay out of it, for Christ's sake. You're the least likely member of this family to have anything useful to contribute.'

Joe tenses. 'This isn't about me. It's about Mum.'

As I watch Joe, I know he's close to tipping point. 'Please. None of this is useful. Richard, why do you have a problem with me giving up my job?'

'If you don't care what I think, do what you like.' He drains his glass. 'On second thoughts, I won't be here for dinner. I'm going out.'

'Before you go . . .' I glance briefly at Joe before I go on, deliberately provoking him. 'The police have some photos. They were taken in 2018 at a charity dinner, raising money for St Margaret's hospice.' When Richard stiffens, I realise he knows what's coming. 'There was a rather nice photo of you with Kat, which made me think back. When Oliver introduced us to her, both of you acted like you'd never met before. I find that distinctly odd.'

'I must have forgotten,' he says in a voice that's entirely different.

'That's what I told the police,' I say calmly, not sure what I've hit on, but knowing there's something in what I'm saying. 'Anyway, you're going out. Don't let us keep you.'

Going upstairs, he comes down a couple of minutes later, ignoring us both as he pulls on a jacket, slamming the door as he leaves the house.

Having stayed in control, now that he's gone, my adrenaline is subsiding. I sit down suddenly.

'Mum, you're shaking.' Joe places a hand on my shoulder.

'I'm fine.' But tears roll down my cheeks. I can't believe how blind I've been. 'I haven't seen it before. How haven't I seen it?'

'What do you mean?'

'Your father, Joe . . . he doesn't care about us, does he? I've seen shades of it over the years, but it's become more extreme. Now, he's nothing but a bully.' Stricken, I gaze at my son. 'You and Oliver have had to bear the brunt of it. I'm so sorry . . .'

I think of Richard's coldness after Oliver died, when I would have given anything for warmth; the way he speaks to Joe, as if he's worthless when Joe is a more decent person than Richard could ever be. Leaning my head in my hands, I feel the blinkers fall away, the guilt and grief overwhelming me, the thought in my head instantly.

I want a divorce.

Hannah

This time, when I changed my identity, I wanted everything by the book — a passport and matching bank account — so that I could rent somewhere to live and apply for a job.

As time passed, Colette assumed it was Leo's death that preoccupied me, and in a sense she was right, if not in the way she believed. With the police investigation now closed, I could relax, but every time I opened my rucksack, his watch ticked relentlessly at me. Not wanting to risk getting caught with it, I almost hurled it into the sea. But I liked the irony that when Andre had lived lawlessly and immorally, perhaps in dying he could do something decent for the world.

There had to be someone who could benefit, I reasoned, which was how I found myself in Perpignan, headed for an off-the-beaten-track place I'd heard about. Growing in recognition, it was a rundown site volunteers had taken over, where they cultivated food and cooked it for the poor in the community in the canteen they were kitting out. When I knew how it felt to have the odds stacked against you, I liked the philosophy that no one should go hungry. I knew also that Leo, as I now called him, would have approved. After all, as he'd told me himself, there was no stauncher supporter of the redistribution of wealth.

It was a cool spring morning, the mimosa trees coming into flower, the air filled with its heady scent as I found the site. Waiting till lunchtime, I watched the volunteers slow-cook sauces, stirring in potatoes or pasta. Having bought a bowl, when no one was looking, I hesitated only briefly before slipping Leo's watch into the donation box. It was as simple as that. I finished my pasta, waiting until I heard a cry of delight go up. Getting up, smiling to myself, I walked out.

It felt like another piece in the puzzle of life had slotted into place. As I caught the bus back to Collioure, I had a sense I couldn't ignore that things were shifting around me, in a direction that was yet to reveal itself. Except that was my major mistake, I decided. I shouldn't be waiting for events to take their course. I should be making them happen.

I started looking at house sits in the UK, until I realised I had to cut ties to everything that had been part of my life here. House-sitting joined the list, alongside stealing, cheating and killing. Those rules I'd spurned long ago about leading a life that was respectful to other people – I'd decided that after all, there was a point to some of them.

When I got back, Colette looked disappointed. 'No shopping?'

'I just walked. It was nice.'

'Come and have a drink with me.' Fetching two glasses, she opened a bottle of red. 'You haven't been yourself since Leo died.'

'I guess not.' I took the glass she held out.

'I always thought you got on so well,' she said quietly. 'You seemed alike.'

'In some ways, maybe.' I resisted the urge to tell her more. 'In others, we were very different.'

'Santé.' She raised her glass. 'To life.'

'To life.' I looked at her. 'Thanks, Colette. I've really enjoyed being here.'

'But you are going, non?' A look of disappointment crossed her face.

Suddenly I realised that, in the course of that glass of wine, the moment had arrived. 'I think I am.'

'Where?'

'England, maybe. But nothing is certain.' I rolled my eyes exaggeratedly, lightening the mood.

Reaching out, she took my hand. 'Well, I hope maybe one day, you will come back.'

'Me too,' I said quietly.

★

Of course, shaking off old habits was never going to be easy. After leaving Collioure and making my way north through France, I stopped off at a hostel in Paris. I didn't know why I hadn't thought of it before, but it was the obvious place to find a new identity. Spending a few nights there, it was worth the wait when this girl checked in. Her hair was different to mine, but her face was uncannily similar. I followed her from a distance, as she walked with her friends towards the Seine.

Finding a quiet place in the park, they dropped their bags on the ground, one of them staying to keep an eye on them while the others went off to get some food. Once they were a safe distance away, I wandered over, glancing at the guy who'd been left behind.

'Bon jour. Quelle heure est-il?'

'Pardon?' He looked at me blankly.

'English? Ah, fantastique!' I pretended to be elated. 'Where are you headed?'

As he told me about their trip, I put my rucksack down, enthusing madly, all the time eyeing up the bag the girl had been carrying.

'I hope you have a really fantastic time.' Leaning down again, I picked up the wrong bag, and as I'd predicted, he didn't notice. 'See ya.'

I made it back to the hostel as fast as I could, picking up the rest of my stuff, before getting out of there pronto, knowing I needed to get out of Paris as quickly as I could. I still had the passport I'd left the UK with, but I didn't want any record of my return. When I handed over the stolen passport, no one queried it, but a young woman travelling alone probably wasn't a profile they'd be suspicious of.

As the ferry left Calais, I felt a pang of regret. There had been a freedom to these last years that I didn't expect to find in England. But thinking of the passport I'd stolen that I was going to use to open a bank account, I knew I'd been lucky. It possibly wasn't the name I would have chosen for myself, but it could have been worse.

Planning ahead, I'd booked into a cheap hotel on the Kent coast. I'd no idea what kind of place it was, but it was comforting to know I'd have the sea close by. As soon as I was there, I'd open a bank account and change some money, before the girl discovered her passport was missing and cancelled it. Then . . . I wondered what the start of the rest of my life would bring.

I watched as the English coast came into view, taking in the white cliffs of Dover, the hovering seagulls under an already grey sky streaked with clouds. It felt weird to think about how long I'd been away and what had happened in that time, while life in England had gone on as before, pretty much unchanged.

Disembarking from the ferry, I headed for the station. I didn't *have to wait long for the next train and speeding through open countryside, I gazed out at the green fields, the distant sea I'd so recently crossed. Less than twenty minutes later, I arrived in Deal. My new life was about to begin.*

26

Ana

After seeing Richard outside, in the days that follow, unease hangs over me, enough that I keep the curtains half closed, and each time I go out, I'm constantly on the lookout for his face. At home, I put myself in Katharine's shoes. Someone like her would have had her eye on everything. I don't buy for one moment she didn't know what was going on. With Oliver conveniently out of the way, she can say what she likes, however fantastical. But what fascinates me most is why she lies.

If I were her, I would have been obsessively going through his pockets; opening his post; logging in to his laptop and checking his emails, his photos, his bank account. There is no doubt in my mind that she was onto all these things. I know enough from Oliver to know what makes her tick, that in her skewed mind, the world is against her, instead of the reality that she's simply another twisted person playing the victim.

But we all choose the face we want to present to the

world. Gazing out of the window, I look at the sea. After everything that's happened in my life, Oliver was supposed to be my new beginning; a chance to live a simple, peaceful life. But as happens every time, it's been taken from me. With nothing to keep me here, once I have Oliver's money, I'll be free to go anywhere in the world. *Anywhere*, as long as it's far away from here. I imagine somewhere warm, near the sea – a little house with a sun terrace, set in its own private garden with views of the ocean between the trees. But without the people you love, all the money in the world can't buy you happiness.

A knock at the door brings me back to the present as my heart starts to race. Praying to God it isn't Richard, I call out. 'Who is it?'

There's a brief silence, before a woman speaks. 'It's Jude. Jude McKenna.'

Taken aback, I hesitate before opening the door. On the doorstep, Jude looks terrible.

'Do you want to come in?' Holding the door open, she comes in.

She nods, once. 'I'm sorry to turn up like this.'

I close the door behind her.

'I'm amazed you found me.' Actually, given Richard already has, it probably isn't surprising at all. I gesture to the sofa. 'Would you like to sit down?'

She perches on the edge. 'I found your address in one of Richard's pockets.'

I fold my arms defensively. 'That stands to reason. I saw him outside recently, in the street.'

Jude looks startled. 'He's been here?'

'He hasn't actually knocked on the door. But he obviously knows where I live.' I watch her for a moment, this most unmaternal of mothers; the woman who raised the man I loved. 'Would you like a cup of tea?' It's an AA holdover – tea the curer of all ills. If only.

'Thank you.' She seems overtly grateful, but that's probably because she was half expecting me to turn her away. 'I drink it black.'

Same as me. Going to the kitchen, I make two cups, then take them back to the sitting room, passing one to Jude.

She looks guarded. 'If I'm honest, I suppose I'm curious to know who my son was allegedly leaving his wife for.'

I put my tea down. 'What is it exactly that you want to know?'

She frowns. 'Did you ever stop and think that you were breaking up his marriage?'

'Excuse me?' I look at her in astonishment. 'Have you ever stopped and thought the state of his marriage was the reason we met? Not all marriages are meant to stand the test of time, Mrs McKenna. Sometimes it's easy to lose sight of that.'

'It's Jude.' She sighs. 'I'm sorry. It's all such a mess, isn't it? I don't know what to think anymore. Our lives seem to have been turned upside down.'

'Yes.' Guarded, I wait for her to go on.

'I suppose I've realised I've got a lot of things wrong. It's why I wanted to talk to you.' She hesitates. 'What I don't understand is how Kat and Oliver had always seemed so happy. She and I used to be close. Of course, she's going through a terrible time. I can't imagine how she must feel.

But there are still so many unanswered questions.' She sounds doubtful, I can't help noticing. 'It's another reason I wanted to talk to you.'

Hallelujah, I feel like saying. Reading between the lines, Jude has doubts about Katharine. At last someone sees her the way Oliver did.

Jude goes on. 'We used to have such a good relationship. She lost her mother when she was young – while for me, she was the closest I had to a daughter.'

'You are sure about her mother?' I ask gently. 'Oliver had his suspicions that she's still alive. He said Katharine used to get these phone calls. She always went out of the room so that he couldn't overhear.'

Jude looks startled. 'Kat wouldn't have lied about her mother. It must have been a client.'

I shake my head. 'Not according to Oliver. He was convinced it wasn't a client. Though talking of clients . . .' I pause, wondering how far to go. 'He also used to check her diary. It had gotten quieter more recently until it was pretty much empty. He didn't know what she was doing all day, but she wasn't working.'

A frown crosses Jude's face. 'That can't be right. They had a joint mortgage. She had to be getting money from some-where.'

'Isn't it entirely possible', I say archly, 'that she had money of her own?'

Jude looks surprised. 'Surely not.'

'Look, it isn't for me to say, but how well do you know Katharine? I mean really know her – where she went to school, where she studied, her parents' names, any siblings she had.'

Jude looks puzzled. 'I know her childhood wasn't happy. But the only other person she's talked about is the grandmother who died when Kat was eighteen.'

'How do you know any of it is true?' I was starting to lose patience. I mean, it really isn't hard to find these things out.

'I had no reason not to believe her.'

'But unless you can be sure you can trust her, if I were you, I'd forget everything you think you know about her and start from the beginning.'

Jude looks shocked. 'You're probably right. But it isn't just Kat I'm concerned about. You said Richard came here?'

'The other afternoon, he was down there.' I point down towards the street. 'He was staring up at me. I assumed he was trying to frighten me.'

'That's Richard's style,' Jude says quietly. 'He isn't a nice man.'

Her words are music to my ears, but also astonishing. 'Then how come you're married to him?'

'I've been asking myself that very question,' she says grimly. 'Since Oliver died, I've seen the light about a lot of things. I suppose it's made me take stock.'

I try to hide my surprise. 'I think death has that effect on many of us,' I say gently.

'Tell me what Oliver was like,' she says. 'When he was with you, I mean. I'm starting to think I didn't really know him.'

I give her the filtered version. 'He was strong and vulnerable at the same time. He was sensitive, too. It mattered greatly to him what you and Richard thought – too much, in my opinion. He hated the thought that he was letting you down. It's why he couldn't talk to you. But he was troubled,' I say honestly. 'His relationship with Katharine was impossible, and at work, he was struggling with the pressure. Drinking relieved it. He talked to me about it, a lot. He appreciated that I understood and that he didn't feel judged.' I pause. 'I'm sorry. I hope that isn't too brutal.'

'I just want the truth, whatever that is,' Jude says quietly.

'I do, too.' I pause. 'Which takes us back to who sabotaged the car. Have the police said any more to you?'

Jude shakes her head. 'No. But they're not at all convinced that Kat wasn't the intended target.'

Irritation flares inside me. 'If that was the case, don't you think whoever did it would have been back for another try?'

Jude looks at me curiously. 'It is all rather odd, isn't it?'

'Very.' I'm silent for a moment. 'How long before probate should be granted?'

'Hopefully not too long.'

I try to sound generous. 'At least Katharine will know where she stands.'

Jude looks worried again. 'I have a feeling it isn't going to go the way she wants it to.' But she doesn't elaborate.

When Jude asks me for my mobile number, I give it to her. 'I probably won't call, but it's nice to know I have it. You're one of the few links I have to Oliver.'

After she's gone, I realise she didn't get around to asking if I loved her son, more evidence that love hasn't figured highly in the lives of the McKennas. Needing some air, I put on my coat and the boots Oliver bought me, pulling a black knitted hat over my hair, before going outside. It's a wintery scene, the air sharp, the cold sun low in an opalescent sky. As I walk, my breath freezes in clouds, as I wonder if the police have spoken to Beatrice and what she might have said to them.

Uncannily as I'm thinking of them, my mobile rings.

'Ms Fontaine? It's DS Stanley. Do you have a minute?'

'Of course.'

'It's about the car Mr McKenna was driving. Is there anyone else who might have travelled in it? Only we ran the prints again. As well as Mr McKenna's, his wife's and your prints in the car, there's a fourth set – of glove marks, which is probably why they were missed the first time around.'

As revelations go, it isn't exactly an impressive one. 'I don't know of anyone. But it has been cold, Detective Sergeant. I often wear gloves. I expect Katharine does too. Maybe they belong to a friend of hers. Have you asked her?'

'We've already spoken to her.'

'You think this could be the person who sabotaged the brakes?'

'We're not ruling anything out, but it's possible.'

After the call ends, I feel nauseous. Glove marks are inconclusive. But there's the more sinister possibility that whoever was wearing them didn't want to be identified. Turning towards the sea, I feel myself shiver.

If it was up to me, I'd put my money on Katharine, and as it turns out, the police reach the same conclusion. Later that day, I get a call from Jude.

'I've just found out the police have arrested Kat.'

Even though I've had my suspicions about her, I'm taken aback. 'Are they charging her?'

Jude sounds anxious. 'As far as I know, they're keeping

311

her in for questioning. Richard was going to speak to them, not that there's anything he can do.'

Bloody Richard again. 'She needs a lawyer, not Richard. Can you let me know what happens?'

But as she ends the call, instead of feeling relieved that they've established it was Katharine, I'm uneasy again. Wherever you go with this, whoever you talk to, somewhere in the background there's always Richard.

27

Katharine

I keep quiet on the way to the police station, but once we're there, I realise how ridiculous this is and as we go inside, I can no longer control myself. 'This is outrageous. I shouldn't be here. I demand to speak to someone.'

'Mrs McKenna, please stay calm. Would you like to call your solicitor?'

I think of Mark Osborne in his exclusive office as he told me about Ana Fontaine. He's exactly the person I need. 'I would.'

While we wait for Mark to turn up, I'm left in a small interview room, with a young PC who looks about sixteen. Calming down, I try to gather my thoughts. Whatever evidence the police have found, surely they'll realise they've got it wrong; that I'm innocent in this; that there's something they're missing.

Mark turns up surprisingly quickly – testament, no doubt, to the vast fees the McKennas have paid him over the years.

'I'm sure we can get this sorted quickly,' he says reassuringly. But he doesn't quite meet my eyes.

I'm not sure he appreciates the complexity of what's happening. 'You have no idea, do you?'

I fill him in on my suspicions that Ana Fontaine is setting me up, as he looks slightly taken aback.

'When she sabotaged my car, she didn't imagine that Oliver would be driving it. By getting rid of me, she stood to gain Oliver as well as his money. When you put it all together, it adds up.'

He looks uncertain. 'Let's see what the police have to say. Shall we get started?'

As DS Stanley comes back in with Constable Ramirez, the young PC leaves. Starting the tape, DS Stanley recites the date and names of those present, before she starts to speak.

'Mrs McKenna, can you tell us where you were the night before your husband died?'

I think back to the last few hours before this nightmare started. 'I was at home.'

'Your husband came home at approximately what time?'

I remember Oliver walking in, carrying his flight bag, his uniform jacket over his arm. He leaned down to kiss my cheek. I asked what kind of day he'd had. His reply was that it had been good. 'He wasn't late. He had a flight the following morning.'

DS Stanley is straight in there. 'Except he didn't, did he, Mrs McKenna? As we now know, he'd lost his job.'

She knows perfectly well what I mean. 'At the time, I thought he had a flight. Of course, now I realise he was maintaining the illusion of having to take minimum hours off before going to work again.'

'According to Ms Fontaine, he'd started training with Skyro at this point, the company that had offered him a job recently – a job you didn't know about.'

I frown at her. 'I knew he'd been offered the job. I found out after the accident. But I didn't know he'd started working there.'

'You're sure about that?' She pauses. 'Some coincidence, isn't it, that no one knew that you used to work there, too? No one would ever have known had those photos not been found, though I can understand from the way you lost your job why you didn't want to draw attention to it.' DS Stanley makes a note. 'Regarding your relationship with your husband, you told us it was good, is that correct?'

I swallow. 'I've already told you, on the whole, yes. Like anyone else, we had our ups and downs, but nothing we couldn't have resolved.'

'You didn't know at this point he was seeing Ms Fontaine.'

I shake my head. 'No. I didn't find her photo until after the accident.'

'So even given he was away much more than usual, you didn't suspect anything had changed?'

'No. The thing about flying . . .' I pause. 'Each week is different. There is no set pattern of working hours.'

DS Stanley pauses briefly. 'Obviously, we've established your husband had alcohol problems and subsequently lost his job. You've maintained he didn't have a drink problem and that you didn't know he'd left. Is this correct?'

Knowing how this sounds, I hedge. 'It's what I believed at the time.' Pausing, I add, 'There is still no proof that he had a problem with drink. It's possible it had become confused with his symptoms of diabetes. And of course, there's the possibility that Ms Fontaine is lying.'

'Which begs the question: why she would lie?' DS Stanley says crisply. 'But that's irrelevant. We've found links to AA in his search history, as well as dates of meetings on the calendar on his phone.'

I hadn't realised they'd checked.

DS Stanley pauses before going on. 'You claim your marriage was solid, but you didn't know your husband was having an affair, or about his drinking problem and that he'd been going to AA meetings, or that he'd lost his job and had been offered another one.'

'I didn't.' I glance at Mark. 'But it isn't how it sounds.'

'How is it then?'

I sigh. 'Oliver was hiding things from me. I don't know why, but there was no way I could have known.'

DS Stanley frowns. 'Isn't it possible that you'd got wind that something had changed? You're a therapist, Mrs McKenna. It stands to reason that if there had been changes in your husband's behaviour or routines, you would have picked up on them straight away. I think you knew exactly what was going on. The idea that he had met someone else was unbearable to you. But what was far worse was the thought of losing the money you'd got so accustomed to.'

'That's not how it was,' I say despairingly, before taking a breath. I remind myself to stay calm. 'I have my own business. I loved Oliver. It was never about money.'

'About your counselling business, how many clients do you see regularly?'

'I don't know.' I'm flustered all of a sudden. 'It varies all the time. On average, around fifteen.'

'Not overly busy, then.'

'It isn't just a question of seeing people. Each session requires time to write up notes, and there's housekeeping.'

'You presumably have a diary and a client list.'

I open my mouth and close it again, because since Oliver's death, my diary is empty. 'Yes,' I say quietly. 'But I've been quieter lately. It hasn't been easy.'

'If that's the case, you must have had considerable time on your hands. What do you do all day?'

'The same things anyone else does. We've been renovating the house, working on the garden, I catch up with friends occasionally.'

'On the subject of friends, it would be helpful to talk to them. Could you provide us with some names?'

My stomach feels queasy. 'I could . . . but I haven't seen any of them for a while. You know how it goes sometimes.'

'Why was that?' DS Stanley's eyes seem to bore into me.

'The truth?' My voice wavers. 'I suppose Oliver had alienated us from them. When you cancel plans too many times, people start to give up on you.'

Frowning, her eyes don't leave my face. 'I'm going to tell you what I think the truth is. It was you, rather than your husband, who alienated people. You spent most of your time alone, didn't you, Mrs McKenna? It gave you plenty of time to obsess over your husband's affair with Ms Fontaine, and to educate yourself about how to cause enough damage to your brakes to render them useless. You had probably worked out the brakes on your car were easier to get to than your husband's. The night before the accident, it was easy. You ensured your husband drank enough wine so that he wouldn't stir, which in the circumstances, wouldn't have taken much persuasion. While he was sleeping, you crept downstairs, did what you needed to do to your car, then disabled the battery on his, a simple enough task, making sure there was no way his was going to start. With that done, you went back to bed. I think you knew all along he'd lost his job and that the next morning, when he supposedly went off to work, in reality he was going to see Ms Fontaine. At home, all you had to do was wait. Then of course, a little while later, we turned up with the news of the accident.'

'No.' As everything starts to close in, I feel light-headed. She's a million miles from the reality of this. But as I sit there, I realise, without evidence to the contrary, everything points to me. In DS Stanley's mind, everything she's said makes perfect sense and there's no way I can prove otherwise.

There's a silence before she looks at me. 'Mrs McKenna, you are free to leave for now, while we carry out further investigation. But please don't go far. We may well need to speak to you again.'

★

As I walk out of the police station with Mark, a tentative feeling of relief settles over me that for now I'm free, but it does little to reduce how worried I am. Being questioned by the police has shaken me. After finding a taxi to take me home, the interview replays in my mind. My only consolation is that, so far at least, they don't have evidence.

Trying to distract myself, I turn my mind to what I'm going to do next, still conflicted about whether to sell the house or not. When I get home and walk inside, it's cold, littered with half-filled packing boxes, the smell of cardboard pervading the air, the decision made for me as I know instantly I can't stay here.

Locking the door behind me, now that I'm alone, my fear escalates. All I've done is try to protect my position. But from the start, every interaction with the McKenna family has been layered with deception. From my first meeting with Richard, to Joe's determination to seduce me. From the start, Oliver and I had little chance of surviving. Only Jude is different. Though, no doubt they'll have closed ranks since Joe told her what he'd found out. I haven't heard from her in recent days.

Self-pitying tears prick my eyes. What comes next, I have no idea. Everything in my life has fallen apart – my marriage, my future, even my business. Despite my efforts to better myself, I've learned the hard way I'm not cut out to be a counsellor, while in her mind, DS Stanley has the events around Oliver's death all worked out.

Lying in bed that night, there's no escaping my thoughts. I cast my mind back to the day Oliver and I met. I'd seen a charismatic man with a successful career, good-looking, from a well-off family – who had everything I didn't have, everything I craved.

While I was driven by a need to make my life safer, easier, more comfortable, Oliver had an innate desire to live up to the expectations of his family. It seemed too much to hope for that we could be the missing pieces in each other's lives, forgetting the single most important thing: that beyond affection, a physical attraction to each other, there was no love. But while I was too used to living without it, Oliver was too damaged to notice.

28

Jude

With Christmas on the horizon, for the first time, there is no room in my head for elaborate presents and seasonal food. The combination of Oliver's death and Richard's behaviour has destroyed what used to make this house a home.

Getting out the artificial tree, I wonder for whose benefit I'm hanging the decorations. They're expensive, bought a couple of years ago when the colour scheme in the sitting room was changed. There is no sentimentality, no memories of my children's childhood attached to them. They're simply part of a tradition that this year feels utterly meaningless. I contemplate taking myself off for a few days, the thought of Joe preventing me from booking anything. In the past I would have told myself that Joe is a grownup, he can look after himself, but after losing Oliver, I'm not comfortable leaving him alone with his father.

Forcing myself to go through the motions, I do an online food shop – Richard always takes care of the wine. But when it comes to presents, inspiration evades me. Given this house is bursting with material goods, I have no desire to buy more of them. If I could choose anything in the world, it would be one more day with the son I've lost. I'd lavish him with the love he never felt, tell him how proud of him I am, how I will always regret not being there for him, how I wish I could have made things different for him. Thinking of my two small sons watching me go to work, their faces sad, too scared of their father to tell me not to go, to stay, a tear rolls down my cheek. In this moment, I'd do anything in the world to have that time back.

I have to focus on what I do have, and that's Joe. His is the only present that preoccupies me, but I want to give him something personal. Upstairs, I go to my jewellery box. Opening it, I take out the watch that used to belong to my father. It's a cheap watch – my parents weren't well-off, but as I hold it in my hand, I conjure an image of it on his wrist, then his face, the eyes that were always filled with love.

Holding it to my lips, the tears start to flow. How did I get so much so wrong? How did I become this awful, money-obsessed middle-aged woman for whom position was more important than family? Sitting on the bed, I give way to my grief – for Oliver, for my parents, for the life I could have had, for the woman I could have been. With all the choices I was privileged to have, I could have done something great with my life.

Looking up, my eyes rest on a photo of me and Richard. Younger, our eyes are bright. We're smiling, but even then, our faces are hard, devoid of love. We were a transaction, I'm realising; a deal just like any of his other business deals. Glancing at another photo of Richard, something in his eyes repulses me. There's a look of superiority, an arrogance I haven't recognised before, as the realisation hits me that Richard displays all the classic traits of a narcissist.

Instinctively I know he's hiding something. Placing my father's watch to one side to wrap to give to Joe, I go downstairs to Richard's study. Opening the door, I hesitate. There's an unspoken rule in this house that no one goes in here unless invited by Richard. But this is just as much my house and I'm not playing by his rules anymore. Going in, I study his bookshelves, packed with titles related to business, investing, money. Sitting at his desk, I can't help feeling like a voyeur as I open the top drawer. There's nothing notable in there – a couple of expensive pens, a leather-bound notebook. In the drawer beneath are some letters. Sifting through them, there are some from his accountant, plus a couple of invitations to corporate dinners that he hasn't told me about.

Given how ordered Richard's study is, the bottom drawer of his desk is uncharacteristically untidy. There are a couple of folders, underneath which are more letters, and a collection of chequebooks. Picking them up, some are old, the cheques used up. Picking up a newer one, I flick through the stubs, astonished not only at how recently they're dated, but that in these days of online banking, Richard even uses cheques. I study the names of the payees, none of which I recognise, but then I come to one I do. *Mrs K McKenna*. When I read the amount, I gasp out loud. Why is Richard paying Kat thousands of pounds?

A horrifying thought comes to me. Surely Richard hasn't been sleeping with her. Shocked, as I contemplate the possibility that Richard's been screwing his son's wife, I know it isn't beyond him to do that. But isn't it beyond the Kat I know? Returning to the chequebooks, I carefully go through them, soon realising that it isn't a one-off; that over the last four years, he's been making regular payments to her.

I'm startled by the sound of a car pulling up outside. Dreading that Richard's come home, I quickly put everything back in the drawer, before closing it again. But as I get up, something in the bin catches my eye. Leaning down, I pick up the copy of the Order of Service from Oliver's funeral. My hand goes to my mouth, my heart twisting with grief as tears fill my eyes.

Oliver was his son. How could he be so callous? As my loathing for my husband plummets to new depths, I realise what a despicable human being he is, who only cares about himself. And whatever he's done, I am guilty too, for looking the other way. Instead of challenging his behaviour, I've enabled him.

But as I walk out of Richard's office, it isn't my husband standing there.

'What are you doing, Mum?' Joe looks at me suspiciously.

'I'm trying to work out what kind of man I've been married to,' I say fiercely. I hold out the Order of Service.

'Guess where I found that?' Taking it, Joe looks flummoxed as I go on. 'It was in the bin.'

An expression of shock crosses his face.

'I don't know if you know, but your father has been paying Kat a lot of money. For years. Do you have any idea why?'

He looks at me sharply. 'How do you know?'

'Chequebooks,' I say simply. 'It's all there, in his handwriting.'

A frown crosses his face. 'Why?'

'I have absolutely no idea. Can you think of a reason?'

'God knows.' Joe's face clouds over. 'You shouldn't have gone in there, Mum. You know what he's like.'

I stare into Joe's eyes. 'But why shouldn't I? Why has he

always made such a thing of this room being off limits to the rest of us? I'm his wife, Joe. We're his family. Don't you see? He's bullied us all into doing what he wants and we've been stupid enough to go along with it.'

But Joe hedges. 'We're all allowed privacy.'

As he defends his father, I look at him sadly. 'Don't make excuses for him, Joe. He's paying Kat a lot of money, on top of denying he remembers meeting her all those years ago. Ever since our marriage, I've gone along with what he expects—no, *demands* . . .' I find the right word. 'All this time, he's been taking me for a fool.'

Suddenly Joe looks shocked. 'Last time I saw Kat, she'd had an email from the mortgage company. The mortgage was in arrears. I said if she couldn't settle it, I'd lend her the money. She accepted. Of course she did,' he says cynically. 'But in light of this, she hardly needed it.'

'She obviously doesn't want anyone to know that she has money. I suppose it stands to reason, given it came from Richard.' I pause. 'You need to make sure she pays you back.'

'Don't worry, I'm going to.' Joe pauses. 'Are you going to ask Dad about this?'

'Him or Kat.' I hesitate. 'Maybe I'll talk to her first. See what she says.'

*

I turn down Joe's offer to come with me, wanting to see Kat without anyone else there. As I drive, the gloom is brightened by colourfully lit Christmas trees, fairy lights in windows, that this year, fail to touch me. I imagine cosy homes, the exchange of gifts, the sense of anticipation. Until now, I've never stopped to imagine Christmas being anything else.

But this year, I've learned how it can as easily be a time of isolation, of loneliness. There are no welcoming lights in Kat's driveway when I pull in. The windows are dark, the garden stark, the autumn leaves left to rot where they've fallen.

When she opens the door, her eyes are lifeless.

Instead of going to hug her, I stand on the doorstep. 'How are you?'

'Surviving.' As she looks at me, she seems to have picked up on the change in me.

'Are you busy?'

'I've started packing stuff. I'm putting the house on the market.'

I nod slowly. 'It's probably for the best.'

She remembers herself. 'Come and have a cuppa. I'll put the kettle on. I'm waiting for someone to come and pick up the sofa.'

As I walk towards the kitchen, I notice the array of half-packed boxes. 'You've been busy.'

'Not as busy as I'd like to have been.' She pauses. 'The police took me in for questioning.'

'I heard.'

She glances at me briefly before going on. 'They couldn't charge me. They don't have sufficient evidence. But since coming back, I've been thinking.'

It explains her defeated look, her air of preoccupation. 'I'm sorry you had to go through that, Kat. It can't have been pleasant.'

'No.' There's a tremor in her voice. 'I'm going to leave, Jude. There are too many memories. Too many—' She stops herself.

'What were you going to say?' I'm curious to know what it was.

'Nothing important.' Remembering the tea, she gets out a couple of mugs and teabags. 'I remember you saying to me to take each day at a time. That it would gradually get better. The problem is, I'm still waiting for that day.'

'It takes time,' I say, trying to sound sympathetic, as I remember the reason for my visit. 'There's something I wanted to ask you. I'm hoping there's an explanation. I know Richard has been giving you money, Kat. A lot of money.' I watch her cheeks tinge with pink.

'How?' Her voice is low.

'I found his chequebooks.'

A look of terror crosses her face. 'Jude, please don't go there. He's ruthless. He'll stop at nothing to get what he wants.'

'What's this about, Kat? What is there between you?' I watch her closely.

'There's nothing.' Her voice is hard. 'Really,' she says more calmly.

But as I think of the way she accepted money from Joe to pay off the mortgage arrears, suddenly I'm angry. 'So what is this money about? And why did you accept Joe's help with your mortgage?'

When she looks at me, there's fear in her eyes. 'I can't tell you, Jude.'

'You have to. Kat, don't you see what a mess this family is in?' I pause. 'Is this in some way connected to Oliver?'

'Please, Jude.' Gathering herself, this time she speaks coldly. 'It would be better if you just forgot you knew anything about this. It's nothing personal to anyone in the family.'

I stare at her. There's no trace of the daughter-in-law I welcomed as one of our own, whose wedding dress and flowers she asked me to help her choose. This woman is distanced, in whatever this is, only for herself. But for some reason, she's clearly terrified.

I find my voice. 'That's where you're wrong. When it comes to trust, it is personal. Whatever else you're caught up in, that's your business, but I welcomed you into our family and you've deceived me, Kat. Don't you dare stand there and tell me it isn't personal.'

Her face is ashen as I look at her.

'Don't bother with the tea.' Suddenly I want to get out of there. I turn to leave, but as I walk down the hallway, there's a knock on the door. I reach it before Kat, to find a couple of burly men standing there.

'We in the right place for the sofa, love?'

'Talk to her.' Gesturing behind me towards Kat, I push past them and go out to my car.

As I drive away towards Deal, I have no desire to go home. Somehow, I have to get to the bottom of this. Whether it's relevant or not, the police need to know that there's some connection between Kat and Richard.

If she hasn't already told them, they also need to know about Kat's allegations that Oliver abused her. Putting my foot down, I drive fast until I reach the edge of the town. Slowing down, I pull into the police station. I park, taking a deep breath before getting out, standing there for a moment, gathering my thoughts.

Walking towards the building, I open the door into the reception area, where there's a young PC behind the desk.

'Is DS Stanley available?'

'I'll check for you. Can I take your name please?'

'Judith McKenna.'

After talking briefly on the phone, he turns to me.

'She's going to be a few minutes. Would you like to come back in a bit?'

'It's fine. I'll wait.' It's stuffy, airless, the chairs look uncomfortable, but I've no desire to go anywhere else.

Hannah

Hannah Price didn't die quietly. Hers was more of a lingering death, the kind where the spirit holds on, where breath fades slowly. But when she eventually went, my dreams went with her. I tried to love this life I'd returned to, to channel Hannah's enthusiasm, her determination. When I failed, I tried conjuring Margot's voracious appetite for life, Gemma's untiring sense of adventure, until realising with a sinking heart, not one of them belonged here.

Unforeseen by me, everything had changed. Gone were my aspirations to live the sparkling, exciting, risk-filled high life. Instead, the person I'd been before I first left the UK was back. An ordinary girl no one would look twice at; who would have settled for an ordinary life, had she been lucky enough to stumble across it. I thought about Edie's cleaning company, wondering if it was still going strong. I even contemplated starting my own. But the truth was, I wouldn't know where to start.

For two weeks I wandered around, a lost soul among other lost souls, until a narrow escape from death started my blood pumping again. When I stepped out in front of a car that missed me by inches, my near miss revitalised my will to live.

But this time was going to be different. I was going to invest in myself, build the future I knew I deserved. I thought I'd been lost, but I'd rediscovered myself. The last two weeks, I'd simply been through a metamorphosis, the same way a caterpillar does, somehow absorbing Hannah, Margot and Gemma, assimilating their anger and pain, their joy and powerlessness, until I was ready to emerge as me.

Investing some money in a couple of online business studies courses, I pored over notes, learning new vocabulary, quickly realising I'd found something I was good at. It would take a little time, but hell, the one thing I did have was time.

Newly fired up, I went to a hairstylist, emerging sleek and shiny. Next came my clothes – up-to-the-minute British fashion, the latest makeup, feeling my heart beat with a renewed sense of purpose. Gazing in the mirror of my hotel room, I saw a stylish young woman, her eyes telling a story or two, one who exuded a quiet kind of confidence, who deserved a future, to find love, even. I smiled at myself. Not only was I back. Stretching out newly unfolded wings, I was ready to fly.

29

Ana

After the conversation with Jude, I'm aware of a momentum building, as events gather pace around me, a feeling that's amplified the following day when I hear a knock on the door. Suddenly I'm wary.

My heart races as I go over to it, hesitating before opening it. 'Who is it?'

'Richard McKenna.'

Hearing his voice, I feel a rush of fear. Surely he can't imagine I'm going to let him in. But what if he tries to break in? Thinking quickly, my eyes rest on my phone. Picking it up, I set it to record. 'What do you want?'

'I think we should talk.'

His voice is mild, vaguely affable, but I know enough about him to realise that this amiability is faked. Putting the chain across and holding the phone out of his eyeline, my heart thuds as I crack the door open.

'What about?'

'I wondered if it might be you.' A fleeting look of

recognition crosses his face as he remembers me from the wake. 'A funeral is hardly the time to be snooping, Ms Fontaine.'

I stare him out. 'You know perfectly well I was there to pay my respects to your son.'

'Whatever,' he mutters. 'That's not why I came here. I think we both know there have been some misunderstandings.' Up close, he's more repulsive than I'd realised, but it's his eyes that disturb me most. Cold and empty; the eyes of a monster.

'I'm not sure I know what you're talking about.'

He continues the affable act. 'Look, we both know there are some old photos doing the rounds. They're a little unfortunate.'

I raise an eyebrow. 'You mean the ones of you with your daughter-in-law at a charity dinner? Let's see, 2018, wasn't it? Before she met Oliver?' I can't resist it. 'They're harmless enough, aren't they?'

Fighting himself, he manages to stay calm. 'It really would be better if I came in and we talked about this properly.'

'Seeing as this is my flat, that decision is up to me,' I say coolly. 'I'm not interested in your photos, Richard.'

He visibly grits his teeth. 'There's a little more to it, as I think you know.'

'Everything I know, I've already told the police,' I tell him, flinching as he tries to jam his foot in the door.

His eyes narrow, glinting at me as he mutters. 'How much for you to get the hell out of our lives and never come back?'

'Excuse me? Aren't you forgetting that I'm quite a wealthy

woman?' Trying to hide my fear, I stare at him with distaste. 'Nice try, Richard. But you can fuck off. I'm not for sale.'

When he shoves his weight against the door, suddenly I'm terrified. But behind him, one of my neighbours calls out.

'Ana? Is everything OK?'

'Fine, thank you, Ed.' I try to stop my voice from shaking. 'This is Richard McKenna. He was just leaving.'

Stepping back, Richard glowers at me. 'You haven't heard the last of this.'

'Whatever.' Shrugging, I push the door shut.

As I go to sit down, my heart is thumping. When seconds later there's another knock on the door, I'm terrified.

But it isn't Richard's voice that calls out.

'Ana? It's Ed. I just wanted to check that you're OK.'

Getting up, I hurry over. Opening the door, I glance up and down for Richard.

'Your friend has gone.'

'I can assure you he's no friend.'

Ed frowns at me. 'He seemed to be giving you a hard time.'

'He's a nasty piece of work.' Still shaken up, I look at Ed. 'If you're not busy, do you think you could do something for me?'

After explaining I'm frightened that Richard will be hanging around, I ask Ed if he'll walk with me to the end of the road. But when he goes one step further and offers me a lift to the police station, I accept gratefully.

As I walk inside reception and go to the desk, the young PC looks up.

'I'd like to speak to DS Stanley if she's available.'

'Ana?' The voice comes from behind me.

Turning round, I do a double-take as I meet Jude's gaze. 'I've just had a visit from your husband.'

Her eyes widen, but before she has a chance to speak, a door opens and DS Stanley comes in.

'Good afternoon, ladies. Who's first?'

I gesture to Jude as she gets up. 'I'm not in a hurry. I'll wait.'

Sitting there, I'm conscious of my phone in my pocket. The recording isn't great, but hopefully good enough for DS Stanley to make her own interpretation. While I wait, I go back over Richard's visit. He must have felt pretty desperate for him to have behaved like that.

Twenty minutes pass before Jude reappears. She comes straight over to me. 'Do you mind if I wait for you?'

'Not at all.' In fact, I'm relieved. After what's happened today, the prospect of leaving here alone isn't an appealing one. Seeing DS Stanley come through the door, I get up.

'Ms Fontaine? Would you like to come with me?'

In the interview room, I tell her about Richard's visit. 'As you already know, I've seen him before, outside my flat, in the street. That time, other than stare up at my window, he didn't do anything. But I realised then, I couldn't trust him. Anyway, today, he knocked on my door. He was really most unpleasant. I didn't let him in, obviously. I had the chain across. But I managed to record the conversation. I thought you should hear it.'

Listening intently, DS Stanley glances at me now and then. When it's finished, she sits back. 'So he's tried to pay you off to conveniently disappear.'

'It seems that way. He was actually trying to force his way in when fortunately, my neighbour turned up. I think it was the idea of being named and shamed that made him leave. But I am slightly worried that he might come back.'

'If he does, call us. We'll send someone over.'

It's only mildly reassuring, but at least they're aware. 'Thank you.'

'Be careful, won't you, Ms Fontaine? He seems oddly obsessive over a couple of photos.'

Back out in reception, Jude gets up when she sees me.

'Do you have time for a chat?' she asks quietly.

I nod. 'I know this place.'

In Jude's car, we drive in silence into the town, as I direct her to the community centre. After parking in a nearby street, we walk together.

'Did Richard tell you why he'd come to see you?'

For a moment I pity her, being married to such a vile, overbearing man.

'Basically, he wanted to know how much he'd have to pay me to move away from here.'

'Foolish man,' she says quietly. 'Has he forgotten about the money Oliver's left you?'

'He probably thought I'd be tempted by more. I mean, he's the kind of person who can never have enough money, isn't he? He probably assumes everyone is the same.' I turn to Jude. 'But I'm genuinely not. I never expected what's coming to me from Oliver. I certainly don't need more money. I just want this to be over so that I can have a life again.' I pause. 'So what brought you there today?'

'Richard,' she says simply.

'Surprise, surprise.' My sarcasm is thinly veiled.

'I discovered he's been making payments to Kat. We're talking tens of thousands, over a period of years, and I've no idea why. She refuses to tell me. All she said was that it would be better if I just forgot about it.'

I'm astonished. 'What a strange thing to say. Have you challenged Richard?'

'Not yet.' She sounds hesitant. 'I went through the drawers of his desk and found some old chequebook stubs – that's how I found out. Richard's study has always been out of bounds to everyone else. I'm slightly concerned as to how he'll react.'

'Not well, I should imagine.' I frown. 'I would make sure you're not alone when you talk to him. So what has Katharine been doing with the money?'

'Saving it, I guess. It explains how she's been contributing to the mortgage when her business is quiet. But recently, she let Joe pay off her mortgage arrears. From what Richard's been paying her, she shouldn't have needed to take money from Joe.'

'Sounds like she's out for what she can get.' As we reach the community centre, I point to the entrance. 'We're here.'

When I first met Oliver here at the AA meeting, I could never have imagined that months later, I'd be coming back here with his mother. But so much that's happened since then is unimaginable. Going up to the bar, I order two black teas. Taking them over to a table near the window, we sit down.

I hesitate before telling her, but then I figure she'd want to know. 'The AA meetings are held here. There's a room at the back.'

'This is where you met Oliver?'

Watching her face, I nod. 'The first time he came, he left as soon as it was over. The next week, he didn't come at all.

His third week coincided with my last week. Most people say something at their final session. I stood up and said coming here was the best thing I'd done, and for those who were just starting, they would never regret it.' Unexpected tears fill my eyes. 'I was thinking of Oliver as I said it.' I paused. 'After, we left and walked to the beach. I remember telling him he'd have to get used to drinking a lot of tea because it was a prop. Then he started talking.'

As I glance at Jude, her eyes are filled with sadness.

'I'm glad he had you,' she says at last. 'Even for that short while.'

'So am I.' I wipe away my tears. 'Sorry. It's been a bit of a day. Your husband . . .' I try to play it down, but the truth is Richard's frightened me.

'He has a lot to answer for,' she says quietly.

'Do you know if the police plan to talk to him?'

'DS Stanley said they would be bringing him in for questioning.'

'Good. He's going to love that.' I can only hope there aren't repercussions on Jude. But with the chequebook stubs as proof, I can't help but wonder how he's going to wriggle out of this one. My eyes are drawn to the flashing Santa suspended from the ceiling.

'It isn't going to be much of a Christmas this year.'

'I'll be glad when it's over,' Jude says. 'But I just want all of this over.'

As she sits there sipping her tea, I realise how brave she is. Oliver's dead, Kat's let her down, fuck knows where Joe is in all this; leaving her alone to take on the worst of all of them. Richard.

30

Jude

By the time I get home, Richard's car is parked in the drive. Wondering why he's home early, I find Joe in the kitchen.

'Dad's in a vile mood,' he says quietly.

'Probably because he didn't get his own way earlier today.' I tell him about Richard's attempts to buy Ana's silence.

Joe looks slightly shocked. 'Are you sure?'

I nod. 'He doesn't know it yet, but she recorded him. Apparently he tried to force her door open.' Hearing the door of Richard's study open, I shoot Joe a warning look.

Coming into the kitchen, he doesn't say anything. But he doesn't need to. The stench of his mood fills the room. Switching on the kettle, he gets a mug, slamming it down on the worktop, before making a cup of tea and storming out again.

About half an hour later, the police turn up. I wonder if Richard knows they're coming, if that's the reason for his mood, but apparently not. After letting them in, I knock on the door of his study to tell him.

He looks furious. 'I'm quite within my rights not to talk to them. Tell them I'm busy.'

'You're going to have to tell them yourself.' Leaving the door open, I go back to the kitchen.

'I've told him you're here,' I tell DS Stanley. 'Please, have a seat. I'm sure he won't be long.'

Sitting down, after a few minutes, DS Stanley checks her watch pointedly. Another five minutes pass before Richard appears. Instead of sitting down, he leans against one of the worktops belligerently.

'Yes?' His face is like thunder.

'Apologies for turning up unannounced, Mr McKenna. We have tried to call you several times. We also left you a message.' DS Stanley looks at him pointedly. 'There are one or two questions we'd like to ask you. We can do it here, or you can come with us down to the station. Your choice.'

'I'm not coming to the police station. I'm a busy man, Detective Sergeant.'

'Would you like us to leave?' I ask her.

She glances from me to Joe. 'I think you should stay.'

Richard glares at her. 'What is it about this time?'

In spite of his blatant rudeness, DS Stanley stays admirably cool and unflustered. 'I understand you paid a visit to Ana Fontaine earlier today.'

'I went to see her. It's a free world.' But some of the bluster has gone out of him.

'She said you tried to intimidate her, before trying to bribe her to move away. When she told you she wasn't for sale, you tried to force your way into her flat.'

Richard's face goes pale. 'That really isn't at all how it

was. I simply asked her to leave our family in peace. We're grieving.'

Listening in disbelief, if I didn't know better, I'd have almost fallen for his act.

But DS Stanley doesn't. 'In case you've forgotten, so is Ms Fontaine,' she says drily. 'The nature of the conversation you had is not in doubt, by the way. She recorded it. I've heard exactly what you said to her. I can play it back to you if you've forgotten.'

When Richard doesn't speak, she goes on. 'What were you planning to do once you'd forced your way into her flat?'

Richard sighs heavily. 'I just wanted to talk. That was all.'

DS Stanley moves on. 'In addition to this, some new information has come to light. It appears that you've been paying Katharine McKenna some quite large sums of money. There's no point in you denying it. Your wife's seen your chequebooks. Can you explain the reason for this?'

Glaring at me, he turns to blustering again. 'I think you'll find there's been some mistake, Detective Sergeant. I've given her money from time to time – she's family. It's a personal matter, nothing more.'

'There's no mistake. Your daughter-in-law has admitted it. But so far, she refuses to explain why. To quote her words, she said *it would be far better to forget about it*. Seeing as the money came from you, perhaps you could elaborate.'

Richard's face visibly pales. 'This interview is entirely voluntary. I'm under no obligation to answer your questions.'

'Dad . . .'

Richard turns on him. 'Shut up, Joseph.'

How could I ever have interpreted affection from this

man? He is devoid of empathy, cold, unfeeling. I wonder if he has any idea of the damage he is doing. Getting up, Joe's face is ashen as he walks out.

'You do realise we can apply for the right to look at your financial records.'

He holds up his hands. 'Be my guest.'

With Richard refusing to cooperate, the police soon leave. After they've gone, I wait for the backlash, but there is none.

'I think it would be better for you to move out.' Richard's voice is ice cold.

'As a matter of fact, so do I.' Getting up, I walk towards the stairs, relief flooding through me that after thirty years of marriage, it can come to an end so easily. But I should have known he wouldn't leave it at that. When I'm halfway up, he starts shouting after me.

'What the fuck did you think you were playing at, snooping around my desk?' Standing at the bottom, he's angrier than I've ever seen him. 'Never mind talking to the police behind my back? After everything I've given you, don't you think you owe me a little gratitude?'

I pause halfway up. 'You're forgetting, Richard, I've worked just as hard as you have. And this is not about money.'

'That's exactly what it's about.'

'It's always about money with you.' I raise my voice. 'Well, this isn't. It's about lies, deception, intimidation, bullying. Whatever you say, you know exactly what I'm talking about. I should have left you a long time ago.' My heart is thumping as I reach the top of the stairs. Glancing down as Joe comes back, I catch an angry exchange between them, before Richard turns around and storms away.

Fetching a couple of suitcases from one of the spare rooms, I go to our bedroom and start to pack.

An hour later, Joe is nowhere to be seen when I take them out to my car. Going back in, I pick up my laptop and a framed photo of the boys when they were young, but there's nothing else I want. Picking up my coat, I go outside and stand there for a moment, gazing at the house that could have been the most wonderful of family homes, just as Joe comes out.

'Mum, don't go.' He looks devastated. 'This is our home.'

I smile sadly. 'It's our house, Joe. But it was never a home.' Pausing, I touch his cheek. 'I'm sorry you're caught in the middle. I know it feels brutal, but it will be OK, I promise you. I can't live with your father. And this is the only way things are going to change.'

He looks worried. 'Where will you go?'

'I don't know. But I'll find somewhere.' I get in my car. 'I'll let you know where.'

It's the hardest thing I've done, driving away. In the rear-view mirror, Joe's face reminds me of when he and Oliver were children. But Joe isn't a child. And he might be upset, but there's a lesson in this for him, too. If I'd stayed, Richard would have won, yet again, when what Joe needs is to see his father lose.

Driving into Deal, I park near the community centre where I went with Ana. It so happens there's an AA meeting about to start and as I watch people arrive, I imagine Oliver among them, grateful at least that he had somewhere to go.

Inside, I drink a cup of tea and google hotels, then B&Bs, eventually finding one in a village a few miles out of Deal. Booking it for a week, I feel more peaceful than I have in a long time as I finish my tea and get on my way.

31

Katharine

The day after the police interview, I know I have to pull myself together. After showering, I make a list to work through and while the kettle boils, the first thing I do is call some estate agents.

Having set up some appointments for them to come to value the house, I'm starting to feel more in control as I check my phone. Already there are a number of replies to my marketplace adverts.

Later that afternoon, as I'm typing a reply to someone who wants to pick up the coffee table, I hear a car pull up outside. Dreading the police have come back, as I finish the message, there's a knock on the door.

But when I go to the door, I'm wishing it was the police. As I open it and see who's standing there, I feel my heart plummet. 'What are you doing here?'

Coming in and closing the door behind him, Richard stands there, glowering at me. 'What the fuck did you say to Jude?' he says nastily.

'Nothing, Richard. She already knew about the money. She came here because she wanted to know why. But I didn't tell her.'

'Fucking woman.' He's jumpy, like a coiled spring.

Seeing him like this, I'm suddenly worried about Jude. 'Don't do anything stupid, will you?'

He rounds on me. 'How can I? The bitch has gone.'

'Gone?' I'm shocked. 'What do you mean?'

'She's left me.' His voice is bitter. 'As if bloody Ana Fontaine finding the photos wasn't enough, now the police have them and they refuse to let it go. The fact that you worked at Skyro,' he shakes his head, 'I never imagined that would come out.'

When photos on social media are there for the world to see, it beggars belief that he can say that. 'Then you should have made sure those photos were taken down.'

'I know that now,' he snarls. 'But I didn't imagine some nosey-parker fucking bitch would be trolling through the past determined to look for them.'

He's made no mention of Oliver dying, and suddenly I can't stop myself from challenging him. 'Don't you care – even the smallest bit – that your son has died?'

The question brings him up short. 'Of course I do. But I can't bring him back,' he snaps. 'I just have to deal with the consequences.'

But I know from the way he speaks, it isn't true. Shaking my head, I stare at him. 'You're lying, Richard. You couldn't care less. You've never cared about anyone other than yourself.'

It seems incomprehensible that Jude would have left Richard. Or maybe it isn't. Suddenly I admire the courage it must have taken; realising that it's what I need, too. 'Maybe you should tell the police what you should have said at the start of all this,' I say, knowing he won't go for it. 'The truth.'

'You can imagine what will happen if I do.' Richard paces over to the window. Standing there, his eyes narrow as he turns back to look at me. 'Actually, you're right. Maybe I should. I wonder what they'll say when I tell them you've been blackmailing me.'

An iron hand grips my insides. 'You conned me, Richard. You told me you were taking Skyro to court. When they realise what you've been involved in all this time, do you honestly think anyone will listen to you?'

It doesn't matter what he says. Given he's been investing in illegal arms, whichever way Richard plays this, he's caught.

For a moment, he's silent, then as he looks at me, the expression on his face is one of pure evil. 'You think you have it all worked out, don't you? Well, let me tell you. After your part in this, you deserve nothing, Katharine.'

I try to stop myself from shaking. 'My part? You have a fucking nerve, Richard. What would your family think if they knew where your money had really come from? No wonder Jude left you.'

He comes towards me, until he's standing right in front of me, his face inches from mine, his eyes menacing. 'Don't you fucking dare speak to me like that,' he hisses. 'You owe me everything.'

As he stands there, I know I've pushed him too far as fear washes over me. Wondering if I should call the police, I glance around for my phone, but he sees it before me.

'Don't even think about it.'

I feel myself start to shake. 'I don't owe you everything. It could have been a whole lot worse, if I hadn't come to you.'

'You. Know. What. I. Mean.' With icy calm, he says each word deliberately. 'Just keep your fucking mouth shut, or I will see to it that you lose everything. Because if I go down, you, Katharine McKenna, are coming with me.'

As he speaks I feel nauseous. It's like my eyes are opening to how abhorrent he is, as I realise what a fool I've been. Unable to listen to another vile word, suddenly I'm desperate to get him out of here. My heart is hammering as I glance at my watch. 'I have someone coming to pick up some more furniture in a minute.' It's a lie, but he reacts as I hoped he would.

'Don't worry. I'm going. But I'll be back.'

Slamming the front door behind him, he revs his car, before driving too fast out of the gate, sending up a spray of gravel. Locking the door, I go back into the sitting room.

With the sofa now gone, the house is bare, unwelcoming. Staring around the bare walls, I'm shaking as I sit on the floor, trying to get my thoughts together. I should have steered clear of him, shopped him to the police before I left Skyro and walked away with a clear conscience.

But I didn't, and now it's caught up with me.

That night, I lie awake. The house feels soiled by Richard's presence, the walls rebounding with the echo of his words. Still conflicted about what to do, over the dark watches of a long night, I finally work it out. Something has to change. Whatever comes next, I can't go on living like this.

After a couple of hours of sleep, the next morning my mind is clear. I'm done with all the lies. As I said to Richard,

I can see only one way forward and if there are consequences, I have to accept them. Picking up my phone, I make a call.

★

After showering and changing into clean clothes, I'm oddly calm when I open the door to the police. 'Thank you for coming. Please, come through.'

DS Stanley and Constable Ramirez follow me through to the kitchen.

'Do sit. I'm sorry about the state of the place.' But it's as if a fog has lifted. I no longer care about the house, nor about Richard or Joe. Instead, I'm doing what I should have done a long time ago.

Sitting down, I look at DS Stanley. 'I can only apologise for keeping this from you. I told myself it wasn't relevant, but I realise now that it probably is.'

They stay silent, only occasionally interrupting to ask questions, for the most part listening intently as I talk about the confrontation I was involved in at Skyro that led to me losing my job and everything that's followed since.

DS Stanley frowns at me. 'So once he'd realised you knew about his involvement in exporting illegal firearms, Richard McKenna effectively paid you to stay silent?'

I shake my head. 'It didn't seem like that at first. When I lost my job, I didn't know he was involved. I thought the paperwork I'd seen listing his name was a mistake. He was a man I knew through charitable causes. I couldn't believe he'd be involved in shipping illegal arms. When I told him, I honestly believed he was as shocked as I was. When he offered me money, he said he felt the same way I did and it was compensation for the circumstances in which I'd lost my job. In exchange, he asked me to be a witness when he took Skyro to court.'

'Which of course, he had no intention of doing,' she says quietly. 'When did you work that out?'

'Not that long ago. I can't believe I didn't see it before. I was married to Oliver by then.' My voice wavers. 'I'm not saying I was right to stay quiet, because I wasn't. But if I'd challenged Richard . . .'

'I can imagine.' DS Stanley's voice is grim. 'But staying silent about a crime as serious as this one is perverting the course of justice, Mrs McKenna. You should have told us.'

'I know that now.' I stare at the table. 'But what I still don't know is how Oliver fit in with all this.'

DS Stanley glances at her colleague. 'Skyro offered him a contract, didn't they? I imagine he would have done his homework. What came next, I think we can probably work it out.' She pauses. 'There was another matter we wanted to discuss with you.'

My heart misses a beat. 'Yes?'

'Your mother-in-law told us that your husband was abusive towards you.'

'He was.' I shake my head. 'Of course now, given everything we've found out, I think he was stressed and simply taking his frustrations out on me. I'd always hoped we'd come through it. It's obvious now, he didn't feel the same.'

'Again, you should have told us, Mrs McKenna.'

'I know. I suppose I felt, if I did, I'd be tainting everyone's memory of him, mine included. Whatever was going on between us, I really did not want our marriage to be over, Detective Sergeant.' My voice wavers.

She frowns. 'I have one more question. When you and Oliver met, did you have any idea who his father was?'

I shake my head. 'None whatsoever. It came as a complete shock.'

'I bet it did.' She looks around. 'So where are you moving to?'

'I'm not sure. But it won't be for a while. I'm still waiting for probate, and the house has only just gone on the market.'

'This money that Richard McKenna has paid to you, given the circumstances, there may be some attempt to reclaim it.'

But where exactly Richard got it from, is nothing to do with me. 'As far as I know it came from his personal account,' I say quietly.

'In that case, there's nothing more to say on the matter. Please don't leave the area, Mrs McKenna. It's likely we'll be needing you as a witness.'

I nod. 'I'll be here.'

Having been in Richard's thrall for so long, I can't believe how long it's taken me to see him for what he is, to find the courage to expose him. But as I've found out the hard way, there is nothing more dangerous or seductive than the twisted dance of a psychopath.

32

Jude

By chance, I'm at the house collecting a few more possessions when the police turn up looking for Richard.

'I don't know where he is,' I tell them. 'Just for your information, I've moved out. I've come back to collect some more of my things.'

If she's surprised, DS Stanley doesn't show it.

'I spoke to him earlier and arranged a time to meet him here.' DS Stanley glances at her watch. 'Supposedly about ten minutes ago.'

'He's making a point,' I say calmly.

She looks less than impressed. 'He's also wasting police time.'

Just as I gather the last of what I came here for, I hear Richard's car outside.

DS Stanley turns to me. 'It might be wise if you wait through there.' She nods towards the open door to the sitting room.

'How did you get in?' he growls.

'Your wife let us in.' DS Stanley is matter-of-fact.

'Where is she?' He sounds furious.

'Collecting some of her possessions, I believe. Mr McKenna, we have some questions we'd like to ask you.'

His voice is typically abrupt. 'I have nothing to say.'

'In that case, you give me no option other than to arrest you.'

'On what grounds?'

'Perverting the course of justice, suspicion of attempted murder, fraud. Unless you know otherwise.'

There's a brief silence. 'What is it you want to know?'

'We know about your association with Skyro, Mr McKenna. There is no point denying it. We have witnesses who are prepared to testify against you.'

He speaks abruptly. 'I have no idea what you're talking about.'

'I'm talking about the investment in the shipment of illegal firearms. These things usually come out. Surely even you must realise that. Your daughter-in-law told us how you blackmailed her. She was brave, wasn't she? Standing up to the company who employed her because she'd found out what they were involved in. She was fired, but after, she came to see you. She'd discovered a confidential file implicating you in some deal involving the shipment of illegal arms – a very lucrative one, by all accounts. Having met you at a charity event, she wanted to let you know. She believed there'd been a mistake, or that you were being set up. Having convinced her she was right, you told her you felt sorry for the way she'd been treated, that you felt the same way as she did and you'd like to compensate her, as long as she was prepared to be a witness when the time came, because with her help, you had a plan to bring Skyro down.'

'She's not being straight with you. I can tell you every word of that is complete rubbish.' Richard sounds furious.

But as I listen from behind the sitting room door, I'm staggered, remembering the evening shortly after Oliver died, when Richard came home from work with the file on Skyro, the performance he put on as he showed it to me. The way he expressed disgust that Oliver had gotten caught up in something so corrupt. All of it faked, to save his own skin.

DS Stanley goes on. 'It's why neither of you acknowledged each other, when she was re-introduced to you as your son's new girlfriend. You gave no indication that you'd met before. In spite of how shocked she was, she played along, because you'd impressed on her the importance of keeping this between the two of you, until the case went to court. Of course, there was never going to be a court case, was there? There were far too many more lucrative deals to be done. Our officers will be going through your affairs with a fine-tooth comb, Mr McKenna. Illegal deals involving firearms are taken very seriously.' She pauses. 'Going back to your daughter-in-law, you bought her silence, didn't you? Just as you tried to with Ms Fontaine, but unlike Ms Fontaine, Katharine went for it. She had no job, no family to help her. You saw her desperation and took advantage of her, the master puppeteer pulling the strings. But then you have been all the way through this.'

'You have no idea how wrong you are.' Richard's voice is mutinous. 'She's lying. Can't you see that? I haven't been blackmailing her. It's Katharine who's been blackmailing me.'

'Why would she do that?' DS Stanley sounds disbelieving. 'All this time, she's been prepared to be a witness when you took Skyro to court. Unlike you, she wanted justice, Mr

McKenna. It's there in black and white, in the press release, while all you wanted was to continue making money, no matter the human cost, which brings me to the last part.' Her voice changes. 'Your son's death. We know it was you who tampered with the brakes. It's only a matter of time before we find proof. After going for an interview with Skyro, Oliver started finding out more about them. We've seen the history of searches on his laptop. Very much his father's son, by the sound of things, only he dug a little deeper than you had. Your son discovered the link between you and Skyro. He'd read about them being arrested on suspicion of flying illegal firearms. Then he stumbled across something that linked them to you. I can only imagine how disgusted he must have felt. Unlike you, it sounds as though your son had a moral code. Already feeling under pressure, he challenged you. Tried to pay him off, too, didn't you? But I'm guessing it didn't work. You, of course, were never going to back down. It matters little what the content of that conversation was. What matters is the outcome. There was only one way to save your skin. You knew you had to ensure Oliver's silence.'

33

Ana

It's February before the case against Richard goes to court. From the back of the courtroom, I listen, detached, as the list of charges against him is read out. It's a lengthy trial during which Richard denies both blackmailing Katharine and the allegations about the gloves and Oliver's murder, but after hearing the evidence, the verdict is unanimous and as he's led away, my feeling of relief is palpable.

A couple of days later, I meet Jude in the community centre. Since leaving Richard, she seems to have come into her own. But knowing her husband killed her son has broken something in her.

'It's good to see you.' I hug her lightly.

'You, too. Tea? Or something stronger?'

I'm tempted, but I've come too far along the road of sobriety to give in now. 'Tea,' I say as she realises her faux pas. 'It's fine. It would have been a problem once, but not anymore.'

I watch her go to the bar to order our drinks. When she

comes back, I quiz her about Richard. 'I still don't know how they reached the conclusion they did.'

Jude sighs. 'Skyro was always the common denominator. It seems ridiculous that none of us realised sooner, but with all the smoke and daggers, we were distracted, and Richard used that to his advantage.' She shakes her head. 'To think it was Richard who supposedly found out that Skyro had offered Oliver a job. He made such a thing of it. You'd have thought he would have kept it quiet.'

'Probably in the hope he would deflect the police and stop them digging further.' But even so, his behaviour is unfathomable. 'Why the fuck did Katharine go along with it?'

'Richard has this saying: every person has their price. Kat had hers, and he paid it. That's what the money was about. Of course, if she'd said no, it might have turned out very differently.'

'So she betrayed her principles for the money. Nice,' I say sarcastically.

'She didn't intend to at the start. She genuinely believed that he was taking Skyro to court. But by the time she'd realised he wasn't, if she'd shopped him to the police, they would have charged her with perverting the course of justice. Of course, in the end, in order to expose Richard for what he is, she had to come clean anyway.'

I'm silent, thinking. 'It's just so awful that Oliver stumbled across his father's involvement.' My eyes mist with tears. 'I can only imagine how he must have felt, having to carry that. But I can understand now why he refused to talk about it.'

'It adds up, doesn't it?' Jude looks at me sadly. 'Oliver was always anti-war, as I'm sure you know. Once Richard knew he was onto him, it didn't matter that he was his son. Richard was merciless. He did what he had to in order to save his neck, and his money.' A tear rolls down her cheek. 'You wouldn't have imagined it was possible, would you?'

But as I know to my cost, there are too many men like Richard in this world. 'It happens, sadly.'

She shakes her head. 'The police found knitted gloves matching the marks they found on Kat's car stashed in his own car of all places. Can you believe it? He must have believed he was completely above suspicion.'

But sadly, I can. People like Richard believe they are above the law. It doesn't cross their minds that they could get caught out. 'I still think it's weird how Kat had a sudden change of heart.'

Jude looks troubled. 'I don't think she realised the gravity of what she'd done. Perverting the course of justice is a serious offence, particularly in relation to a murder enquiry.'

'She got what she deserved.' I wasn't going to lose any sleep over Kat being charged. 'She was lucky to get off with a fine.'

Jude looks sad. 'But it was always Richard pulling the strings. Kat was just weak. She had no idea it was him who'd tampered with the brakes. The police clearly knew that. When she spoke to me about it, she was convinced you'd done it.'

'If you'd seen me attempt anything mechanical . . .' I show her my manicured hands. 'So, now that Richard is out of your way, what will you do?'

'First, I'm going to find myself a house.' Jude looks hesitant. 'Then actually, I'm going to train as a therapist.'

'Oh no,' I can't resist rolling my eyes. 'Not another one.'

For the first time today, she smiles. 'The first year of training is general. But after that, I think I'd like to specialise in addiction counselling.'

'That's wonderful, Jude.' My sentiment is genuine. 'You'll be great.'

'That remains to be seen.' But I can tell she appreciates my encouragement. 'I've a lot to learn. But I thought it would help me start to understand what Oliver went through.'

I swallow the lump in my throat. 'Thank you.'

As she looks at me, for the first time I see something about her that reminds me of Oliver. 'So what about you?'

It's the million-dollar question. 'I'm giving up my flat. Now that I have Oliver's money, I was thinking about moving away and buying a little house somewhere near the sea. But after everything that's happened, I want some time to take stock. Losing someone you love is painful.' But I don't need to tell Jude that. In her own way, I know she did love Oliver. Trying to lighten the mood, I smile. 'I might go away for a while – give men a miss and rescue hundreds of cats or children or something like that.'

She looks at me sympathetically. 'After everything you've been through, it would be good for you.'

She pauses.

'You have such a pretty name.'

'Thank you.' I'm taken by surprise. 'I adopted it.' Seeing her face, I elaborate. 'It isn't a crime. There were one or two memories I wanted to leave behind. Oliver knew all about it.'

I can tell she doesn't understand when she's silent for a moment.

'You know, I've never asked you anything about your life before you and Oliver met.'

I breathe in sharply. Is this where I tell her what a mess I was? About the trail of destruction that seemed to follow me? How after too much went wrong in my life, I never imagined I'd be able to love again? About the superhuman effort it took to turn my life around, how falling in love with Oliver was both the greatest and worst thing that ever happened to me. No. The past is in the past, and it's best left there.

'There isn't much to tell.' I hold her gaze. 'I was a nobody.' But I'm touched that she's thought to ask. Getting up, I lean down and kiss her on the cheek. 'Good luck, Jude.' Turning around, I walk out.

34

Katharine

The court hearing triggered a cathartic shedding of everything related to the McKenna family. The problems Oliver and I had, Richard's relentless manipulation, the way Joe played on my emotions. I went over them, again and again, until they no longer had any impact on me, and I knew I was rid of them. The only one I had time for was Jude.

I know I'm potentially in line for a prison sentence. But luck is with me when I'm let off with a fine. Substantiated by the press release, the story of me leaving Skyro holds up well. After hearing the lengths Richard went to for his own selfish gains, the fact that he'd deliberately exploited a vulnerable woman and blackmailed her, as well as sealing his fate, had secured my freedom.

A couple of weeks later, I catch up with Jude over lunch in a restaurant that's just opened up, around the corner from the fancy beachside apartment she's renting. Our relationship has changed, but so have we. There is more honesty, less agenda; a shared sense of relief that Richard is inside.

'I only want to talk about this the once,' she says. 'But I want to have an honest conversation with you. I'm completely done with Richard, and if Joe has any solidarity with his father, I'm afraid the only way he's going to learn any different is the hard way. But that aside, you and Oliver . . .' She looks puzzled. 'When you met, did you love him?'

I take a deep breath, staring at my coffee for a moment. 'If we're being honest, I loved the idea of him. We were attracted to each other, but in reality, I think we were two damaged people who didn't really know what love was. Subconsciously, I guess I saw him as having the family and security I'd always craved, while for him, I was the potential wife he knew you and Richard expected of him. We were swept away by the idea of it all. Genuinely, I wanted the happy ending.' I look at her. 'But as we both know, life isn't always like that, is it?'

'Rarely.' Jude sits back. 'Have you thought about talking to someone? A professional? You were alone for so long. It might help.'

To think I once believed I could help other people. 'Maybe I will.'

There's more to it than I've told Jude, but it's in the past now. Anyway, I've been doing some self-counselling of late, mostly amounting to a brutal character assassination of myself. Bizarre, but oddly therapeutic.

'There's one thing I would like to ask you.' Jude hesitates. 'Ana said Oliver had suspicions that your parents weren't dead. Is that true?'

I sigh. 'I wanted them to be.' I look at Jude, wondering if she'll be angry. 'I wasn't lying to you when I said my childhood was unhappy. But people don't understand the reality of abuse. We had a big home, they were well-off. Cutting a long story short, they should never have become parents.'

'Like me and Richard,' Jude says quietly.

I shake my head. 'I could tell you things.'

I think of the cat I loved. Iris. How I came home from school and my mother told me she'd gone off with another cat; how later I found a bill for her being euthanised. God knows how my mother got the vet to agree to put down a healthy cat, but my mother was capable of anything. The lavish party my parents put on for my eighth birthday that was an oasis in the desert of my childhood. My pink dress and glittery silver shoes. The way, as soon as my friends left, they ripped down the balloons and decorations and threw my cake away. How I never wore that dress again. I could go on.

'For reasons I've never understood, my mother took pleasure in seeing me suffer. She found out where I was after our wedding – she must have been looking online. She has called, but only once or twice. Each time, I blocked her. Having turned my life around, I couldn't risk them coming back and ruining it.'

'It must have been wretched.' Her voice is full of sympathy. She has no idea how much so.

'It was. Most of the time I don't think about it.'

Jude shakes her head. 'I still can't believe the way Richard tried to twist it and make it look as though you were black-mailing him. He must really believe we're stupid. Even the idea . . . it's preposterous.'

Is that what she really thinks? I watch her for a split second to make sure, before nodding my agreement. 'I know. Thank goodness the jury realised.' I quickly change the subject. 'I've never said thank you, Jude.'

She looks surprised. 'What for?'

I look at the woman who's been a big part of my life, who in spite of her failings is the closest I've known to a mother. 'You've always been good to me. I really wanted to be the perfect daughter-in-law. I suppose I'm trying to say I'm sorry. I let you down.'

'Perfect doesn't exist,' she says quietly.

'I know that now.' I frown slightly. 'Have you heard any more from Ana Fontaine?'

'I met up with her just after the trial. She was going to sell her flat and go away. She wasn't sure where exactly. I did just recently hear something about her. I'm not sure how true it is, but if it is, it's a terrible story. She was on holiday with her husband and daughter in the south of France. There was a fire in the hotel where they were staying. Ana had gone for a run. Both of them died. Poor woman. It's probably why she changed her name – to avoid being recognised.'

An expression of shock crosses my face. 'You're sure it was her? I mean, it's terrible, obviously. But strange that she'd change her name.' Though it explains why I could never find anything out about her.

'Who knows what she was thinking? After losing them, she must have been beside herself. I don't know how you ever get over something like that.' Jude's silent for a moment. 'So, what about you? Now that your house is sold and the paperwork sorted, what are you going to do?'

'I've given it a lot of thought.' I sit back, still thinking about what Jude said, about Ana Fontaine. 'I haven't decided yet, but I've been thinking about some friends I've lost touch with. I thought I'd give them a call. Last I heard, they were quite scattered. Then maybe I'll plan a road trip and see where I end up.' I'm lucky I don't have to worry about money for a while. 'Then when I find somewhere to settle, I'll buy a house.'

Jude's eyes are warm. 'Good for you.'

I'm not sure if Jude's approval is laced with relief that I'll be out of her hair.

'It feels like the right time.'

She goes on. 'Do I know any of them?'

I smile at her. 'I don't think so.'

Life can be complicated, but it always would be, as I was finding out. After Oliver's increasing lack of interest in me – our arguments, stumbling across Ana Fontaine's photo as my marriage grew more distant – it turns out that life can also be unexpected. Just when I'd believed Oliver had success- fully hidden the rest of his money from me, his life insurance had paid up. There was the way that no one in court believed that it was me who'd been blackmailing Richard. How the gloves I wore when I sabotaged the brakes found their way into Richard's car, combined with the fact that Richard had no alibi that night. I may have made a lot of money from him, but after investing in illegal arms, Richard deserves everything that's coming to him.

Knowing this whole episode will soon be behind me, at last I can start to look forward again. And I suppose, in a sense, I've come away with something. I am Katharine, now, complete with matching passport and bank account that I'm keeping, just as I'd intended the day I stepped off the train that pulled into Deal. That part, at least, has gone to plan.

It's ironic that in running from the family I detested, I'd

ended up surrounded by similar people. But that was the attraction of wealth, I was learning. However much I used to despise it, life was much harder without it. Now, however, thanks to Oliver's money, Richard's too, I'm no longer running away. I've been given another chance to start again; to maybe live a better life this time. I think of the friends I mentioned to Jude: Gemma's thirst for adventure, Margot's desire to party, poor Hannah who was reluctantly taken in by a friend she'd believed was dying. But there's no need for Jude to know about any of that.

I came to Deal in search of a new start, with the hope of finding love, and while it didn't work out, I do at least have money in the bank. But most importantly, however, I have my freedom back.

It's time to get the hell out and hit the road again.

Acknowledgements

My first thanks go to everyone at Avon, in particular to my editor, Lucy Fredericks. It's been our one and only book together – I've loved working with you and your brilliant touch has completely transformed it.

Another huge thank you goes to my amazing agent, Juliet Mushens, and the whole Mushens Entertainment team, for everything you do for us authors.

To my readers, thank you so much for buying my books, for the reviews you write, for spreading the word. I'm so grateful to you – none of this would be possible without you.

This book was inspired in part by our travels through rural France, and the many beautiful houses we've seen since coming here. There's something about the way they seem rooted into the landscape and I wrote this in a lovely old house in a peaceful part of the Dordogne, where the words just flowed. Frances Sewell, thank you so much for our time there.

As always, I'd like to say a massive thank you to my family and friends. To Laura Stanley for allowing me to use her name! To Martin for sharing this road trip, and for doing absolutely everything else when deadlines are looming.

And to Georgie and Tom, who inspire me every day. I am the proudest mumma of both of you.

Don't miss the
#1 bestselling thriller

'A sinister, twisty tale you won't want
to put down'
Sam Carrington, author of
The Open House